A REQUIEM FOR CROWS

A NOVEL OF VIETNAM

Dennis Foley

OPEN ROAD
INTEGRATED MEDIA
NEW YORK

978-1-5040-7318-9

This edition published in 2021 by Open Road Integrated Media, Inc.

180 Maiden Lane
New York, NY 10038
www.openroadmedia.com

"Let every nation know, whether it wishes us well or ill, that we shall pay any price, bear any burden, meet any hardship, support any friend, oppose any foe, in order to assure the survival and the success of liberty.

"This much we pledge—and more."

John F. Kennedy
President of the United States
Inauguration speech
Jan 20, 1961

PROLOGUE

NOVEMBER 1965

Finished with deliberations, the officers shuffled back into the courtroom. The grinding sounds of their combat boots and the scuffing of their chairs on the raised platform, built just for the trial, broke the silence. Two colonels, three lieutenant colonels and one major flanked Brigadier General Ben Stratton. They silently took their seats.

Stratton slipped on his reading glasses, opened a piece of paper folded only once at the midline and read to all assembled in the room, "As President of this court-martial, it is my duty to inform you that the members of the court, two-thirds of which were present at the time a secret written ballot was cast, have reached their verdict. As to the charges and specifications, the court finds the accused . . ."

Scotty Hayes braced himself for the reading of the verdict.

CHAPTER 1

BELTON, FLORIDA
—APRIL 1963

Scotty Hayes walked down the hallway at Palms High as if he didn't have a care in the world. There was a bit of James Dean in his walk, Elvis in his smile and Jerry Lee Lewis in his attitude.

Here and there classmates nodded, said "Hi" or gave him a quiet smile.

He didn't seek out eye contact with classmates, but didn't fail to acknowledge anyone who recognized him with his winning smile or a wave, or even a quiet, "Hi there." Though not a member of the scholarly elite or athletic royalty, he was popular enough.

Scotty stopped at his locker, spun the worn combination dial on the warped door with a snap of his wrist and a hint of body English and popped it open with ease. He ignored the fact that the inside of his locker was chaotic and in need of a good cleaning. Crushed, ripped and crumpled notebook pages peeked out of the spaces between rarely used textbooks stacked at reckless angles.

He pulled a pencil from behind his ear and flipped it end over end at the triangle opening formed by stacked math, history and chemistry books. He was pleased with himself when the pencil landed inside the small opening on the very first try.

"Hayes. You goin' to practice, man?" A classmate slid into a spot against the adjacent locker, a move designed to allow him to speak with Scotty without having to take his eyes off the girls walking the halls and stopping at their own lockers.

"Mal, have I ever missed a practice?"

Malcolm Striever jabbed his thumb over his shoulder toward the vice principal's office. "No, but just about anything might a' happened in there. For all I know, you might be on your way to solitary for ten years."

Scotty looked around for other students who might be in earshot. "Hey," he whispered, "why don't you broadcast it over the intercom, man?"

Malcolm lowered his voice. "Well, he didn't throw ya' out of school, did he?"

Scotty smiled. "What? For cutting a few classes?"

"It could happen. I'm guessing Old Man Skerritt's about had it with you. Did he give you his 'Good students are not truant students' speech? I've heard it about once a year since I was a sophomore. I can almost repeat it word for word."

"Let me worry about Skerritt." He playfully punched Malcolm's shoulder. "Relax. No big deal."

Malcolm looked at his watch. "Scotty, we better get on over to practice before Coach Huffman has our asses. Anyway, we get there early I can check out girl's cheerleading practice and watch long-legged Jeanie get all worked up over you."

Scotty pulled his letter jacket from his locker and slammed the door, spinning the combination dial in one fluid move. He threw the jacket over his shoulder and shook his head. "I got about as much chance with her as I do with Marilyn Monroe."

"The Marilyn who's been dead for over a year?"

"That's my point."

The two walked down the hallway to the exit, Malcolm struggling to control his notebook and several textbooks, Scotty empty-handed.

Track practice over, Scotty sat on the long narrow bench in a canyon of athletic equipment lockers. He kicked his spikes into his own with one foot while putting on a dry t-shirt. Like his book locker, his gym locker was a messy collection of dirty socks, some textbooks, knotted Ace bandages, and equipment from three different sports. All of it smelling of sweat.

Malcolm dropped his towel on the bench, pulled a comb out of his own locker and began combing is wet hair, naked.

"Hey, man! Put some clothes on. It's bad enough we all got to see your skinny ass in the shower. You can put something on now. Give us a break. There's only so much ugly we can take."

"Fuck you, Hayes. You're just jealous."

Scotty laughed. "Malcolm, you are really not from this planet, are you?"

A booming voice interrupted them. "Whoa! Hold on, ya'll. Check this shit out."

Scotty and Malcolm turned to find Paul Wynn standing at the other end of the bench still in his track sweats wearing a bright green windbreaker with the word Tulane emblazoned across the chest.

Scotty knew Paul as an okay athlete who always did his homework for classes. He was not unpopular, and as a jock, he was unlikely to set a state record or be named to an All-American team. But as a football lineman, he had the advantage of being big and nearly impossible to move. Beyond that, he was no one special.

Malcolm tried to speak while wobbling on one foot and stepping into his briefs. "Where'd you get the jacket, Wynn? You steal it?"

"Screw you, Striever. A guy from the Tulane's Alum Association left it with the coach." He mugged, modeling the jacket. "Cool, huh?"

Scotty looked back to his locker and pulled out his street clothes, saying nothing.

"Why you, man?" Malcolm laughed. "You wash his car for him? Or what?"

"No, *asshole*. He brought the jacket so he'd have a pocket to put this in." Wynn held up an opened envelope and waved it for all to see. "My ticket, ya'll. This is it. Can you believe it? A full ride at Tulane. I'm goin' to play football for the Green Wave. What are you doing next year, Malcolm?"

A few cheers and some good-natured remarks came from different corners of the locker room. Everyone except Scotty appeared to be happy for Paul Wynn.

No one noticed the coach watching the whole thing through the doorway to his office. Leaning back in his chair he yelled out, "Hayes? In my office. Now!"

Malcolm stuck his head through the neck of a sweatshirt. "Shit, Hayes. What did you do, now?"

"Yes, Coach?"

"Close the door, Hayes." Coach John Huffman was twice Scotty's age and more than twice his size. A West Virginia State baseball hat was perched on the back of his head. He nodded at a straight-backed chair on the other side of his cluttered office. "Sit. I want to talk to you, Hayes."

Scotty quickly searched his memory for something he might have done wrong at practice. He sat stiffly, waiting for the coach to set the tone, watching him for some clue, if only to get out in front of whatever the bad news if only for a fraction of a second.

With his back to Scotty, Huffman asked, "What do you think about all that out there?"

"All that, Coach?"

"Wynn's good news."

"Oh . . . Good, I guess. He wanted to get into Tulane. To play ball there. Yeah. Good."

The coach lifted a sheaf of papers from his desk and then dropped them back onto it. "Grades."

"Grades?"

"Yep. Semester grades. Wynn's, Striever's, yours, and every other senior's grades. Wynn's got 'em. Good ones. And he's a pretty fair football player on top of it all." The coach spun his chair around and looked directly at him.

Scotty knew whatever Coach Huffman would have to say next, it would not be praise for his grade point average.

"You aren't settin' any records. Are you, son?"

Scotty looked down at his shoes and shook his head. "No, sir. I guess not."

Coach Huffman sighed and pushed his cap farther back on his head. "I had pretty high hopes for you when you walked onto my ball field three years ago. You were good. I thought we had the time to get you better." He hesitated and picked up a football wedged between a file cabinet and his in-box. He rolled the ball around in his fingertips as if looking for the laces, about to make a pass then he stopped and looked back at Scotty. "But, son, you never got any better.

"You see, the difference between you and Wynn is he worked. He didn't even have the moves you had when he started here, but he lapped you, son. That's why he's going to Tulane, and you aren't."

Scotty had no reply.

"Boy, you got t'go into life like you need to go into a football game—with your hair on fire and smoke comin' out your ass. I was hopin' you'd do that by now."

"I'm sorry, Coach."

Huffman pointed out at the door to the locker room. "That's not going to be you."

"What's not, Coach?"

"I'm sorry no one's going to send you a letter or bring you a school windbreaker. You're not getting a jock scholarship to some college. Ain't that right?"

"I guess not, Coach."

The coach took a breath and exhaled his disappointment. "You're a good kid, Hayes. But there's no fire in you. Colleges recruit boys with ass-kicking ball playing moves and okay grades or better. Can you honestly say you qualify in either category?"

Again, Scotty didn't reply. He just stuck his hands into his letter jacket pockets and stared at his shoelaces.

"We both know the answer, don't we?"

Scotty summoned up some optimism but was unable to deliver it with much conviction. "Coach, I'll find some way to play ball at some school. I'm sure there's someone who'll take me on."

"Son, you're a senior and time's pretty much run out for you. You frittered away your chances. You can't create a reputation with what's left of the school year. Heck, you only got a decent chance of making my track team before you graduate. I'm sure high school has been fun and filled with great memories, but it's not some place where you've done much to launch a sparkling career at any goddamn thing, far as I can see."

Scotty didn't argue.

"Hell, even if you made the sports page of every paper between now and graduation you got a transcript filled with some pretty shitty grades you can't ever change. Your record won't ever go away. And how were your SATs?"

Scotty looked up and shrugged.

"I'm not surprised. Nobody makes crappy grades and then goes out and smokes the SATs.

"Look, I've enjoyed having you on my teams. You've always been easy goin' and even helpful to some teammates. But I don't know how to advise you now. You're going to have to get serious about things or just plain starve to death. If I could, I'd help you, 'cause I like you. But you've got to admit you haven't been leaning into it much. So you go on home and get those wild thoughts of being invited to some college somewhere out of your head. It'll jus' mess you up to think it's gonna' happen. 'Cause it ain't. It just ain't gonna' happen for you."

"I'm goin' back some day, come what may, to Blue Bayou . . ." Scotty tried to sing along with Roy Orbison's voice squeezing through the small speaker of the AM radio perched on the windowsill in his room, but soon gave up when he could no longer reach the high notes.

He finished stuffing a few things into a tired duffel bag once owned by his father. It was one of only two things Scotty had to remind him of Jake Hayes. The other was encased in a small blue box trimmed with gold. He picked it off a makeshift bookshelf in the converted sun porch which served had as his bedroom all through his high school years.

He opened the box with great care and held it securely in both hands. Inside a blue ribbon, trimmed with red and white, held the brass Distinguished Service Cross Medal against the fake velvet backing. His father, who never even knew he had earned it, only wore it on his uniform at his burial. Jake Hayes was killed in action the day before his twenty-second birthday in Pusan-Ri, Korea. He was a medic with an airborne infantry company decimated by wave after wave of North Koreans. For his actions, he was awarded the country's second-highest award for valor in battle.

Scotty held the open medal box and thought about taking it with him. With effort, he could summon up his father in his uniform, wearing highly polished paratrooper boots. He was tall and lean. More Scotty couldn't pull from his memory. Everything else he remembered about Jake was from yellowing photos with scalloped edges Kitty had kept anchored to the black craft paper pages of a few albums.

Placing the box back on the shelf over his perpetually unmade bed, Scotty looked around his room. The things he would leave behind were a schoolboy's things—track medals, a football letter certificate on the wall, his baseball glove. His small homemade closet was half filled with clothes he would have no use for where he was going.

He swung around on the edge of his bed and looked at the things on the nearby desk. It had been a catchall and not a place where he'd done any real homework. He fingered the track medal hanging by a ribbon from his desk lamp. He won it at a Divisional meet running the 440 relay with Joe Blithe who was now at State. Below it, the baseball photo of him and the junior varsity team reminded him only two of the eleven boys on the team were still in Belton.

The only high school in the area, Palms High managed to graduate nearly three hundred students that year from all over the county. For graduates, there was little to keep them in Belton. There was no industry and few jobs. The population was mostly farm workers and retirees who couldn't afford to enjoy the luxuries of towns like nearby Sarasota.

Graduation and Scotty's summer had passed without event. He had a couple of part-time jobs. Each ended quickly. Suddenly, the friends he just assumed would be around weren't. They'd gone off to college, moved away to jobs that filled their days, or left Belton for the service. Now it was Scotty's turn to leave.

He clipped the strap to the closure on the top of the duffel bag and dropped it into the center of his bed.

"Scotty? Scotty, you still here, honey?" His stepmother's voice, husky from chain-smoking Pall Malls and drinking too much Wild Turkey was fading from sixteen hours of working two jobs. Her voice came from her bedroom at the opposite end of the small tract house.

"Yeah. I'm here."

"You won't leave without sayin' good-bye to me, will you, honey?" Kitty Hayes asked.

"No. I won't." He checked his watch. "I'm not leaving 'til morning."

It was well after midnight when he made one final check to be sure he had everything, and then found his way to Kitty's bedroom. He wasn't looking forward to saying good-bye to her.

His stepmother had come home from work while he was packing and grabbed something to eat on her way through the kitchen. Scotty could see she hadn't even taken the time to take off her shoes or finish her sandwich. She had dozed off on top of her built-in Hollywood bed in her small bedroom.

Careful not to wake her, he gently pulled a lit cigarette from her fingers and crushed it in the overflowing ashtray balanced on a small ledge on the wall near her bed.

He looked at the tiny tired woman half covered by a throw, still wearing her apron from work. Kitty meant continuity for Scotty. Even though she wasn't his real mother, she'd been loyal and loving. He had no memory of his real mother who died when he was an infant in a freak railway crossing accident. As long as he could remember, Kitty had been there.

After Jake died, Kitty worked days and nights tending bar, waiting tables and taking odd jobs to pay the rent and keep food on the table for the two of them. She had no other skills and traded her smile, her figure and her energy for a paycheck. Scotty hadn't noticed how the years had slowly aged her and taken their toll on her. His memories of the two of them playing catch, swimming in the Gulf and watching Bonanza together were as fresh as if they had done those things that week.

Still, time and loneliness wore on her. He ignored the changes and how she had long since learned to soften the sharp edges of her life with too much bourbon and too many painkillers.

He unfolded the throw she hadn't had the strength to spread out before she drifted off and covered more of her small torso only inches from being more off than on the bed. He didn't want to wake her, but he didn't want to leave either. He picked up the magazine left open and face down on her small makeup table stool. *Reader's Digest*—flipping it over he noticed she had also turned down the corner of a page. It was Kitty's attempt to improve herself. She had kept a promise to herself to read each issue for as far back as he could remember.

He sat down to spend a quiet minute with her before he had to get serious about the last details of his departure. He would miss her. He remembered how she had looked when he was a small boy. She was pretty then. Her bright smile came sparingly now. Her hair was stiff with too much hair spray. Gone was the warm straw color he'd remembered from a decade earlier. Now, it was brassy. Her makeup was caked and smudged— applied in successive layers as she had gone from one job to the other during her long day. He didn't care about those things. For his entire life, there'd only been one person he could count on, one person he could trust, one person who hadn't left him—Kitty Hayes.

She had no one, and he had her. He worried about her health, the stream of losers she took up with and her ever-present loneliness. He was torn over leaving, but he couldn't stay. He had to report to Fort Benning, still a whole state and over five hundred miles away.

He looked around the room, knowing he might not see it for a while. On her messy makeup table, she'd wedged a portable record player between an oval mirror balanced on the corner and the wall of the small bedroom. The script on the side of the record player proudly announced Hi-Fi. The box itself was laminated with grained vinyl in an alligator skin pattern. On the spindle stood three more 78s ready to drop down on top of the Johnny Mathis album resting on the flocked turntable. Scotty had heard those same albums over and over again, complete with the popping and scratching unique to each.

The room smelled of Kitty's perfume and was overpowered by something in the makeup she used liberally to hide imperfections in her once smooth complexion. Scotty noted the compact containing pressed powder showed more shiny bottom than product, reminding him how short the money had always been. He wondered how much he would be able to afford to send her once he was actually in the Army.

She stirred without waking up. He still had things to do, but first leaned over to gently kiss her on the forehead before he quietly slipped out of the room.

He had waited for Kitty to wake up, but hesitated to rouse her just to say goodbye. She needed her sleep more than she needed an emotional goodbye. Hell, he was only going to be gone for nine weeks, and he'd be back on leave before he would be stationed somewhere for any length of time.

He looked at his watch one more time and made up his mind to call her later on during the day after she got to work. He picked up his bag to leave but stopped at the front door to look around the cramped quarters.

He wouldn't miss much, especially the plastic laminate furniture or the couch so sunken in the middle getting out of it was a chore. The aluminum foil on the rabbit ears of the Emerson black and white TV was less effective than wishful. And the kitchen floor was in bad need of new linoleum. What was there had given way to worn spots where most of the traffic had broken through to the cream colored fiber beneath the speckled yellow and maroon pattern. Maybe he'd try to replace it while he was home on leave. Leave—it seemed such a long way off. For sure, he had slept his last night there. Once he walked out the door, he'd forever come back as a visitor.

He was excited about going somewhere new but anxious it was off to the Army as he opened the door and stepped out into the humid Florida morning. He walked to the end of the front walk, which died into a curbless side street and stepped through the small wire gate in the fenced-in front yard. He took a moment to glance back at the aging, mildew stained Florida cottage with its cracked jalousied windows.

With his entire summer's savings—thirty-nine dollars—in his pocket, Scotty stuck out his thumb along the interstate snaking its way north to Georgia. A trucker whose most distracting feature was a large, bobbing Adam's Apple gave Scotty his first ride and spent the first two hours telling Hayes how he was making a huge mistake by not enlisting in the Marine Corps, as the driver had done. He hammered on about how wimpy soldiers were when compared Marines and how the Marine Corps made a man out of him.

Hayes tried to politely nod in agreement, but the Army wasn't his idea, it was his local Draft Board's.

The truck driver dropped Scotty off in Waycross about the time the roads were filling up with people threading their way home from work. He was cutting off toward the coast, and Scotty would have to find another ride to Columbus.

As the truck pulled out, Scotty looked around. There was nothing close by except warehouses and the railhead. He had no idea which direction would be most likely to take him to food and lodging, so he just set out toward the brightest lights, all neon.

The signs on the wall said pizza and Budweiser. Scotty looked around inside the small bar before picking out a stool. The place was almost empty and smelled of beer and stale cigarettes. A jukebox at the far end of the room pounded out a Beach Boys tune still high on the charts, often repeated on radio stations across the country.

The bartender, a withered woman in her fifties, wore a stained apron to protect her as she washed glasses in the bar sink and stacked them on the drying rack next to it. She looked up at Scotty, "What'll it be, sugar?"

"A Bud. And a slice of pizza," he said as he threw his leg over a stool right in front of her.

As she wrote the order down, he pulled a five out of his pocket and placed it on the bar between them.

She stuffed the order up under a clip on a hanging wheel connecting the bar to the kitchen through a small window. "Guess you're over eighteen, hon," she half asked and half announced then picked up two glasses and dropped them into the sink.

"Yes ma'am," he said, suddenly feeling a little foolish for emphasizing the difference in their ages. He reached into his shirt pocket for his Camels, a new habit he had thought would make him look older. He lit a cigarette with a cough and experienced a wave of nausea.

The barkeep looked up at him, her arms elbow deep in sudsy water. "You gonna' make it there?"

Covering, Scotty blew a small amount of smoke skyward and touched his tongue with his fingertips. "Loose tobacco. I'll be okay."

She wiped her arms on her apron and a bar towel and nodded toward the two taps behind the bar top. "Draft or bottle?"

Scotty tried to sound worldly, "Draft. That's my poison."

She poured his beer and tilted the excess head off before finally topping it off. "It'll be a bit for y'er pizza."

The beer was cool and welcoming. He was no stranger to drinking. Around Palms High, he had enjoyed the reputation as one who could hold his liquor. He didn't get wild or hostile when he drank. Still, he wanted to look like having a beer in a bar was routine rather a relatively new experience.

While he waited for his pizza, Scotty crossed the room to the pay phone and called Kitty at work. Actually speaking with her was nearly impossible. The noise in the background at her bar coupled with the Johnny Cash record on the jukebox in Scotty's bar and marked the conversation with pleas on each end to repeat things. He was frustrated by the call, knowing there'd probably not be many chances to speak with her once he got to Fort Benning.

The pizza came with a second beer and Scotty enjoyed both, half watching a black and white television on the corner of the bar top. Customers came and went but mostly stayed. Soon all of the stools at the bar were occupied, and the noise level completely drowned out the jukebox and the television.

Scotty played with the ring of water on the bar top. Should he continue to thumb his way to Columbus, Georgia that night or find a place to stay? Before he could decide, an argument broke out behind him.

A drunk was trying too hard to convince a woman to sit down and have a drink with him. She kept refusing, and he kept insisting. Finally, he grabbed hold of her wrist and tried to force her to sit down.

Before he realized it Scotty heard himself say, "Hey, leave her alone." It wasn't like him. The words just spilled from him without warning.

The drunk tried to focus on Scotty. "Butt the fuck out, asshole." He tightened his grip on the woman and pulled her toward a chair at his table.

Scotty looked around the room hoping to find someone else willing to get involved. No one was volunteering. He took a sip of his beer, not wanting to get in the middle of it but wanting even less to look like he was backing away. He stood up from his bar stool hoping the gesture would be enough.

The drunk thrust his chin out defiantly. "What? You got a problem, asshole?"

Scotty stepped toward the drunk and tried a less confrontational tone. "Listen, pal. Can't you see she wants to be left alone? There must be a dozen other women coming here tonight who'd like to have a drink with you."

The drunk dropped the woman's wrist and made a failed attempt to stand up in Scotty's face. He fell back into his chair and became even angrier because he had made himself look so stupid. On his next attempt, he leaped to his feet and overshot his mark bumping into Scotty's chest, headfirst.

Scotty hit the man's shoulders with the heels of both hands, stopping his forward momentum and propelling him backward, over his chair and onto the floor.

Unsure of how the man would react next, Scotty braced for a fight, but the drunk only got up on his hands and knees and began to vomit.

Scotty threw his arm out to ease the woman away from the splatter.

The bartender cried out, "Shit, Earl. Your ass is out of here this time. Get out of my bar! Now!" She flipped up the hinged section of the bar top with a bang, ran into the middle of the room and bent over Earl screaming at him, pointing out *someone* would have to clean up after him, and she wasn't going let him into her bar ever again. She finally threatened to call the cops as Earl staggered out the door.

"How do I ever thank you, hon?"

Scotty turned to find the woman from the argument standing next to him, her hip leaning against the bar. Up close she wasn't as young as he would have guessed. Maybe twelve or thirteen years older than he was—in her early thirties. He wasn't sure what to say. "It's nothing.

Don't worry about it. Ah, I'm sorry he was such a jerk." He stumbled over his words.

She was tall which added to her nice shape. He quickly recognized he was staring and hoped she hadn't caught him eyeing her.

"Buy you a beer?" She hopped up onto the stool next to his and reached for his pack of cigarettes.

He looked around the landing at the top of the stairs leading to her apartment, uncomfortable. The place was quiet and clean and even had a carpeted hallway. But he was too excited by the prospect of spending the night with her to take in more of her place. He tried to act like going home with her wasn't a big thing for him. But he, like his friends, had talked more about sex than they'd actually experienced. And spending the night with an older good-looking woman was simply unheard of. Still, he didn't want her to know the night could be a milestone for him.

It wasn't as if he had never been with a girl. He'd enjoyed some stolen moments in the back seats of cars and more than a little hurried petting in forbidden places, but he had never been with a woman. Not a woman like her.

Her name was Liz. Inside the apartment, she excused herself and told Scotty to make himself at home while she showered. The apartment was very small—one room with a hotplate in the corner and a bathroom. He picked up a magazine off a table near the bed and flipped through it without anything grabbing his attention. He could smell the freshness of a woman in her bath coming through the door left ajar. He wondered if she expected him to join her or if she was just letting the steam escape from the windowless bathroom trapped in the center of the apartment building? He opted to wait for more encouragement from her.

He felt a flutter in the pit of his stomach when he heard her turn off the shower. Whatever the evening held was going to happen as soon as she came out of the bathroom.

He'd been so sure she was coming on to him in the bar but wasn't quite so sure as they walked to her apartment and she had chosen neutral topics to talk about.

He looked up from the magazine to find Liz standing in the door, her hair wrapped in a towel, drying her naked body with another. She seemed so comfortable. Her body was toned and just short of muscular but very feminine. Long legs and a very small waist set off her breasts.

He'd never seen a totally naked woman before. And he'd never been completely naked with one either. This wasn't like exposed body parts with nervous high school girls worried about being caught.

She smiled, stopped drying herself and nodded toward the bathroom. "Your turn, honey. Want me to wash your back?" She laughed.

Scotty wasn't sure if he should just exit the bathroom naked or if he should wear his jeans. Still unsure of her intent, he opted to wrap a towel around his midsection and see if it wouldn't provide him some middle ground to go either way.

He opened the door only to find her already in bed, still naked. Her damp hair brushed her shoulders. Her arms were gently crossed over her midsection, the sheet just covering her lower torso. Scotty felt awkward and didn't know exactly where to look.

"You coming to bed?" she asked, pulling back the covers for him.

As he stepped to the side of the bed, she reached up and untucked the corner of the towel around his waist, letting it fall to the floor. She placed her other hand on the back of his upper thigh and gently pulled him toward her.

CHAPTER 2

By noon the next day Scotty was still looking for another ride out of Waycross. He spent eighty-one cents on a Coke and a bag of salted peanuts at a truck stop along Highway 41. His money was running very low, but he'd get twenty dollars as soon as he got to Benning to be deducted from his first month's seventy-eight dollar paycheck. He'd never much thought about money before. They didn't have much money, but Kitty had taken care of most of the money in his life. He'd never thought of money from his few odd jobs as paying for essentials.

"Hey, you need a ride?"

Scotty saw an enormous woman wearing a muumuu and a scarf covering her hair. She pumped gas into a two-gallon gas can sitting on the fender of her Corvair. "Sure do," he said.

"North or south?"

"What?"

"Which way you goin'?"

"Columbus," he said.

"You stationed there?"

Hayes felt cramped in the small Corvair. She was so large she spilled over her bucket seat, across the divide, onto the side of his seat. "No. I mean, yes. I'm reporting in tonight."

"My boy went through basic there and what's that thing you go to after basic?"

"AIT."

"Yeah, advanced training, or something. He's in Germany now. Who'd a thought my boy J.D.'d ever be over there in Europe? Hell, he'd never been out of Waycross before the Army. You ever been away from home?"

"Sure. Plenty of times," he lied, not wanting to admit his lack of worldliness. "But I don't know where I'll be going after basic."

"Your momma gonna miss you?"

Scotty was uncomfortable with the woman, not sure what she had in mind. He felt like she was pumping him to tell her more about himself than he wanted to. He tried to recall what he'd packed in case he had to bail out and leave his bag in the trunk. "My mom died when I was a kid."

"Oh, I'm sorry, honey," she looked over at Scotty.

Her eyes seemed sincere. He guessed she was really just a mom herself giving a kid a ride. He relaxed a bit.

"What ya' want to do in the Army?"

"Don't know. It really wasn't my idea."

"Drafted?"

"Yeah. But it would have happened sooner or later anyway. Just about everyone from my graduating class seems to be getting draft notices."

"Maybe you can learn a trade."

"Like what?"

"My boy's in the Signal Corps now. He puts in phones and stuff. Seems to me he could do the same thing when he gets out if he was a mind to."

He hadn't thought about being a student again. "I'll just be happy to get through basic without killing myself."

"Oh, you'll be okay, baby. Think of all the boys who've gone through basic. Why would you be any different?"

He thought about how many times he had failed—at school and a couple of jobs. He hoped this time would be different.

It began to rain.

"My name is Asa Russell. We're going to spend the next two months together. And you're not going to like me. I won't lose any sleep over that," the tall Negro sergeant said, his hands on his hips standing squarely in front of the assembled ranks of new recruits.

Scotty was relieved the sergeant's eyes quickly sought out another recruit at the opposite end of the ten-man file to hassle. He tried to blend in and dodge some of the hazing and yelling going on all around him from several cadre NCOs. He had come close to being the object of Sergeant Russell's attention twice in the last hour as they ran from building to building filling out forms, drawing equipment, signing for weapons and getting assigned to squads. Each time, just before Russell pounced on him for some minor infraction or failure to follow instructions, another soldier committed an even greater sin drawing the sergeant's attention and his wrath.

Scotty didn't know much about the Army, but he knew a few things about Russell from few glimpses he had stolen. Russell outranked the other sergeants by a simple count of the large yellow stripes on his shirtsleeves. And he must have been a parachutist because he wore bright, shiny black paratrooper boots like his father had worn. But mostly he had eyes like a bird of prey. He didn't miss a move, a twitch or a mistake committed by one of the recruits.

The best possible way to avoid becoming Russell's object of ridicule was by not getting noticed. Which was what Scotty was trying to do. He knew he had to work on lowering his profile, except he stumbled, fell onto the asphalt and spilled his armload of bedding in front of him. The other recruits kept running in formation, none of them willing or able to stop to help Scotty Hayes spread-eagled on the parking lot outside the company supply room.

"What the hell is your problem?" Sergeant Russell yelled, leaning over Scotty, his hands on his hips, chin jutted out.

Scotty looked up at the face only inches from his own. "I, uh. I just tripped."

"Tripped? You tripped?" The sergeant pointed back at the building. "What the hell's so hard about double-timing from the door to the barracks across the street? Are you some kind of fucking spastic, boy?"

Scotty felt a sudden flush of panic in his chest as his heart pounded and he checked the urge to jump up and run. "I'm sorry."

"'Sorry?' You're sorry as hell. You're the sorriest piece of shit I have in this platoon, boy." The sergeant looked up at the others and yelled, "We can all get some sleep sometime tonight if this young lady here can get off her ass and get with *her* platoon."

Embarrassed and angry with himself for getting singled out, Scotty propelled to his feet. He scooped up the rolled mattress, sheets, pillow, mattress cover and blankets from the street and stared through the sergeant.

"You gonna' be a wiseass now, son?"

"I'm not your son," Scotty blurted out. As soon as the words left his lips, he knew he'd made a mistake. He knew he'd pay for it. He hadn't meant to confront the man. He was confused, out of his element and completely rattled by it all.

"We'll see just whose son you are, boy. I'll deal with you later. Now, fall in with the others and quit holdin' all of us up. Move!"

Scotty ran and stumbled to catch up with the others in the formation. But he couldn't miss the look of disdain on the faces of the others. He could not avoid hearing the grumbling. From within the ranks, a voice said something about Hayes causing trouble for them all.

Even though it was nearly two in the morning, the World War II barracks was still abuzz. The forty new recruits were making bunks, shining boots, folding newly issued clothing and stuffing everything into cramped lockers while all talking at once.

The door at the end of the platoon bay opened with a bang, and Sergeant Russell stepped onto the waxed linoleum. Scotty saw him before he had even cleared the doorway.

"Where's Mister Stumble Dick?" Russell yelled.

With Russell's arrival, everything stopped. And except for the sounds of Russell's voice and his combat boots on the floor, it was suddenly silent. There was no doubt, he was looking for Hayes.

Scotty stood up and stared at the blank wall across the center aisle of the platoon bay—not at Russell, unsure of how to calm his situation.

"You don't answer when an NCO is looking for you, asshole?"

Still staring at the wall, not looking at Russell, Scotty said nothing thinking it would be better to play dumb than to antagonize the sergeant.

Russell walked into Hayes' line of sight and got nose to nose with him. "You know, boy, every new cycle of trainees has one problem child in it just like you. And every time I have to square his ass away. You see, it's my job to handle these little episodes where dickheads like you just don't get it. And I have to make sure you understand who runs things around here and how this man's army works."

Hayes broke his stare and looked Russell in the eyes. He tried to send some kind of signal he was listening and not trying to piss the sergeant off, but it wasn't working.

"What? You want to tell me something? You feelin' froggy? 'Cause if you are you can go ahead and jump now. And I'll put you on your ass so fast you'll wonder if it was a truck or a bolt of lightning. You got me?"

Hayes unsure of what Russell expected of him, didn't answer. He felt his face begin to flush.

Russell got closer, his nose two inches from Scotty's and deliberately raised his voice, "You got me?!"

Still unsure, Scotty tried to think of an appropriate reply.

Before he could pick one, Russell started in on him again. "Looks to me like you need some *extra training*, boy." He turned and grabbed a rifle from one of the arms racks straddling the centerline of the aisle between the rows of double bunks and threw it at Hayes.

Hayes saw it coming out of the corner of his eye and awkwardly caught it. Unsure of what to do with it, he waited for Russell to make the next move. Sweat formed at his neck and trickled down his back between his shoulder blades. His breathing became labored as his chest tightened. He was getting rattled. More rattled than he'd ever been.

Russell grabbed the collar on Hayes' fatigue shirt and pulled him to one of the windows. He tapped the glass and pointed out at a grassy field next to the barracks. "See that?"

Before Hayes could reply, Russell continued. "That's a parade field. It is one point seven three miles around it. Most days you'll use it for physical training, and you'll get plenty. But you're getting a head start tonight, boy.

I want you to go out there and find the beaten path that runs 'round the whole field and start double-timing around it with your rifle held over your head. You got it? Double-timing, that's running for a dumb-ass civilian like you."

"For how long?" Hayes asked.

"'For how long?'" Russell mocked Hayes' nerve for even asking. "Until I get tired. That's how goddamn long."

Sweat poured down Scotty's face from under his helmet and burned his eyes. His new boots rubbed blisters in several places on his feet, and his arms felt as though they were made of wet sand.

He regretted having started smoking before leaving Belton. His lungs burned, and he was exhausted from lack of sleep. Rage, confusion and something resembling depression boiled up inside him as he staggered along the worn path, holding the eight-pound M-1 rifle over his head.

His pain wasn't anything like he'd experienced in football or track. The sensation wasn't like the pain from a muscle pull or a sprain. It was bone deep in his feet, shoulders and his knees. In school, he could bounce back in minutes. But in the hours since starting Basic Training, pain seemed to stack up on pain. Even the joints in his hands were stiff with swelling and becoming tender. It didn't feel like pain from training alone. It felt like it was deliberate. To punish him.

His skin was on fire in several places where his sweat soaked fatigues constantly rubbed into his neck, ankles, crotch and waistline. His eyes burned from sweat running down his face during the unending hours of two days of crawling, running and pushups.

What had he done to cause Russell to single him out? Why was he suddenly the pariah of his platoon? Everyone in his platoon looked at him like he was wrong, not the sergeant. He knew Russell owned him for the next eight weeks and could make his life even more miserable for him. Scotty knew for sure he had to get out of Russell's gun sights. And it wasn't going to be anything like pacifying his former high school vice principal.

As Scotty continued to struggle around the parade field's beaten path he caught sight of Sergeant Russell standing on the porch of his barracks, arms crossed, watching. From somewhere deep he summoned up the strength. He stiffened his arms to support the rifle and raised his head. He found the reserve to pick up his pace and steady his gait as he ran on into the dark Georgia night. He might drop; he might die out there, but he wouldn't quit.

In the dark of the platoon bay, all he could make out was the deep shadows hugging the corners of the cavities between the floor beams holding up the second floor. The recesses were unlit by the promise of dawn soon to spill through the rows of windows running along the long walls of the open platoon bay.

Unable to quickly fall sleep, Scotty stared up at the exposed joists just over arm's length from his upper bunk. How many others had slept in the same bunk and how many of them stared at the very same beams.

He wondered if anyone else in his platoon was suffering as much as he was. And with each day they seemed more and more like strangers than comrades in arms.

Fatigue tugged at him and his problem with Russell dogging him and singling him out for ridicule weighed down his mood and begged for a solution. He had never been so exhausted or felt so alone. In the middle of a room filled with almost two dozen other soldiers, he felt like an outsider.

Gone was the support he counted on from high school classmates when he was singled out by teachers. Gone was the chance to talk his way out of trouble with a smile and a promise. The others were getting along okay, and he seemed to be the only one Russell just wouldn't let up on.

He tried to laugh it off in front of the others when Russell wasn't around, but it didn't work. He tried to solicit sympathy and got no response. He even tried a few handy excuses. Nothing was working for him. None of his well-honed skills at getting out of work or excuses for not being prepared from his high school days worked in G Company, 1st Battalion, 2nd Training Regiment.

Scotty was coming to realize his two problems, Russell and the platoon, were going to continue for the rest of basic training—almost two more months. He didn't know if he could take it for much longer. And he couldn't see any way to appease Russell or divert his attention to allow Scotty to quietly slip back into the obscurity of just being one of the trainees in the platoon. He was certainly Russell's pet project. And it made no difference whether Scotty was screwing up or doing okay, Russell watched his every move, stayed on his back and made his life miserable.

Problem solving wasn't one of Scotty's talents. His whole life had been ad hoc, on the fly and without deliberate actions on his part. He'd never been a planner or even a plotter; never worried about trying to get out ahead of problems. He'd always been able to disappear into the crowd, but he no longer enjoyed the luxury, and it frightened him. He had to come up with something. But what?

While everyone else was sleeping, Scotty had been cleaning the latrine. Punishment for something he had done earlier in the day. He'd even forgotten what it was. What looked like an hour's job turned into four, and he didn't finish until nearly three a.m.

He was so drained he couldn't find the strength to take off his boots or uniform before climbing into his rack to steal some sack time before the next training day officially started. For him, the days were beginning to feel as if they were all braided together into one long, unending ordeal dedicated to breaking him.

He tried to get comfortable atop a three-inch mattress supported by a wire mesh grid looking more like garden fencing than bedsprings. He still hadn't adjusted to sleeping less than five feet from overhead beams layered with many coats of paint. He knew he wasn't going to get completely comfortable, so he settled for what he could get.

He thought of home and Kitty. He couldn't even quit. There he was in Georgia—on his own and missing Belton and even high school. And another day of it was about to start all over again. He felt the pressure to hurry up and get some rest because it was just minutes before the platoon would have to fall out of the barracks for the morning's scheduled run and physical training. And he had no plan.

"Hayes," an angry voice whispered from above his head, behind Scotty's bunk.

Drifting, Scotty wasn't even sure if he heard his name being called or if he dreamed it.

"Hayes!" He heard it again and started to get up on one elbow to look around in the darkened platoon bay when the voice cautioned, "Don't move. Just keep looking at the ceiling, asshole. Don't even think about looking back at me."

Unsure of whose voice it was or if there was a threat attached to the whispered words, Scotty tried to decide what to do. He opted to lie still and listen.

"We're already tired of you being a fuck-up, Hayes."

"Who's we?" Scotty asked, now sure it was another trainee.

"Don't be cute—the whole goddamn platoon. We don't want Sergeant Russell or any of the other cadre on our asses because of you. You're making us look bad, and we're tellin' you if you don't shape up we're going to kick your ass. All of us.

"Every time you fuck up we end up getting shit for it. We're tired of doing pushups because you screw up. We're tired of being the last platoon in the chow line because we have to wait for Russell to quit tearing your ass up. We're tired of being the last for Mail Call because of you and we're tired of being thought of as a bunch of fuck-ups around the battalion because of you!"

Scotty could feel others standing near his bunk. They were all there. What could he do? Who could help? *Russell.* Maybe he could help. The same Russell who had been busting Scotty's hump was the Russell he needed right then. No. Russell couldn't really protect him from them. If they wanted to get him, they'd find a time and place. "You can't—"

"Shut up. We're gonna' have a blanket party. You keep it up, and you'll be the guest of honor."

Scotty had heard about blanket parties coming through the Reception Station his first two days in the Army. They jump you, throw a blanket over your head so you can't identify anyone and then pummel you.

He could feel his stomach tighten as he gripped the metal rails of his bunk and tried to calm his racing heartbeat.

"We'll just tell the NCOs you tripped and fell on the stairs comin' down from the second floor. And you know they'll buy it because they're fucking sick of your sorry-ass attitude too.

"Then we'll be through with you, Hayes. You'll end up in the Post Hospital and you ain't our problem no more. They'll recycle your ass. But we'll be rid of you, you fuck-up. We'll be graduated, and you'll just be startin' Basic all over again."

Recycle. One of the other dreaded words he had heard. Rumor had it any trainee who was recycled to another training company to start all over again was in for harder treatment and was certain to be an outcast in a group he hadn't started with, no matter how popular he'd been in his old training company. Scotty already knew how bad it was, he couldn't imagine it getting worse in another company.

The voice asked, "You got it?" Then he kicked the metal frame of the double-bunk for emphasis.

"Yeah. Yeah, I got it," Scotty said.

He didn't move. He just listened. The voice went silent, and his sense of the others standing around his bunk disappeared too. Scotty strained to hear something, anything. Only the sounds of the Army broke the silence. From the windows, open three inches top and bottom by regulation, First Call played over a tinny loudspeaker, the bugle call provided by a scratchy record player at regimental headquarters. But it wasn't loud enough to drown out the pounding of his own heart he felt deep in his throat and could hear pulsing in his ears.

In what seemed like only a few minutes First Call was followed by Reveille. Another day at Fort Benning had begun.

The sun pressed down on Scotty, as he sat with the forty other basic trainees in the bleachers tucked into the slash pine and scrub oak woods on the north side of the Sand Hill training area. Sweat from under his helmet collected on his shaved head and trickled down the back of his neck and down his forehead into his eyes. He tried to fight off sleep and hold his focus on the instructor standing in front of the bleachers, but he kept drifting in and out of the netherworld between awake and asleep. As quickly as he felt alert and winning his battle, he would feel his head fall backward only to snap back forward by some reflexive muscle response to the loss of consciousness. It was a special hell. The more he fought to stay awake, the more unsure he was if he was awake or dreaming.

He'd picked his place in the bleachers because he thought he could hide among the others. The classes and the constant smothering of supervision by sergeant after sergeant from one training area to another was becoming a blur for Scotty. But he was getting a little better at ducking the cadre NCOs in his own company. His new problem was the instructors who came and went with each new class on weapons, first aid, dismounted drill, and physical training were all unknowns to him. One was as likely as another to leap on Scotty for any number of infractions for technique, not following instructions, safety violations, uniform problems or just not paying attention. All of which he seemed to be able to commit with frightening regularity.

Sleeping in class was one of the cardinal sins, especially if the subject had to do with life and death on the battlefield. He soon recognized every class was about the same central theme somewhere at its core. Even so, he kept nodding off and recovering, slipping deeper. Losing control.

Suddenly, he felt a sharp pain as something smacked him in the back of the head. His helmet flew forward, off his head and into his lap.

Russell! He was standing right behind the bleachers. The tap on the helmet was a warning to Hayes. Either he had to stay awake or deal with Russell after the instructor lecturing on rifle marksmanship finished his class.

"Sergeant Russell?" the instructor called out in a forceful military voice a form of handoff of the class to its own cadre.

"On your feet!" Russell yelled as he walked around the bleachers to the gravel apron in front and stopped facing the instructor.

Responding to Russell's command, the entire platoon of trainees leaped to a rigid position of attention in the bleachers.

The instructor waited for Russell to position himself in front of him. "This concludes the instruction. You can take 'em home." He then saluted.

Russell returned the salute. "Thank you," he said and then turned to face the standing trainees. "Where's Hayes?" he hollered out.

At the sound of his name, Scotty was shocked to discover he'd been singled out again. For what? He was just standing there with the others, hidden in the mass of bodies. He blurted out, "Here . . . Sergeant," without thinking about it.

"Get your ass down here. Now!"

Hayes snatched up his rifle and threaded his way down the rows of the bleachers to Russell. He slipped and caught himself, then nearly tripped over another trainee's rifle butt as he bumped and stumbled to the bottom of the bleachers.

What was it? What could he want? What was Russell upset about—this time? At the bottom row, he finally leaped awkwardly from the bleachers and landed in front of Russell. He wasn't sure if he should say anything.

"Glad to see you are with us and *awake*, Hayes," Russell said, looking over Hayes' head at the others above and behind him.

Again, Scotty didn't know what he should say to Russell's remark. Or if he should say anything at all. He started to say a mollifying "Yes, Sergeant," and then checked himself for fear sure to create more problems for him.

"Hayes," Russell said, shifting his focus to Scotty. "I think we just might be able to keep you awake if we give you a little added responsibility." He looked at the others and added, "Not like your day's already filled with it."

The others laughed nervously.

Scotty didn't know what Russell was getting at, but he knew it wasn't going to be good. Again, he opted to say nothing.

"Turn around, Hayes."

Scotty turned to face his platoon, still standing at attention in the small bleachers.

"Hayes, I want you to take charge of this gaggle here. Then, get them into a marching formation behind the bleachers—ready to double-time home."

Scotty stood mute.

"You got that, Hayes?"

Scotty couldn't believe what he was hearing. He didn't know anything about giving drill commands to soldiers. What was Russell trying to do? Was he just trying to find new ways to embarrass him? That had to be it. But why? Up till then, he'd been sure Russell was just singling him out to ridicule him or amuse himself. But asking him to give drill commands was sure to make him look like the biggest fool in the training regiment. Why couldn't he just yell at Scotty? Or make him do pushups? Why did he have to make him perform like a trained seal?

"Well?" Russell asked. "What are you waiting for, Hayes? You've been in and out of enough military formations by now to know how it's done. So do it, Hayes. Just do it. And do it now!"

Scotty felt panic clamp onto his chest. More sweat ran from his armpits down his sides to his beltline inside his fatigue shirt. He'd never been in charge of anyone, and certainly not a group of soldiers. He'd never even spoken to any group other than a book report he had to do in the ninth grade. And then the fear of public speaking almost caused him to throw up before the class.

They were all looking at him. Everyone in the training area was watching to see him make an idiot out of himself. Nearby, NCOs were elbowing each other to make sure no one missed Hayes' performance. And Scotty knew in a fraction of a second Russell was sure to yell at him again.

He tried to gather his thoughts. He tried to remember what the commands were to get the job done. *Attention?* No, that couldn't be it. They were already standing at attention. *Fall out?* No. That couldn't be it either. That would only get them out of the bleachers—then what? They were still looking at him, daring him to screw up again.

Russell leaned forward, his face mere inches from Hayes' ear and whispered, "Try 'At my command, fall to the rear of the bleachers and reform for movement.'"

Scotty's mouth was dry. He felt his tongue thicken. He repeated Russell's words. But they did nothing.

"Louder! They can't hear you, *Miss* Hayes."

He tried it again. Louder, this time. "At my command, fall to the rear of the bleachers and reform!"

Still nothing.

Russell leaned over to Scotty again and added: "Now, give them the command to fall out."

Scotty took a deep breath and forcefully bellowed, "Fall out!"

The platoon leaped out of the bleachers and ran to the rear where they quickly reassembled into a platoon formation of four uniformly neat ranks all standing at attention, one man precisely behind the man in front of him, waiting for the next command—just as they had been taught since the very first week.

Scotty was stunned. They did it. They did what he told them. And they did it perfectly. And they did it because *he* gave them the command.

"Hayes?"

Scotty didn't know what Russell wanted, and he expected harsh criticism. He ventured a neutral reply, "Yes, Sergeant."

"What are you waiting for, son? They're over there—behind the bleachers. And you're here. Now get your ass over there and take command of my platoon so you can march them back to the company area."

CHAPTER 3

It was still weeks before the colors would burst and the New York rolling hills overlooking the Hudson River would put on a display of golds, reds, and brilliant yellows. It wasn't cold enough for a topcoat, but those days were coming soon as the academic year had begun to spool up in earnest.

Preoccupied with his thoughts and barely aware of those around him, Major Eldon Haywood Pascoe exited Thayer Hall. He started his walk home, to his Army quarters on the other side of West Point's huge manicured parade field known by every cadet and every graduate as *The Plain*.

His regular path to and from work took him along the concrete walk overlooking the river, around Trophy Point and past the flagpole holding the huge Post Flag still up until the end of the duty day.

The sidewalk outside the building was awash in the bodies of cadets in motion and faculty members all rushing to be somewhere else. To the man, they all moved with a purpose, as they had been trained to do from the first day they entered West Point as lowly *new cadets*.

The mass of student cadets and a few junior officers he passed each snapped sharp salutes to the tall, angular Army major. Pascoe returned the salutes as if on autopilot but failed to utter the appropriate responses to the frequent, "Good afternoon, sirs" from those saluting him. It was the first time he had failed to do so since his own cadet days thirteen years earlier. Neither did he make eye contact with more than a few of the dozens of officers and cadets rendering him the traditional courtesy.

As he let his gaze drift downward from the faces of other officers passing him he was reminded of the disparity evident in the number of combat ribbons on the blouses of many of his peers and the absence of any on his own chest. Each day since graduating from the Military Academy he had regretted taking the option of going on to graduate school while his classmates went directly to the Korean War.

So many of their blouses were brilliantly colored by decorations for gallantry in battle, wounds received in combat and awards for excellence in the most demanding of leadership roles. His own ribbons were for meritorious service—none of it in combat. His proudest insignia of accomplishment was the silver aviator's badge he had earned at flight school.

He had often rationalized his actions, his less than aggressive efforts to join his classmates in Korea, by telling himself he couldn't have known Korea was going to turn out to be a war instead of a *police action*. Neither could he have known the level of respect shown to his classmates who had distinguished themselves there.

He distanced himself from the crowd that thinned as he got farther from the center of the campus on his way to his quarters. On The Plain cadets were already formed up in rehearsals for the coming Saturday's parade—a weekly ritual. For a moment he was reminded of his time on the same grassy field. It didn't feel all that long ago. Suddenly, he was aware of the cadets who had stopped as had the cars along the road encircling The Plain—each driver getting out and standing at attention alongside his car turning his attention to the Post flag.

It was the end of the duty day. The six-man color guard at the base of the flagpole began the ritual of firing the salute cannon and lowering the flag as the bugler played Retreat Call.

Pascoe stopped to join the others standing silently, saluting while his country's flag moved slowly down the mast to the waiting hands of soldiers dressed in pressed, polished and perfectly fitting uniforms.

He held his salute, listened to the bugle call, and felt a tingle of patriotism in his chest, which always accompanied such ceremonies as old as soldiering itself. If someone were to tell him within three years that very same flag would be burned and spit upon in the streets of America he would have laughed at them.

Only a six-minute walk took him the rest of the way to his quarters. The Retreat ceremony was completed, the flag perfectly folded and retired for the day.

He entered his antebellum quarters by crossing the white column-flanked porch, which took him through the heavy and ornate front door. Immediately inside the door, something on a small table caught his eye. He was irritated to find Karen's dirty gardening gloves tossed carelessly on the table. This served to lower Pascoe's mood even more. It wasn't just the gloves. It was the fact she just tossed them on *that* table. The table holding *the* tray—the silver tray where official visitors left their calling cards.

Calling cards were another tradition in the old Army and still lived on at West Point. But again the symbolism was lost on Karen. The gloves were just another reminder of how he kept failing to impress upon her the importance of decorum and tradition at West Point. A major's wife did *not* leave gardening implements in the foyer. And Eldon Pascoe's wife certainly wouldn't leave dirty tools there.

It bothered him the way she always treated the Army as if it was just a part-time job he would soon leave and go on to find a real career. She didn't get it. He had always wanted to be a West Point grad and an Army officer. He had told her many times the Army was where he intended to stay and where he would excel. It was his career, his calling and not just a job for him until something better came along. At least those where his goals until that morning.

His arm on the oak balustrade, he leaned across it and craned his neck toward the second-floor landing, "Karen?"

No answer.

Still trying to set an example, he took off his service cap and carefully placed it squarely on the top of the hall tree on his way past the bead-board skirt of the sweeping staircase to the butler's pantry tucked behind it.

The pantry was an early 19th Century relic of a time when servants staged entire dinner parties from its cramped confines. The pantry separated the kitchen from the large formal dining room. The service area was complete with glass cabinetry to hold the family's china and silver, good linens and serving dishes.

In those earlier days, the household staff readied meals on the new oak surfaces and lined up everything to be served, cleared or refreshed from the long narrow room lit only by gas lamps and a single window at one end.

Pascoe scanned the cluster of liquor bottles crammed into the corner of the countertop. He had told Karen more than once they looked disorganized and to him—sloppy.

As much as he wanted a drink, he was compelled to rearrange the bottles, taller ones in the back, shorter ones in front, equal spacing between them, labels all facing him and readable. He took half a step back and checked his work before pulling his favorite brand of single-malt scotch from the huddled collection.

The top unscrewed, he reached for a glass and was pleased to find the tumblers on the shelf above in neat rows and ranks, upside down, ready to be pressed into service—just how he had left them the night before. He poured half a tumbler full of scotch. No ice, no water, no soda. He gulped most of the contents in one swallow.

Pascoe leaned against the counter and dropped his head, his chin nearly touching his chest. Deep in thought, enjoying the warming feeling of the scotch, he was unaware Karen had entered the far end of the pantry.

"Eldon, honey. What's wrong?"

He looked at her. She stood confidently, wearing a light turtleneck sweater under her bib overalls. The baggy form of the denim couldn't conceal her tiny waist—a cheerleader's body. A body that would never suggest she had just passed her thirty-third birthday.

His peers and superiors thought she was cute, perky and playful. He'd heard the word *delightful* used too often for him to feel comfortable about it. They considered her an asset. He refused to accept the notion that her sex appeal and personality might have added some modicum of job security to his career. He preferred to think that all he had achieved was the fruit of his hard work and dedicated performance of duty. He had appreciated how once outside their home she had never embarrassed him, but she still didn't consider herself part of the Army's family.

Pascoe had known officers whose careers ended because of completely inappropriate behavior on the part of their wives. And there were those who failed to get promotions because their wives didn't fit the mold. Field grade officer's wives were defined by very strict standards. Those who didn't meet them could compound the problems of a mediocre officer's career.

Karen's appeal was not how he wanted to become tenured. The fact she had a cute little behind other men admired had ceased being a source of pride to him and often provoked feelings of jealousy. He had to guard against his growing compulsion to confront other officers who stole a desirous glance at her for fear it could be blown out of proportion. Once out of proportion, an incident could end up mentioned in a performance report where any negative comment could be career ending.

He knew her appearance alone didn't guarantee him a place in the Army, but he suspected there were instances where her attractiveness might have resulted in invitations they might not have received had he been married to a woman with a less attractive body. Anyone who didn't know him well would assume their frequent appearances at social and official functions were a sign he was on the right track and was someone to watch, someone on his way up.

He took another drink and refused to put the thought out of his mind. He was convinced he was young to be a major and selected to teach at West Point because of his competence, not because of the size of her breasts. "Karen, you left your gloves on the hall table."

She ignored his comment and offered a neutral reply. "Honey, I didn't hear you come in. I'm so glad you're home." She raised a small basket. "I've decided what we should do this weekend is go have ourselves a nice picnic before the weather gets ugly again."

He refused to reply to her silly suggestion. He picked up the bottle. "I don't suppose you want a drink."

"No," she answered. "What is it? Is something wrong?"

He tilted the bottle, pleased to find the amount he poured stopped exactly at the point he had intended it to—at the glass' midline. He raised the drink to his lips and sipped slowly, controlled, focused.

"Well, when you want to tell me whatever's bothering you, I'll be in the kitchen, Eldon."

"Harris showed me my fitness report today. He crucified me. That worthless bastard!"

"Your what?"

"My Efficiency Report."

She waved her hand as if shooing his comment away. "Oh, don't be silly. Nobody cares about those kind of things. I used to get them all the time when I worked at Kroger's before we were married. It was just a joke around the store—"

"Karen, we've been married ten years, and you still don't know a god-damn thing about the Army. Would it kill you to learn something about what I do? You and your picnic baskets and flower arrangements. Don't you ever pay attention to anything? Don't you know what this means? How important this is to my future?"

"Well, I may not know everything about the Army, but I don't see how a silly old supervisor's rating can be all that bad."

"Because it isn't a max report! Because it isn't first tier. Because it doesn't say I walk on water. I don't get anything but the highest ratings. I won't settle for less. And I won't accept less from him or anyone else."

She always did know the point at which it was better for her to be silent and he had crossed the mark. "I'm sorry, Eldon. I didn't know you and Colonel Harris weren't getting along."

"Neither did I. Asshole. Who does he think he is giving me a report like that? He's a goddamn campus rat. He's been here what, six years, teaching history and he's going to give *me* a shitty report?

"We'll see about this. I'll shove my report up his ass before I'm through." He poured still another drink and Karen left the pantry without saying another word or making a sound.

Pascoe sat in the straight-back chair in front of Leggett's desk and waited for him to get off the phone. Pascoe looked around the office to fill the time. Offices for instructors at West Point were interesting amalgams of academic and military trappings.

Leggett's was no different. Bound volumes of classic books related to instruction stood in regimented, perfectly arranged bookcases flanked by colorful enameled wall plaques representing the unit insignia of some previous posts Leggett held. His desktop sported a pipe rack holding Meerschaums and handmade briars in precise upright ranks near a large brass ashtray crafted from a spent artillery shell.

An umbrella stand held pointers and rolled maps since officers never carried umbrellas by custom. The coat rack which might otherwise hold woolen suit coats and tweeds with leather elbow patches on civilian campuses held only Leggett's Army green uniform tunic, hung precisely, the left shoulder facing out, this too by custom.

Each office projected the military and academic resume of its occupant complete with framed awards, certificates, and degrees. Only a few small, inconspicuous framed family photos revealed a personal life.

Lieutenant Colonel Paul Leggett was a bull of a man with a proud reputation as an All-American fullback in his cadet days—when West Point had a winning football team. He had been an upperclassman when Eldon Pascoe arrived as a new plebe. They had known each other since then and had even been assigned to the same stations twice since Pascoe graduated.

Leggett hung up, and Pascoe plowed headlong into the conversation without so much as even a passing effort to measure Leggett's mood or to determine if Leggett was even the slightest bit interested in his problem with Colonel Harris. Nothing was more important to Pascoe than safeguarding his chances for advancement. Still, he tried to conceal the extent to which Harris' report had shaken him. Holding his cards close to his chest was a habit he had developed early—as a cadet.

Concealing as much as he could always seemed to work to his advantage. Over the years he had tried to perfect the art of withholding information about himself. In his mind, it was the other side of the caution—information is power.

Leggett's generosity was widely known. Many of his peers, as well as cadets, sought him out for advice. Pascoe too knew he could come to Leggett and had done so more than once over the years. But never before had he come to Leggett in trouble. Their usual discussions centered on Pascoe's choices and aspirations—career strategy and career development, void of any real problems.

In all the times Pascoe had asked for Leggett's advice, they had never gotten beyond a business level of conversation. They had never shared as much as a beer together. And, on every occasion, the topic had always been Pascoe or his career. Pascoe had never asked about Leggett's family or even if he had a pick in the Army-Navy game.

Pascoe didn't recognize Leggett could set his personal feelings aside while he tried to offer his best advice to a subordinate even if they were not good friends. Pascoe mistook this as sincere involvement in his future and was encouraged to return over the years. He spoke carefully, guarding against inflammatory words or a level of volume, which might give away his near panicked state over his sinking career.

"I'm tempted to challenge the report because Colonel Harris hasn't counseled me on anything I've done wrong. He should have at least given me a chance to fix whatever he took objection to before the report was due. Shouldn't he?"

Leggett had been listening while watching the river of gray-clad cadets pass under his office window hurrying to and from morning classes. He turned back to the room, took his pipe from his mouth and pointed the shaft at Pascoe. "It might garner some sympathy with the Records Review Board if he had pounded your ass, El. But, he gave you a *superior* rating. Numerically, he gave you a 108 out of a possible 110. You might have gotten some traction out of a 30 but not a 108."

"It's still the kiss of death. There's no way I can have a chance at early promotion to lieutenant colonel with a less than *outstanding* report to go along with the others I've received. I'm screwed!"

"Look at this from the Army's perspective. They want officers with proven track records to put their money on. They don't want to promote people with iffy reports or put them in positions of higher responsibility. They want to work good horses to death."

"So, where does that leave me?"

"What you have to do is look like a thoroughbred on paper. In the long view."

"But what about the report Harris just wrote?"

"Pattern, Eldon. Pattern. It's just one report."

"What are you getting at?"

"Get off trying to challenge Harris. It's not going to accomplish anything for you except pissing people off. Harris is good and has been teaching here long enough to leave a positive lasting impression on every cadet and every other faculty member he has met.

"Hell, there's even a rumor the Superintendent is considering making him the Dean of Students. He's solid here. Pete Harris was one of the first Rangers to climb the cliffs at Point du Hoc at Normandy on D-Day. He's a legend around here among the cadets.

"And if isn't enough, he's commanded a rifle company in the Wolfhounds in Korea and was wounded twice in battle. He's a decorated, well-respected soldier who just happens to head the History Department here. You aren't going to discredit him on qualifications or his method of observation. Anything you do to bring him down will only come back to bite you in the ass."

Pascoe dropped his head into his hand. "Okay. So what's left?"

"You have to make one less-than-perfect report look like a complete fluke. Like there was some personality mismatch. Like it doesn't belong with the others. Isolate it. Surround it with more *outstandings*. More max reports. Let it get lost in the pile of good reports."

"How?"

"First, get away from Harris before he can do it to you again. Six more months and he's obligated to give you another report. You don't want to give him a chance to repeat this. You could get caught with a second bad report. But, if you can get out of here in less than six months, you'll be able to dodge a second report from him.

"Then, you have to spend the next several years working your way into the toughest jobs you can find. Much tougher than the one you've got. Good soldiering kind of jobs in ass-busting combat units. And while you are in them you *must* get good reports in each of them."

"I'm not sure I'm following you."

"Like I said, think of the Army's perspective on this. In a few years, when you come up for consideration for lieutenant colonel they'll ship your file over to the promotion board at the Pentagon for review. Half a dozen colonels and a brigadier general or two will go over your personnel jacket for the jobs you've had and the job you've done in each.

"Suppose you have a fat file made up of a string of good reports from increasingly tougher and tougher jobs and only one report in the middle of the pile out of step with the others. Wouldn't you guess the single atypical report from a job teaching history, a job with no command responsibility, no risk, no serious professional challenge, might be discounted or dismissed in favor of the trend indicated by all your other reports?"

Pascoe let it sink in for a moment and then looked up at Leggett who was emptying out the bowl of his pipe into the large metal trashcan next to his desk.

Leggett continued. "You got to get going on this, Eldon. You've got to get out of here right away and find those hard jobs. You've got to make a solid career plan and work it. No screw-ups, no compromises, and no shortfalls. Nothing else will do this. You've got to pick the tightest spots in the toughest fights and win them all. You're in charge of the pattern you set from this day forward, and the pattern will show up on paper. And it's paper that'll get you promoted early or get you an invitation to leave the Army.

"It's in your lap, Pascoe."

"Christ, where the hell do I do all this?"

"You've got to volunteer to go to Vietnam."

CHAPTER 4

Rain came and went in waves—normal for Georgia. That morning a short cloudburst contributed to the constant state of wetness experienced by trainees every year at that time. They were wet from rain, or sweat or the heavy night's dew. Either way, they stayed wet and uncomfortable.

Scotty tried to force his discomfort out of his mind as he sat in the middle of the bleachers, with the others, but this time he was locked onto Russell's words.

Sergeant Russell stood close to the lower row, centered on the bleachers. That day, serving as an instructor, he wore a steel helmet rather than the more ornamental and less protective shiny black lacquered helmet liners worn by the cadre. He spoke forcefully, reaching for clarity and understanding, determined to get his message to every man in the platoon. He was able to make eye contact with each soldier over and over again as he paused for important points and searched for signs of recognition in those soldiers' eyes. He knew from experience that failure to instruct his charges could be fatal.

He held a small egg-shaped, olive drab object up above his head. "This, gentlemen, is the Army's standard fragmentation grenade. It is the M-26 hand grenade." Nomenclature was always delivered in a laundry list of characteristics and capabilities. Nothing omitted, precise and complete to the smallest details.

He continued. "After the rifle and the bayonet, it is the basic fighting tool of the Infantryman. It weighs twenty-one ounces, has a four-second delay and is filled with flaked or granular TNT. The body of this grenade is made of thin sheet metal, and when detonated, it produces thousands of fragments, which come from the serrated wire coiled inside the body.

As he spoke, he held the grenade up in front of his face and pointed out its components. "Function is simple. The thrower pulls the pin and throws the grenade. Once the grenade leaves the hand of the thrower the safety spoon held down by the thrower's fingers springs free—arming the grenade. Four seconds later the grenade explodes.

"Fitch."

A soldier in the top row of the bleachers stood quickly. "Yes, Sergeant."

"How far away from me are you?"

Fitch looked at the six rows of bleachers below him then the short span of gravel between the bleachers and Russell. "My guess is thirty, maybe thirty-five feet, Sergeant."

"Sit. I want all of you to look over your shoulder at the yellow stake in the ground behind the bleachers."

They all craned their necks and looked between the legs of the soldiers above and behind them at the worn wooden stake, three feet high, otherwise unmarked, that had been driven into the ground in the training area.

"Gentlemen," Russell paused again for emphasis. "This grenade will kill everyone within fifteen meters and wound as far away as eighty feet. That stake is exactly fifteen meters from where I am standing.

"Accordingly, these distances require the thrower to be outside these distances to avoid becoming a casualty of his own grenade. So forget all the John Wayne shit you've seen in the movies about pullin' the pin with your teeth, lobbing a grenade into a room and flattening yourself against the outside wall of a shack until it goes off. You try that and your ass is an instant fucking casualty."

He paused to allow the image to sink in.

Scotty's gaze wandered from the stake to Russell to the grenade range behind Russell and then to the others around him. They were all wide-awake, all paying attention and all worried about the training day ahead of them.

"This grenade produces casualties by its high-velocity projection of fragmentation and blast. Now, if you'll direct your attention to my assistant instructor in the grenade pit, he'll demonstrate."

The young sergeant assisting Russell stood on the near side of a shoulder-high wall of the grenade pit beyond Russell. It was a three-sided concrete stall with the open end toward the bleachers and the target area beyond the wall on the opposite end.

From Scotty's vantage point he could see over the wall to the chewed up dirt impact area pockmarked by tens of thousands of grenade explosions over the years. Nothing grew there. Nothing dared.

The assistant instructor raised his elbows to shoulder level holding a grenade tightly to his chest. He slowly slipped the index finger of his down-range hand into the grenade pin ring and held the body of the grenade firmly with the other.

"Pull pin!" Russell yelled.

The assistant instructor pulled the pin on the grenade and assumed a quarterback's passing stance, the grenade near his ear, his free hand pointing over the wall and down range.

Scotty's heart started to pound, anxious to have the armed, now lethal grenade, on its way over the wall and away from them. He glanced down at the ground and estimated the distance between his platoon in the bleachers and the grenade thrower to be less than seventy-five feet—still within the effective casualty-producing range of the grenade.

"Throw grenade!" Russell yelled.

The thrower lofted the grenade over the wall and watched it wobble through the air. Once out of his hand the safety spoon he had been holding down with his palm flew off and started the fuse's short delay. The grenade landed nearly a hundred feet away from the thrower. Once it landed the sergeant dropped to the ground on the nearside of the wall and waited.

Scotty listened to the unspoken count in his head, two-three-four and the grenade exploded, throwing red Georgia clay in a plume in all directions. The crack of the grenade was sharp and precise, unlike movie explosions. Dirt fell back to the ground in clumps, and Scotty felt himself begin to breathe again.

If the regular routine of demonstrations followed by practical exercise held true, Scotty knew it would just be a matter of time before the trainees would each be ushered into the grenade pit, one at a time, to throw a grenade.

As the assistant instructor got to his feet and Russell returned to the front of the bleachers Scotty was surprised to hear his name slip from Russell's lips. "Hayes. Get your ass down here."

"Yes, Sergeant," Scotty said, leaping to his feet. He quickly threaded through the others and found his way to the ground in front of the bleachers. This time careful not to get tripped up and determined not to get rattled—despite knowing Russell's summoning had something to do with the grenade range.

Russell walked over to a wooden box in the corner of the grenade pit and snatched a fiber canister from the box. Opening it, he dumped a live grenade out into the palm of his upturned hand. His back to Scotty, who stood at the base of the bleachers unsure if he should have followed Russell into the pit, Russell spoke. "Everyone stay where you are. Everyone except Hayes. Hayes, get into the pit." He turned and stepped into the center of the concrete enclosure through the open end.

At Benning, Scotty had learned to move everywhere at double-time. He ran to the pit, getting there the same time Russell did.

Russell pointed down at a four-inch diameter opening in the low spot of the bowl-shaped bottom of the grenade pit. "You know what that is, Hayes?"

Scotty looked at the hole, which appeared to him to be the opening of a pipe of some sort sunk into the concrete slab. "A hole?"

"No shit! It's a goddamn grenade sump, Hayes." He looked toward the bleachers and raised his voice again. "Listen up," he said to the platoon. He pointed to the pipe. "This sump is buried under nine inches of concrete and is thirty-six inches long. It's designed to contain most of the fragmentation of a loose grenade. All the rest is directed out the open end. Should one of you numb nuts drop a live grenade today I want you to do three things: Yell '*Live grenade!*' kick it into the grenade sump, jump away from the sump and hug the ground until the grenade goes off.

"It won't do you any good if you can't get the grenade into the hole. You got it?"

They all yelled in unison, "Yes, Sergeant."

"Clear, Hayes?"

"Clear, Sergeant!"

"Good." He turned back to Scotty and looked him directly in the eyes. "Look at me and do *only* what I tell you to do. You got it, Hayes?"

Scotty could feel sweat forming under his arms. And his sense of things closed in on him. He was suddenly not conscious of anyone or anything but Russell and the grenade he held. "Yes, Sergeant." His words came out in a near whisper, his chest and throat tightened. Inside he kept trying to convince himself he could calm down and stay focused. He suddenly thought of the fat woman who gave him a ride on his way to Fort Benning. How many others had done what he was about to do?

Russell grabbed Scotty's upper arm and turned him slightly, so his left shoulder pointed at the front wall of the grenade pit. He then grabbed Hayes' right hand and forcefully stuffed the grenade into his palm and closed Scotty's fingers around the body of the grenade. "Do not drop this."

"Yes, Sergeant," again slipped from Scotty's lips as he held his eye contact with Russell.

"Don't do anything, yet. I'm going to tell you to pull the pin. That's when I want you to pull the pin and cock your arm like you're Johnny Unitas of the Colts. Then, at my command, I want you to throw the grenade over the wall, watch it land and then hit the concrete here in the pit. *Don't* get up until I tell you it is clear. You understand?"

Scotty nodded. He felt cotton mouthed.

"Goddamnit, Hayes, don't nod your head. Speak, boy. Speak!"

"Yes, Sergeant. I understand."

"Good," Russell said, then he stepped back a few inches to give Scotty more room to throw. He next looked around the range and over the wall to make sure the target area was clear. Without looking, he reached out and wrapped his hand around Scotty's.

Scotty's hand trembled as he held the grenade tightly and rested the index finger of his opposite hand inside the pull ring attached to the arming pin.

"Steady, son. You'll be okay," Russell whispered. He let go and stepped back, watching Scotty's eyes and not his hands. "Pull pin!"

Scotty yanked the pin and took up a throwing stance, knowing the only thing between him and death would be measured in seconds should he drop the grenade or open his hand. His breathing became rapid and shallow. Sweat flowed down the bridge of his nose and fell to the ground in droplets.

"Throw!"

Scotty lobbed the grenade up and over the concrete wall into the target area. As it flew, the spring-loaded spoon ejected firing the fuse with a small pop. The grenade's flight ended with one clumsy bounce and then stopped rolling a foot and a half from the initial point of impact.

Scotty watched the grenade until Russell's hand slapped him on the back of his neck to remind him. "Down!"

They both flattened out on the concrete just as the grenade went off with the distinctive crump only a grenade emits.

Scotty suddenly had an unaccustomed feeling of accomplishment, of having done something almost perfectly.

"Clear! On your feet, Hayes," Russell stood and dusted off the front of his fatigue shirt. He then turned and pulled another grenade canister from the case and unpacked it. "Swithins!" he yelled over his shoulder to another soldier in the bleachers. "Get down here. You're next."

Scotty turned to leave the grenade pit and give room for the next trainee.

"Whoa! Where you going?"

Surprised and a bit confused, Scotty looked at Russell to see if there was something else he should be doing or something he'd forgotten.

Russell thrust the next grenade into Scotty's hands. "Take this and teach Swithins how to do it."

"What?" Scotty wasn't sure he heard what he heard.

"This is how it goes in the Army, Hayes. This is how it always goes. You learn something, you do something, and then you teach that something to other soldiers. Now, you've learned it and you've done it—show Swithins how to do it. I'll be over by the bleachers having a smoke."

＊＊＊

As the training day ended the rain returned.

Because it took so long to get everyone through the grenade training, they slept in the training area, eleven miles from their Sand Hill barracks. Several hundred yards behind the grenade pits, G Company had set up two-man pup tents, neatly aligned in precise rows and tightly staked to the ground so no wrinkles remained in the tent walls. Each of the tents was encircled by a two-inch deep trench dug around its base to allow water running off the tents to flow away from the tents instead of into them and under their occupants.

Scotty stood in the chow line with the others, his aluminum mess kit and canteen cup ready for the dinner meal. He had learned to carry his empty mess kit upside down to keep the rain from collecting in it before he even got to the serving line. Balancing the mess utensils was made more difficult by having to carry his rifle at sling arms, the canvas strap refusing to stay put over a rain-slickened poncho. His hands filled, Scotty could only shrug in an attempt to get his sling higher on his shoulder and less likely to fall.

Rain began to run off the lip of Scotty's steel helmet and down the front of his poncho. He tried to ignore it as he moved forward into the footprints of the soldier in front of him.

The food line was set up using Army versions of thermal food containers designed to keep the food hot and dry. Neither of which they managed to do. Scotty stepped up to the first server, a soldier from another platoon, and flipped his mess kit right side up meeting the spoonful of lime Jell-O on its way down. The green glob hit the wet bottom of the mess kit and began to seek the low point in the shallow pan's bottom.

The next server plopped mashed potatoes into the same spot previously occupied by the traveling Jell-O, and it immediately began to thin out as rain pelted it and turned it from a solid into a milky paste.

The meat was a large slice of roast—equal parts beef and fatty venous highways crossing the red-to-brown, unevenly cooked fat-ringed slab. At the end of the line, Scotty picked up wet bread, butter, a small unrecognizable dessert square from a sheet cake, and filled his canteen cup with hot coffee.

He found a spot under a pine tree to sit and eat his meal. Alone. The others had stopped threatening him about his screw-ups, but were still a long way from embracing him and accepting him into the ad hoc friendships that had formed in the platoon.

Trainees were not permitted to eat in their tents for the same reason they were not allowed to lie on their bunks in the daytime. It was a
matter of good order and discipline with a supporting rationale having
to do with sanitation. To the trainees, it was all just more Mickey Mouse
treatment.

Scotty ate as the rain turned into a Georgia downpour. His food was
cold, awash in rainwater and tasteless. But he didn't care. It was food.
He was hungry, and the anxiety about throwing his first hand grenade
was behind him. And he had done a good job talking Swithins through
throwing his first grenade. He felt good about the day.

As he blew on the coffee and tried to avoid the scalding lip of the aluminum canteen cup, he looked around the training area at the clusters
of trainees collected into two, three and four-man groups under trees,
under the bleachers and just out in the open, too tired to seek relief from
the rain.

A jeep pulled into the rock lined parking lot at the end of the mess
area and one of the NCOs he had seen around the battalion but didn't
know, jumped from the driver's seat and ran over to Russell. He handed
Russell something and they spoke briefly.

Russell quickly gathered the other cadre members from G Company.
Whatever it was generated shocked expressions and gestures of surprise.
Scotty hoped it had something to do with canceling training due to the
weather. He had heard when the threat of lightning got high enough they
would stop training and return to the barracks. He thought for a moment
at just how appealing his lumpy mattress had become at the end of the
long training days.

"Listen up!" Russell stood on the hood of the jeep to be seen and
heard by all. "Stay where you are. I have an announcement to make." He
looked at a small piece of paper the courier had brought him and read. "At
midday today the President was shot by a gunman in Dallas while riding
in a motorcade."

All of the trainees began to react and comment on the news. Russell
raised his hand. "At Ease! I'll tell you when to talk, and it won't happen until I'm through here." He continued to read. "The President died
of his wounds at one-thirty Dallas time. The Vice President has been
sworn in as President, and the Armed Forces have been placed on a
higher defense condition.

"That's all," Russell stepped down from the jeep and turned his back to the group, obviously shaken by the news.

As he entered the building, Eldon Pascoe took off his service cap and snapped it against his leg to dislodge the rain drops before they soaked into the wool turning it soggy. He wound his way up the stairs to Colonel Leggett's office and interrupted him with a polite knuckle rap on the door frame.

Leggett looked up from his desk, "Pascoe?"

"Sir, it's important I speak with you now."

Leggett put his pipe in the large ashtray centered on is desktop and looked at the cadet seated in front of the desk. "We'll finish this tomorrow."

The cadet snapped to attention and with a "Yessir" turned and left the room.

Pascoe stepped into the office and pulled a copy of the New York Times from under his arm. He waved it at Leggett. "This is awful! Kennedy—dead. What a shock."

Leggett took off his reading glasses and dropped his gaze in what appeared to be a moment of reverent reflection over the loss. "It's sad. I kinda' liked him. Even if I didn't, I'd still feel sick about this."

"Yeah, well, I'm screwed!"

Leggett looked up at Pascoe. "What?"

"I'm screwed. Kennedy gets killed—it means for sure we're going to pull out of Vietnam."

Leggett took a deep breath and measured his response. "*Excuse me*, Major?" It was the first time he had ever addressed Pascoe by his rank. "Are you telling me the death of JFK is causing you a personal problem?"

Pascoe realized how it sounded and tried to back-peddle. "No. No. It's not like that. I didn't mean it like that, but you have to admit Kennedy was behind the advisory build up in Vietnam. And it's sure to be reversed under Lyndon Johnson. What am I going to do? This is going to make my plan almost impossible."

"What are you going to do? What are *you* going to do?" he repeated. Leggett pounded the bowl of his pipe on the edge of the ashtray to dislodge the charred contents while he tempered his tone. "You, Major, are going to do what the Army wants you to do. You are going to stand by for the changes resulting from this terribly unfortunate turn of events. And you are going to do your duty—whatever it turns out to be."

Leggett's note of sarcasm was not lost on Pascoe.

"You see, the Army, the White House, and history aren't really all that preoccupied with repairing your damaged career, Major. In spite of what you might think."

Pascoe was taken back by Leggett's tone. "But you told me I ought to—"

"Well then, let me tell you something else. Over the years you've often blown by my office or buttonholed me in a hallway somewhere, and the topic of every single conversation was you and your future. Not once did you talk about anything but you.

"And each time I became more and more disappointed with the officer you were becoming and hoped it was just something you would work through. I made the mistake of thinking you might recognize this because you are terribly bright and you are quite skilled. But I'm afraid I've been a very bad judge of character in your case. Each time you walked away from me, you did so as a much smaller man in my eyes.

"And I walked away angry I hadn't called you on it."

Pascoe's face flushed as he listened to Leggett's assessment of him. "Well," he said, taking a tone to dismiss Leggett's words, "you've obviously misunderstood my questions and don't appreciate why I sought you out for your advice because I admire you and respect you."

"Get this straight, Pascoe. We come from different sides of soldiering. I always place the mission and the men and the Army at the top of my list of considerations. You always place Eldon Pascoe at the top of yours. So I suggest you find yourself another career advisor. At this point, I'd be inclined to suggest you just might consider resigning your commission for the good of the Army."

"Me consider resigning? You can't be serious," Pascoe said.

"Let me put it to you this way. It's a good thing you aren't working for me because I'd give you an Efficiency Report to make Colonel Harris' look like a fucking Valentine's Day card, mister."

The company returned to the cantonment area after three days on the grenade range and even more rain. Scotty was running through the company area with an armload of clean bed linen when he heard his name called. Recognizing the voice, he stopped, came to attention and answered. "Yes, Sergeant."

Russell stood on the porch of the WWII era clapboard building that served as the company headquarters—the Orderly Room. "Come here."

Scotty searched his memory for something he should have done or something Russell would be on him about as he ran. He reached the steps of the Orderly Room with no idea what Russell wanted and repeated, "Yes, Sergeant."

"Let's go inside and talk, Hayes."

Scotty knew no good could come from a private conversation with Russell. What could they possibly talk about not ending up being trouble for him?

He followed Russell through the Orderly Room's open central area surrounded by clerks, desks and file cabinets to a small corner office containing only a single desk with a chair squared off in front of it. Russell took the chair behind the desk and pointed to the straight-back. "Sit."

Scotty either mumbled "Yes, Sergeant," or thought he did. He watched Russell move around to the other side of the desk, searching for some clue. He'd never even been in the Orderly Room. Trainees didn't go to the company headquarters unless they were in trouble. And Russell had never spoken to him alone. Being singled out by Russell was unnerving enough in front of the others, but a private meeting with him brought on a completely new set of fears for Scotty. All of this was made worse by the harsher tone in Russell's voice.

Scotty watched as Russell picked up a manila folder and silently thumbed through the contents. "Tell me you aren't tired of me being on your ass every day."

Scotty sputtered, "I ah—"

"Ever wonder why I don't get on everyone's ass same as I do yours?"

Not wanting to sound picked on, Scotty was quick to reply, "No, Sergeant. I never have."

"Bullshit!" He scanned the papers again and laid them down on the desktop, side by side. "Know what these are?" He didn't let Scotty reply. "Your test scores. They tell me everything about you on paper. But the Hayes in these tests and Hayes in my platoon are two different animals. The scores tell me you are capable of more, but you aren't showing me shit."

Scotty broke eye contact with Russell and looked at the tiled floor unable to find a suitable response.

"Where do you come from, Hayes? You got a pile of money some-where? Got a good job waiting for you when you get back to," Russell glanced at one of the forms and found what he was looking for, "Belton?"

Scotty looked down at his cap twisted in his fingers. "No. But I have plans."

"Yeah, you got plans. Big ones, I'm sure. What kind of plans? You're going to go back to Belton and drive a truck? You going to work in a ware-house? Just what are you qualified to do? I'll tell you, Hayes. Nothing. You're a screw off. A fuck-up.

"I've known kids like you who never thought any farther ahead than the next day. They thought they had the world by the balls and they were wrong too. They were just about your age when they walked right out of Basic Training into the Pusan Perimeter in Korean. You want to see something that'll pull your head out of your ass? It's being in a fucking foxhole in knee-deep snow and living at twenty below zero for weeks on end. Seeing guys in your squad shoot themselves in the foot to get off the line. Your days are hell and your nights are worse than nightmares. You stink from weeks without soap or water. Your feet freeze.

"One day you're a private in an eleven-man rifle squad. The next you're one of the few left alive, and you're in charge—responsible for the lives of others. All that time you are up to your chin bad guys trying to shoot holes in your ass.

"Responsibility's a burden you've never had. It's your ticket to growing up. It could just be the best thing ever happened to you. Or you just might not be man enough. I could see you goin' either way, Hayes. The tests don't tell me if you've got the stones to lead, only that you have the po-tential. Something tells me you've heard this pain-in-the-ass lecture about potential before. But it don't mean shit if potential's all you got."

Palms High and his vice principal and his coach's words came back to bite Scotty. How many more desks was he going to sit in front of while someone told him there was a boat leaving and he wasn't going to be on it?

Russell continued. "You see I know things about you, Hayes. I know you been travelin' light, just gettin' by. You think all you need to do is smile, laugh and slide through. You know how far that'll get you in combat?"

Russell picked up his file and waved it at Scotty. "You've got a shitty high school transcript and great Army entrance exam scores. Do you know that? With your scores, you can do about anything in the Army?"

Scotty was caught by surprise by the contradiction. He shook his head. "No." He barely remembered the tests he had taken at the Reception Station his first few days in the Army.

"But you aren't likely to do shit until you wake up, pull your head out'a your ass and get some motivation. I can't give it to you. Now, personally, I don't really care, one way or the other. It's up to you. No one's going to hand you anything just because you have some test scores. For that you have to work. And you haven't shown any interest in working. Have you?"

Scotty kept his head down, not wanting to reply.

"You see, Hayes, where you get started in the Army depends on three things—scores, performance and the recommendation of your company cadre. It's some amazing shit to me, but on paper you've shown aptitude in electronics, clerical, mechanical and more important—leadership.

"It's time for you to decide if you want to just piss your time away as another duty soldier painting rocks and hauling garbage or if you want to become a leader and take on some responsibilities."

Scotty was having trouble taking in what Russell was getting at. "But I don't know anything about leadership, Sergeant."

"Can't argue with you there. From where I stand, I don't know how you lead yourself to the latrine in the morning. But we're going to find out." He dropped the papers back onto the desktop, stood up and walked around the front of the desk and looked down at Hayes. "Stand up!"

Scotty responded to the tone of Russell's voice and jumped to his feet.

"Look at you," Russell said. "You look like you slept in your uniform and shined those boots with a fucking Hershey bar. You aren't a soldier. You are an embarrassment."

Scotty straightened up and met Russell's eyes. "Yes, Sergeant," was all he could think to say.

"Tuck your shirttail in and button your pocket."

Hayes fumbled with both, wondering what Russell was going to find wrong next.

Russell walked back around the desk and opened the center drawer. He pulled out a dark blue armband with bright yellow sergeant's chevrons sewn on it. He threw it on the desk. "Put this on. Starting today, you're the Platoon Guide. It's an acting sergeant's rank with none of the pay, none of the privileges and all of the responsibility.

"I'll expect you to get 'em up, get 'em ready for training, keep a running account of where every man is every minute of the day, make sure they get fed, get medical attention if they need it and make sure no one gets stupid on you.

"At the end of the day, you will make sure they all clean their weapons, the barracks and themselves before you worry about Scotty Hayes.

"This means you will be getting' up earlier than every other trainee in your platoon and you'll hit the rack later. You'll set the example in everything you do from attitude to performance of duty. Your boots will be shinier and your uniform will be neater. Your bunk will be tighter, you'll be a better rifle shot, a better bayonet fighter, and you'll max the physical fitness test. In short, you will become a better soldier than any other man in the platoon and look like a walking fucking billboard for Army recruiting.

"You got it?"

"Yes, Sergeant."

"And if you let me down, just know I haven't even started to get on your ass. If you let me down, I'll show you what being on your ass really is."

CHAPTER 5

The dark blurred the faces but didn't muffle the noise of the trainees spilling from the barracks. Scuffling across to the company street to find their places on the ground, they fell out of the barracks for their first formation of the day.

The first man there, Scotty had stood on the same spot each morning in his new post as Platoon Guide for over two weeks. There, in front of his platoon, he waited for them to assemble and form up—transforming them from a crowd to four even ranks of carbon copy soldiers so the morning's head count could begin.

"Let's go!" Scotty urged. "We don't want to be last. Last to formation and we're last to the chow hall!"

The whole company, grumbling, coughing and scuffling settled down as the more than two hundred trainees created six precise platoon formations of four squads each. Each fronted by a trainee Platoon Guide like Scotty.

The new silence was quickly broken by the sharp bark of commands shouted by each Platoon Guide demanding the squad leaders report their charges present or accounted for.

Scotty received replies from each of his squad leaders and turned his back to the platoon to face Sergeant Russell standing centered in front of the six trainee platoons, stretched out for half a city block. He then reported his platoon all present.

"At Ease!" Russell commanded. He looked up and down the trainee company, sizing them up. "Are you all ready for PT?" he challenged them.

In unison, they all yelled the obligatory response, "Yes, Sergeant!"

"Good. Can't get too much physical training. Only civilians hate PT. A day without PT is a day without sunshine. Right?"

Again in unison, "Yes, Sergeant!"

"Right!" Russell raised his voice even louder and gave the preparatory command to turn the formation for movement as a column along the roadways to the exercise area. But before he snapped the execution command of *face* he stopped. Instead, he yelled, "As you were," to cancel his command.

He looked over to Scotty's platoon. "Hayes!"

Scotty was caught off guard. Listening to Russell, he was sure the morning would follow its normal course: they'd double-time to the PT area, do their calisthenics, back to the company area for breakfast and then off to training for the day. And he would just guide his platoon through it all, staying low under the radar trying not to aggravate Russell. But at the sound of his name, he was unsure if he was being singled out for some infraction.

Loud enough for the entire company to hear, Russell adopted a mock tone, "You know, I'm starting to get too old for all this. Time for you young bucks to carry more of the load."

Scotty still wasn't sure who Russell was talking to and again decided to make no response.

Russell continued. "So I've decided Hayes here will drive this group of potential fighting men to PT." He looked directly at Scotty. "Hayes. Get your ass over here and take over the company."

A chill ran through Scotty though he was already clammy from the moist Georgia morning mist. He had to march the entire two-hundred-forty-man company to the PT field? A platoon was hard enough to move from place to place, but the entire company was a driving lane wide and a football field long. Could he do this? There was no way out of it. Russell wasn't going to ask him if he wanted to do it. He had to do it, and he had to do it right the first time—or face Russell's wrath and ridicule from the others.

"What the hell are you waiting for, Hayes? I'm not getting any younger here."

"Yes, Sergeant," Scotty replied. He then ran over to Russell.

Barely three feet from him, Russell looked at Hayes for what seemed to Scotty to be an uncomfortably long time then spoke is a slightly sarcastic tone. "Hayes, do you think you can shepherd this bunch to the PT area without causing a car wreck, killing someone or bumping the formation into a building?"

Scotty was lying when he answered. "Yes, Sergeant. I'll try."

"*Try?* You'll try? Son, we don't try around here. We do. We get shit done. We accomplish. We prevail. Now, take over this company and move them to the PT area before this company is late for lunch."

Scotty saluted, as was customary after accepting charge of a formation of soldiers, did a well rehearsed about face and looked at the six platoons stretched out to his left and right.

But before he gave his first command, he was distracted by some mumbling and motion in the second rank of his own platoon.

Fitch. He obviously had something to say under his breath about Hayes to all the other trainees around him.

Scotty had been able to figure out just who in the platoon had been behind the late night threat of a blanket party early in training. But he also knew at least five of the forty thought he was a victim of Russell's, six or eight who could care less one way or the other, and two dozen who did have a problem with him causing trouble for them.

It hadn't taken him long watching and listening around the platoon to figure out whose voice he had heard in the barracks the night he was threatened. It was Jeffery Fitch.

Scotty looked over at Russell who uncharacteristically failed to call Fitch on his misbehavior in ranks and rip into him. Instead, Russell raised an eyebrow and looked at Fitch and back to Scotty, as if to ask what he intended to do about the errant soldier. It suddenly became obvious to Scotty Sergeant Russell expected Scotty handle everything—including Fitch.

Fitch stopped talking and straightened up. The entire company waited, listening to what was happening though few could see it—all facing to the front. The only noise was the crunching of Scotty's combat boots as he began the several long strides in the dry cinders of the company street to take him from his position to Fitch's.

As he walked, he could feel his face flush and knew every man in the company, Russell and the other cadre standing near the formation was waiting to see how he would handle Fitch. His heart pounded. His throat became dry. He was not sure yet what he would do when he got to Fitch. The thought caused his chest to tighten, and his breathing became labored.

Scotty stopped abruptly, squarely in front of Fitch and forced his face up into Fitch's eye line—only inches separating the two. He lowered his voice but spoke with emphasis and authority. Like he had seen Russell do many times. "Listen to me, you dickhead. You fuck me up here, and I swear I'll kick your ass. You got that straight?"

Scotty had no idea what he would do if Fitch didn't toe the line or if Fitch took a swing at him or even gave him some backtalk. He also didn't know just how much authority was his to exercise or if Russell would back him up.

Everything was silent. No one moved. No one spoke. Fitch stared through Scotty without making a response or acknowledging his words.

Out of ideas, without a next move but not wanting anyone to know it, Scotty turned and quickly walked back to his post in front of the company. His blood pulsed in his ears as he walked. He found it hard to swallow and was aware of the fact every man in the company was still watching.

He reached his position in front of the company and picked up where he had left off, preparing to move the company to the physical training field. He looked at the others. As he prepared to bark out the commands to move the huge formation out of the company area, he realized he was holding his breath.

"Hayes?" Russell called out. "We going to training or not, son?" He didn't wait for Scotty to reply. "Get this bunch out of here and do it before I retire. Now, Hayes. Move, boy. Move!"

Russell was right. The problem with Fitch was behind him, for now, and the company was still standing there waiting for a command. Waiting for him to lead them; which he did.

Scotty wiped the rain off his watch and checked the time. He pulled his shirt collar up to keep the rain from running down the back of his neck.

It was nearly two in the morning when he hung up the pay phone located in the middle of a bank of twenty of them mounted on the wall outside the PX annex in his company area. It was the only time he could call Kitty. She was home during the day when he was in training, and there were no phones in the training areas. Even so, he wouldn't be allowed to make a personal call during the duty day. His only option was to wait until she got home from work.

He stuffed his hands in his pockets to ward off the chill of the cool Georgia night and his soaked fatigue uniform. Scotty headed back to the barracks, unhappy about how the call had gone. Kitty tried to put up a good front for him, make him believe she was okay and everything at home was fine. But he pressed her until she explained the strange heaviness in her voice. She finally admitted she was getting over pneumonia but insisted she was okay and he shouldn't worry.

Scotty knew her job, her smoking and her drinking were certainly the cause of her repeated bouts of illness. It was not her first brush with pneumonia. She didn't mention it, but he knew pneumonia meant more expenses for medication, expenses she couldn't afford. She was getting deeper in debt, and he knew there were no better job prospects for her in Belton. As he walked to the barracks, he knew at best she would eat Wheaties and milk after work.

He crossed a wide road to the city block–size area taken up by the six two-story barracks, an orderly room and supply room belonging to G Company. As he mounted the few steps leading into his platoon's barracks, he heard his name. Russell! Doesn't he ever sleep? Reflexively, Scotty snapped back a reply, "Yes, Sergeant."

"Come over here. Hustle."

Scotty spotted Russell standing near the corner of the barracks under the overhanging hip roof looking as freshly pressed and spit-shined at almost three in the morning as he had looked twenty-one hours earlier. He broke into a trot for the few strides he needed to take him to Russell.

Scotty stopped and assumed a rigid position of attention. It had become nearly automatic in the weeks he'd spent under Russell's demanding eye.

"What are you doing out here at this hour, Mister Hayes?"

Scotty jabbed his thumb over his shoulder in the direction of the Post Exchange. "I had to call my stepmom. She doesn't get off work 'til late, Sergeant."

"Give. Let me hear it. What's your problem?"

"Oh, there's no problem, Sergeant."

Russell raised his hand and pointed to the roadway. "Hey, who do you think you're bullshitting? You think you just walked across Victory Drive like a man with a purpose, a smile on his face and a place to be? Cut the crap. You got a personal problem?"

"No, Sergeant. I mean, yes, Sergeant." Scotty was quick to change up and make eye contact with Russell. "But it's not a problem. I mean, I can handle it."

"Stand at ease, Hayes."

Scotty relaxed from the position of attention.

"Smoke if you got 'em."

Scotty was surprised at Russell's suspension of the rigid, near-scripted dialogue normally exchanged by trainees and cadre. He searched his pockets and found the cigarettes he kept promising himself he would quit smoking and lit one up.

"Let me hear it," Russell said.

"Well, it's no big deal, Sergeant."

"Family problem?"

"Ah, yes. Sure. But, really, it's not a big deal to the Army."

"Is it important to you?"

Scotty shrugged. "Well, sure."

"Let me tell you somethin,' Hayes. The Army works or doesn't 'cause of soldiers, not weapons, equipment, bands, parades, uniforms or generals. How a soldier feels about his unit, the leadership, himself and the righteousness of his mission is part of what makes him combat effective. The other part's how he feels about things back in *the world*—in his personal life. That means family. That's home. The best soldier in the Army won't have his heart in it if he's worried about his wife or a sick baby or some asshole putting moves on his girlfriend.

"And you need to understand how important this about you and about the men in your charge in the years to come."

Men in your charge. Scotty was momentarily stunned at the thought soldiers might ever be in his care.

"So what's your story, Hayes?"

"My stepmom's having trouble."

"Men?"

"Money. She's a widow and doesn't have much goin' for her to get a good paying job. When she gets sick, she can't work and doesn't get paid. When she can, she waits tables and works in a bar. She pretty much lives off tips." Scotty shook his head. "And Belton, Florida isn't a place where high rollers hang out."

"Is this a hardship case? You need to apply to get out to take care of her?"

"No. Not as if she's an invalid or nothing. She just doesn't make enough to pay the bills."

"And let me guess. You're thinkin' you'll just take out an allotment and send her money every month out of the big paycheck you're getting' from the Army. Right?"

"That's right." Scotty nodded. "I was thinking a little extra money each month might just make it okay for her."

Russell took off his glossy black helmet emblazoned with a bright yellow five-stripe sergeant decal on the front and wiped the morning's humidity from his forehead. "How much you make, Hayes?"

But before Scotty could answer, Russell did. "Seventy-eight bucks a month before taxes. That's what you make. Just how much money do you think you can part with and still get to the end of *your* month?"

Scotty hung his head, silent.

"You might be able to get away with it for a few months, but soon you got to pick up the tab for new uniforms, new boots—and the costs keep rising. Not like you can take on a second job. Uncle Sam's got your ass for at least twenty hours a day for the next year or so."

"But I've got a place to sleep, clothing and food and she's only got . . ."

"You want to be able to afford money for your family you'll have to find a way to make more."

"How do I do that? I'm just a Private E-1."

"You know how much more a three-stripe buck sergeant makes? How's a hundred forty-five a month sound?" Russell waved his helmet off in the general direction of the Main Post. "You know they'll pay you an extra sixty-five a month just to jump out of perfectly good airplanes. All you have to do is go through Airborne School first? Son, you lean into it a little, and you could more than triple your pay in no time. But you got to step up and take on more responsibility. You got to get your head out of your ass, and you've got to work—hard."

"But I'm just a draftee. I got just over twenty-two months left in the Army."

Russell put his helmet back on and crossed his arms over his chest. "Aha! So you thinkin' you've got no money now, and you aren't going to stay around or try hard enough to make more. Then you're gonna get out and find yourself on the street with no job and no real skills to sell. That your plan? How's that going help your stepmother?"

"But, Sarge, I can't . . ."

"You can do anything you want, Hayes. You want to lead or follow? You want to be able to step up to your obligations or not? Up to you, son."

Scotty finished his cigarette. As if on auto-pilot he field stripped it, tearing the paper down the side and scattering the tobacco into the grass near the barracks steps then rolling up the small scrap of paper and sticking it in his pocket.

"Think it over, Hayes. You're the man in charge of what happens to you now. You ain't a schoolboy anymore." Russell turned to leave and stopped after two steps. He looked back at Scotty. "Oh, about Fitch. Don't ever let 'em know you aren't sure what *you're* gonna do if they don't do what you tell 'em to do. You tell a man you're gonna kick his ass, better bring your lunch and be ready to follow through. The first time they call your bluff and you can't come through, you're done.

"Now get in the barracks, we've got a new day starting in an hour. And you've got a lot to do."

"Let's go! Let's go! Get out—now!" Scotty stood in the doorway to the barracks and yelled to the others. He wanted to get them out of the barracks and into formation quickly enough to keep the platoon from being penalized for moving too slowly and forming up last.

Scotty looked back inside and found only Jeffery Fitch still in the barracks, obviously taking his time just to piss him off. "Fitch!"

With a burst of speed, Fitch blew by Scotty as if he had been hustling all along. "Fuck you, Hayes."

Scotty let it go. From the landing at the top of the barracks steps, he looked out toward the horizon, over the tops of the cream colored buildings, their green shingled roofs and beyond the fifty-year-old oak trees planted in the early days of Camp Benning. He looked for a sign of the day's weather. Like a farmer, he had come to worry about what was ahead and what he needed to prepare for. But the skies weren't giving up their plans. It was pleasant enough. Still, he had learned how quickly west Georgia could turn cold, wet, and nasty.

He looked back onto the company street. It was a different formation than their first, seven weeks earlier. Now, the trainees were able to find their imaginary spots on the ground, which placed them in four precise ranks of ten. It had become a well-oiled routine at formation time. Each man could leave the barracks, run to his own spot and almost immediately find himself exactly one arm's length from the man in front of him and the same distance from those who flanked him.

On this morning all the trainees were weighed down with field gear they would need for a week out in the elements. Scotty gathered up his own combat gear and ran to his place in front of the platoon.

For all of them, except Sergeant Russell, it was the first time in the heavy field combat gear. Steel helmets gave them the look of boys in men's battle garb. Their equipment rode awkwardly on their backs, hung loosely from their shoulders and each item crowded another for a place on each trainee. But not for Russell who looked prepared, organized and comfortable in the very same equipment.

To Scotty, every item of Russell's field gear had been custom tailored for him. His pack, bedroll, canteens, ammunition pouches, gas mask, and even his large rubberized poncho were perfectly fitted, rolled, tied, fastened and folded to ride well on the long march ahead without hindering his movement or causing him to tire. Somehow Russell avoided the packhorse look the trainees seemed to have mastered.

Russell, walking among the ranks, finally stopped in front of his assembled platoon. "All right! Listen up. Bivouac ain't French for a fun camping trip, gentlemen. You better be ready for simulated combat conditions. We ain't goin' to be roasting marshmallows out there." He then continued to walk through the ranks of trainees checking each man's gear. "You think Basic's been tough so far, don't you?"

Silence.

He raised his voice even louder. "DON'T YOU?"

The trainees responded in unison. "No, Sergeant."

"Bullshit. You've all been whining and draggin' ass lately. Acting like a bunch of disorganized civilians. More than a handful of you've been riding the sick book." He stopped in front of Fitch. He flexed his knees to get eye to eye with the shorter trainee. "You wouldn't know anything about that. Would you, Mister Fitch?"

Fitch stumbled over his reply. "No, Sergeant."

"In a pig's ass, Fitch. You lay down on me this week, and I'll recycle your ass so far back you'll be going through basic training with astronauts headed for Mars some day."

He moved on not waiting for a reply from Fitch. Inspecting each man's backpack and equipment, he worked his way forward and finally stopped at Scotty, in his solitary leadership post out front of the platoon. He lowered his voice. "You ready, Hayes? Because if you aren't you better get that way, fast.

"You got an accurate platoon roster?" Russell walked around Scotty and checked out his equipment—pack, canteen, entrenching tool, shelter half and ammo pouches.

Scotty pulled a folded roster from his pocket.

"You going to get this bunch to the training area in one piece today?"

"Yes, Sergeant."

"I don't want to lose anyone on the way 'cause they can't hack it. You got it?"

"Yes, Sergeant." Scotty had heard all the trainee lore. Stories were told and retold, but every trainee would later learn they were mostly gross exaggerations. The rumor was the seventeen-mile march to the Bivouac Week was so grueling trainees fell out from sheer exhaustion in large numbers, many needing to be hospitalized. There were even stories of deaths due to exhaustion. The only thing Scotty would find to be true was the day's march was more of a run than a march, and it was exhausting.

"Hayes, you flake out today and nobody in this platoon will even follow you to the shit house." He tugged at Scotty's loose and sagging shoulder harness. "Tighten this up. You get to double-timin' and your gear starts sliding around you'll be one sorry ass trainee. You'll have blisters where you didn't know you had places."

"Yes, Sergeant," Scotty said.

Scotty had not really paid much attention to the stories. It seemed to him if they were true certainly something would have leaked out of Fort Benning to the newspapers and mothers across the country would be incensed by the treatment of their sons. Maybe it was not wanting to believe the stories or maybe he thought how bad could it really be?

Anyway, he knew he had enough to think about keeping up with the extra duties as acting Sergeant. It was enough for him to be worried about getting through one day at a time and being responsible for the other thirty-nine trainees in his platoon. And lately he had even started thinking about graduating soon and the few weeks leave he'd get—and about going home.

But now the day had come to march out to the bivouac area. Getting there was the first hurdle. Once there it would be a week of advanced field training—live-fire exercises, the gas chamber and testing on their knowledge of first aid and map reading and then their final qualification on the rifle range. Failing any of these tests would mean being recycled—to Scotty a much bigger worry than a march to the training areas.

As he stood there waiting to move out, he recognized he really hadn't prepared for the march—the extra weight he had to carry, rigging everything so it would be comfortable and travel well. It was as if the day would never come or he wouldn't be there long enough to see it. But it had come, and he now recognized he would have to deal with the weeks of little sleep. That alone would be a big problem. He would need more than average endurance to make the march.

Toward the center of the company formation the Field First Sergeant, senior to Russell, yelled the commands which turned the entire company in the right direction and started them marching in a long and neatly formed column of six platoons of four even files per platoon.

As they left the company area, Scotty's thoughts shifted to his responsibilities. He had to keep every man in his platoon in line and in step. He had to keep them moving at a steady pace with the others to keep the rigid formation from falling apart once the going got tough and the trainees tired.

In the first half hour on the march, they threaded their way through the regimental cantonment area, blocking intersections while they passed.

Scotty noticed some in his platoon were already hacking and coughing with what the medics called URI—upper respiratory infection. It was something every trainee experienced. So many trainees from so many different parts of the country coming together late in the year, being forced to live together, sleep in cramped barracks and sit jammed into bleachers in outdoor classes provided just the Petri dish needed to exchange and spread the viruses. Almost every trainee suffered some kind of URI before Basic Training was over.

By the third mile, the buildings and asphalt roads gave way to the apron of the training areas. The range road was the forty-mile-long central artery, which every trainee took to get to the firing ranges and training areas. Wide enough for a school bus and topped with crushed gravel, the roadway sliced its way through the trees and Georgia Kudzu on its lazy arc around the numerous rifle, tank, and grenade ranges—all of them firing into a common impact area in the center large enough to hold a small city.

After less than an hour on the range road, Scotty's feet already hurt. The tender bones bumping up against the inside of his combat boots had never adjusted to the constant pounding since his first day in the Army.

His rifle, slung over his shoulder by a stiff canvas strap, felt much heavier than its actual eight pounds. His steel helmet pressed down heavily on the top of his nearly bald head and made his neck ache just holding it up.

In spite of the aches and pains, Scotty wasn't going to let on to anyone else he was feeling the effects of the march. He might have felt differently were he still a trainee hidden somewhere in the ranks of the platoon, but as a trainee leader he was visible out in front and his pride wouldn't let him whine or quit.

His platoon was third in the order of march. Already trainees were starting to drop out. On either side of the roadway sergeants from other platoons were yelling at pale-faced soldiers collapsed in the drainage ditches or leaning against tree trunks suffering from the demands of the march. Some were favoring painful feet. Others were bent over, vomiting heavy mess hall breakfasts.

From somewhere behind him, Scotty heard Russell bellow, "Hayes!"

Without looking around from his position up in front of his platoon, Scotty kept marching. "Yes, Sergeant."

"You already got some damn stragglers fallin' out in the back a' the platoon, boy. We *don't* have stragglers. You hear me? Get on it. Now!"

Scotty peeled off and let this platoon pass by until the tail end came abreast of him. The platoon's rear ranks were ragged and no longer held the precise alignment they'd started out the morning with. He came alongside the last row of shuffling, staggering trainees and fell into step with them. "What's the problem back here?"

Two of the three stragglers didn't respond, but Fitch turned to face Hayes. "Fuck you. Get your ass back up front where you can keep sucking up and kissing Russell's ass."

Kissing Russell's ass? Without thinking Scotty reached over and yanked Fitch out of the formation by his pack suspenders.

The two stood by the side of the road while the entire company moved on. Fitch glared at Scotty. "What are you gonna' do? Huh?" He nodded at the sergeant's stripes pinned on Scotty's sleeve. "You think those put some weight in your ass? If you don't let go of me now I'm gonna' lay you out here in the street, you asshole."

Scotty could feel blood rush to his face. He let go with one hand and quickly felt it tighten into a fist ready for what was to come. Russell's words suddenly echoed in his head: *Don't let 'em know you aren't sure what you're gonna do, Hayes.*

"Fitch! There a problem? Hayes? What's the story?" Russell yelled from fifty yards up the road. He didn't wait for a reply. "Get your asses back into formation before *I* come back there and sort you two out. Now!"

Clearly focused on Scotty's eyes, Fitch lowered his voice. "We aren't through with this."

All Scotty could think to reply was, "No. We aren't. Anytime. You just say when." He shoved Fitch toward the formation now a hundred yards up the road. "Move."

Fitch turned and started a half-hearted shuffle somewhere between walking and jogging to close the distance between him and the platoon.

"Hayes," Russell yelled. "You get your ass back up where you belong. You can't honcho a forty-man platoon from back there. A marching platoon's like spaghetti. You can't push it. You got t'get up front and pull it."

Two hours into the march a sergeant up at the head of the column yelled out the command to change the pace from a fast march to a double-time, and the entire trainee company broke into a synchronized run.

Running in step was hard enough but carrying a rifle, pack and gear made it much harder. Everything Scotty carried clanked and rattled as he ran. In no time he started to doubt his ability to keep up the pace for the remaining eleven miles ahead. He remembered track in high school and tried to feed his straining leg muscles with oxygen by forcing himself to exhale, clearing his lungs to allow room for as much oxygen as he could take in on the next breath.

Ahead Scotty heard the first trainee completely lose it, fall and pancake onto the gravel pathway. The sound was immediately followed an unseen cadre sergeant yelling at the unseen trainee to get back up on his feet and catch up.

Scotty's platoon was in no better shape than the others. He turned and awkwardly double-timed backward so he could see them. He mimicked the encouragement he heard up ahead, "Close it up. Stay in formation!"

There was some grumbling in the rear of the platoon directed at Scotty.

"Okay, knock off the bullshit," Scotty yelled. "We're going to finish this march one way or the other. Bitching won't help." He turned back around, nearly tripping over his own boots and got back into step.

As Scotty ran his stomach soured and he felt light headed. Suddenly the thought of falling out himself fired a flash of panic through him. He couldn't fall out. He couldn't quit. They were all watching him. No. He had to hold on and finish—no matter what. He struggled with his load and gulped in as much air as he could. He tried to command his body to relax and ignore the pain of the forty pounds of clanking combat gear.

CHAPTER 6

After an hour of double-timing, a cadre sergeant halted the company and gave them their first break.

"Hayes. What are you sitting down for? Huh?"

Scotty quickly capped his canteen and looked up to Russell's dark eyes peering out from under his helmet—his hands on his hips. "We were told to break for chow, Sergeant."

"Not *you*, Hayes. You eat *after* you've checked every man in your platoon.

"You ever see any member of the cadre go through the chow line before every trainee's been fed?"

"No, Sergeant. But—"

Russell pointed to the soldiers seated along the shoulder of the road "'But' shit, Hayes. Get off your ass and go check their feet. You find someone with blisters you send him back to the meat wagon. You got it?"

"Yes, Sergeant."

"Make sure every man changes his socks. You find a man without any socks, you dig into your pack and give him a pair of yours. You got it?"

"*My* socks?"

"That's right, your socks. Kick his ass later—when we get back. But you won't have anyone in this platoon falling out a' this march because of feet. You hear me?"

"Yes, Sergeant."

Scotty looked at the platoon. Most of them eating C-Rations, some stretched out on the grassy margins just off the gravel path trying to regain their strength. Still, others slept—a skill learned early by every Army trainee.

"What are you waiting for, Hayes?"

"Nothing, Sergeant." Scotty jumped to his feet, dropped his gear in a pile and started toward the others.

"Hayes!" Russell yelled again.

Scotty turned. "Sergeant?"

Russell pointed at Scotty's gear on the grass. "Where the hell you going?"

"To check feet, Sergeant. Like you told me."

"Put on your gear. We're in simulated tactical mode from the time we left Sand Hill until we return to the barracks next week. You go somewhere, you wear your helmet, your gear and carry your rifle—everywhere. And it goes for every man in your platoon."

Scotty turned back and picked up his backpack and pistol belt and rifle. "Yes, Sergeant."

Though his own feet hurt, Scotty was completely surprised at what he found among the other trainees. A forced march in boots only a few weeks old affected each trainee differently. Some had no mark save the crosshatch pattern the bootlaces traced up the front of each ankle. Others were bleeding from blisters, which had grown, burst, and drained into socks not completely clean before the march.

He stopped in front of a boy from Louisiana and made him take off his socks—already suspicious of what he would see. The sock on one foot was wet with blood, and the other showed the start of another growing stain.

As he got closer, the smell of dirty feet and dirty socks assaulted Scotty's nose. "Damn! You ever wash those feet?"

The boy took off his socks and threw them on the ground next to where he sat. "What's it to you? You my mother?"

Scotty surprised himself with his reply. "Yes. I am your goddamn mother until we get out of Basic. And I told you all last night to bring *clean socks*. Do you remember me telling you to bring clean socks? You think I just made that up to make your life miserable? Why do you think I said that, huh?" Scotty pointed at the soldier's bloody feet. "To keep this from happening. Now, get your gear and let the medics decide what to do with you."

He watched the soldier hobble barefoot to the ambulance parked behind the last platoon. Inside he felt responsible. If he'd just checked their socks before they started the march.

"Hayes."

Scotty turned to find Russell next to him also watching the bleeding trainee who had reached the ambulance and was pointing out his blisters to one of the medics.

"His socks were dirty, they bunched up and just rubbed the skin right off his feet."

Russell turned to Scotty. "His status?"

"Pardon me?"

"Where's your roster? Keeping track of your people is every leader's job." He pointed to the blistered trainee. "After we get to the bivouac area and I ask you for a status report I want you to be able to account for every man by name, by status, by location. You need to write all this down. You may think you can remember where he went and he's with the medics or evac'd to the post hospital but by the end of the day there may be ten of them. Your memory all that good, Hayes?"

"I, ah—"

"No, Hayes. Nobody's memory's that good, and when you are doin' this in a shootin' war, it gets harder than woodpecker's lips. You can't rely on your memory. You have to be right, and you have to keep good notes. Be exact. There's mommas, wives and babies back home who want to know for sure what happens to their men."

Scotty watched Russell walk away, not having waited for a response. A shootin' war? The man was such a puzzle to Scotty—sometimes rough and demanding and other times he seemed to treat Scotty like an equal.

He turned to look at the others. Every man in the platoon watched as Russell passed through the clusters of trainees changing socks and caring for their feet. His authority over them was absolute, but his concern for their welfare seemed to be strong and ever present.

The break was way too short. Scotty's uniform was soaked through with sweat even though the cooling winds of a Georgia fall had been in their faces all day. As quickly as Scotty finished checking all the feet and tending to those who needed medical attention the company was back on the range road running toward the bivouac area still miles away. And Scotty never found the time to eat.

Another hour and a half of running and more trainees gave out or gave up. Those who couldn't continue were scooped up by the cadre and ushered off to the ambulance creeping along behind the company. Those already in the ambulance would be shuttled to the post hospital as soon as a replacement ambulance arrived. Some of the casualties would rejoin the company by nightfall, but most would recycled to other training companies.

With the sun getting low on the horizon and the end of the march only a mile off Scotty heard a rifle, steel helmet and trainee crash onto the gravel behind him. Without even thinking about it, he pulled out of his slot up front and looped around to the back of the platoon.

There, on all fours, was Fitch—vomiting. The color had drained out of his face.

Scotty dropped to one knee next to the fallen trainee. "Fitch. Fitch! Look at me." He wanted to see exactly how bad it was.

Fitch mumbled something unrecognizable and tried to lay down in the gravel.

Scotty stood, straddled Fitch and looped his arms under Fitch's shoulders to lift him to his feet.

Fitch stood, but he was very shaky. His bluster and bravado were completely gone. His fatigue shirt was soaked with perspiration and stained with vomit.

"Can you walk?"

"Dunno. Just leave me here," was all he could seem to master.

"Give me your gear," Scotty said.

"Huh?"

"We only got a mile to go. You can make it." Scotty reached down, picked up Fitch's steel helmet. Then his rifle. He slung the weapon over his shoulder next to his own.

"I can't," Fitch said. "I can't make it."

"Sure you can. Your gear, Fitch. Gimme."

Fitch fumbled with the large buckle on his pistol belt. Once loose, he shrugged his backpack and remaining combat gear.

"Hayes! Don't make a career out of it back there!" Russell yelled.

Scotty didn't respond. He took Fitch's harness holding all his gear and slung it over his free shoulder doubling his own load. "Let's go. Easy." He held Fitch up, and the two moved forward at an awkward shuffle.

Freed of his gear, Fitch regained some strength.

The two hobbled along for two hundred yards—Scotty holding up Fitch, managing to carry all his added gear.

Russell bellowed from the front of the platoon, "You going spend all day back there, Hayes?"

Hayes got Fitch to within a few yards of the tail end of the running platoon. "Parks! Johnson!" Scotty yelled to two other trainees. "Come take Fitch."

The two trainees dropped out of the formation and moved back to Scotty and Fitch. Fitch's color was slowly coming back into his face.

Others in the rear of the platoon looked around to see what was happening and without prompting from Scotty three fell back. The first two trainees each took one of Fitch's arms around their shoulders to support him while he ran. The other trainee rushed to Scotty and relieved him of the burden of all of Fitch's gear, splitting it up between them all three of them.

In less than ten more strides all were caught up and back in their places in the formation. Scotty picked up his pace and ran around the platoon back to his place in front. Once back in his place and in step, Scotty looked over to Russell, running alongside the formation.

Scotty was disappointed Russell didn't seem to show any sign of approval. Approval of the fact the platoon was intact and working together while the other platoons were losing stragglers and looking more ragged. But just as Scotty was about to look back to the front it seemed as if Russell gave Scotty the slightest nod of his head. Or was he just imagining it?

And an hour later, Russell's command voice echoed the command of the Field First Sergeant, "Platoon . . . Halt!" The words every man in the company wanted to hear.

Scotty stopped with the others and looked back over his shoulder quickly making a head count of his platoon. They made it. They *all* made it. His was the only platoon to not suffer any permanent dropouts or quitters on the run. Exhausted, sore, nauseous, and hot, they had made it to the bivouac area. Scotty felt a sense of pride he'd never felt before. Not at football or track in school. This was different. He wasn't on winning team; he had led a winning team.

"Hayes . . ."

"Yes, Sergeant. I'm on it," Scotty replied. He turned around to the platoon. "Okay, everyone on your ass. Now! Get those boots off. Feet. I want to see 'em."

Russell walked up behind Scotty. "That's right. Feet." He pointed off toward a truck arriving with the cooks and large thermal containers cans filled with supper. "Then get 'em in the chow line. Then I want to see you with a headcount and a list of injuries. All before you eat. Got it?"

The night overtook them, and soon Scotty found himself squeezing into the small opening of the pup tent he would share with another trainee. He was more tired than he had ever been and he hurt in several places. The skin on his feet burned and the bones ached. His hipbones were rubbed raw from the constant motion of his pistol belt during the day's march, and his shoulders were bruised from the burden of his combat harness. Still, he felt better than ever before.

He looked forward to getting some much-needed sleep. His platoon was all bedded down in the bivouac area, tents all scattered randomly in a simulated protective pattern so as not to make them easily identifiable from the air which would make them an easy target for enemy artillery or mortars. And Scotty had done it. He got them there, got them fed, cared for them, set them up for the night and sacked out. In the morning they'd all begin the long hours on the firing ranges where each man, including Scotty, would qualify with a rifle—an absolute requirement for graduation.

Three days later Scotty jumped out of the back of the deuce and a half truck. He had hitched a ride into the company area. He'd been told Russell wanted to see him back at the barracks where he had been taking care of some platoon business but wasn't given a reason why.

He entered the platoon barracks and found it strange. He'd never been in the two-story building when the others weren't there. It was silent. Empty and hollow. He walked down the center of the platoon bay between the rows of double bunks, their bedding stripped and stowed in lockers, their mattresses rolled on top of the springs at the foot of each bunk.

In each platoon barracks, there was a single nine by twelve room set off from the open bay, windowless on the interior, windowed to the outside. He'd never been inside Russell's cadre room. It was in this room the senior cadreman in charge of the platoon's training stayed unless he was married and lived in quarters with his family. Russell's room was marked with an eye-height nameplate reading SFC ASA T. RUSSELL in block letters centered on the door bearing many coats of gray-green enamel.

Scotty raised his hand to knock and checked himself. He tucked the uneven blousing of his fatigue shirt into his trousers and smoothed out the wrinkles by running his thumbs around the inside of the waistband from his navel to his kidneys. He straightened his gig line—the line made up of the running edge of his shirtfront, the end of is brass belt buckle and the hemmed edge of the fly on his trousers. These items in vertical alignment were an important indicator of attention to detail. Misaligned they were a sign of a sloppy soldier.

Finally, Scotty rubbed the dust off the toes of his combat boots on the backs of each opposite trouser leg, took his helmet off, tucked it under his left arm and knocked.

"Come!" Russell boomed from inside the small room.

Scotty turned the highly polished brass knob and opened the door, unsure what he'd find inside.

Russell sat at a small Army field desk next to the door, intent on the paperwork before him.

"I was told you wanted to see me, Sergeant." Scotty stood in the open doorway sure he was not to step on the highly polished tile without Russell's permission.

Russell poked the Army ballpoint pen over his shoulder in the direction of his bunk. "Sit. On the footlocker."

Scotty moved to the Sergeant's personal footlocker with one stride and sat without trying to mark the linoleum tiles as he turned on them.

"You know why you're here?" Russell spoke without turning to look at Scotty, his pen still marking up the document before him.

"No, Sergeant. I don't." Scotty stole a look around the room. He wanted to take as much of it in as he could out of sheer curiosity. The inside of the room was covered in many coats of paint but was clean everywhere he looked. The unfinished stud walls had shelving and equipment hooks placed in convenient and efficient spots.

The room was all Russell. A private yet professional enclave almost never seen by a trainee but no less prepared for inspection at any time.

The room had its own special smells, unlike the large platoon bay just outside the door. Scotty could make out the distinctive smells of waxes—car wax, floor wax, and a furniture polish Russell must have used on the single four-drawer Quartermaster dresser, which stood in the far corner of the small room. These smells were mixed with the light oil Russell used on his pistol and Brasso, the polish every soldier used to clean and shine all his brass insignia and belt buckles.

Though it was nearly ten at night, the bunk, identical to Scotty's, was perfectly made, tight and precisely positioned two inches from the wall at the top and far side. Over the bunk, a small shelf held Russell's headgear. A steel combat helmet sat squarely on its half of the shelf. Its olive drab paint was even and free of chips; the canvas chin strap was pulled behind the back lip of the helmet and fastened securely. Next to it sat Russell's cadre helmet in striking contrast. Unlike its combat counterpart, it was a glossy black lacquered garrison helmet adorned with full-color decals over each ear—each a replica of the First Army patch worn on the left shoulder of each cadreman assigned in the Training Regiment. Centered over the front lip of the helmet were sergeant's chevrons—three inverted gold V-stripes up and two rockers below. The helmet gleamed under the harsh light of the single overhead bulb—buffed to a high shine by hand with a fine car polish.

While Russell's back was still turned Scotty's eyes darted to the few photographs on the walls. One was Russell in full paratroop gear, parachute on his back as he stood ready inside a huge cargo plane.

Another photo showed Russell standing at a rigid position of attention in front of a formation of other Green Berets. A senior officer was pinning a medal on Russell's crisply starched and ironed khaki shirt. Russell's eyes clear and fixed under the brim of his beret on an imaginary point straight out in front of him—through the officer.

Scotty realized in the seven weeks he had known Russell he had never seen him in Class A uniform, one on which ribbons were normally worn. In Basic Training the uniform of the day was fatigues. In the picture Russell had several rows of combat ribbons and special skill badges Scotty was unaware of, all indicating Russell's broad experience as a combat soldier and leader.

Russell dropped his pencil on the papers on his desk. "Looks like you fired Expert on the rifle range and you've qualified in the gas chamber and the infiltration course—everything you need to graduate. How you doing as a trainee leader?"

Scotty looked down at his helmet he fiddled with between his knees. "I'm not very good at this."

"What? You think leaders are born? You think it's some God-given talent? Leaders are trained. They are molded and pounded into shape. That's what we do in the Army, Hayes. Especially here at Benning. This is where combat leaders are made."

Again, Hayes wasn't sure how to respond.

"You up for it?"

"It?"

"You want to lead or follow, Hayes?" Russell didn't wait for Scotty to reply. He turned back to his desk and picked up a sheaf of papers stacked neatly on the corner. He jabbed them at Scotty. "I want you to fill these out. You're applying to NCO Candidate School."

Scotty wasn't sure what he was hearing. "Pardon."

"They're running new a test program here at Benning. Candidates come from companies like this. It'll be ten times as tough and three times as long as basic. But in six months, if you can hack it, you'll graduate as a sergeant and be sent to a combat infantry unit as a squad or fire team leader."

Scotty took the papers and made eye contact with Russell for the first time since he'd entered the room.

"You'll have to suck it up. You'll have to do a little more growing up, but I think you can do it.

"Now, go fill out these applications and give them to me before you head back out to the bivouac area." He looked at his watch. "And you'd better get it in gear if you're going to get back out to the field and put your platoon to bed."

Scotty found himself propelled to his feet, half in surprise and half in disbelief of what he'd just heard. He stood to take the folder of papers from Russell.

Russell stood and put out his hand to shake Scotty's. "And if you flunk out I'm going to kick your ass, Hayes."

CHAPTER 7

After five days of waiting for a final assignment in Camp Alpha, a tent city for the newly arrived, Pascoe's orders came through. He'd gone to Vietnam with orders to report to the major US Headquarters, Military Assistance Command, Vietnam—known largely by its acronym, MACV.

Even before breakfast he was summoned to MACV headquarters in northwest Saigon and told he would be assigned to an advisory job and paired up with a Vietnamese staff officer.

"But I was hoping for something else," Pascoe told the personnel officer who didn't look up from the paperwork on his desk. He stole a glance at the colonel's hand, searching for the single item that could give him some cachet. He needed a connection with the colonel, which just might allow him to negotiate a better assignment before the decision was final. But Pascoe was disappointed to find no West Point ring on the colonel's finger.

The overweight assignments officer appeared to be nursing a hangover. "Yeah, Major, and I was hopin' to be a brigadier general by now too." He pointed at the floor. "But I ended up here. And I can tell you this is no general's job. Life's tough everywhere. Get used to it, because Vietnam's gonna' jerk a knot in your ass for sure if you don't relax."

"I was kind of hoping to advise a Vietnamese regimental commander," Pascoe said.

The colonel laughed, took a drag off a mostly smoked cigar and blew the smoke from the corner of his mouth toward the ceiling. "Yeah. And I'd like to be assigned to Hawaii for the last two years I got in the Army. Now, you got your choice, Major. You can have this job with the Viets and get your ass out of Saigon and out into the field, or I got one other job screaming to get filled. It's in Graves Registration here in the city."

Working at the mortuary was the very last thing Pascoe wanted. He let it go.

The colonel leaned over the arm of his chair to see beyond Pascoe into the outer office. "Parsons? Is Colonel Minh here yet?"

Pascoe was completely unprepared for the cartoon vision who walked into the office. Though a small man, Lieutenant Colonel Minh made a grand entrance wearing a tight, tailor-made flight suit with a lavender scarf at its open neck. He wore huge reflector aviator sunglasses which dwarfed his face.

"I am here, Colonel," Minh announced as he first saluted the colonel and then turned to stick out a welcoming hand to Pascoe. "You must be my new American. No? I'm so very happy to meet you, Major. Welcome to Vietnam."

Pascoe tried to peel his gaze from the Vietnamese officer's long pomaded black hair to take the hand of the man easily seven inches shorter than he was.

In his very best Vietnamese Pascoe replied. "Yes. Yes, sir. I'm Eldon Pascoe, sir." He was sure to smile and had prepared himself for the limp handshake he got. He'd been warned of this too. He'd heard all the horror stories about advisors not getting along with Vietnamese counterparts and being fired over causing them to lose face. It was the last thing Pascoe wanted to add another negative report to his personnel file back at the Pentagon. No matter what, if he hoped to redeem himself in the Army's eyes, he'd have to get along with Minh.

Minh had gone ahead while Pascoe collected his belongings. Since his days as a cadet, Pascoe had not had to carry his own bags. En route to Vietnam, he quickly discovered if he wanted to get anything of his anywhere he had better do it himself. There were no skycaps, cab drivers or baggage handlers once he left San Francisco.

The two Vietnamese soldiers standing guard outside the helipad entrance to the headquarters hardly looked up when Pascoe struggled through the doorway with his three overstuffed bags. One listened to squawking sounds coming from a tiny transistor radio pressed to his ear. The other seemed to be fantasizing over a vision across the busy street. A beautiful young Vietnamese woman in her traditional ao dai silk top and pants bent over a motorbike, tying a parcel to the seat.

Rather than set them down, Pascoe dropped his bags hoping to get some attention from the two enlisted soldiers but got no response. He looked out across the chopper ramp for Minh only to find eleven choppers—some with crews, some without. The airfield was already crowded beyond its capacity. A pillow of curry colored dust hugged the strip, ramps, and nearby roadways; a cloud that stayed in place all day, every day for nine more years.

"Colonel Minh?" he asked.

The soldier with the radio didn't miss a note of the Vietnamese ballad which sounded more like pain than a love song. He nodded at a nearby chopper parked on a helipad marked V.I.P. and then spat a stream of muddy betel nut juice across the top of the sandbagged security post never once making eye contact with the American major.

Pascoe knew the soldier had walked a fine line between simply voiding his mouth of pooled saliva and showing his disdain for yet another foreigner arriving in Saigon.

Raising his hand to shield his eyes, Pascoe squinted against the brilliant morning sun beginning to climb bringing with it the day's oppressive heat. He could already feel his fatigue shirt beginning to stick to his back.

Through the plexiglass of the chopper's windscreen Pascoe made out Minh's outline in the command pilot's seat of the helicopter. It was not where he'd expected to find the colonel. He gathered his bags and limped clumsily toward Minh's aircraft, one outsized bag awkwardly banging against his leg with each step.

As he approached the aircraft, his concern about Minh being at the controls was compounded by the appearance of the airframe. It was plain to see very little maintenance had been performed. The aging chopper had dents and tears in the paper-thin hull. The large sliding doors were missing, as were the seats normally found in the cargo. Navigation lights were broken, the rotor blades were excessively worn and there was no sign of a crew chief normally standing by with a fire extinguisher should there be a problem on start-up.

Any other flight Pascoe would have refused. He couldn't challenge Minh's preflight inspection and had no other options. Still, he knew it was unlikely the chopper's outward appearance didn't mirror the care given to the engine, transmission, rotor assembly and flight controls.

Hoping he was wrong about the chopper's readiness to fly, he threw his bags in the back. He opened the door and climbed up into the right seat—the co-pilot's station trying not to show his concern.

The blinding sun bounced off the geometric rice paddies as Pascoe looked down from the helicopter. The tiny farm plots speeding by beneath the chopper were separated by thousand-year-old roads and trails, caramel in color and hard packed by centuries worth of travelers taking their produce to market each day. Here and there, on the portions of each farmer's land least likely to produce good crops, families built their homes and penned up their livestock leaving the best of their small acreage for crop cultivation.

The soil was rich where Asia's Mekong River became a delta before spilling into the South China Sea. Each year several million tons of topsoil arrived with the monsoon floods and left behind invisible magic adding fertilizing properties to the province. Everywhere, what wasn't brown water, dirt or thatched houses was rich vibrant green—rice, cabbages, and manioc. In the fields, little boys rode the backs of huge water buffaloes like shepherds on the other side of the globe.

Pascoe looked west over the raised dual clusters of instruments arrayed for each pilot to use. For as far as he could see the terrain was flat and wet and it was not yet the rainy season. Dotted with small hamlets, the countryside below teemed with busy villagers, travelers, and livestock. But only a few miles short of the border there was no sign of civilization, only a huge grassy marsh absent any signs of human life—an unmistakable indication of the danger to be found there.

Where the population began to flag the concentration of often overlapping bomb craters increased. Each crater was a small perfect pockmark with raw dirt edges half filled with blue-green alkaline rich water. Some had been taken over by small families of mud ducks. Where the craters had damaged trails, Pascoe could see the traffic had simply been rerouted around the damage to make a new trail. Life went on in Hau Nghia Province. These were people who had never known peace. Never in their lifetime.

Pascoe looked across the chopper at Thi Van Minh. In spite of Pascoe's efforts to avoid it, Minh was now his new counterpart—a recently minted term invented for Americans assigned to advisory jobs.

Minh's actual post was Operations Officer for the Vietnamese 6th Infantry Division. It would be Pascoe's job to help his counterpart improve combat planning and operational techniques peculiar to infantry division operations—something Pascoe had been trained in. For most advisors, counterpart relationships were strained and unsteady. Americans found it uncomfortable working with Vietnamese officers whose jobs were often political appointments. Promotions were frequently influenced by family relationships and political considerations rather than merit or experience. To this was added the differences in culture in general and the less-than-aggressive style of combat operation conducted by the South Vietnamese.

A greater problem was their tendency to confuse their personal and professional lives making most American advisors uneasy with the appearance of impropriety. Pascoe was already uncomfortable with the man, his appearance, his shaky flying and his unwillingness to allow Pascoe to try out the Vietnamese he had studied hard to learn.

Minh blended French and passable English. He seemed to take delight in practicing his English and had spoken nothing but since they met. Pascoe had learned to expect all this in advisory training at Fort Bragg, but he would never let Minh know of his dissatisfaction. He couldn't.

Minh's kept talking without added focus on the task at hand as he wrestled the chopper into an abrupt turn just after they passed over a military compound.

"Welcome to the 6th Infantry Division. This is our headquarters," Minh said as he set the chopper up to land on the large H formed by sand bags laid out on the hard baked center courtyard of the compound. The chopper cleared the dual flag poles flying faded US and Vietnamese flags, both flapping furiously in the rotor wash.

Pascoe hadn't expected much, but the headquarters at the Sugar Mill was a shock. It was all one color—beige, from years of road traffic dust on the adjacent unsurfaced highway, which passed the gated headquarters. The only real color in the compound was the large red and white barber-striped pipe horizontally spanning the compound's single lane entrance. It rested on a stop in the fencing at the small end of the pole and was counterbalanced on the other by a huge block of concrete.

Three Vietnamese soldiers wearing American helmets dwarfing their small heads stood in a sandbagged guard house topped with a corrugated tin roof to keep the sun and rain off of them and provide for their comfort.

As Minh awkwardly settled the chopper onto the helipad, a thick donut of dirt blown up from the earthen compound boiled away from the rotor blades bathing each building and the guard post in a whole new shower of dust. Such dustings happened as many as twenty times a day, with each chopper taking off and landing at the busy headquarters.

Pascoe popped his seatbelts free and looked around the chopper as Minh shut it down. He was sure the first order of the day for him was to brush up on his own flying techniques. If he was going to continue to fly with Minh he wanted to be able to take over control of the chopper if he had to.

Glassless windows provided only marginal ventilation in the wooden building originally designed as a large sugar mill. After the French owner's left the Vietnamese division commander moved most of the mill's employees to smaller buildings in the nearby town then moved his headquarters to the Sugar Mill which controlled the area to the west—toward Cambodia. Still, the buildings were nowhere near a perfect fit for an infantry division headquarters.

Minh led Pascoe deeper into the warren of small rooms and crowded hallways. Clusters of uniformed Vietnamese clerks and headquarters staffers were crammed into corners too small for any clerical or combat functions. It looked as if the takeover of the headquarters had happened in uncoordinated and unplanned phases. There was no apparent method to the assignment of space and no consideration given to facilities or utilities. Extension cords threaded through holes in walls and draped over door tops. The lighting alternated randomly between harshly lit pools and dark corners. Glaring fluorescent lighting fixtures were scattered haphazardly around the office spaces, some humming, some flickering.

Everywhere field desks were piled with paperwork and occupied spaces not otherwise dedicated to headquarters functions or storage. Just walking through the crowded corridors was difficult. And the mood seemed to be light and uninvolved in the war effort. Many of the soldiers playfully laughed and lounged about, completely unconcerned about the war going on outside the high-walled, concertina-topped fences surrounding the compound.

Minh stopped at a desk manned by a sergeant who, unlike most of the others, diligently sorted paperwork. The Vietnamese fascination with bureaucracy—a leftover of the French occupation—would soon become apparent to Pascoe. The sergeant leaped to attention on seeing Colonel Minh. Minh spoke too rapidly for Pascoe to catch it all, but he did understand something about an appointment Minh needed to see the general. He turned to Pascoe. "Major, one of the soldiers will take your things from the chopper to your quarters. Come." He opened the first closed door Pascoe had seen in the building.

Minh led them to an anteroom more claustrophobic than the others. There another Vietnamese sergeant spoke rapidly into a radio hand microphone. "What is the problem?" Minh asked.

The sergeant continued to argue with someone on the other end having trouble convincing the Vietnamese artillery headquarters in the provincial capital of Tay Ninh to approve a request for supporting fires. They were refusing to fire on some targets listed on the request Minh had submitted earlier that morning.

"Give it to me," Minh said to the sergeant. With one hand he grabbed the mike, and with the other he pointed in the direction of still another room. "Major, I will only be a short time with this. Please be comfortable in my office."

Inside, Pascoe stood in the center of Minh's office trying to take it all in. It was more like a shrine to Lieutenant Colonel Tri Van Minh. Only one wall was set aside for the business of war. There a canvas drape concealed what Pascoe thought might be a map or bulletin board. The other three walls were covered with carefully posed photos of Minh. One large one with Minh in full uniform standing against a limbo background. It had been taken in a photo studio complete with all the strategic lighting to highlight Minh's glossy hair and give the appearance of a stronger chin. Minh appeared to be wearing makeup as he stood stiffly, his new chin raised with a hint of arrogance above the high collar of his dress white mess uniform.

Many of the other photos were of Minh in America—at Fort Rucker, the Army's Flight School. Minh with choppers. Minh with American classmates. And Minh accepting his graduation certificate from some American general Pascoe didn't recognize.

Pascoe walked around the room. It smelled of dust and smoke and mildew. Scattered among the framed photos were several certificates from Fort Benning's Parachute School, The Infantry Officer's Advanced Course and an out-of-context proclamation from a mayor in Enterprise, Alabama proclaiming Vietnamese-American Friendship day—Minh's photo prominent in the attached newspaper clipping.

The single worn desk took up a large amount of floor space in the office. The desk must have been nearly fifty years old and had probably seen service in other government buildings. A new coat of varnish failed to conceal the blue ink stains tattooed deep into the grain of the desk's top.

Pascoe couldn't resist picking up the gold plated ceremonial dagger, which held a position of honor on the desktop. Handmade, it was decorated with an engraved serpent extending from the hilt to the knife's point. In the blood groove, which ran down the center of the blade, was an inscription to Minh from General Nguyen Cao Ky, the Commanding General of the Vietnamese Air Force.

Worried Minh might catch him, Pascoe put the dagger back and turned to look at the rest of the office. The décor throughout the room was a strange amalgam of Asian and military furnishings. A flat-topped ceramic Chinese dragon served as a side table for a folding lawn chair with woven webbing of bright colored plastic. A small table in the corner of the room held a cluster of American liquor bottles. Next to them four small shot glasses stood upside down on a clean white napkin.

Minh's voice startled Pascoe.

"Sit." Minh pointed at a straight-backed chair centered on the desk. "We talk." He pulled out a blue pack of French Galouise cigarettes and offered one to Pascoe.

Though Pascoe didn't smoke, he took one of the cigarettes and put it to his lips. Turning down the offer would be taken as an insult by Minh.

Minh produced an America Zippo lighter with an enameled flag of the Republic of Vietnam in orange, red and green stripes—the national colors. He lit the cigarette and then lit his own as he walked to his desk. "Bui!" He called out for the sergeant in the outer office.

Almost immediately the sergeant knocked respectfully and, not waiting for a reply, entered carrying a tray. He placed the tray on the top of the ceramic dragon and served each officer hot tea French style—in glasses instead of cups. He left as quietly as he entered. Personal servitude was common in Vietnam. Something else Pascoe would have to overlook.

At first, the sight of the tea troubled Pascoe. He could plainly see something resembling a knot of worms gathered in the bottom of the glass of golden-brown liquid. A closer look revealed the tea had been cut into long thin strips, like American chewing tobacco. It was dropped loosely into the glass and covered with the hot water to steep. The tea was served with the shredded leaves still in the glass.

Minh picked up his tea by the rim avoiding the heated glass. In a toast-like gesture, he pointed the glass in Pascoe's direction. "Welcome, Major. May we enjoy a productive time together."

Pascoe braced himself for the first sip. Though he found the tea very hot, the flavor was pleasant and absent the biting aftertaste common in American teas. It was strange to drink hot tea in a climate already draining his energy and soaking his new jungle fatigues with sweat. "This is very good, sir."

Minh beamed. "Good. Good. I'll have some sent to your quarters for you. I hope you will like many things about my country."

Minh leaned back in his chair, savoring his tea and his cigarette.

The moment felt awkward to Pascoe who wasn't sure if he should restart the conversation or wait for Minh. He opted to take the initiative. "How can I best help you here, Colonel?"

Minh waved his hand indicating the unseen outer offices of the building. "As you can see, we are a very poor division. We need many, many things. We are far from Saigon. And they do not think about our needs out here—out here where the Viet Cong control the night."

In advisory training, Pascoe had been warned the Vietnamese were more likely to ask for resources and equipment than actual tactical advice. He mustn't make promises he couldn't keep because nothing he said would be taken as idle conversation. He selected his words carefully as not to suggest any promise at all. "Maybe, after I get settled in, you can show me around and point out what is lacking."

Minh stood, smoothed out the wrinkles in the front of his flight suit and stepped to the drape on the wall. He pulled it back revealing a tactical map of the area of combat operations for his division. Unit locations were well marked on the clear plastic overlay in blue grease pencil. Enemy positions in red and imaginary boundaries between regiments in black.

He picked up a wooden pointer from the narrow tray below the map, tapped the clear plastic overlay and began as if giving a performance. "This is where my war is, Major." He circled the center of the map with the tip of the pointer. He tapped a point on the border with Cambodia jutting toward Saigon. This we call the Parrot's Beak. At the top of the map he moved the pointer over a gentler curve in the black border, "And this is the Angel's Wing. Oh, yes, and now it is your war."

Pascoe tried to act interested but not ignorant of the situation. Minh couldn't know he'd read every book he could find on Vietnam, its history and culture, the French war and the communist insurgency eating away at South Vietnam like a cancer. He knew young Vietnamese men, women, and children had been dying in the area adjacent to the border for centuries over differences in religion, border disputes, land, power, and money.

Minh traced the length of the thick black boundary between Cambodia and Vietnam and continued speaking in the pattern Pascoe was becoming accustomed to—as if Minh was first thinking in Vietnamese and then searching for each equivalent English word. "We are responsible for this section of border. Seventy-three miles long and not possible to seal. Communists soldiers from the north travel hundreds of miles down small trails inside Cambodia to come to South Vietnam.

"Cambodia gives them safe passage because we cannot strike them there." He flatted the pointer out against the border. "Here they break into small groups. They become farmers and woodcutters and fishermen. They infiltrate into my country and then reform later to attack government outposts, towns, and military bases."

Minh put down the pointer and lit another foul-smelling cigarette.

"From the looks of the terrain it appears to me slipping across the border would be hard to do without being detected," Pascoe said.

Minh laughed. "These are cunning men. They are dedicated, and unlike you Americans, they are very patient. They learned from their fathers and their grandfathers. They can sit in the marshland all day and not move. At night they move in the darkness. We set out many ambushes, but they slip through. We conduct aerial reconnaissance each day by helicopter and all we can find are the trails through the mud where they moved at night."

"You don't sound like you are having any success at all," Pascoe said.

"Oh, do not mistake my words, Major. We kill many, many Viet Cong here. But for every one we kill ten get into Vietnam and take the lives of our brothers and our children." His eyebrows drew together over his eyes, and his tone became very dark. "They burn our homes, and they steal our rice. Then they get drunk after they kill the men, and they rape the women and young girls. They are animals, Major. They are all animals."

Pascoe noticed it was the very first time Minh's smile had faded. "What kind of surveillance do you have on the border?"

"We send out small patrols—into the swamps, but we cannot always see VC or hear them." He threw his hands up in the air. "There are hundreds of square miles out there where my enemy can hide, and we only have a very small number of helicopters to patrol the skies and few combat soldiers to set up ambushes at night. And we suffer many, many casualties.

"The terrain out there is very hard on my soldiers. Even when they do not make contact with enemy forces, they suffer from mines and booby traps. Malaria, Dengue Fever, and dysentery take my men. The worst is the marsh water. Even in the dry season, they become casualties from the being wet all day and night. They have to move and hide in the low places to keep from being seen by the enemy. This keeps them in stinking bogs and filthy water—"

"Let me guess," Pascoe said. "Then the leeches open sores on them and then bacteria sets up housekeeping."

"Yes, Major. They make, ah . . . how you call them . . . ulcer—?"

"Ulcers. That's right, Colonel. Skin ulcers," Pascoe said.

"A soldier with these infections is often gone for many weeks before he can go back to the field to search again for VC."

Pascoe thought about what to recommend to Minh that wouldn't involve trying to overcome the problem with hardware or American money. But before he could come up with something Minh continued.

Minh turned back to the map, reached up and knuckled a number in red in the corner of the map. Ashes fell from his cigarette. "And this is our combat strength as of today."

Pascoe could understand Vietnamese well enough to get by if someone wasn't speaking it too rapidly. In the few minutes he'd been in the headquarters, he could see he'd have to work harder at understanding the heightened speed of dialogue. And he was not very good at reading Vietnamese handwriting, especially acronyms. Still, what was immediately apparent to him on the map's acetate was the number—forty-one, followed by a percentage mark. It was enough to be understood in any soldier's language. It was the division's foxhole strength—the number of combat-ready soldiers. Less than half of their authorized strength.

After Minh finished his informal briefing, he pointed to Pascoe's flight bag still sitting by the doorway to the office. "I have taken too much of your time. I must get you to your team house. You will want to meet Colonel Wills, the Division Senior Advisor, before dinner in the General's Mess."

"Thank you for the briefing, Colonel. Would you mind if I spend some time going over your recent After Action Reports to get myself oriented on some of the details of what the division has been doing?"

"I will make them available. You are welcome to read anything you wish."

***

Pascoe looked around the team house located on the opposite side of the helicopter pad. It must have been a storeroom of sorts before being pressed into service as the quarters for the small advisory team. The large cavernous building had been broken up into small single rooms by the amateur construction of stud walls and wallboard, a combination of plywood and bamboo matting. Together they offered a modicum of air circulation and some privacy.

Someone had put his other bags in one of the empty rooms. He stepped inside to look around. It was more than Spartan-like with a single tropical slatted window he could neither open nor close, a single light bulb hanging from a twisted cord in the center of the room and a single cot topped with a rolled mattress and no pillow or bedding.

Some previous occupant had fashioned a series of hooks along one wall to hang gear and clothing. Other than the hooks and the bunk there was nothing in the room save a small field table with a large upturned metal ammo can pressed into a second life as a desk chair.

Outside a chopper landed, and more dust blew through the room adding to the layers already there. Pascoe was becoming accustomed to the constant sounds of choppers and nearby howitzers firing huge steel artillery rounds off in the direction of the border but not the dust. He opened one of his bags and began to look for places to put his things.

"Major Pascoe in here?"

Pascoe heard his name being called by an American. "Yo. In here," he answered as he stepped over his bag to open the wobbly plywood door to the room.

There, standing in the hallway was his new boss, Lieutenant Colonel Jasper Wills—a man clearly ten years older than Pascoe—a tall, lanky man more Adam's apple and awkward limbs than career officer with an impressive command presence. His face was heavily tanned from the neck of his t-shirt to just above his eyebrows. The rest was pale and untouched by the sun due to the constant wear of hats and helmets.

His jungle fatigues hung on him. Sized by height alone, the uniform had more bulk in the girth than Wills did, and his arms seemed to dangle from the sleeves rolled above his elbows as if they were pinned into the rolls.

"Hot damn! Just what I need," Wills said. He stuck out his hand to shake Pascoe's. "Welcome to Veet Nam," he said. "I've been waiting for you to get here for about a month, Pascoe."

Pascoe stumbled over trying to render a customary salute first and then take Wills' hand. "How are you, sir? It's Eldon. Eldon Pascoe, sir."

"Got a minute?" Wills asked.

"Sure. Sure. Come in," Pascoe waved Wills into his small room. He nodded at the ammo can. "Please. Make yourself at home."

Wills shrugged off his combat harness holding his leather holstered pistol, canteens, and his first aid, compass, ammunition, and survival pouches. Dumping the added twenty pounds of gear on the scarred concrete floor, he sat and arched his back as if he could stretch some of the tension from it. He pulled an olive drab handkerchief from his pocket and wiped the sweat and grime from his neck. Then he took off his wire-rimmed glasses and wiped the dust from them. "Whew! This is hotter than home. You can even sweat in the shower this time a year here 'bouts."

Pascoe sat on the corner of his bunk. "Where's home?"

"Nesmith, South Carolina. Sure do miss it. My people are all from Nesmith." He looked at his watch then waved off in the direction of the border beyond the Sugar Mill's perimeter. "Listen, I only got a minute to say hello and get back out with the general. It's gonna be like this most times. That Viet general don't fart without me nearby, and if you see me at all, it'll be a rare thing in your duty day.

"Listen, you gonna have to get tight with Colonel Minh and don't let him talk you into shit you don't think you or he oughta' be doin'. I'll try to back ya' up when I can, but get used to these little folks takin' every chance they can to play poor mouth and complain they need things to win the war." Wills leaned toward Pascoe and lowered his voice. "What they need most is to get their little asses out of their base camps and out there into Indian country."

Pascoe was surprised at Wills' candor. "I appreciate all that, Colonel, but how do I do that and still gain Minh's confidence?"

"Throw the boy a bone now and then. He'll be one step ahead of you, though. Every Viet knows what has arrived at the docks in Saigon to support the advisory effort even before we do. So he'll know what he's asking you for is already available somewhere in the supply system. Don't let him catch you tellin' him something's not available when he knows damn good and well it's already in-country. You'll catch on."

Pascoe shook his head. "I sure hope so. This seems a whole lot more complicated than I thought it was going to be when I got my orders."

"It's new ground for all a' us. If we tried to run our army the way they run theirs we'd all be a British colony or probably speaking German now."

Outside, the chopper, which had brought Wills in, cranked back up to flight idle again. Wills checked his watch. "Look, I got to go. I'll try to bring you up to speed in bits and pieces where and when I can find the time."

Wills stood, picked up his field gear with one hand, and half-slapped Pascoe on the shoulder with the other. "You'll be okay. Just do what you think's right, son. That's the best I can tell ya.'"

Pascoe opened the door for Wills. "Thanks for the vote of confidence, sir."

Wills stopped in the open doorway and lowered his voice. "Oh, you need to know no matter what you or I do, no matter how this war goes, Minh's gonna be a general soon. He's got big-time pals in Saigon. A brother-in-law who's a general on the Premier's staff. You just watch your back. You hear?"

"Will do," Pascoe said as he unconsciously straightened his posture.

"Okay, I'll prob'ly see you in the General's Mess for chow later."

Pascoe watched Wills walk down the narrow hallway to the brilliant rectangle of light leading out into the compound. He sensed he just might be able to have a chance at redeeming himself with Wills as his supervisor.

CHAPTER 8

The few days Pascoe spent in Saigon at Camp Alpha didn't prepare him for his first nights at the Sugar Mill. The heat was more stifling than Saigon's, denying him any level of comfort allowing him to sleep. Not moving and not covered, Pascoe stretched out on his bunk under the draped mosquito net wearing only his GI boxers shorts. Sweat pooled in the hollow of his throat and ran down the sides of his face only to fall on the pillow he had fashioned out of two folded towels.

The nearness of the great swamps and the Vam Co Dong River flowing just outside the compound made the humidity that much more oppressive. Occasional bursts of rifle fire and the teeth-rattling howitzers frequently interrupted the din already put up by insects in the farmlands surrounding the mill.

He began to question the wisdom of volunteering for Vietnam. With the exception of Colonel Wills, he hadn't met anyone he had any confidence in and wasn't really sure what lay ahead. He had no idea if he'd be confined to the Sugar Mill working in the Operations Section or if he'd be allowed to go forward—to the troop units' battle positions and patrol bases. He wouldn't be able to make these decisions alone. He'd be expected to follow Colonel's Minh's lead, and Minh would determine how he would spend his year. He hated the fact his degree of risk would be in the hands of someone else.

The bunk was uncomfortable; mosquitoes buzzed around the netting, and he yearned for sleep to overtake him. But it wouldn't come. He thought of West Point and how many thousands of miles away it now seemed. He thought of Karen, who he had left with her family in Pennsylvania. Picturing her he felt an urge for her between his legs. He hadn't even thought about a year without sex. A year without being able to touch her. He missed her naked body next to his, the weight of her breast against in his palm as he had become accustomed to sleeping with her. He loved to encircle her with his arms, snugging his hips against her tight bottom, taking in the smell of the skin in the crook of her neck.

He became aware of the blood rushing to his groin and quickly felt a sense of panic at having no release for the sensation. How could he spend a year without the pleasure she gave him? No matter what small disagreements they might have had during their day, Karen never let her mood determine her availability. She never denied him sex or withheld it to punish him. She always enjoyed sex, and it seemed to him giving him the pleasure he craved was her responsibility.

He remembered the ease she felt with sex and her lack of self-consciousness. She loved being naked and exciting him with her fingers and lips. She took pride in her breasts set off by her tiny waist. She loved to pin him to the bed while she sat up. She controlled the pace of their sex, straddling him and encouraging him to caress her body while she carefully gauged her movements to tease him, never failing to bring him to a delicious climax before they slept.

Frustrated at her distance and his discomfort, he pulled one of the towels from underneath his head and wiped the perspiration from his face, neck, and chest. The radium dial of his watch heightened his anxiety. It was ten minutes to two, and he was nowhere near sleep. There was nothing he could do. There was no kitchen for something to eat which might make him sleepy. He had been unable to exercise while in transit and waiting for his final assignment in Saigon. He felt thick and leaden. Since leaving the US, he had been denied the opportunity to run, an activity which not only kept his weight down but burned off many of his frustrations and cleared his head. Now, at the Sugar Mill, there would be no place to run and leaving the compound to run along the dangerous roadways was out of the question.

His diet had only added to his discomfort. Airline food then mess hall food—he'd not been able to find food which either satisfied him or calmed the knotty feeling in his gut.

After another hour of restlessness, sweating and lack of sleep Pascoe got up and searched for the dry towel hanging over the foot of his bed. He didn't bother to turn on the light as he left the room to follow the hallway out to the makeshift shower set up next to the building.

Each day in Vietnam was a reminder of what every American left behind. His old quarters at West Point, his B.O.Q. rooms while he was in schools in transit to Vietnam, all were marvels of engineering, comfort, and sanitation when compared to the toilet and shower facilities throughout the war zone.

Pascoe slowed his pace as he approached the showers. Water pooled on the hard-packed compound—evidence of the poor design of what was not much more than a scaffolding of four-by-four posts holding up large garbage can sized water barrels. Each of the four barrels was a shower. There was neither a pretense of privacy, a thought given to removing the run-off, nor any effort to provide those small things necessary to shower. There was no place to put a towel, rest a bar of soap or even shave in or near the shower itself. Pascoe had discovered he would have to either shave blind in the shower or in his room using a small plastic bucket he had found in the Team House. Even then, the bucket was of such poor construction he would have to walk very gingerly to keep the walls of the bucket from buckling and spilling the water he need to shave.

Worse than the shower's poor design was its placement. Pascoe's nose was assaulted by the smell of human waste, urine, gas and diesel fuel. The

GI outhouse was a four-holer. A large plywood box with four uncovered ovals cut into its top served as the only toilets in the compound. The latrine was enclosed only by screened walls and topped with a corrugated tin roof—again offering no privacy. The odors came from the empty oil drums placed under the holes in the wooden box. Waste would collect in the drums until someone dispatched a Vietnamese soldier to pull them out, pour in a mixture of gasoline and diesel and set them aflame. Allowing them to fill the air with dense, black smoke put a distinctive smell in the compound, all the offices, and even Pascoe's room. The ceremony was known throughout Vietnam as *burning the shitters.*

It wasn't much as offices go, but Pascoe would make it work and try not to complain. It was very small, had a single shuttered window, a desk, chair and a Japanese electric fan emitting a hum. He ran his fingers across the desktop and felt the dust and grime, which settled on it in the few hours since a soldier had wiped it down. Through the small window, he could see the brown stripe of the Vam Co Dong River as it hugged the outside wall of the Sugar Mill on its way to the South China Sea. He wiped the sweat from his neck and longed for his air-conditioned office at West Point overlooking the steely blue Hudson River and Flirtation Walk where cadets had taken their dates for two centuries to steal some private moments together.

"Sir?"

Pascoe turned to find a lanky American sergeant standing in the doorway to the office, his cap in his hand. "Yes?"

"Sir, I'm Sergeant Caruthers. I'm your Ops NCO."

Pascoe smiled, leaned across the small desk and stuck out his hand. "Well, I'm glad to see another American face around here. Seems like we are outnumbered." He pointed to a stool on Caruthers's side of the desk. "Sit. Tell me what you do around here."

As Caruthers maneuvered the small stool to a spot where he could sit on it and face Pascoe without being out in the hallway, Pascoe quickly sized up the soldier. He read his military resume off his fatigue shirt. His embroidered Combat Infantryman's badge had two stars atop it—meaning he was a World War II and a Korean War veteran. It was a plus for Pascoe. Pascoe also recognized Caruthers was a master parachutist, which had always been a problem for Pascoe, who when offered the chance to go to the Airborne School passed up on it. Ever since paratroopers had made him feel like he was not a real Infantry soldier.

"So, Sergeant Caruthers, tell me, what do you to earn your pay?"

Caruthers pulled a package of Redman chewing tobacco out of the cargo pocket on his trouser leg and held it up for Pascoe. "You mind, sir?"

"No, go ahead." Pascoe watched as Caruthers opened the pouch, rolled up a ball of chew half the size of a golf ball and pushed it into the space between his teeth and his cheek. He then moved the ball of tobacco around a bit making the wad smaller. A hint of the dark brown tobacco juice appeared at the corner of his mouth, and he wiped it away with the back of his hand.

"So?" Pascoe reminded him there was still a question.

"Oh, Yessir. Well, dependin' on what it is you want me to do I pretty much do what you want."

The answer didn't tell Pascoe much. "Well, let me put it this way, what have you been doing up to now?"

"Major Smith, you know, the advisor you replaced, had me sticking close to him and keepin' an eye on these V'namese. They can be some kinda' slippery, y'know. And if you don't boot 'em in the ass they sit on theirs all the time. But then Major Smith went home early 'cuz his wife was sick, and we had two months with nobody in y'er job. I pretty much ran errands for Colonel Minh and tried to say out of sight."

"Why's that?"

"Well, ever' time Minh sees me he wants something. So I figure if he don't see me he can't be busting my ass about stuff he wants me to scrounge up. He's always tryin' to get me to buy stuff for him at the PX in Saigon or the Class VI Store."

Pascoe could only imagine what Caruthers was referring to since he had neither been to the Post Exchange in Saigon nor the Class VI Store, the Army's version of a liquor store. Not wanting to endorse the sergeant's actions Pascoe simply said, "I see."

"But now you're here I don't think I need to be hidin' as much because he'll be after you like he was after Major Smith."

"So how do we help Colonel Minh plan and execute combat operations around here?"

Caruthers leaned forward and lowered his voice a little. "Major, can I be honest with you?"

"Absolutely."

Caruthers tapped his Infantryman's badge on his shirt. "Sir, I'm a grunt. I been a soldier now, man and boy, goin' on thirty years. One time or another I been a rifleman, squad leader or a platoon sergeant and this here's my third war. I been rode hard and put up wet. But I got to tell you, sir, I'm just plain uncomfortable with all this headquarters stuff."

"Politics?"

"Yessir, whatever you want to call it. I'm a ground pounder. I belong with young soldiers, not these V'namese pussies. They is damn near worthless."

"All of them?"

Caruthers moved the chaw in his mouth to the other side and looked up at the ceiling. "Well, no sir. I'm thinkin' there's a few I'd be callin' pretty good soldiers. But most a' them are just lazy little bastards."

"I see. Well, I'm going to need your help getting used to how things work around here and I'll be interested in hearing who you feel is reliable and who isn't."

Caruthers straightened his back a little, pushing out his chest. "Yes, sir. Be happy to do it for you."

"How much longer you here?"

Caruthers rolled his eyes. "Lemme see. The way I figure it I got ninety-seven days and a wake up left in country. I've already got alert orders to report to my terminal assignment." Caruthers leaned back and smiled. "I asked to be stationed somewhere near home, so they're sendin' me to Fort Leonard Wood, Missouri."

"Where's home?"

Caruthers smiled showing the brown staining on his teeth. "Right outside the front gate—Waynesville."

"And you are going to retire there?"

"Yes, sir! I'm willin' to hump these boonies with these little people while I'm here, but this is it. I'm getting closer to fifty than forty and I still got some real good fishin' years in me. I want to spend 'em at my end of a rod on my bass boat."

Pascoe didn't know why he had expected Minh to send someone to tell him before Minh fired up the chopper. But he hadn't bothered. He had hoped to be there to help Minh preflight the aircraft before their first real orientation flight. He wanted to feel better about flying in the aging chopper. At least an inspection might let him know what to worry about.

Racing from his office to the idling chopper, he knew there had not been enough time for Minh to properly inspect the chopper in the few minutes since he had seen Minh pass by his doorway.

He saw but tried not to see, the excessive buildup of greasy black soot on the huge exhaust port of the powerful turbine engine. Any aviator knew this meant either improperly burning fuel or a chopper that simply hadn't been adequately cleaned in quite some time. Either way, it was not a good sign.

Pascoe crawled up into his seat on the right side of the cockpit, buckled up his waist and shoulder harnesses just as Minh looked outside the chopper at a Vietnamese soldier standing behind the chopper giving Minh a thumbs-up to take off.

Tucking his ears into the built-in headset cups of his helmet, Pascoe watched the temperature gauges and RPM indicator. What if Minh needed him in the event of a hot start? A fire was second only to a crash landing in the litany of pilot's nightmares. He tried to catch up with the flight startup procedure by quickly memorizing the indicators on the myriad of dials and gauges arrayed in front of him. He needed to have something to compare the readings to in the event of some in-flight problem.

Minh's voice over the intercom startled Pascoe. "We go now." He slowly raised the collective, pushed the left peddle to keep the tail of the chopper where it belonged and eased forward on the cyclic stick between his knees. Immediately the chopper got light on its skids.

Almost out of reflex, Pascoe looked out his side of the chopper for anything which might cause them to abort the takeoff. "Clear right."

The chopper raised slightly off the pad, subtly shuddered then hesitated as Minh changed its direction from up to forward in the most critical transition in any chopper's flight.

Pascoe held his breath as Minh crossed the rolls of barbed concertina wire on top of the walls surrounding the compound allowing only inches of clearance. Pascoe forced himself to relax. Minh was in control of the chopper. He considered offering some suggestions to improve Minh's flying techniques but decided the risk of offending Minh was the more likely outcome than Minh actually taking his suggestions. How could he ease Minh into a conversation about flight safety to discover how much Minh knew about the subject or how important it was to him? Maybe after they had flown together a few more times. Maybe after they got more familiar with one another. Maybe then.

Quickly the chopper reached a more comfortable altitude for Pascoe and leveled out. At least, if the engine failed at fifteen hundred feet and Minh wasn't prepared for it, Pascoe could wrestle the aircraft to the ground in a controlled autorotation.

Cooler air filled the cockpit and Pascoe wiggled around to free his uniform where it had glued itself to his skin from the humidity. "I didn't go through any flight orientation training for Vietnam," he said still hoping to draw Minh out. "I had no idea I'd end up with a counterpart who not only had his own chopper but was a qualified aviator."

Minh laughed. "We have Vietnamese way of flying here. Not like America. Here we try not to get shot down."

Pascoe laughed uneasily. "Any special evasion technique you use? I mean do you set a minimum altitude or fly different routes so you won't set up a pattern or avoid certain situations?"

"Oh, yes. We fly that way." He smiled and glanced at Pascoe. "Sometimes we not fly that way."

Pascoe gave up on trying to get Minh to explain his flying. He'd have to watch him if he wanted to find out just how competent a pilot he was.

They flew west for less than two miles when Minh released the cyclic long enough to point out over the instrument panel. "Everything you see is our area of operations."

Pascoe scanned the vast flat flood plain interrupted by tufts of Nipa palms sheltering mostly abandoned thatched roofed houses. Streams and small rivers coiled and gently flowed toward the Mekong Delta before merging and spilling into the sea. Again, the closer they flew toward the Cambodian border the fewer the signs of civilization.

Pascoe covertly stole a glance at the duplicate set of instruments arrayed in front of him, not wanting Minh to think he was watching his flying too closely, but he was unsuccessful.

"Would you like to fly, my friend?"

Pascoe was surprised at the offer. "Sure." He lightly placed his feet on the co-pilot's pedals and his hands on his duplicate collective and cyclic controls clearly announcing the traditional trade-off command, "I've got it."

Minh released the controls on his side of the cockpit and raised his hands in an exaggerated gesture for Pascoe to see out of the corner of his eye Minh had relinquished command of the aircraft, and it was now up to Pascoe to control the chopper's every move.

The chopper made a slight wobble as the tail rotor shimmied first right then left while Pascoe searched for a sense of feel to the pedals. He hadn't flown in almost a year, and each chopper was different. Like the unique feel of a clutch or the brakes on an older car. Pascoe felt the moisture gathering again under his arms. "Where we headed, Colonel?"

Minh checked the spinning compass and then pointed off to the northwest. "Stay above fifteen hundred feet, heading two-eight-five."

"Roger that," Pascoe said, gingerly leaning the chopper over into a gently arcing turn and bank to his right, holding it until the compass spun to the desired heading before leveling off again.

"Look to your right. Three o'clock."

Pascoe looked at a black smudge on the ground—burned out remains of some small buildings in the center of a tiny hamlet surrounded by many new pockmarks from friendly bombs and enemy mortar rounds.

"That was one of our command posts. The Viet Cong attacked two weeks ago. They kill everyone and tied the battalion commander to the flag pole in front of the building."

Pascoe picked out the flag pole almost perfectly centered on concentric circles of barbed wire and neatly laid out though destroyed sandbagged bunkers.

"Before they kill him they cut him open and his insides fall to the ground." He paused and then added, "His wife and children watched this before they were killed."

Pascoe tightened his jaw as he eased the chopper over into a tight right turn and took a long look at the bomb craters and burned thatched houses below. On top of the carnage, Pascoe recognized he would have to understand a war where soldiers took their families with them since nowhere in Vietnam was there any escape from the battlefield.

"Come. I show you Duc Hue. Over there." Minh pointed off at a small geometric feature on the horizon. The construction was French and elaborately engineered as a defensive compound prepared to sustain long sieges. "It is a Special Forces camp. Every night the VC they come."

Leveling up the chopper, Pascoe quickly scanned his instruments to check on the performance of the lumbering chopper. He was surprised to find the rotor and turbine RPMs were okay as were the critical temperature gauges. "Are they trying to overrun the camp?"

Minh laughed. "Oh, no. They think we are very worried about Duc Hue. We know they do not want to take Due Hue. They attack so they can move people through here at night." He swept his hand to indicate the vast expanse of the swamps and marshland south of the camp. "Every night they come. Go down."

"What?"

"I show you. I've got it," Minh said, quickly snatching control of the chopper from Pascoe.

He slammed his cyclic stick over to its limit forcing the chopper to heel over abruptly into a tight descending left spiral and bled off altitude so quickly Pascoe soon felt the warmer air. In flight school, the maneuver was called a yank and bank and was grounds to fail a check ride with a flight instructor.

Minh pulled out of the spin with the same lack of finesse and maneuvered the chopper off into a flat orbit at two hundred feet.

Pascoe suddenly became conscious of his dangerous proximity to the small clusters of trees which could easily conceal enemy gunners. Gunners who might be trying to get their chopper in their gun sights. He had never felt so vulnerable. He wondered if his year would be like this every day.

"There. Out your door," Minh said.

Minh jerked the chopper over into a right turn to allow Pascoe to look straight down. There Pascoe saw a newly made trail cut into the marshy ground. The path headed east, away from the Cambodian border and deeper into South Vietnam. Reeds were bent over, and footprints were easy to pick out in the mud, each filled with water. One person had made the tracks during the night.

"They come."

A few hundred meters from the trail Pascoe saw other trails, all solitary ones, all heading in the same direction. It appeared to him a small squad of eight or fewer Viet Cong soldiers had spread out over and area several football fields in width to infiltrate.

He nodded at the small hamlets and villages behind them. "And they end up back there?"

"They hide in every hamlet in Vietnam. Then they mass to attack."

***

In the distance, a single and dominant terrain feature stood out of place in the flatness of the immense Mekong River delta which formed the bottom third of Vietnam for thousands of years. Pascoe pointed at the solo and nearly cone-shaped mountain ahead of the chopper. "What's that?"

"Ah, this is a special place for us. I will show you. We go there. It is a good place for you to see much," Minh said. He flew the chopper directly to the mountain.

As they got closer, Pascoe glanced at the altimeter in the aircraft to compare it with the summit of the mountain. His guess was somewhere in the neighborhood of three thousand feet high, and it looked to him to cover about fifteen square miles—standing out from the hundreds of miles of pool-table-flat countryside surrounding it.

Even closer, Pascoe could see that it was more rock than earth—large granite boulders seemed to have been piled up by nature. Near the base, stands of bamboo and banana palms separated it from the flat land.

"I must practice pinnacle landing," Minh said. He raised his glove hand and waved it around the flat land. "You can see I don't get many chances to do that."

Pascoe remembered learning pinnacle landings in flight school. It put the fear in the hearts of all flight students. Just the thought of landing on the top of a mountain or a rooftop was fraught with the possibilities of over or undershooting the landing and tumbling down the side of a pinnacle. The instructors took delight in making Pascoe do it again and again. Still, he didn't ever get completely comfortable with the technique. He felt his legs stiffen as if putting on the brakes in a car as Minh shot his landing approach to a very small flat spot on the top of the mountain.

"Hold on, my friend. I not good at this."

In spite of his words, Pascoe was pleased to find that Minh did a fairly skilled job of putting the chopper down on top of the mountain—on a spot less than half the size of the Huey chopper's length.

Minh reached up to the bank of switches in the overhead console and began to shut down the chopper's turbine engine. "Come. We get out."

Pascoe wasn't comfortable with getting out of the chopper in an unsecured area. He reached down and checked his pistol.

Minh didn't miss it. "Do not worry. The Viet Cong do not occupy this mountain. They only come here when we sometimes put radio relay teams here. When we are not here, they not here too."

The two soldiers got out of the chopper and looked out and down over the green and brown flatland below. Pascoe was surprised to find evidence of one encampment after another everywhere on the top of the mountain. "I can see why you would want to use this to support operations near here."

Minh kicked a wooden box rotting in the sun marked with French writing on its side. "You see? Many soldiers have been here."

"I can see how you would easily adjust artillery fire from here. How much help is it as radio relay?" Pascoe asked.

"It is good if you have good radios with the soldiers. If you do not have someone here or in an airplane you cannot reach radios near the border from," he turned and pointed in the direction of the Sugar Mill, "our head-quarters."

"This is so strange. No mountains for miles and then this one alone," Pascoe said.

"It is said in Vietnam legend there was a young girl named Ba Den was to marry a brave young soldier. On the day of their wedding, her fiancé was called away to battle, and he never returned. Ba Den waited and waited. She cried herself to death right here. To us, this is a holy place."

CHAPTER 9

Newly minted Sergeant Scotty Hayes walked up the front steps of the Fort Benning Non-Commissioned Officers' Club for the very first time. His stride was steady, his carriage erect. He had taken on a bit of a swagger he had not brought with him when he left Belton, Florida. In the year he had spent in Advanced Infantry Training, Ranger and Airborne School and NCO training he had shrugged off much of his boyish uncertainty, ambivalence and self-consciousness. Training NCOs had taught him to stand proud, be proud and move with a purpose. Others had hammered decisiveness into him. And still others had made him aware of the necessity to look sure, sound sure and be sure. He had learned his lessons well.

As he stepped through the large glass double doors of the club he pulled off his overseas cap, the large red, white and blue glider patch sewn to the front of the hat known to all paratroopers as a piss cutter. Just inside the club his highly shined paratrooper boots suddenly went silent on the carpeting. As a graduate of NCO school, he was proud to be a new sergeant, making him eligible for admission to the club reserved for non-commissioned officers only.

Scotty crossed the lobby and braced himself for what he would find on entering the main room. He stopped at the doorway to allow his eyes to adjust to the room and immediately enjoyed the air-conditioned relief from the mid-summer Georgia heat and humidity.

Buck Owens' voice filled the main barroom with *Together Again* and laughter punctuated it all. A single row of sergeants stood at the bar along the wall nursing drinks. Others clustered at small tables marked by solitary candle flames struggling against the air conditioner's draft at the bottoms of colored containers.

"Hayes!"

Scotty searched the room for the voice.

"Over here."

On the far side of the parquet dance floor, an arm waved to Scotty. He quickly recognized Sergeant Russell but was surprised to see him in civilian clothes. He had never seen Russell out of uniform. Everything was always in place, always pressed, always polished and always perfect. To see him in slacks, loafers and a crisp and perfectly ironed cotton, buttoned-down collar shirt was different, but it was still very Asa Russell.

Scotty threaded his way through the crowd, conscious of the heads turning his way—some mumbling, others nodding with a *there goes one of them* expression. He was completely aware most other soldiers were in their late twenties before qualifying for promotion to sergeant. His rapid advancement was the result of a program designed to fill the thinning ranks of mid-level NCOs. NCOs who were leaving in large numbers having been through World War II, the Korean War and unwilling to get on the ride Vietnam promised.

"Well, well, well," Russell said as he stood to meet Scotty. He held out his hand to shake Scotty's, and put his other on Scotty's shoulder to keep him from sitting right away. "Let me look at you. Son of a bitch! You really did it."

Feeling uncomfortable with Russell's praise Scotty tried to play it down. "It really wasn't as hard as being in your platoon in Basic. If I could live through eight weeks of Ace Russell, I could live through anything."

Russell laughed and gestured for Scotty to grab a chair. "Seems to me we only lost about five out of forty who couldn't hack it in your trainee platoon. What would you say, about forty-five percent of your NCO class washed out? And more than half of your Ranger class?"

Scotty sat, careful not to bend his knees under the chair to avoid spoiling the sharp creases he'd spent time pressing into his trousers. "How'd you know—?"

"You don't think I was keeping tabs on you?" He smiled. Something rare for Russell. "I had a lot a' time invested in you. I wasn't going to send you off to become an NCO and have your ass flake out and embarrass me. If you had a' I would a' come over to your training battalion and kicked your ass the rest of the way to graduation."

Scotty laughed. "You mean like you did when I went through Basic?"

Russell took a sip of his beer and then tipped his glass to Scotty as if a question. "Something to drink?" Not waiting for Scotty's reply he raised the beer over his head, got the bartender's attention and mouthed the words, "Two more."

The beers came, and Scotty reached for his wallet.

"Nope. On me," Russell insisted. He looked to the waitress. "I've got a tab running. The name's Russell."

Pulling the beer and coaster closer, Scotty nodded. "Thanks, Sergeant."

"Ace. Call me Ace."

Since the day Scotty had met Asa Russell, it never occurred to him he might actually address him as Ace like all the other NCOs always did. "Okay. It's going feel strange though."

Russell laughed. "Was I such a big son of a bitch?"

Not sure how to answer, Scotty sought a middle ground. "If you only knew how many nights I saw your face while I was fighting to ward off the cold down in the Florida swamps last winter, or while I was sure I wasn't going to make the last quarter mile of an obstacle course. Or, worse yet, while my mouth was filled with cotton and my palms were sweating when I stood in front of a group of other NCO candidates giving a class for a grade. I kept thinking, that damn Russell put me here."

"No Scott. You put you there."

Russell had never called him by his first name. "I'd probably be a truck driver in Germany today if it hadn't been for you," Scotty said.

"And now you're going off to war."

Scotty was quiet for a moment. He nodded his head breaking the air of self-confidence he had carried with him into the room. "And I don't mind telling you I don't think I'm ready for this."

Russell laughed again. "Boy, do you think there's ever been an infantryman who thought he was ready to go to some God-forsaken butt hole of the world to get shot at by someone he's never met and really doesn't have a hard-on for?"

Scotty smiled. "Guess not. But this is worse because nobody here has any idea just what's going on over there. I only had two Tactical NCOs in school who'd even been to Vietnam, and they were there before any real shooting started."

"I'm guessing President Johnson isn't expecting you to go over there and sort out all the complications, fix everything what's broken and solve all his problems. I'm damn sure he does expect you to go over there and teach those little fuckers how to fight."

"But those guys been fighting somebody or another for a hundred years. Who am I to tell them how to go to war when I've never been shot at?"

"Scott, they've been fighting the North Viets the same way they fought everybody who's ever invaded their country back to the time they were throwing rocks at each other." Russell leaned forward and poked his index finger into the tabletop. "What they need is a lesson on the kind a' hustle you got. They need an attitude change, not new tactics or weapons."

Scotty took a sip of his beer and shook his head. "You sure have a lot more confidence in me than I do."

Russell leaned back in his chair. "You think that's news to me?"

They were silent for an awkward moment while Scotty let it all sink in. He was going to Vietnam and experiencing all the same anxieties known to every American soldier from Gettysburg to the Pusan Perimeter in Korea.

"Hey. You just go over there and do what an old boss of mine told me to do when I was a young NCO like you, 'Act right and do good stuff.' Nobody can expect more of you."

Scotty looked around the room. "Now, more and more NCOs are starting to show up back here after a tour over there, and I want to ask them what it's like, but I get the feeling too many of them aren't happy with us *Shake and Bake* NCOs."

"Forget it. They didn't like it when some of us nineteen-year-olds went from PFC to buck sergeant in Korea either. When wars heat up so do the promotions. If they didn't do it, they'd have an army of privates. Anyhow, since Napoleon, every soldier's war is different than the one the guy in the next foxhole experienced. You just go do your best."

"Sergeant, ah, Ace, I'll do my best. The last thing I want to do is fuck up."

Russell pointed his index finger at Scotty's bright new chevrons. "You earned those stripes because those Tac NCOs thought you could hack it. I don't have to tell you how good those guys are. You know it. If they said you should be a sergeant, then you shouldn't have to worry about screwing up."

Scotty heard him but still wasn't persuaded. "I hope you're right. I sure don't want to embarrass anybody."

"Hey. Speaking of anybody, how's your mom?" Russell said.

"Kitty? I saw her last Christmas. I got to go home on leave for a week. She's just wearing down. She can't work much anymore, but now I've claimed her as my dependent, so Uncle Sam's helping me pay for her and get her some medical help. She's got emphysema, whatever the hell it is."

"Enlargement of the alveoli in the lungs. Eventually, the walls of the tiny air sacs collapse. Usually involves chronic bronchitis, chronic cough and over production of sputum."

Scotty gave Russell a surprised look.

"Hey, don't you think an old war dog like me remembers his Special Forces medical training? You think all I got out of it was a green beret?"

"I forgot. But you're right. That's what it is. She's just having an awful time with it. But she's got a girl who comes in a couple times a week to help around the house and cook some stuff up for her to eat. Still, I'm afraid I'm looking at the beginning of the end. And, I'd rather get my ass kicked than think of not having her around."

"I lost my momma when I was a kid. Let's hope you get luckier."

Scotty spoke up over the heartbreaking sounds of a steel guitar punctuating a Hank Williams song competing with the noise and the laughter only heard on Saturday afternoons in most NCO clubs. His face brightened. "I'm going to see her next week. I've got thirty days leave on the way to Saigon, and I'm going to spend all of it at home." He shook his head.

"I'm sure lots of things need fixing around the house, and I've got to find out just what the story is. If I listen to her tell it, she's 'doin' fine.'"

Russell motioned to the bartender for another round. "That's good. I'm sure you're about ready for a break after over a solid year of training."

Scotty laughed. "I never thought I'd hear you say that."

"You just think I've got a heart of stone and an ass made out of bumpers, don't you?"

They both laughed. Then Scotty asked, "What about you? They going to keep you here pounding out Basic Trainees for the rest of your career?"

"No, sir." Russell killed what was left of his beer and waved back at a friend who pointed at him as he entered the club. "I'm on my way to Southeast Asia myself. Got my orders last week."

"Vietnam?"

"Well, yes and no."

Scotty gave him a puzzled look.

"I'm going to put my green beret back on. I'll be going to 1st Special Forces Group in Okinawa. It means I'll be there on paper but deployed somewhere in Vietnam, Laos or Cambodia. So count on me holding up my end."

Suddenly, a war that seemed so far away and so unfamiliar to Scotty was filling up his life and his thoughts. Others in his graduating class received orders for Vietnam. Around the main room in the NCO club, he could spot NCOs who recently returned from Vietnam by their MACV combat patches worn on their right shoulders. Over the bar, the black and white television had some news footage from Saigon, and now Russell.

Scotty wanted to ask Russell about Vietnam, about what he really should believe. He'd heard it all in training but how much of it was real? What could he really expect?

"Hey? You already there?"

"There?"

"Vietnam. No extra credit for showing up there early. Finish your beer, we'll get refills and order something to eat."

"Sorry," Scotty said. "I was there. I got to tell you it's got my ass puckered."

"That's good," Russell said. "You go over there thinking you're some kind of bad ass and they'll be shippin' your ass home in a tin box courtesy of the Quartermaster."

"I just want to think I can hack it."

He surveyed his quarters examining everything. The few GI furnishings in the single room were cleaned, windows washed, drawers cleaned out, trash and butt cans emptied and the floor swept and mopped.

His blouse hung on the door of his locker ready to be put on as his last act before turning out the lights and locking the door one last time. Satisfied he hadn't missed anything, he turned his attention to his wall locker. He ran his hand across the empty top shelf as a final check to be sure he'd cleared out all the odds and ends stored there, some items to go with him, some headed for the trash.

On the bottom shelf, his duffel bag sat folded precisely to the inside dimensions of the locker. He picked it up surprised to also find his father's old duffel bag tucked neatly under his. He'd forgotten he'd used his father's bag to carry his things from Belton to Fort Benning The very same things the Army made him throw out before his first day in the Army was over.

He unfolded the newer bag, readying it for stuffing. It smelled of an oil unique to all heavy canvas items issued by the Army. On its side was stenciled Scotty's name, rank and serial number. But his eye was drawn back to his father's bag on the bottom of the locker. His father carried it with him to Korea, and someone else had sent it home with his belongings after he was killed. He dropped his bag, and picked up his father's. Faded stenciling on the bleached-out, scarred and scuffed duffel bag read: Hayes, Jacob T., Sergeant, RA11413202.

There had been a day like this one for his father too. He'd finished difficult combat training at Fort Benning and packed his gear into the old bag when it was new and dark green. Jake Hayes too had been a newly minted paratrooper headed off to a war in Asia.

Kitty had photos of Jake in his uniform the day he left for Korea. It was a different uniform than Scotty wore—Ike Jacket and brown paratrooper boots, both a hangover from WWII. But the paratrooper's badge over the chest pocket on his blouse was the same as Scotty's new wings. And at his side was the duffel bag, new then and ready to travel.

Scotty changed his mind. He refolded his bag. He would pack his things in Jake's bag—a combat soldier's bag.

During all these preparations to leave Fort Benning the sergeant across the hall played *The House of the Rising Sun* over and over again on a portable record player with a speaker less than a third the size of the 45 RPM record itself. At first, Scotty enjoyed the music. But after the fifth time, the silence was better than more of Erik Burden's depressing song of the seamier side of New Orleans, poverty, despair, and ruin.

He yelled, "Hey, don't you have another record?" A door slammed, and the music stopped.

He quit packing long enough to check his watch. He always thought he was one of those guys who didn't get homesick, but the closer he got to leaving the more he looked forward to Belton and Kitty, sleeping in and even just wearing civilian clothes for a change.

Others in his training platoons had suffered from bouts of homesickness but not Scotty. He'd never been one of those guys who talked endlessly about being home and going home and friends and girls back home. He wasn't the type who shared letters or subscribed to a hometown newspaper, which always seemed to arrive after a showdown with a Doberman.

He never let thoughts of home torture him. When it crept into his mind on the long nights on field operations or during training in the neck-deep black and slimy oatmeal of the Georgia swamps he tried to think of something else. If he longed for anything at all, it was for Kitty's laugh.

He was eager to walk in his front door feeling he'd accomplished something, proud of something. Something difficult. Something few other new soldiers had done. Even playing ball in school, he'd never walked into his house with a feeling of pride, a feeling of singular accomplishment.

Forcing the last of his clothing into the bag, he envied civilians who could carry as many suitcases as they wanted. Soldiers were restricted to wearing uniforms while they traveled and carrying only one duffel bag to get a military rate on planes and buses. He slammed the duffel bag on the floor several times to make room for the last item.

"Hey! Hayes?"

Scotty heard the voice from the floor below. "Yo," he replied.

"Your ride's here, Sarge."

"Thanks. Tell 'em I'll be right there." Scotty quickly stuffed his shaving kit into the bag, snapped the hook on the strap closing the top of the duffel bag and made a quick check of his lockers for anything left he might have left behind. He pulled his blouse from the hanger and put it on but not before jumping up once to see if anything remained on the top of his wall locker.

From below he heard the same voice, "Hey! You miss this ride to town, you miss your bus, man!"

Finding nothing there, he took his cap from the top of his footlocker and placed it squarely on his head, measuring two fingers from the top of his right eyebrow to the lowest point on the brim of his overseas cap—as regulations required the cap to be worn.

He hoisted the heavy bag by its strap and took one last took around the room, partially to say good-bye but also to look for anything he might have left behind.

The room had to be cleaner and neater than when he moved in. It was the Army way of doing things: Leave it better than you found it. It would never have entered Scotty's mind before Fort Benning, before Sergeant Asa Russell, before Army training. Now he wouldn't ever think of leaving a room with something out of place, something needing cleaning up, no matter how late he was.

"Hayes. This is your last chance, man! This truck has to get over to the motor pool now!"

"Be right down," Scotty replied.

CHAPTER 10

He'd decided to get the straight story before seeing Kitty. She'd been dodging his questions in his letters and phone calls about how she was feeling and what the doctor told her. "Not as bad as you think," she kept saying. "You don't have to worry about me, baby. Just got a little cough."

The doctor took his glasses off and cleaned them with a handkerchief he produced from his jacket pocket. "You see, emphysema is an enlargement of the tiny air sacs in the lungs and the destruction of their walls."

He put his glasses back on but still peered over the top of them at Scotty. "You need those sacs to transfer oxygen into your bloodstream and take away the carbon dioxide."

"Destroyed sacs? It all sounds pretty awful, Doctor," Scotty said.

"That's only part of it. Most emphysema patients suffer from other complications, some scarring, excess mucus and occasional muscle spasms. It seems to be more fatal in men than women if it's any consolation for you."

"You mean Kitty can live with this?"

"I mean she's less likely to die if she behaves herself."

"Can't you heal her or cure this? I mean, is there a shot or something?"

"No. We can manage it. We can't cure the disease, but we can treat the symptoms. Unfortunately, the damage is done. No medication or treatment can return her to the way she was before her lungs started to turn to leather."

"Shit! So what can she expect?"

"Respiratory complications, bacterial infections, bouts of coughing and production of some disgusting sputum. Patients like Kitty can expect to suffer from shortness of breath, lethargy, bronchial attacks, influenza, pneumonia and even weight loss and possible swelling of her legs as the disease causes her heart to malfunction.

"I'm prescribing appropriate medications for her condition, and from time to time I may need to put her on portable oxygen."

Scotty heard the words—cold and clinical as the doctor spoke them, but he could only think of all these things happening to Kitty, his Kitty, not just any patient. He interrupted the doctor. "What do I do?"

"First and foremost, keep her away from cigarettes and smoke filled environments." He raised his finger and waved it at Scotty. "Before you say anything, I've known Kitty damn near as long as you have, son. She's trying to convince me, and she'll try to convince you, she'll quit smoking, but she needs to keep tending bar—"

Scotty held up his palm. "I've got it, Doc. You don't have to paint a picture for me. If I have to tie her leg to the kitchen stove, she's not going back to Murphy's."

"Good. Now, if she feels up to it, she can wait some tables now and then. But make it an outdoor restaurant. Absolutely no smoking or smoke-filled rooms. Remember, her lungs don't care if she's in a smoke-filled bar or a smoke-filled restaurant. Got it?"

"Roger that."

"You know the very best thing you can do for her?"

"What's that?"

"Make her want to get better. Give her some good reasons to live life and enjoy it. Get her moving and keep her attitude on the right side of this thing. Depression's as much of a killer for her as her damaged lungs."

Scotty stood and stuck his hand out. "Doc. Thanks for what you're doing for Kitty. Count on me to hold up my end. But I'm . . ."

"But you are leaving again."

"Yes. Vietnam."

"I'll medicate her. You do what you can to motivate her. Call, write. Whatever you can do. If it gets bad enough, I'll contact the Red Cross, and they'll clear it with the Army for you to come home on compassionate leave. That's how it works."

Scotty stared down at his boots and thought about what the doctor had just said. "How bad does it have to get?"

"Near the end."

Scotty hoisted his duffel bag up on his shoulder and walked along the sidewalk outside the medical office. Two blocks to the bank. He had to make sure his allotment would continue to go to Kitty's checking account. She'd go under without what he was sending. And he wanted to open a safe deposit box for Kitty where he could leave a copy of his will. He needed to be sure the bank knew how critical it was for the money to get to her account uninterrupted. Mostly, he wanted a face and name he could contact from Vietnam.

He patted his blouse to make sure the envelope containing the will was still tucked into the inside pocket. His will. He'd be twenty his next birthday and words like *will, life insurance,* and *survivor benefits* were new and awkward for him to think about. What would happen to Kitty if he didn't come back from Vietnam? She had no one else.

The bank staff understood his needs. He tucked the two banker's business cards into his wallet and slipped it back into his hip pocket.

"Scotty? Scotty Hayes?"

He looked around for the voice and saw someone standing backlit by the blinding sun coming through the huge glass window of the bank's front. He thought he recognized the voice. "Mal? That you?"

Malcolm Striever stepped closer to Scotty and stuck out his hand. "How the hell you been, man? Jesus, look at you!" He stepped back and mugged at Scotty's uniform as if trying to decide if it was right for Scotty and if it met with is approval. "Shee-it, man. You look like a regular fucking Audie Murphy, Hayes!"

Scotty waved at Malcolm to stop the theatrics. As Malcolm circled Scotty and made more of a fuss, Scotty recognized the patch over the pocket on his coveralls. Orange State Plumbing. Malcolm's hands were blackened; his nails broken and dirty. He even seemed to be making an attempt at growing a Beatles' haircut. But with his tight curls, it wasn't working. Finding Malcolm working for a plumbing company was the last thing he expected to find on his return. Scotty searched for the right words. "Yeah, it's me. How you been, Mal? You good?"

Malcolm waved an opened envelope ragged at the edges. "Just dropped in to cash my paycheck. You know. Got to pay those bills. They just keep coming. So, how long you gonna' be here, man?"

"Few weeks. I'm on leave. On my way to Vietnam."

"No Shit! I been watchin' all that Tonkin Gulf stuff, man and I'm startin' to get worried they're going to tag my ass. Every time I get the mail I expect to find a letter from the Draft Board." He laughed, "So I try not to go to the mailbox."

"I'm sure they can handle things over there without your help," Scotty said releasing his old classmate's hand.

"Look, you headed home?"

"Yep. I just got in town."

"Hold on. Just lemme cash this check, and I'll give you a ride."

Scotty waited outside the bank, half thumbing through all the copies of all the paperwork the bank officers had given him. Through the large window, he noticed Malcolm kept looking back at him from the teller's cage and he suddenly felt a bit conspicuous in his paratrooper boots and Army green uniform.

Malcolm waved a handful of cash at Scotty and mimed something about being rich as he walked to the doorway. Outside, he made a sweeping gesture, "This way if you're goin' with me."

They crossed the small parking lot. Malcolm stopped and began patting his pockets. He nodded at a truck. "This is my Cadillac." He dug around in the front pocket of his coveralls looking for the keys to the twenty-year-old plumbing truck marked with a company logo on the door.

Scotty threw his duffel bag in the back of the truck on top of a bundle of copper pipes and next to a wooden toolbox. "Man, you always did know how to go first class, Mal."

"Fuck you, Hayes."

Scotty opened the passenger door only to find Malcolm already cleaning off the seat. Malcolm's black metal lunchbox and a hat matching his coveralls sat on top of a work order clipboard. He waited while Malcolm took everything and shoved it behind the seat.

Before Malcolm started the truck, he leaned over and popped open the door to the glove compartment. Sitting on top of a pile of dog-eared papers, a pint bottle of Old Crow rested on its side, half empty. "What do you say? Want some?"

Scotty was surprised at the offer, so he laughed it off. "Whoa! Too early in the day for me. Remember, I've been locked up for over a year. Hardly ever had a chance for more than a beer now and then. I'm gonna pass."

Malcolm had already pulled the bottle from the glove compartment but quickly threw it back in and slammed the door shut. "Okay. Maybe later."

There was an awkward silence between them as Malcolm pulled away from the curb. Once they were at the next light, he turned to take in Scotty again. "Damn, man. Who are you now? What is all this?" he gestured at the uniform with its badges, patches, insignia, and chevrons.

"You knew I'd been drafted."

"Yeah, but I didn't know you were going to become a paratrooper and whatever else all that stuff means."

"Ranger. I went through Ranger School too."

Malcolm looked at the chevrons on his sleeve. "And this? Are you some kind of general now?"

"Sergeant. I'm a sergeant. Don't you know anything about the Army, Mal?"

"No. And I'd just a'soon not learn. You ain't talking me into a haircut like yours."

They were quiet again until Scotty decided it was his turn. "How about those plans, baseball scholarship and all? Didn't you ever get accepted to Florida State?"

"I did. But I only lasted half a semester. I got drunk one night trashed my knee going home from a party on my motorcycle and found myself back here in a heartbeat." He tapped the embroidered patch over his pocket. My cousin, Junior, works for these guys and got me this job. I hate it, but what the hell else am I going to do in Belton?"

Where had the rest of his classmates gone? Scotty wondered how many had gone on to college as planned and how many had stumbled, like Malcolm. He realized he had not stayed in touch with anyone but Kitty since joining the Army. There just wasn't time. His days had been filled with sergeants like Russell, training, desperate attempts to get caught up on sleep and the constant demands of cleaning things: the barracks, his gear, his weapons, his uniforms to get ready for training sure to trash everything and start the cycle all over again.

He watched Belton go by as they passed through town. The Orange Coast Apothecary was still there, and kids were still inside at the counter. He wondered if was the same for them—a place and an excuse to get together, to hang out with something to do other than just standing on the street corner.

They passed the Phillips 66 station where he had worked changing tires and pumping gas one summer. He remembered the seventy-five cents an hour he got and laughed to himself.

It all seemed so different to Scotty. It wasn't his childhood town anymore. There were faces he didn't recognize and high school kids in cars who must have been in grade school when he was a student.

"Kitty's?"

"What?"

"You're going to Kitty's. Right?"

"Oh, yeah. I haven't been home yet."

Malcolm waved at a friend passing in the oncoming lane. "I saw Kitty last week at Kroger's."

"You did? How'd she look to you?"

"You know Kitty. She was asking about me and telling me about you. She looks tired." He shrugged. "But I guess she looked okay to me."

Scotty checked his watch. "You sure I'm not going to get you in trouble?"

Malcolm laughed. "My boss won't even miss me. He spends all day on the phone bettin' on the dogs and Jai Alai. It'll be okay."

"How does it feel?"

Unsure what Malcolm meant, Scotty looked at him. "How does what feel?"

"Being home."

"Different."

"I'll bet. You don't look anything like the guy I spent four years with at Palms High. Just what did they do to your hair, man?"

They both laughed.

"The Army doesn't have much use for hair."

"I'll say. I got more hair on my butt."

"They never asked me about my butt."

They laughed again, and Scotty started to realize he really was home and he didn't have to get up the next morning well before dawn.

It felt so strange to be away from Fort Benning, where he'd only been surrounded by things Army: men in uniform, geometric landscaping, clean and painted buildings, whitewashed rocks trimming walkways, manicured lawns, hedges and tree wells. He had forgotten how Belton was. He'd forgotten old friends like Malcolm.

Malcolm pulled up in front of Kitty's with a heavy foot on the brake pedal. "Here you go, man. That'll be nine dollars."

Scotty reached over and lightly punched Malcolm on the leg. "Thanks. I owe you, Mal. Let's get together before I leave. You know. A beer or something. Anything but bowling. I hated it when you used to drag me to the bowling alley in high school."

"I'd like that. We can go chase some women like the old days. But the bowling alley's still a good place to find them."

Scotty got out, slammed the door and walked around the driver's side of the truck. He laughed at Malcolm. "Women? What are women?"

"If you don't remember I *know* I really don't want to go into the Army. We're going to have to help you reenter the world, man."

"I could go for that," Scotty yanked his bag off the ground and slipped his shoulder into the loop.

Malcolm hesitated. "You really got to go over there?"

Scotty grabbed his bag from the bed of the truck. "Yep. That's what it says on my orders: Saigon, Vietnam. Do not pass Go."

Malcolm waved out the window as he drove off.

Nothing had changed. The small yard was a little overgrown, and the mailbox was bent at an odd angle, but the house looked the same. Scotty stood in the roadway thinking about all the long nights in training when he had thought about standing on the very same spot and had to put the image out of his mind. He just didn't want to think about coming home. About being away from Benning and away from Russell. But now he was home. He was flooded with mixed emotions—happy to be home and anticipating the worst.

He covered the distance from the street to the front steps in five long strides and found himself standing at the front door. Only then did he realize he didn't have a key. He tried the door and found it open and unlocked.

Not wanting to wake Kitty if she was resting, he half called out and half spoke up, "Mom? You home?"

He heard a muffled cough from the bedroom and found his way down the hallway.

Scotty stopped at the open doorway to Kitty's room. Many things had changed. And she appeared smaller, curled up on her bed, a throw covering her even though the temperature had to be in the eighties.

The room wasn't at all like he remembered it. There was much more light. It was clean. Gone were the ashtrays spilling over with cigarette butts. The dark floral wallpaper was gone, or maybe just painted over with a light peach color. It warmed up everything else in the room. The clutter had disappeared, and there was a sweet smelling breeze originating in the Magnolia tree outside, passing from one jalousied window to the matching one on the opposite side of the room. The throw rug was gone leaving waxed checkerboard green and gray linoleum tiles he couldn't remember ever seeing.

"Scotty? Is that you, baby?" Kitty rubbed the sleep from her face and tried to sit up.

"Yeah. It's me, Mom."

She propped up the pillow behind her back. "Oh, my! Look at you." Tears flooded her eyes and quickly ran down both her cheeks. "You look just like your daddy, honey. Just like he did when he went off to Korea."

Scotty stepped over to the bed, bent and kissed her on top of the head. Her hair smelled of soap and lavender. Gone was the smell of cigarette smoke always surrounding her like a halo.

She took his hands and held him at arm's length to look at him some more. "Your daddy would be so so proud of you, baby." She touched the stripes on his sleeve and tried to continue but not before coughing and sti-fling another. "You been gone so long. I really, really missed you so much. But you're home now, and we're going to catch up. Okay, sugar?"

Feeling a little self-conscious, he pulled a few tissues out of a box on the nightstand next to the bed and handed them to her. "You bet. I've really been looking forward to this too, Mom."

She wiped the tears from her face and then was overtaken by another small coughing bout.

"You okay? I mean, do you feel okay?" He looked around the room. "Can I get something?"

She waved and dismissed it. "Oh, course I am. Just too many years and too many cigarettes. But y'know I've quit now."

Scotty squeezed her hand for encouragement. "That's great. That's really great."

She dropped her voice to a more conspiratorial tone. "But truth be known, I'd kill for just one cigarette right now."

"And I'll kill you if you have one. You know cigarettes got you into this fix. How about we go out and jog around the block until your craving goes away?"

Kitty laughed, coughed and laughed. "Stop. That's hitting below the belt."

He sat on the corner of the bed, pulled the throw up where it had fallen off and tucked it in. "Seriously, you want to get some more rest? I mean . . . I've got to unpack and get cleaned up. So, if you want to—"

"No. Let me up. You must be hungry. Let me make you something to eat, hon."

"Nope. You stay right there." Scotty lied. "I had a big lunch on the road. You just get some more rest, and I'll come back and check on you after I get settled in."

"Promise?"

She slid down in her bed, and he tucked in a loose corner of her blan-ket. She held his hand as he pulled away. "I promise. But don't be takin' too long, now."

He stood and crossed the room, stopping at the doorway. He made an X across his chest. "Cross my heart."

She finished wiggling back down into a more comfortable position and smiled at Scotty. "I'm so happy to have you home, baby."

She closed her eyes again, and he took one last look around the room more slowly and then back to her. As much as it had brightened, she had darkened. Her skin had taken on a bit of gray. He could see other changes —new hollows in her cheeks, the loss of shine in her hair and the thinness of her neck and wrists.

He walked through the house toward his bedroom, stopping to pick things up and put them where they belonged and to throw things away that were beyond their usefulness. The place was a mess. It probably wasn't any messier than when he had left, but he'd picked up so many new habits. Habits of orderliness, neatness, and cleanliness. Habits had become part of Scotty Hayes, the sergeant. Habits Scotty Hayes the boy hadn't given a moment's thought.

At the doorway to his old room, he saw it was smaller than he remembered and far more cluttered. He promised himself along with all the other things he'd promised himself he would do while he was home, he'd give cleaning up the house a good try.

CHAPTER 11

A shower alone was a luxury Scotty had forgotten about. There was no one yelling for him to hurry up. He sucked in the smell of a clean shower stall filled with the aroma of Kitty's shampoo and scented soap.

Scotty washed his hair for the second time and found himself half-singing, half-humming The Animals' *House of the Rising Sun*. He couldn't seem to shake the song.

The water started running cooler. He remembered the water heater was not only small, it was old. But he didn't care. It was a warm Florida day and even lukewarm water by himself was better than steaming water in a shower room full of loud-talking, grab-assing soldiers.

He looked in the steamed-up mirror over the small bathroom basin. It was the first time he'd really had a chance to look at himself in over a year without other guys standing nearby. In an Army latrine, no soldier dared to examine his own image in the mirror without taking a lot of teasing from the others in the room.

The Scotty looking back at him was different than the boy he had seen many times in the same mirror. His skin was tanned where his uniform didn't cover it; his shoulders were broader and his waist was smaller. The Army, Airborne, and Ranger School training had been far more physically demanding than high school sports.

When Scotty reached for his shaving kit and remembered he hadn't unpacked it. He wrapped his hips in a towel, tucked the end of it into itself to keep it snug around his waist and walked back toward the front door to find Jake's duffel bag. As he approached the kitchen, he heard pots and pans clanging in the sink and prepared himself to chide Kitty for not staying in bed as she had promised.

He stepped from the hallway into the kitchen and was completely surprised at what he saw. There, her back to him, was a young woman in some kind of waitress uniform washing dishes. The shortened skirt of the uniform showed off her well-formed legs and a bottom sure never to fail to generate a whistle or a compliment.

She turned with a start. "Scotty!"

"Eileen?" It was the Eileen Carter he had fantasized about in high school. Eileen Carter the plain yet pretty Eileen Carter. The quiet Eileen Carter from his American history class. The same Eileen Carter whose name never came up among his friends without the words beautiful and tits being mentioned in the same sentence. The Eileen Carter who while she was never rude to him never knew he existed. The Eileen Carter who always smelled so good. It was that same Eileen Carter.

"Of course it is. Didn't Kitty tell you I was helping her out? I didn't know you were home."

He suddenly realized he was standing there with only a towel wrapped around his waist. "No. I mean, yes. Ah, give me a minute. Let me get something on."

"Sure," she smiled at his embarrassment. "Take your time. I've got a whole sink full of dishes to keep me busy."

Jake Hayes' duffel bag was heavy. Scotty dropped it on the floor in his room it stood upright like a wet bag of sand. Without thinking, he unbuckled the top and began unpacking its wrinkled compacted contents. With his shaving kit in one hand, he looked at what he was dropping onto his bed and laughed. There was nothing in the bag he'd be wearing while in

Belton. The only civilian clothes he owned were already in his closet. And he recalled how he'd looked forward to wearing something other than a uniform after a year of nothing but.

He quit unpacking and walked through the connecting doorway to the bathroom. As he lathered up his face to shave, Scotty couldn't help but think about Eileen Carter still in his kitchen. Eileen Carter from school. Pretty but distant, Eileen Carter.

He remembered her well. There wasn't much about high school he looked forward to each day, but a few sports and his American history class were the exceptions. He remembered sitting just behind her over her left shoulder. This put her in profile whenever she looked up at the teacher. Even though Scotty knew he had no chance with her, he enjoyed watching her in class. She was a good student, quiet and more private than a loner. She came and went with little fuss or fanfare and limited her conversations with most classmates to the exchange of pleasantries but not much more.

Scotty spun the jaws of his double-edged razor closed and began at his left sideburn. He thought back about after-school events during his senior year and recalled how he never saw her at parties, ball games or even impromptu after-school gatherings.

He rinsed his razor in the sink and thought of how she looked then, always wearing a large boy's class ring on a small gold chain around her neck. Everyone assumed she was going steady with someone from another school and just traveled in other circles. There were various rumors she was dating a college student who had never attended Palms High, and she often spent weekends traveling to see him. It would explain her not being around much for weekend social gatherings.

Scotty raised his chin and began the dangerous attack on his neck and vulnerable Adam's apple. More than once his Blue Blade had left its painful marks on the boney parts of his face and neck. He stopped for a moment and leaned on the wash basin trying to imagine a clearer picture of Eileen Carter from school. She was one of those girls who frequently clutched her three-ring binder to her breasts as if she was uncomfortable or self-conscious.

She had a great shape and nothing she should have been uncomfortable with, but somehow he'd known it would be a waste of time for him or any of his buddies to try get close. Still, Eileen was pleasant and always met him with a warm, if only a small, smile.

She was one of those students who never came to school unprepared, seemed to be any teacher's favorite and would always supply the right answer when called upon. But never more. She was brief and never smug about her grasp of the material. But she was unlikely to raise her hand to insert herself into the discussions. When classes were over, she'd be one of the first to leave the room and immediately get swallowed up by the crowds of students shuttling to their next classes. Even if she wasn't available, he still enjoyed killing time in history class by watching her.

Scotty finished shaving, dried his face and rinsed the sink he wouldn't have thought to clean up in his high school days. He was looking forward to a friendly pair of soft worn blue jeans and a comfortable cotton shirt without starch. He suddenly realized he was thinking of Eileen when considering what to put on.

He'd forgotten how comfortable it was to walk around his own home barefoot in jeans and a loose fitting shirt. It had been a while. But there was a reason for it. Bare feet in any Army barracks, shower room or latrine was an invitation to infection. And infections caused more than a few trainees to be recycled after those infections got out of hand and caused them to drop out of forced marches and long morning runs. Even if it were not the case, the grit and sand never seemed to disappear from the floors, no matter how often they mopped them. He wiggled his toes and reminded himself he was home.

Scotty straightened his back as he reentered the kitchen. "Sorry. I didn't mean to blast in here and scare the crap out of you. I just didn't expect—"

"To find me in your kitchen?" Eileen didn't turn around from the kitchen counter she was wiping down. "No problem. Like I said, I knew you were home."

He pulled a chair from the small lime colored dinette table, spun it around, straddled it, sat down and folded his arms on its back. He didn't take his eyes off of her. "So tell me how this happened?"

She toweled off the dishes she had just washed and began putting them away. "How what happened?"

"How you ended up here—at my house, working for Kitty."

"Well, it wasn't your house when I got hired to help out your stepmom. It was just Kitty's house."

Her answer didn't tell him more than he already knew. "I mean, I thought you'd be gone—out of Belton."

She turned around, and he got his first good look at her. Her hair was a bit shorter than he remembered and the waitress' uniform looked so out of place. He didn't know if it was some dress code thing, but she wasn't wearing the ever-present class ring on the chain around her neck.

Eileen folded up the dish towel and draped it over the faucet. "Nope. I'm still here."

She pointed at the percolator on the sideboard. "Coffee?"

Scotty had forgotten how much he had enjoyed home-made coffee with Kitty. "Sure. If you're going to have some."

She turned her back to Scotty and reached up to an overhead cupboard for a coffee mug. The move forced her up on her tiptoes to make up for her five foot four frame.

Scotty resisted the urge to steal a look at her legs and jumped up from his chair. "Here, let me help you." He reached over her and pulled down a second mug. The smell of her hair was an unexpected surprise. He couldn't remember when he had smelled someone so fresh or so clean. He handed her the mug.

Eileen filled one mug and half-filled the other. "I can only stay long enough for a splash of coffee. I have to get to my job over at Ronnie's."

"Ronnie's? Ronnie's Restaurant? The Ronnie's where everyone in town goes after church? The Ronnie's where everyone takes their mom on Mother's Day? Ronnie's Restaurant?"

"Yep. The Ronnie's known for low pay. The Ronnie's not known for overtime pay. The Ronnie's known for serving gallons of grits and bushels of greens every day—that Ronnie's. Anyway, I'm there from five to eleven every night. Every night 'cept Sundays."

It wasn't what he wanted to hear. "Oh. I'd hoped we'd get a chance to talk. You know, catch up." He searched her face hoping she felt the same way. "We could talk about old times or you could tell me where everyone ended up after graduation or something . . ."

"Well, I'd love to sit and talk with you, but I got to work, Scotty."

He had no idea what made him think she might say yes, but he asked anyway. "Some other time? How about after work? Could we grab a burger or something? After you get off? Tonight?"

She was quiet for a long pause and then smiled, meeting Scotty's gaze. "Yeah. Yeah, okay. If you don't mind hanging out at Ronnie's while I close the place up."

"No. Not a problem for me. I've got nothing but time. I'll be there. At eleven. I'll be there." He suddenly heard his own voice. It sounded to him like he was babbling. He shifted his focus to his coffee mug and took a sip. "This is good. You can't believe the coffee I've had to put up with in the Army. One day it's watered down and the next it's more like motor oil. Thanks."

Eileen brought hers to the tiny table and sat down with Scotty. Scotty motioned toward Kitty's bedroom with his mug. "So, how's she doing?"

"Kitty?" Eileen smiled. "She's one of the sweetest people I've ever met. She's worried she might be a burden on me. And I'm trying to help her. You're lucky to have her."

"Oh, I know. You know she's not even my real mom?"

"I know. She told me all about your dad and everything. She's mighty proud of you, you know? Get her started talking about you, and she lights up."

"It's about time I did something. I didn't set Belton on fire while I was in school. Now it's my turn to take care of her.

"I talked to her doctor already. What do you think? She doing okay?"

"She's tough, Scotty. I'm no expert, but I think you just being home is going to help. She's never going to be a hundred percent again, but if she takes her medicine, stays away from cigarettes, and gets her rest, I think she's going to do pretty good. You, me and Doctor Gordon have to corner her and make sure she can't do anything but what's good for her."

"She seemed pretty tired when I came in earlier."

"She's only good for so long," Eileen said. "She needs a nap every afternoon. It helps. She'll be up and around in a little while. Except for her coughing now and then, you'll think she's okay. But don't let her get overtired and don't let her push it. Rest is her very best friend."

Eileen got up again and opened a cupboard over the sink. She took out three large plastic pill bottles and put them on the counter. "She's got some of these in her bedroom, but if she runs out, here's the rest." Eileen raised one container filled with yellow pills. "You have to force her to take these. They make her sleepy. But they help her breathe. So don't let her talk you out of taking them."

Flipping another cupboard open, Eileen tapped a schedule written on lined notebook paper and taped to the back of the door. "Here's the schedule. You'll need it. There's no way you can remember she needs to take some pills twice a day and others three times a day."

Scotty stabbed himself in the chest with his index finger. "Me make Kitty do anything? I'll try. But this is a new role for me for sure."

"Scotty, she needs you, and in the six months I've been working for her, I've never seen her more excited about anything than she is about you coming home. She'll listen to you. She's your biggest fan."

He finished his coffee and took his mug to the sink. He picked up the bottles of pills and shook his head. "I hate this."

"I know. So do I," Eileen said. She pulled the apron from around her waist, folded it up into a neat little square and placed it on the kitchen counter. "I've got to go. I'm gonna' be late for work if I don't get out of here."

"Oh," Scotty searched for words. "Is there something I can do? Can I drive you over there?" He thumbed the door to his room. "I can get some shoes on and take you over there with time to spare."

"No. I'll take the bus. And you should know Kitty's car isn't running again. I don't know what; it just doesn't want to start for her or me. And thanks, anyway, for offering, but I've got to go."

Scotty followed her to the front door and stepped out onto the small landing immediately feeling the warm, smooth concrete step with his feet. He watched her move down the short sidewalk to the street. "Tonight? Eleven? Right?"

She turned, shaded her eyes with her hand. "Sure. That'll be nice. Oh, and, welcome home, Scotty."

He watched her as she walked toward the bus stop and suddenly realized he'd never seen her at a distance greater than a few yards. She'd always been in a classroom or swallowed up by the river of students in the halls passing the classroom door. He liked the way she walked. Her walk was more confident than he would have guessed.

It was the same Eileen but a different Eileen walking down the road. She hadn't run from him. She wasn't in the same kind of hurry to get to work as she had always been to leave history class.

He felt more comfortable around Eileen the waitress than Eileen the classmate, even though he'd stammered and looked pretty stupid in the kitchen. All he knew was he couldn't wait to see to see her that night.

He raised his hand to his eyes and watched. Though the outfit wasn't at all flattering, she was prettier than he remembered. He felt a pleasant flutter in his gut.

The carport hung loosely from the side of the house as if eager to sever its connection and be on its way. Scotty made a mental note to do something about it before Florida's regular tropical storms finally took it away and caused some serious damage in its flight.

He stepped under the overhang and looked at Kitty's 1947 Studebaker two-door sedan. It scowled back at him under the large metal visor bolted over the windshield like a long eyebrow. The visors were common accessories in a state with so many sunny days and the only thing to help bring the interior temperature down in a time before cars were air-conditioned.

He opened the door to the smell of damp, musty upholstery mixed with the irritating aroma of just plain old Florida dust. Tufting peeked out of splits and tears in the aging bench seats. They looked more like sofas than car seats. He could see the concrete slab beneath the car through a small hole rusted into the floorboard on the driver's side.

Scotty remembered Eileen's words, which weren't much help. *Won't start* could mean plenty of things. He leaned inside the car and looked over the steering wheel to find the keys, as always, still in the ignition. Turning the key, he watched the gas gauge fail to crawl away from its resting point.

Scotty threw his butt into the seat, his foot up under the dash and pressed in on the clutch as he centered himself under the steering wheel. Yanking the gear shift into neutral, he pressed the starter button and pumped the accelerator.

Nothing. Not a sound. Not a response. He tried it again and got the same silence, broken only by the small chain on the keys clinking against the dashboard.

He knew the next move was under the hood, but he sat for a moment and remembered learning to drive in the old Studebaker. He'd been worried he couldn't see over the hood to the hidden right fender and was never sure if he was too close to something or might do some damage. But Kitty taught him how to use the hood ornament to gauge his distance from the roadside or a curb. She made it fun and reminded him if she could see over the dash, he could too. Back then, he was fifteen and was already a foot taller than she was.

"Okay. Time to get serious," he pronounced to the car as he took the keys, got out and walked back to the bulging turtle shell of a trunk lid. It surrendered to the keys and after giving off a sound of stuck rubber weather stripping it opened wide enough for Scotty to step into it if he'd wanted to.

Inside he grabbed a small sandbag. It was like sandbags found everywhere in Florida, but it was oil-stained and filled with hand tools. Getting a stranglehold on the gathered neck of the bag he carried it around to the front of the car and rested it on the salt-pitted chrome bumper. He didn't bother to look for a hood release. There was a small length of rope sticking through the large grinning grill. It served as the makeshift hood latch since the real one had been broken for several years. He untied it and lifted the heavy hood, putting up the long rod to support it.

He surveyed the greasy engine for anything obvious. It was a mess. Oil, grease, and some pine needles covered almost everything in the engine compartment. Dust hugged the surfaces unclaimed by the oily splatter. There was even a cobweb stretching from the steering column to the fender well. And the leaking radiator had a collection of long-dead bugs stuck in its tight mesh teeth.

Scotty strained to reach over a bulbous fender flaring back from the headlight to squeeze the radiator hoses for signs of fatigue in the rubber, but he finally had to step up onto the bumper to reach the hoses.

As he suspected, they were soft and mushy and would definitely need replacing before he left for Vietnam. The thought of Vietnam flagged his troubleshooting process, but as fast as it popped up, he thought of Kitty and what else needed doing. Suddenly, time was important. Important where it had never much concerned him in the past.

Once up and leaning over the engine, Scotty spotted the mushroom shaped, beige colored corrosion encircling each of the battery's posts. He pulled a pair of pliers from the sand bag and spread the handles open holding onto the jaws. With his free hand, he scraped some of the corrosion off the posts then blew some more of it away. He steadied one side of the open pliers' handle on one post and quickly tapped the other post with the other handle. Scotty jumped as sparks shot from the point of contact confirming there was juice in the battery. It just wasn't getting to the starter.

After a trip to the kitchen to track down some baking soda and water, an old toothbrush and some rags, Scotty cleaned the battery top and posts, added water to the three thirsty cells and reinstalled the cables. He finished the process by greasing up both posts and cables with a coat of Vaseline to keep the corrosion from returning before he did.

Coming in from the bright Florida sunshine the kitchen seemed dark at first. Finding Kitty leaning against the sink with coffee in hand surprised him. "Hey, you're up. Great! How are you feeling?"

Kitty quickly put her cup and saucer down, stepped toward Scotty and threw her arms around his neck. "Forget how I feel. Give me a hug, baby."

He embraced her and discovered how frail she was, how brittle she felt and how thin she'd become since he left. He was almost afraid to hold her too tight. When she quickly broke the embrace, it was obvious she was trying to keep the extent of her deterioration from him.

"I've been waitin' for so long for you to come home, hon." She held him at arm's length and examined him moving the focus to him. "Look at you. Your hair . . . Did they need to shave it all off?" She patted his shoulders at their wide points. "What are they doing to you? You must have put on twenty pounds of muscle, sweetie."

"In the Army, they just like to call it *good training*. Now, why don't you sit down and let me get you something to eat and some more coffee?"

Kitty ignored him, leaned forward, just out of reach and gave him a peck on the lips. "Baby, I missed you so much."

Scotty shook his head at it all. "It's really, really good to be home, Mom."

She stepped back. "Golly, you've changed so much, hon."

He mugged and struck a pose as if competing as a weight lifter, flexing. "Okay. I'm a bit older. I weigh about fifteen more pounds than when I left. But I'm okay, and they didn't break anything."

He reached down and pulled the waistband of his jeans away from his stomach. "And I've even lost inches. Go figure."

"Well, honey, the ol' army sure put some bulk on your bones. Look at your arms." She tried to wrap the fingers of both hands around one of his biceps. "What the hell do they feed you up there in Georgia?"

"Snakes."

"Snakes?!" Her hand flew to her mouth in surprise. "They make you eat snakes?"

"No. Not really. It's just a nickname. They just call us snake eaters."

"Us?" Kitty made a face, confused. "Us who?"

"Rangers, Mom. Some call us *snake eaters*."

Kitty took a sip of her coffee and put it back down, the cup rattling a bit as she returned it to the saucer as she thought over the nickname. "So you *didn't* have to eat snakes?"

"Well, no. I mean, yes. We did have to eat snakes, but it was only for survival training in the swamps. Not like we have to eat 'em on a regular basis."

Kitty waved her hand in front of her face as if it would expel the taste and smell of snake. "Oh, sugar. How could they make you do that? It's so awful!"

Scotty laughed. "It wasn't all bad. Honest."

She pointed her finger at him. "Now, don't you go an' tell me it tastes like chicken."

Scotty smiled and laughed again. "Would you feel better if it tastes like chocolate?"

Kitty slapped Scotty playfully. "Now don't you tease me, Scott Hayes." She laughed harder and began to cough a little, then harder. She pulled a handkerchief from her bra by reaching through the arm hole of her sleeveless dress and covered her mouth to conceal the mucous she had coughed up.

Scotty pulled up a chair. "Sit. Can I get you some water or something?"

Kitty doubled over in an extra effort to control a cough. "No, no. I'll be okay. It'll pass."

Scotty felt helpless watching her struggle to regain her breath. He tried to get her to smile again. "Okay. Okay. I surrender. No more snake stories."

Kitty smiled and looked Scotty directly in the eyes. "Honey, oh my lord." She paused for a long time before continuing. "It's so, so good to have you home."

The two went on to finish a whole fresh pot of coffee. Scotty got Kitty a slice of melon, insisted she take her medication and ended up bribing her with a promise he'd cook her a steak on the grill in the back yard for dinner. He'd also insisted she rest in the living room while he cooked—telling her he'd take care of everything.

Later, Scotty came in the kitchen door with two well-charred steaks. "Hey. Soup's on." Once inside, he was surprised to find a new Kitty.

Kitty had rested, changed clothes and put on some makeup. "Want a beer?"

"Sure." He put the steaks on the kitchen table and pulled out a chair for Kitty. "You look terrific."

She sat, reached over and rubbed his arm. "Thank you, baby. I feel better. Funny what a shower and a nap can do. Even at my age," she said, completely sidestepping her medical condition.

"The pills help?"

"You know, they do a bit. But I hate those big ones. They're hard for me to swallow."

"How 'bout if I cut them in half for you. Will you be sure to take them then?"

"I promise."

They talked, laughed and got caught up on lost time. He tried to find the right time to bring the subject up, but it never came, so he just blurted it out. "About you working—"

Kitty raised her palm to him. "I know what you're going to say, but I'm okay. I can work. I just need to not work so much and to rest when I'm not working."

"And take your medication."

"I know, I know. I promise. I'll take the pills. But I'll starve if I don't work. Worse yet, I'll go plum crazy if I just hang around here all day. Especially with you gone."

"I'm getting parachute pay now, and as soon as I get to Vietnam, I'll be getting combat pay too. I'll be able to send you more money then."

Kitty reached over and caressed his cheek. "Baby, I don't want your money. I can take care of myself if I don't go crazy spending my money."

He didn't want an argument and sought the middle ground. "I'll make you a deal. Let me help you and then you won't have to work full-time—"

"But I—"

He interrupted her before she got on a roll. "No. You need to scale back the work. You can't work less and pay the bills too. I can't send much, but I can send enough to let you have enough free time to get some rest. "But here's the promise I want from you: No more late nights. No more bars and you've got to start sleeping like regular folks, get some sun and some fresh air—and take your pills."

Kitty raised both hands in the air. "Okay. Okay. I surrender. I'll try. I promise."

"I'm serious. No more Murphy's bar. It's got to be a day job if you're going to work at all. You're not a vampire. You know you can work while the sun's up?"

Kitty laughed. "Honey, just having you home is helping me feel better." She jabbed her fork toward his beer bottle. "You want another?"

"No. I've got things to do and then I'm going to meet Eileen later for coffee."

"Eileen! Ain't she 'bout the most precious thing you ever met?"

"Between you and me, she was my secret love in high school."

Kitty looked puzzled. "And she wasn't interested in you?"

"Mom, she wasn't interested in anyone at Palms High. She had a boy-friend or something. I even heard she was engaged. But, no matter what, she wasn't interested in me."

"All I can tell you is she's been a blessing. Doctor Gordon knows her momma and knew she was looking for some part-time work. So he put us together. Wasn't 'til after I met her that I found out you two went to school together. Didn't I tell you about her in my letters?"

She hadn't mentioned it was Eileen, but Scotty couldn't see any point in saying so. "Sure, I just forgot. Anyway, she's another thing you need extra money for. So don't argue with me."

Kitty smiled. "Okay. I'd forgotten how much trouble it is having a man around the house."

"There's another thing you ought to be working on."

Kitty wasn't following. "What?"

"You've been single too long."

Kitty started to laugh, then started to cough. She raised her hands as if to signal him to wait for her to catch her breath. Tears of laughter spilled from her eyes while she struggled.

She finally got the cough under control. "Enough! I promise. I'll take the pills. I'll get some rest. I'll quit working at Murphy's. But I'm drawin' the line at getting married again."

They both laughed, and she added, "Now *you* get finished with your dinner and go see that cute little girl. You're the one who's been single too long."

CHAPTER 12

Between the near-smothering humidity of Belton, Florida and spending a few hours tinkering with Kitty's car Scotty needed another shower. He tried to search for some options and came up short. He was happy to be able to get the car running again, but it was only a matter of time before it would need to be replaced. He stepped out of the shower and rechecked his fingernails for any remaining grease from the car.

Finding no grease, he wiped the steam from the mirror, leaned on the sink and examined his image. He really didn't see what he was looking at. His head was filling up with a list of things. Things needed to happen before he left and while he was gone. And he'd have to be the one to do them. Kitty's car, her care, things around the house still needing attention doing all banged around in his head.

And he was bothered he hadn't been completely truthful with Kitty about money. After she was diagnosed, while he was still at Fort Benning, he'd officially declared her his dependent. It would entitle her to a small allotment from his Army pay each month, and he could make survivor benefits available to her in case the worst happened to him in Vietnam.

He would have to think of a way to explain to her why the monthly checks would be from the government and not from him personally. He just didn't want her to think she was depending on him. But he had no choice. It was just the bureaucracy and paperwork.

He knew he wasn't going to have to explain the survivor's benefits if he was killed. The Army would send someone to tell her. By then there'd be no one for her to argue with.

He shook his head. *Eileen.* He forced the Kitty concerns out of his mind while he lathered up by shifting gears to Eileen. He found the change in focus was matched by an immediate shift in mood. He liked the new feeling stirring inside when he thought of her. It was different. He'd dated girls in high school but never for any length of time.

There wasn't an old love or a steady in his past. And he realized how long it had been since he'd been around a woman he could be excited about.

***

The streets of Belton were almost empty as the hour neared eleven. But tradition still held sway. It was Saturday night, and here and there Scotty passed a carload of teenagers still out cruising. He remembered when he and Malcolm used to do the same. When Malcolm could talk his father into letting him drive the family car. His dad's Chevy station wagon somehow took the cool out of cruising Belton, but it was better than no car at all. And Scotty could never get Kitty's car since she needed it to work nights.

He smiled as he remembered how hard it was to scrape up the money they needed to put gas in the car and still hang out with friends. They would cruise through the Dairy Queen, park on the apron of the lot and then jump into cars with friends camped out in the parking slots reserved for customers ordering food delivered by the car hops. They would sit for hours talking, laughing and watching the girls come and go.

Downtown Belton was the place to be on any Saturday night, and it hadn't changed much since he'd left.

Scotty pulled into the parking lot in front of Ronnie's Restaurant as several cars were leaving. A car pulled out in front of him opening up a spot right in front of the long row of restaurant windows.

The radio on, he found himself singing *Mr. Lonely* along with Bobby Vinton but dropped out when his range couldn't keep up with Vinton's. As he parked and turned off the engine, the radio went dead.

Scotty checked his watch to make sure he hadn't arrived too early. It was two minutes to eleven. Still, he decided to wait a few more minutes before going inside. He clicked on the ignition to listen to the radio again even though he knew he was flirting with danger, considering the battery troubles he'd overcome earlier in the day.

He spun the knob lit by the yellow light on the dial searching for more music and found mostly news on the hour. Someone named Martin Luther King was getting the Nobel Peace Prize, LBJ had been sworn in, and Scotty paused long enough to listen to an announcement attributed to Secretary of Defense McNamara—stating the US had no plans to send combat troops to Vietnam. Scotty finally found what he was looking for—The Supremes. He tried to pick the song up with Diana Ross. ". . . come see about me."

He looked through the windshield into the restaurant and could see the room was nearly empty. A couple of tables had diners lingering over coffee. At one a woman was searching the bottom of her purse for exact change to put on the small tray holding her check. She placed the money on the tray one coin at a time.

He saw Eileen come through the swinging doors leading to the kitchen with a coffee pot in her hand. Scotty felt another tingle as he watched her cross the room and top off a customer's coffee. The customer smiled, and his lips moved as he thanked her and she smiled back.

Scotty suddenly realized what a great smile she had and how he couldn't remember ever really seeing beyond her polite smile. This one was friendlier and much more giving.

He found himself turning off the ignition again to sit in silence and watch Eileen. She made several trips across the room clearing plates, dropping off checks and saying good night to customers as they left the restaurant.

It was hard for him to imagine the Eileen Carter from school was the same Eileen Carter in his kitchen earlier and on the other side of the large plate glass windows at Ronnie's.

With the car door only half open, Scotty stopped, suddenly overwhelmed with doubts. His breath? He looked down at his jeans and shoes. Was he overdressed? Was it too early? What the hell was going on? After all, he was only going to have coffee with her or go get something to eat. It wasn't like he was going to try to get her interested in him romantically. She already had some guy, somewhere.

He sat back in the seat for a moment to calm himself, feeling a little silly. Hell, he'd done far more frightening things recently than have coffee with a pretty girl. What was it about Eileen that put him off his game? His first parachute jump, the Florida swamps, demolitions training—none of the things he'd done since leaving Belton had made him as anxious as he felt then. He raised his chin, took another deliberate breath and let it out slowly.

Scotty looked back through the window, and she was smiling at a couple settling their bill and thanking her. He found himself wiping his palms on his trousers and craving a cigarette after six months without one. "You can do this, Hayes," he whispered, That done, he threw the car door open wide as if breaking from a huddle and stepped out in the muggy Florida night. Without thinking of it, his fingers went to his gig line, forgetting he was in civilian clothes and the alignment of his shirt, fly and belt buckle weren't going to be scrutinized by anyone. Somewhere Sergeant Asa Russell was smiling.

"Hi, Scotty." Her face seemed to brighten as she looked up from a table, seeing him walk through the door. "You did make it after all."

"Sure. I told you I'd be here. I'm not too early, am I? 'Cause if I am, I can wait for you outside or something."

In what seemed to be a kind of autopilot, Eileen moved effortlessly arranging new place settings at a table she'd been clearing without taking her eyes off of Scotty. Eventually ending up on his side of the table. "Nope. Look around." She motioned toward the large dining room behind her. "It's my very favorite time of the day—closing time."

Only two tables were still occupied—one by a young couple deeply involved in a conversation over coffee, another by an old man hidden behind a newspaper. Scotty hooked his thumb over his shoulder toward the doorway. "I don't want to be in the way. Really, if you want me to wait outside till you're finished—"

She flagged him with the napkin in her other hand. "No. Uh uh. Now go on over and take a stool at the counter. I'll be finished here in a few minutes."

He realized he'd been passing his car keys from one hand to another. He dropped them into his pocket and pointed toward the counter. "Okay. I will. I'll wait. I'll be over at the counter."

Eileen smiled and reassured him. "I won't be long. I promise." She turned straightened out the fresh silverware and took her coffee pot to the two occupied tables to offer the remaining diners their final warm-ups.

She was a different Eileen, cheerful and almost chatty with the customers as she playfully announced it was last call. Not the quiet buttoned up Eileen from history class. He liked this Eileen even better than he ever had liked the Eileen at Palms High.

Approaching the counter, Scotty discovered two options: his back to the room or a stool which would allow him to see most of the room from the short leg as it turned to butt into the wall near the large kitchen doors. He opted for the spot at the counter giving him the best view of Eileen.

He sat down and as quickly as he did Eileen had finished the loop at the other tables and appeared on the other side of the counter with the pot in her hand. She raised it and asked, "Want some?"

Scotty righted an upside down cup, nailed it back into its saucer and pushed it toward her. "Sure. This is getting to be a routine—you, me and coffee."

"If you'd rather have something else . . ."

"Oh, no. I didn't mean . . . Coffee's fine. I was just thinking about you making coffee for me this afternoon—"

"Okay, but if you want something, promise you'll let me know. I already turned on the closed sign outside, but I can still get you a piece of pie or some of our chocolate cake. You just speak up, ya' hear?"

"No." He picked up the filled cup. "This will be enough for me. Don't worry about me."

"Good night, Eileen," the old man with the paper tucked under his arm put on a small brimmed straw hat with a wide and colorful band as he threw his forearm into the door to leave.

Over her shoulder she smiled, "G'night, Mister Joyce. Y'all come back and see us, now." As she turned back to Scotty to say something he nodded at the couple behind her. The couple who had been at the very last table.

"Thank you, Miss," the man said as he opened the door to allow the woman with him to pass through.

Eileen followed the two to the door, said goodnight and locked the door behind them. She turned back to Scotty, untied her apron, balled it up, pitched it on the end of the counter and smiled. "Okay, I'm off now. Let's get out of here."

Holding the door, Scotty waited for Eileen to get into the car. He found his fingers touching her lightly at the small of her back, helping her into the car. And he was suddenly aware the air she moved as she passed so close to him getting in the car took on a hint of her perfume.

She smiled and kidded him. "What a gentleman you are, Scott Hayes."

He rounded the rear of the car, got in, started the aging Studebaker and sighed. "Whew! That's three times in a row that it's started. Looks like my luck's holding."

Scotty eased the car through the curb's gutter separating the parking lot from the street to avoid bottoming out the worn shocks on the car. He stopped long enough to look both ways on Belton's main street, undecided. "What do you think? You in the mood for dinner? Or is there something else you'd rather do. I mean, you must be tired after such a long day."

Eileen laughed. "What if I was hungry? We just closed the last restaurant where you can get a real meal in this town, this time a night."

"Oh, yeah. Well, want a beer? There's always a bar open."

"No. I know I don't want a drink," she said. "But if you want one . . ."

"Nope. I'm good—"

Eileen looked up and down the same boulevard and pointed to lights on a corner two blocks away. "Well, it's not very fancy, but the old standby, the Dairy Queen, is still open."

He laughed. "The Dairy Queen? It's been a long time. Sure. As long as you don't want to cruise it."

"I don't think so."

"Okay, Dairy Queen it is," Scotty said turning down the four-lane roadway.

As he drove the short distance to the fast food spot he was again aware of her presence—only inches from him. He felt obligated to fill the quiet between them. "You have a preference?"

"'A preference?'"

"Outside or in? You want to go inside and sit at the counter or park in a stall for curb service?" he asked.

"Either way's good. Let's park outside. I haven't done that since high school."

"Yes, ma'am. Whatever you say." Scotty swung into the restaurant lot and then into an empty stall in one fluid motion. He stopped, killed the engine, pulled back on the hand brake, flopped his wrists on top of the steering wheel and looked over at Eileen for her approval. "How's this spot?"

She clapped her hands in approval. "Perfect."

Scotty felt awkward again. Unsure of what to say next, he leaned forward, peered out under the Florida eye-shade bolted onto the Studebaker's split windshield. He scanned the huge menu painted on a sign over the island which served as the curb stop for all those eating in their cars. "What's it going to be?"

"My line," she laughed.

"What?"

"You are using my line."

He loved her laugh. "Oh, sure."

She leaned forward and again he saw the profile he so fondly remembered from high school. "I've been a prisoner of the Army for so long I'd give my next paycheck for a plain old greasy all-American cheeseburger, fries, and a Coke."

"Well, you're one lucky guy," she said, "because greasy's still their specialty here."

"Good. In that case, I might even ask for extra grease."

Eileen laughed again and waved her hand in a playful dismissal for him to stop so she could order. "Enough. We keep this up, and this place will be closed before we can even eat. Remember you're in Belton."

Scotty mugged a serious face. "Okay. Okay, what's your pleasure, then?"

"Same thing."

A high school girl in short shorts, a small knit top and a paper hat matching the color scheme of the Dairy Queen with the letters DQ on it stepped off the curb and leaned down to make eye contact with Scotty. "What would you like, sir?"

Scotty gave her the order and then once she got out of hearing distance he turned to Eileen. "Did she call me 'sir?' Me?"

Eileen teased him. "Well, you probably looked real old to her."

"Oh, great. This isn't exactly what I expected coming home. But none of it has been." He then felt as if he'd brought the tone of the conversation down. He rubbed his fingers together and changed the subject. "I must have gotten grease on this steering wheel today. I'll be right back."

Inside the cramped restroom, Scotty washed his hands and peered at his image in the scratched mirror mounted above the sink. It hadn't seen a good cleaning in many hours of use. Bending and tilting a bit, he was able to find the best image, but he shrugged. It wasn't as if he needed to check his hair or could do anything with hair so short. It was just habit.

He washed then dried his hands with the last paper towel in the dispenser and found himself again taking a controlling breath. He looked at his nails to make sure he'd not picked up anymore of the grease from Kitty's car and recalled the days in training when his nails were mostly broken and never clean.

What was it about Eileen making him feel so good and so nervous at the same time? After all, it wasn't like he'd never been on a date before, or like he was a virgin or something. He went into a half-squat and looked through the louvered window near the sink. He could see only parts of Eileen sitting in the front seat of the car. The sun visor cut off the top half of her face, and the dash hid everything from the middle of her torso down.

Her throat and jaw were brightly lit by the car sitting across the service island, lights on to signal the carhop.

Scotty enjoyed the moment free to admire her long and elegant neck without her knowing he was looking. She appeared to be watching a carload of teenagers who had just pulled in across the island and were searching their pockets for money. The kitty had been set up on the hood of the Chevy and was becoming a pile of change and crumpled bills.

Scotty felt an immediate sensation of attraction tempered by a trace of anxiety each time he looked at Eileen. There he was, out with someone who could be the girl of his dreams, but he was going to Vietnam, and she was spoken for. Still, he stole an extra moment to look at her.

The door burst open and a teenager staggered into the single stall, desperate to reach the commode before erupting. He dropped to his knees and encircled the bowl with his arms. Scotty knew what was coming and left before the vomiting began.

Outside the restroom, Scotty found himself straightening his back, tucking in the back of his shirt and walking back toward the car assuming he was being watched. He concentrated on walking confidently so he wouldn't look like he was in a hurry to get back to the car to be with Eileen.

He had to reach through the window to open the door because the outside handle had stopped working years earlier. But instead of grasping finding the handle surrounded by frayed upholstery he felt Eileen's hand.

She twisted the lever releasing the latch. She must have watched him approach the car. He liked the feeling. "Thanks," he said. "Another thing I've got to fix on this on this rolling wreck."

Inside, Scotty settled in behind the steering wheel, wiped it down with the damp paper towel from the restroom and searched for some way to start up the conversation again.

But it was Eileen who took the initiative. "Good to be home?"

The car seat was locked all the way forward making him feel crowded and a little uncomfortable for them to talk. "Your Kitty's sure got short legs." He searched the front and then the side of his seat until he found the control lever, yanked it to the rear and they both slid back with a thunk.

"So, isn't it?" she repeated.

"Everything I used to hate about Belton in school is just great now. I guess you have to leave a place to really appreciate it."

"The Army's bad, huh?" she said.

"No. It's not that. Sure, it's hard, but it's not bad. You never have any time to yourself and forget about any privacy. It's just nothing like going to school in Belton. It's all guys all the time and just so completely army." He felt the flush of color flooding his cheeks, as he listened to himself stammer and grab for words, not finding the ones he wanted, the ones to impress her. He sounded like an idiot. He searched her face to see if she thought so, too.

She bailed him out. "I understand. I can't imagine all the regimentation." She paused and then asked, "And overseas is how long?"

"A year."

"God, a year seems so long," she said twisting slightly to put her back half on the seat and half against the passenger door. "There's fighting going on, isn't there? I don't keep up much on Asia. It seems so far away."

Her knee brushed against his leg on the bench seat. Scotty felt a small electric pulse run up the side of his leg, or at least he thought he did. "Yeah, there's some fighting going on. Guerillas are trying to overthrow the South Vietnamese government. Anyway, I've never been out of the country. So I'm sure it's going to be an experience." He didn't want to imply some heroism was in his future or gush with bravado or even suggest he felt the fighting was not a concern and didn't know how to get himself out of the corner he'd talked himself into. "I only know what I heard in training. And I really don't know what my job's going to be. That'll make all the difference in whether I get near the shooting, I think."

"Are you worried?" she asked. "I mean, about getting a job where the fighting is?"

"You know, I'm mostly worried about doing things right wherever they send me." He shook his head, himself amazed. "I've been through a whole lot of training since I left here and I wonder if I'll be able to do all those things right. Training's one thing, but on a real battlefield, I just don't know if I'm up to it."

"Don't you do what soldiers do if you get shot at? I mean, shoot back."

Scotty smiled. "Yeah, that's what I thought when I left Belton. But it's much more complicated than just ducking and shooting. I guess I saw too many movies as a kid. The Army trains you for all sorts of situations. The expect you to be able to handle all of them. Combat, sure, but they also expect me to do things like calling in artillery and Air Force air strikes or performing pretty complicated medical lifesaving procedures. Then there was a lot of cross training in communications and language training and even classes in civic actions they put me through."

"Civic actions?"

"They call it winning hearts and minds. It's a little like public relations mixed with psychological operations. We're expected to advise the Vietnamese Army and help them do what armies do. But, to top it off, we help the local civilians build roads and bridges, improve their crops, put in sewer systems, dig wells, open schools and set up medical clinics."

She leaned toward him, surprised. "You know how to do all those things?"

"That's my whole point. I lay awake wondering if I can do all those things right."

"Surely, they wouldn't send you if they didn't think you were ready, would they?" she asked.

"I wish it were that easy. I'm worried about doing everything in a strange country with people from another culture mostly in another language I've only had twelve weeks of training in."

"They expect you to speak their language too?" she asked.

"Hey, I wasn't much of a language student in high school Spanish. Believe me, Vietnamese is a whole other thing."

Eileen laughed and touched his arm with her fingertips for a fleeting moment. "I'm sure you'll do fine over there, Scotty."

"You don't know how much I hope you're right."

Out of the corner of his eye, he caught the carhop approaching with a tray piled high with their order. He rolled the window up an inch to give her something to anchor the feet of the tray on and reached into his pocket for some cash.

"How dangerous?"

Scotty peeled off a five and put the rest in his pockets. "What?"

"Some Americans are getting killed over there. Right? Or is it just the Vietnamese and the communists doing the shooting?" She turned her palms up. "I'm confused," Eileen said.

The carhop squatted a bit, dropped the rubber-tipped support arm on the bottom of the tray and parked the loaded tray on the door. "Here's your order, y'all. Anything else?"

"No. I think we're okay for now." Scotty craned his neck to check the tray and passed Eileen's order to her side of the car starting with her shake.

"Whoa!"

He turned to see that even though he wasn't even through passing food across, Eileen's hands were already filled with food. He reached across her to pop the glove compartment open. With the flair of a salesman, he pointed at the flat surface the door offered. "Your dining table, Miss."

Eileen giggled at his impression and put her burger and fries on the glove compartment door, then took the drink he passed her. "You didn't answer me."

"About?"

"About the danger."

Scotty unwrapped his burger only enough to eat it, careful not to let the contents slip onto his lap. He gestured with the burger as if pointing off to an imaginary distance. "Depends on whether they send me to a job out in the field—as an advisor to a combat unit—or if I stay in one of the big cities like Saigon or DaNang at some headquarters job."

"But wait. Didn't I read they bomb the big cities too?"

"No. The Viet Cong don't have an air force, but they do rocket and mortar cities sometimes."

She grimaces, as if in pain. "I hope they give you a job deep in the basement of a building, a big thick one, made of concrete."

Scotty laughed. "What the heck would I be doing down there?"

"Filing something. You know, all the military triplicate copy stuff."

"It'd sure would be a waste of all the training they gave me."

"I still think filing and clerical work would be best," Eileen said from the corner of her mouth, her lips around the straw in her soft drink.

"I'll tell them how you feel when I get to Personnel. That will convince them to give me some job like that. So you won't have to worry."

"Well, I mean, even if there wasn't shooting going on, that's a long way off, and it must be a pretty strange place. And I know Kitty's going to be worried sick until you come back."

Scotty put his burger back on the tray and reached for his cherry Coke. "I guess I'm just going to have to convince her I'm going to be okay and she doesn't have to worry about me."

Scotty pulled up to the curb in front of Eileen's house, killed the engine and the lights. "You need to go in now?" He tapped the small dash-mounted clock only to see the hour hand swing free and pendulum on either side of the six. "I mean it's late, and I'm sure you've had a very long day—"

"No. I don't have to be anywhere until late tomorrow morning. So if you want to talk some more, we can. Anyway, you're the one on vacation, so if you want to spend some more time . . ."

Scotty was confused by the signals. Eileen was beautiful; they had a small history together; they had things in common; she was certainly open to him and appeared to enjoy being with him, but what did she expect? He swallowed and turned to look Eileen in the eyes. "Can I ask you something? Listen, if it's none of my business. Just say so."

"Sure. What? This sounds so serious."

"The guy you were with in high school . . . your boyfriend or fiancé, or whatever he is, what happened to him? He still around?"

"Who are you talking about? What boyfriend?"

"Aren't you going steady with some guy?"

"No. No, I'm not." She broke eye contact with Scotty and looked out the windshield at nothing in particular. "What made you think I was seeing someone?"

Scotty was surprised by her answer. "Well, we all thought you were going steady or engaged or something. You never seemed to be anywhere around in our senior year. We just assumed you had something hot and heavy going outside of school."

"Oh, Scotty, I'm sorry," she said.

"Sorry? Sorry for what?"

She seemed to brace herself for a confession of sorts then continued. "I lied. Well, maybe I didn't really lie, but I misled you and, I guess, everyone else. Same as a lie. Truth is there was no boyfriend. I was never with anyone in school. I never dated anyone. Not at all."

She turned and looked Scotty in the eyes again. "And I've never been to the Dairy Queen with anyone before, either."

To Scotty, the news was what he'd hoped but not at all what he'd expected. "What about the big class ring you wore? And wasn't there a letter jacket you wore too? We all just assumed—"

"Yes, I know. I wanted everyone to think I was going with someone."

"What? Didn't you want to date or hang out with the rest of us?"

"I couldn't."

"I don't understand," Scotty said.

She took another small breath and looked down at nothing in particular, staring at a spot somewhere below the dash. "It was my father. He's a drunk. No, he's worse than a drunk. He's an ugly, ugly drunk. When I was in Junior High, in West Palm Beach, before we moved to Belton, I tried to hang out with school friends, but every time he'd make it a problem for me."

"He wouldn't let you date?" Scotty asked.

"No, but he was so drunk so often I couldn't invite anyone to the house. And I couldn't ever tell when he'd let me go places I wanted to go or see people I wanted to see only to have him explode over something petty and then tell me I wasn't going anywhere."

Scotty put on an even more serious face. "He doesn't hurt you, does he?"

"No, but he hit my mom, and he trashed the house and broke things when he got drunk, which was about every night."

Scotty looked out the window at Eileen's small house. "Why do you stay there? You're out of school now."

"He's gone now. He left my mom about a year ago after she called the cops on him again. They told him they were tired of coming to the house and if they had to come again, he was going to jail. Last I heard he was in New Mexico."

"Great. I mean, it's great he's gone, and you don't have to put up with him anymore."

Eileen looked back at her front door and smiled. "My mom and I have never been closer. Before he left, I couldn't remember the last time she'd ever relaxed or had a good time. We lived in fear of him coming home each night. Some nights he'd come home drunk and tired and just go to bed and pass out. Other nights he'd come home drunk and angry and take everything out on us. And we never knew how he was going to act."

"And he's why you wanted us to think you were going with someone else?" Scotty asked.

"Sure. When I tried to have a real life anyway, he wouldn't let it alone. If a guy came to the house, my father would either go overboard as the concerned father or puke in the middle of the living room rug. I couldn't explain this to anyone—why I couldn't go out with them. So I invented a boyfriend. But I never had one."

"Not at all? Not all the way through high school?' Scotty asked.

She shook her head. "No. Never."

They sat quietly for a moment. She searched the pockets in her uniform and found a wadded up Kleenex she touched to the corner of her eye.

Scotty broke the silence. "Is your father why you didn't want to go get a drink earlier? I'm sorry if I—"

"No. I'm not a prude or a teetotaler or anything. I just don't have any good memories about drinking or drinkers. And what if I'm like my father? What if I'm going to have trouble with alcohol?"

"Can you inherit it?" Scotty asked.

"I don't know. But just in case, I'll stay away from it. Drinking makes people ugly. And I don't ever want to be part of that crowd."

He turned back toward her. "I can't imagine you ever being unpleasant," Scotty said.

Eileen sighed as if relieved to have someone know the truth. "You know, I think it is getting late. Thanks for dinner and the laughs. Mostly the laughs."

He almost ran around the back of the car to get the door for her. They walked up the short sidewalk to her porch, he about half a head taller than she. And he liked the feeling. Scotty gently touched the small of her back again as they walked. She smelled so good, and he wanted to get closer. He wanted to touch her more.

He looked down at his shoes. "I'm not going to be here very long and if you say no I'll understand. But, ah . . ." He tried to find the words to ask her but still walk away with some dignity if she said no. They didn't come easily, so he looked back into her eyes and just plunged ahead. "Well . . . would it be okay if I called you . . . I mean could we go out again?" He started to search for a way to end his questions and not sound so pathetic or so unsure of himself. "Could we do things?"

Eileen stopped him. She reached down and curled her small fingers inside his, gently, tenderly. "I'd like that a lot, Scotty." She then popped up on her tiptoes and kissed him lightly on the lips."

"Well, great!" he said. "I will. I'll call you. Or talk to you when you come around to see Kitty." He realized he was rambling again and tried to end it, but all he could spill from his lips was, "Bye, now."

Scotty got into his car, started it with relief and looked back at Eileen standing on the porch. "'Bye, now.' What the hell's wrong with me?"

He waved, not sure if she could see him in the darkened car and drove off. His timing couldn't be worse. He already knew he would miss her while in Vietnam. Of that much, he was sure.

***

Kitty was asleep when Scotty got home, but she had left a small covered plate of cookies on the kitchen table for him, a glass for milk and a note. He unfolded the note tented next to the glass and read it in the yellow bug light over the back porch spilling through the top half of the Dutch door.

I hope you two kids had a wonderful time. Have some cookies. They probably aren't as good as those snakes you've been eating at Fort Benning, but I'm sure you'll like them. Your favorite—peanut butter. Now, get some rest, honey. Don't you dare get up before ten. I love you, baby. And I'm so so glad you are home. Kitty

Scotty wondered how much Kitty had to do with getting Eileen to help her out around the house, instead of anyone else in Belton who might have been available. He opened the refrigerator for some milk and smiled. He suspected he was being fixed up. And he liked it.

It was almost three when Scotty finished yet another shower, partially to relieve the heat but more for the sheer delight of the luxury. Hot water, privacy, his own schedule and just to be able to sit naked in the dark in his own bedroom.

He couldn't remember the last time he had enjoyed just sitting by himself naked, enjoying the night sounds slipping through the window and the very gentle Florida breeze washing over his body. It was a guilty pleasure, and it added to the enjoyment of thinking about his hours with Eileen earlier.

If he were still in high school, he might write it off as sudden infatuation, like the feelings he always experienced with each new short-term girlfriend back then. With Eileen, the onset was every bit as sudden, but the feeling was more intense, and his gut told him it was different. She was different. He enjoyed being with her, her smile and her laugh. And he looked forward to being with her again.

CHAPTER 13

Scotty couldn't slow down the pace. Time home, with Eileen and Kitty, seemed to scream past him. He could do nothing to put off the date when he'd have to leave for Vietnam—when he'd have to say goodbye to both women.

While he was home, Kitty seemed to brighten and regain some strength and energy she had lost. But he was sure Eileen's insistence that Kitty follow her doctor's instructions had a lot to do with her improvement.

Scotty found being with each alone and both together fun and comfortable. He could see Kitty wanted to do what she could to encourage the relationship between them. She teased him about her and often insisted she didn't need either one around so they could go somewhere together. He was thrilled to know Kitty was as crazy about Eileen as he was.

Still, the days felt like hours and the hours like minutes. He wanted to talk about their future, and it seemed as if Eileen was avoiding the subject, too. It was as if both of them wanted not to spoil the moments with even acknowledging there would be a separation and the danger sure to come with his time in Vietnam.

They laughed and talked and touched and every now and then, they'd grow quiet. He had to go, but they didn't need to spoil their time together by worrying out loud. The awkward moments between them quickly faded as they got used to each other's rhythms and he discovered how wonderful it was to have a woman like Eileen listen to every word he said and show interest in his concerns. He tried to treat her with the respect she was showing him.

In the few weeks they had together she had caused nearly as much of a change in his personality as the Army had made in him physically.

Scotty tried to get caught up on Vietnam by watching Cronkite and reading the papers but not around Eileen. He'd never felt protective about anyone but Kitty before and he wanted to shield both of them from as much as he could. So, unless they brought up Vietnam, he didn't.

Chores and repairs badly needed around the house seemed to occupy every minute he didn't spend with Eileen. He liked fixing the place up for Kitty and enjoyed being outdoors again. It was something he'd never thought much about before joining the Army. Hot sun, a light coat of sweat and sore muscles somehow felt good. And he knew any acclimatization he could do before getting to Vietnam would help.

The goodbyes were awful. With Kitty, it was long and filled with promises. With Eileen, it was short and merciful for both of them. Still, she cried and also made him promise to be careful. But his heart pounded heavily in his chest when she told him she'd miss him every day and she'd write him as often as he'd like.

When he suggested every day was too much, she quickly said she'd do it. They held each other for a long time, quietly taking one another in—no words, no real goodbye.

And then it was over, and he found himself in the front seat of a Trailways bus heading out of Belton before the sun would warm the streets.

Scotty had fully expected to be packed into the back of an Air Force cargo plane for the trip to Vietnam but was surprised by the sergeant manning the desk at the Outprocessing Center at Oakland Army Base. He handed Scotty back his hand-carried personnel records stuffed into a large brown government envelope and pointed to a series of colored stripes painted on the concrete floor of the hanger rechristened the departure point for those headed to Vietnam. "Your paperwork's in order. Now, follow the yellow stripe to the far end of the hangar to begin your processing. You'll go through stations to check your shot record, your dog tags, you be able to exchange money and you'll be issued your airplane ticket, too."

"Ticket?" Scotty was surprised. "The Air Force is issuing tickets now?"

The tired Specialist 5 looked back up from his desk. "Air Force? Sarge, you are flying Pan Am to Saigon."

"What? There's got to be a mistake. Me flying commercial?"

"We don't have enough folks to fill up a flight every week, so you odds and enders go by civilian carriers courtesy of Robert F. MacNamara. So suck it up and enjoy it, Ranger, because it's sure to be the last luxury you're going to have this side of a Viet whorehouse."

Scotty couldn't believe his good fortune as he balanced Jake's duffel bag on his shoulder. He moved forward slowly with the other passengers holding his airline ticket ready to hand it to the stewardess standing at the foot of the ladderway which would take him up into the coach section of the Boeing 707 warming up its engines on the ramp at San Francisco International Airport.

She was tiny, maybe five feet at most, her uniform was as crisp and neat as his, and her smile seemed genuine. She took his ticket, and the smile disappeared. "Well, Sergeant. You're in the wrong place."

Scotty looked up as if he could tell if it was the right Pan Am flight by looking at the aircraft. "Doesn't this flight go to Saigon?"

"Yes it does," she said. She turned and pointed toward the ladder at the front of the aircraft. "But you need to board over there. You are on a first class standby."

"You're shitting me! Oh, I'm sorry," Scotty said, too late to take back the words.

She laughed and pointed to the other stewardess checking passengers in at the foot of the other ramp. "It's okay, hon. You just go over there and see Jeanie. She'll take very good care of you."

Scotty looked down the center aisle of the plane as he stowed his paperwork and his folded blouse in the overhead compartment. There were only two other military passengers on the aircraft, an Air Force officer, and a Navy sailor, both seated near the rear galley.

"Excuse me."

Scotty turned to find a Catholic nun in full black habit pointing toward the inside seat. "I'm the window."

He stepped back to give her room. "Yes, ma'am. Please, go ahead."

In spite of the layers of clothing and veils, she slipped smoothly into the seat and settled back.

Scotty finished closing the overhead bin and swung around to sit only to find the stewardess who took his ticket standing next to his row. "Can I get you two a drink?"

Scotty hesitated and deferred to the nun.

She looked at Scotty and asked, "You going all the way to Saigon?"

"Yes, ma'am."

The sister looked up at the stewardess. "Bring us both Scotch."

He couldn't remember if he'd ever said more than ten words to a nun in his entire life and searched for a way to thank her or break the ice when she took the initiative.

"My name is Sister Bernadine. I'm a Maryknoll."

"My name's Scotty Hayes and I'm a sergeant," he said realizing how silly it sounded as soon as the words slipped from his lips.

"Well, Mister Hayes, we are about to spend twenty-four hours together."

Scotty tried to guess at her age. Her skin was flawless, but her hair, neck, and forehead were covered by part of the white starched cotton frame of her habit so he couldn't get any closer than somewhere between thirty and fifty. "Are you going to Vietnam, Sister?"

"Call me Bernie. Everyone else does. I'm with the Maryknoll mission in Da Lat, north of Saigon. I've been home for some added training. I've already been there for three years. I'm a nurse."

"Oh. Well, I'm headed somewhere in Vietnam. I'm an infantryman."

The stewardess brought four miniatures, glasses with ice and two coasters. She placed them on the tray tables and quickly moved on to the seats behind Scotty and Sister Bernadine.

Bernie cracked the seal on her bottle, poured it into her glass and raised it in a toast. "Well, drink up, Scotty Hayes, because we are both going to earn our pay."

After an hour and two drinks, Scotty felt completely comfortable with Sister Bernie. Soon they were airborne, had eaten their first meal and put away two more small bottles of scotch apiece. He quickly learned to like Bernie and listened intently as she told him about Vietnam and its people. Her take on everything was more candid and more current than what he had received in training.

She was fiercely anti-communist but no friend of the South Vietnamese administration. "They come into my hospital, and I can't tell a communist bullet from a Republican bullet. Neither can the children who get caught in the crossfire."

"What should we do there?" Scotty asked.

"I'm a nun, Scotty, not a diplomat or an expert in international affairs, but we are about the only chance the South Viets have. Still, I don't think there are enough Americans, and I think they're already too late. The communist Viet Cong rules most of the countryside by day and all of it by night."

Scotty was surprised by her grasp of the situation in spite of her denials. She talked to the people in the villages every day and knew what they knew and what they felt, even if they were wrong. "Do you speak Vietnamese?"

"Not well, but they appreciate the effort and treat you differently than Americans who won't even try. Arrogance is something the Vietnamese abhor. Do you speak French?"

"French?" Scotty shook his head. "I only had twelve weeks of conversational Vietnamese and bad grades in Spanish in high school."

"Try to use their languages when you can. They'll help you. Use yours, and they'll clam up. They don't understand why everyone doesn't speak Vietnamese. Everyone they grew up with does."

Scotty liked her laugh. Still, the thought of trying to win over the Vietnamese peasants in their native tongue seemed daunting.

Somewhere out over the black Pacific, they both tired. Sister Bernadine drifted off the sleep while her fingers counted off silent prayers on her Rosary beads and Scotty leaned back and thought all the months of training and the anticipation was now down to less than eighteen hours until he would be in Saigon. He thought of home and looked forward to writing Eileen about spending the night with a nun.

CHAPTER 14

Eldon Pascoe was jarred from a deep sleep to a slightly higher level of confusion in a surreal world making him unsure if he was asleep or awake. Colors alternated between blinding flashes of white light and complete blackness. Over this sounds of deafening thunder finally pulled Pascoe from sleep and he found himself standing in the middle of his room unsure as to what to do first.

He grabbed his pistol belt and pistol from the hook on the wall near the door hesitated for a moment to try to clear his head enough to think if he should get anything else. He was only sure he had to get to the bunker outside the team house fast, before another rocket impacted on the flimsy tin and plywood world he slept in.

Pascoe hardly recognized the Americans and Vietnamese soldiers all crowding the hallways running toward the exit. The flashes of light from the incoming rockets painted each face in grotesque stop-action for a fleeting second only to be plunged into darkness again.

Just as Pascoe looked toward the open doorway to the center of the compound another rocket burst, the light causing him to lose his night vision. Pascoe felt for the wall and walked his way toward the door, hand over hand until he was outside in the darkened compound.

Another rocket overshot the Sugar Mill compound and detonated out in the river. The flash from the rocket helped Pascoe orient himself and allowed him to identify the womblike sandbagged opening to the underground air raid shelter he was looking for.

Pascoe's attempts to walk down the wooden steps cut into the earth turned into a stumble and then a complete tumble leaving him sitting on his butt on the wet floor of the bunker twenty feet below the level of the compound's courtyard.

At the far end of the bunker, someone had fired up a Coleman lantern, which threw a shaky yellow light and gave off a hiss and a petroleum smell mingled with the much stronger smell of burning wood and rocket cordite.

Though the bunker was big enough to hold forty people, it was already sheltering over sixty. Pascoe found a place to sit on one of the six benches running the length of the low-ceilinged structure. Still not accustomed to the light he raised his voice over the buzz of several excited Vietnamese voices. "Any Advisory Team members in here?"

"Yo!" was the only reply. Another muffled rocket burst landed outside somewhere and a silhouetted figure moved through the animated Vietnamese soldiers toward him.

"Caruthers? That you?"

"Yessir." Them fuckin' VC cocksuckers ain't getting' me with two days left. I'm thinkin' I just may start sleepin' in this rat hole until my last day here." He turned to a small Vietnamese soldier seated next to Pascoe and tapped him on the shoulder. "Hey, gimme some room here, will ya, pal?" He squeezed in next to Pascoe and dropped the butt of his rifle on the planked floor.

"How many rockets? We'll need to know for a report to Saigon."

"What?" Caruthers asked trying to yell over the adrenaline-fired cross talk in the underground bunker.

"How many?" Pascoe repeated, raising his voice.

Caruthers raised himself to a half squat. "Hey! Ya'll shut the hell up in here!" The soldiers quieted down, and Caruthers sat back down next to Pascoe. "Goddamn, these little people get to jabberin', and they sound like ducks fuckin.'"

Pascoe didn't want to encourage Caruthers's insults and simply repeated his question.

"I've counted six." He looked at his watch. "But I'm guessin' the last one was it for the night. It's been a few minutes now, and they don't like to stretch these out."

"Why?" Pascoe asked.

"They set up the rockets about five miles out, get 'em all ready to launch, fire 'em all as fast as they can and get the hell out of there before someone can catch them red handed. They know we'll target them and start returnin' the favor."

"What happens now?"

"Soon as we get the all-clear siren we can see what kind of damage they did. Then, when the sun comes up and we can get these little people out of their hammocks and on their feet to go out and find the launch site. If we're lucky, we can track the VC from there."

Pascoe looked out the opening to the bunker for some sign of daylight. The gray-blue of morning nautical twilight was filling the stairway. "You don't sound too optimistic. I mean about finding them."

"It'll just be S.O.S.—same ol' shit. We'll go out there, find their Ho Chi Minh sandal prints, follow them until their path bumps into the Cambodian border. If we could get our asses in gear, we might be able to do something but getting these little people out of the barn and onto the trail is like herdin' old snails."

"Why are they doing this?"

"They's tryin' to distract us," Caruthers said.

"From what?"

"My guess is they're movin' lots of folks through the area tonight, and they need us t'be buttoned up and worried 'bout our own asses. So's not to be discovered."

"Is this their pattern?" Pascoe asked.

"You watch, Major, in a coupla' weeks they'll have enough strength to hit some outpost or camp in enough strength to do some damage."

Pascoe sat at the makeshift conference table in the crowded room and tried to hide his discomfort with the smell assaulting him. The room had had once been used to dry the fish caught in the adjacent river but was later pressed into service for meetings by members of the division commander's staff.

The smell was overpowering for an American but did not seem to register with the Vietnamese general staff members sitting at the slab of plywood which topped the table.

The meeting felt disorganized, unfocused and lacking in agenda to Pascoe, but he dared not interrupt Colonel Minh for fear of offending him. Causing loss of face was about the most serious crime an American advisor could commit in Vietnam.

A Vietnamese captain was stabbing his finger furiously at a plastic covered map spread out on the table. Veins stood out on his neck, and his face flushed as he spoke so rapidly Pascoe couldn't follow him.

Minh seemed to be aware of the problem and chose to interpret. "Captain Nguyen's reconnaissance company searched the area and confirmed the VC had fired the rockets from here." He tapped a spot on the map marked up with red grease pencil and ashes from the cigarette he held in the same hand fell onto the map.

Immediately, his operations sergeant reached up and swept the ashes into his own hand to clean the map for the colonel.

"Did Captain Nguyen find any trails?" Pascoe asked, as if Nguyen wasn't even in the room.

Minh threw his head back in a hearty laugh and replied half in English and half in Vietnamese. "There was hardly any ground around the launch site not trampled with footprints—footprints marched to the west, to Cambodia, in many different paths."

The staff officers around the table took their cue and laughed with Minh.

"This is the game we play, Major. VC rocket or mortar us and then run away. When our soldiers get there, VC trail is almost gone from rain and water in the area." Minh pointed all of the fingers of one hand up toward the ceiling. "Grasses standing up again."

Pascoe had an idea about how to interdict the Viet Cong escape routes back to the security of the Cambodian border and almost slipped and offered it to Minh in front of his staff officers. But he was getting better at thinking before speaking his mind and avoiding the risk of embarrassing Colonel Minh. He would think it over a bit more and then make his suggestion to Minh in private.

CHAPTER 15

Scotty's mouth tasted nasty, his shorts were bunched up from sitting so long in one place, and his neck hurt from sleeping on the plane, but he was sure he was better off than those behind him in coach.

The stewardess had announced their approach into Tan Son Nhut airport in Saigon long before the aircraft had crossed the coast of Vietnam near the coastal resort town of Vung Tau. She also added the local time: 0430. Scotty craned his neck to look through the window at the view still half black in the distance with little success.

"Would you like to change seats?" Sister Bernadine asked.

"Oh, I'm sorry. Did I wake you?"

"No. I've been awake for a couple hours. My eyes are so dry from this flight they felt better closed than open. As soon as we land, you'll see how quickly we regain all the humidity we need and then some." She pointed at the seat beneath her. "So, what is it? Would you like to swap places to get a view of Saigon?"

Scotty thought about how much trouble it would be for her to move, but before he could answer she leaned forward and stood up. She was small enough to stand upright under the overhead bins without having to duck.

They made the swap and Bernadine leaned over and pointed out the important landmarks to Scotty. Through the morning haze, the spidery veins of Asia's largest river filled the small airplane window giving Scotty his first glimpse of the Mekong Delta. Coffee colored browns and rich greens dominated the views. Far to the north, where the flat river delta gave way to the spiny Central Highlands, the intense lights of parachute flares temporarily turned the black valleys of the Annamese Corridor into daylight for some units locked in combat.

As they descended, Scotty could see the beginnings of life. He felt his stomach tightening at the thought that within a minute he would be on the ground in a war zone.

Small boats finished their early morning fishing and villagers walked, bicycled and jammed small Japanese trucks headed to the markets to buy and sell everything from produce to cooking fuel. In the rice paddies, farmers bent over their crops, tending to them in hopes of plentiful harvests to come.

"Beautiful. Isn't it?"

Scotty tapped the window. "What are those?"

Sister Bernadine looked over his shoulder. "Those dark things?"

"Yeah."

"Water buffalo."

"Are those children on their backs?" Scotty asked.

"Children start to work here as soon as they can walk. Tending the water buffaloes is one of their easier jobs."

Scotty thought about how easy his childhood had been in Florida. He could see how little he had in common with the Vietnamese. It didn't much help his confidence in the tasks ahead.

As quickly as Scotty had met Sister Bernadine she was gone. Someone from her religious order picked her up on the tarmac and Scotty was ushered off into the Military Terminal by an NCO wearing an armband reading: *In-Processing.*

The building was made of a single thickness aluminum siding topped with a rippled translucent fiberglass roof which did little to keep the jet and helicopter noises out while amplifying the oppressive heat and humidity.

A floor fan at one end of the basketball court-sized room did little to move the air around inside the crowded terminal filled with American and Vietnamese servicemen all headed to and from different parts of Vietnam—some Americans heading home.

In the less than four minutes Scotty had been on the ground in Vietnam the sweat was running down the hollow of his back staining his shirt. He stood in a short line with five other Americans waiting their turn to check in with a huge Air Force Tech Sergeant mopping sweat from his neck with an olive drab handkerchief.

The sergeant took Scotty's travel paperwork from him and without ever making eye contact began pulling forms and handouts from a bin behind him and dropping them on the ticket counter separating him from Scotty. "This a copy of the Status of Forces Agreement. It governs how you will be treated if you commit a crime punishable by American or South Viet law. And here are three cards you must keep in your wallet while you are in-country." He dealt them out as if playing poker and named them as he did. "The MACV Nine Rules Card lists your duties while serving here; your Ration Card for booze and cigarettes and a Code of Conduct Card listing your obligations if you become a prisoner of war."

Prisoner of war! How could he use the term so matter-of-factly? Scotty took the cards and stuffed them into his shirt pocket thinking he'd look at them later.

"You know where you're assigned, ah . . ." He looked at Scotty's records again, searching for a name. "Hayes?"

"I don't. I was just told somewhere in-country."

The Tech Sergeant mopped his entire faces with his fat forearm and leaned on the counter finally looking at Scotty. He tapped a clipboard in front of him. "Say's here you are going to Military Assistance Command. It could mean anywhere. So don't be surprised if you end up inventorying tongue depressors in Da Nang, boy."

Scotty scooped up the rest of the paperwork laid out on the counter for him to take. "So what do I do now?"

The Tech Sergeant pointed a sausage of an index finger over Scotty's shoulder. "Try to find a seat on one of those benches. Sit and try not to work up a sweat, or you won't be able to make it through the day." He looked at his watch. "It's only zero five forty-five Veet-nam time, and it's already ninety-two degrees. By noon it'll be hot enough frogs'll be fainting from the heat and humidity. You got a whole year here, young Ranger, so pace yourself."

Scotty sat on a bench across from the check-in counter but avoided leaning up against the metal wall already hot to the touch from the sun backing its backside. He watched the faces of those coming and going. There seemed to be some sense of organization and some flow to the traffic flowing through the building parked on the apron of the city's only real airport. Through the window, he could see American and Vietnamese helicopters hovering past on their way to get into the departure pattern shared with commercial jets, Vietnamese Air Force fighters, and cargo planes.

"HAYES—SERGEANT—SCOTT J., sound off if you're in the terminal!" another Air Force Tech Sergeant behind the counter yelled using the customary last-name-first.

"Yo!" Scotty replied, raising his hand and half standing at his bench.

The Tech Sergeant pointed toward an American sergeant standing at the counter.

Scotty stood up, checked his gig line and tried to size up the Sergeant First Class approaching him.

"You Hayes?"

"Yes. Scotty," said, not sure if he should stick out his hand or not.

"I'm Bobby Caruthers." He stuck out his to shake Scotty's hand. He shook it with exaggerated vigor. "I'm really, really glad to see you boy, 'cause you're my turtle."

"Turtle?" Scotty asked.

"My replacement. We call 'em turtles 'cause they are so long in getting here."

Scotty picked up Jake's duffel bag and followed Caruthers already heading through the door to the jeep parked outside.

"I already had two replacements come and go." He moved the large chaw of tobacco from one cheek to the other. "I hope you're a keeper."

Scotty threw his bag in the back of the jeep Caruthers pointed out as theirs. "'Come and go?'"

"Yeah. One got here and turned out he had a pretty bad case of diabetes. So they evac'd him back to the world. The other guy, an SFC from Fort Benning I went through Basic with. He wasn't here two weeks and came down with kidney stones. So he got shipped to Japan and then back home too."

Scotty looked at the five large yellow stripes on Caruthers's sleeve. "Looks like I'm a little junior to be your replacement, Sarge."

"Well, it is an E-7 slot, but we take what we can get around here. And if I don't find a replacement who can stay put long enough for me to out-process I'm never going to get home." He pointed at a TWA jets parked on the apron. "So, Hayes, I'm going to take good care of you until my ass is on one of these freedom birds headed back to the world of round doorknobs."

Scotty jumped into the passenger seat as Caruthers started up the jeep. "What am I going to be doing?"

Caruthers pulled out of the parking lot and into the crowded Saigon streets. "Well, to put it Biblically, Hayes, you're going to help these little zipperhead motherfuckers smite the wily Cong.

"You want a chew?"

Scotty looked down to see the pouch of Redman tobacco Caruthers had pulled from the cargo pocket in his fatigue trousers. He'd first tried chewing tobacco in Ranger School to keep his mouth moist and suppress his constant hunger and to help him quit smoking. He took the pouch from the older sergeant, "Sure." He pulled a plug from the packet and tucked it into the pocket in his cheek and handed it back to Caruthers.

Caruthers looked over at Scotty and smiled. "You know, you gonna' be a'right, boy."

The crowded city streets kept Caruthers from being able to pick up any speed. As they threaded their way through the traffic Caruthers filled Scotty in on all the routine questions Scotty would have eventually asked anyhow—about pay and mail and R & R policies.

Scotty listened and soaked up everything. His eyes searched the road-side stands and the uninterrupted lines of pedestrians balancing loads of varying sizes and wide in variety. He was assaulted by the smells, the heat, and the din. He had never in his life seen so many people crammed into such little space. Florida and Georgia were never like Saigon in December of 1964. He was hardly aware that he spoke out loud. "Goddamn. Where'd all these people come from?"

Caruthers threw his head back and let out a laugh. "Hell, boy, all these people do is fuck and steal from Americans. They sure as hell don't waste much time fightin' the goddamn Cong."

Within the hour they had broken free of the grip the city had on the jeep and cityscape gave way to a rural two-lane highway headed northwest. For Scotty, his Vietnam was there. Saigon was much the same as any crowded city anywhere in the world, except there were Asian faces everywhere. Out in the countryside, Scotty took in the long vistas over a pool-table flat landscape colored in rich greens of the rice fields, punctuated by Nipa Palms and separated by worn brown paths atop the dikes.

Everywhere he looked women were dressed in black or white cotton tops over black pajama bottoms. Each wore a conical hat held in place by a strip of cloth pressed into service as a chin strap. Those who weren't bent tending crops were weighed down with heavy loads of rice or vegetables. Some carrying their loads with a bamboo carry poles on their shoulders carefully balancing their cargo hanging from each end of the pole.

Heat and humidity smothering to most American newcomers felt familiar to Scotty but far more intense. It was the brightness of the day that most surprised him. As they traveled west, the sky was a rich blue for as far as he could see on the distant horizon uninterrupted by the simple farming hamlets stretching all the way to the border with Cambodia nearly thirty miles ahead.

Scotty spat a string of tobacco juice out of the corner of his mouth and looked back at Caruthers. "So how long you been here, Sarge?"

Caruthers smiled without taking his eyes off the ox cart and two farmers walking more in the roadway than on the shoulder narrowed by its rapid transition to rice paddy. "Not thinking any more about how long I been here. I'm too short for memory lane." Caruthers slammed on the brakes and hit the horn trying to avoid hitting a rooster that had escaped from a basket the Vietnamese farmers had placed in the ox cart. One of the men darted out in front of the jeep in a heroic grab for the bird.

"Hey, get the fuck out the road, you dumb motherfucker! I'll run your ass, and your chicken's over in a heartbeat and not lose sleep. Now dee mau, Goddamnit!"

"What's that mean?"

Caruthers let out the clutch and got back into the flow of traffic. "Means get the hell out of my way you dumb ass." He shifted his tone. "How short? Well, let me put it this way, you'll still be pissin' stateside water while I'm unpacking my duffel bag back in The World."

The response wasn't much help for Scotty who was beginning to realize he had a thousand questions for Caruthers he was probably not going to get to ask. "In days?"

"Latest word I got was a little over a month. So you better catch on fast, young sergeant." Caruthers spent the next hour and a half filling Scotty in on his duties heavily laced with cautions about the Vietnamese, Vietnam, the tricky political situation for Americans in and the alien and crippling Asian concept of saving face.

Scotty listened hard but never took his eyes off the constantly changing view of his new home and the people he would be defending. Finally, he focused on two young Vietnamese men standing on the roadside staring back at him and asked, "Sarge, how do you tell who's Viet Cong and who's on our side?"

Caruthers laughed. "Boy, there ain't nobody on our side in-country."

Scotty felt words coming to his lips but stopped himself before he got into an argument over why they were even there. He tried to think of how to ask the question a different way, but Caruthers spat a rope of tobacco juice out of the moving jeep and continued.

"I don't know much about politics or international shit. But I did grow up on a farm near Jefferson, Missouri. Farmers don't have much time to

worry about nothin' bigger or heavier than weather, crops, and money."
Caruthers waved his hand off in the direction of the Vietnamese scattered
across the paddies on either side of the roadway. "These little fuckers got
t'worry about floods, drought, how much fish they can pull out of their
streams, rats in their rice fields, feedin' their kids and goddamn bombs
droppin' in the middle of their lives.

"They don't know nothin' about who's runnin' Vietnam or if they
want to be communists or not. They could really give a shit what the fuck
Ho Chi Minh's doin' in Hanoi. It ain't what they talk about after a long day
bent double in the paddies pluckin' leeches off their nuts.

"Truth is when a VC's in their hootch with a gun, they're all for his
cause. When a South Viet soldier's holdin' the gun, they couldn't be more
beholdin' to him. They've seen the French, Japanese and the French again
come and they seen them go. They prob'bly goin' to see us go too.

"Very practical people these Viets, but they weren't born to be soldiers."

"That one's yours. Used to belong to a kid who had to go home on
emergency leave. His mama was dyin' with cancer or something."

Scotty looked around to see what bunk Caruthers was pointing to.
Seven of the twelve bunks were empty in the NCO hootch, and half of
them were uppers.

Caruthers continued. "The rest of them got broken springs, won't sit
flat on the floor or just plain stink. So it's about the best of what we got
available here at the Shithole Sheraton. Get settled in, and I'll be back."

Scotty waved without taking his eyes off the room. "Sure, Sarge. Later."

Caruthers kicked the screen door open, stepped out in the sunlight
and raised his voice as he walked away. "If you think that place is a night-
mare, wait 'til lunch."

Scotty looked around the team room stuck inside the perimeter of the
sugar mill next to the front gate. Through the glassless window, he could
see hear and taste the dust kicked up by every vehicle entering and leaving
the compound. He kicked the thin s-rolled mattress down onto the single
mesh of springs connecting the four sides of the frame and watched the
dust expelled by the motion.

CHAPTER 16

The first meeting with Pascoe started with a handshake and then got progressively more worrisome. Pascoe was talking to Scotty but seemed to be talking about himself regardless of the topic.

Scotty sat on the wobbly stool placing him below Pascoe's eye line, making him feel like he was in a child's chair in a kindergarten. Pascoe droned on about what their challenge was and how important he thought it was for the Americans in the advisory team to set the example for the Vietnamese soldiers to emulate. Scotty wasn't quite sure if he knew what emulate meant, but he got the drift.

Officers were a little of a mystery for Scotty. The more rank they had, the more they seemed to be a strange combination of soldier and school teacher. Pascoe certainly bore that out, even though Scotty was unaware of Pascoe's West Point background. He kept making references to Vietnam's history and culture. Two things Scotty had never considered while undergoing training at Fort Benning and in the swamps of northern Florida where history and culture. Tactics and survival occupied his thoughts while trying to stay awake on long patrols where he and his classmates crossed paths with hundreds of Coral snakes.

He also couldn't help but notice that Pascoe's uniforms had been tailored to fit him perfectly. Scotty's was baggy and still wrinkled from being packed in Jake's duffel bag. Pascoe's fatigues were starched and ironed, fresh from one of the small laundries he had seen outside the compound walls along the roadway to the Sugar Mill.

Pascoe's words suddenly grabbed Scotty's full attention. ". . . and when Sergeant Caruthers leaves you will be my senior NCO. I'll be expecting you to set the example for every Vietnamese soldier you come into contact with. I will accept nothing less."

"Pardon me, sir. Isn't there a replacement for Sergeant Caruthers? I mean, someone other than me?"

Pascoe frowned, interrupted his own welcoming lecture and looked toward the ceiling. "No. No, there isn't. And this is no small point of aggravation for me." He jabbed his index finger at his own chest. "I'm trying to show our counterparts how important planning is for the smooth transition when replacements are needed, and MACV Headquarters can't even find a single Sergeant First Class to replace Caruthers.

"Just let me worry about that. Until then, I'm going to expect a lot from you. I want you to spend the few days you have left with Caruthers picking his brain and learning the ropes. You'll have his job soon enough."

Caruthers's job. Scotty felt the sweat running down the hollow in his throat. How could he take over from a soldier who had spent thirty years in the Army? He hadn't even completely unpacked yet.

Pascoe wrapped up his welcome making sure Scotty understood his priorities and his concerns and his cautions. All of which were not to do anything that would reflect badly on Pascoe.

Caruthers dumped a cardboard box upside down over Scotty's bunk. Boxes of ammunition, fiberboard hand grenade containers, two hand-held flares, and a couple of flashlight batteries piled up on the mattress. "There you go, John Wayne. Everything you need to kick some Viet Cong ass, son."

Scotty felt his chest tighten. His first real combat patrol. All his training had come down to the day he'd actually face someone bent on killing him.

"Get y'er shit together, young sergeant." Caruthers looked at his GI watch. "You got about two hours. I'll be issuing the patrol order at eighteen hundred hours in the briefing room. Don't be late. Major P will be there, and he don't like it if anybody's late.

"I'm goin' to find some of that fuckin' god-awful Viet coffee. Come git me if you need me." He started to step out of the room and stopped. Reaching in the side cargo pocket, he pulled out a pouch of Redman Chewing Tobacco and threw it to Scotty. "You buy your own on our next PX run when we get back from this ambush."

Scotty caught the paper pouch and looked at it. He hoped he'd be back to do that.

Scotty rigged and rerigged his gear. Counting his canvas rucksack, his web belt that held much of his ammo and grenades, his two canteens, and his rifle, he'd be carrying eighty pounds—more than half his own weight.

He ran over the checklist he had scratched on a cardboard flap torn from a box of rifle ammunition with a pencil too hard to avoid tearing the paper. He had it all: ammo, rations, water, compass, map, notebook, ballpoint pen, grease pencils, water purification tablets, malaria pills and his patrol cap. He slipped the harness of his web gear over his shoulders, grabbed his rucksack by the frame and his rifle in his other hand and looked around the room. On the window ledge was his only snapshot of Eileen. He wanted to take it with him but knew it would be destroyed by the swamps and streams along the patrol route. He paused to look at it for a moment. Eileen smiling at the camera, the Florida breeze blowing her hair. He felt heavy in the center of his chest.

"As y'all know, this is an eight-man ambush patrol. We'll be looking for VC infiltrating in one and two-man teams from Cambodia and through the division area of operations on to Saigon." Caruthers rocked back on his heels and then forward to his toes. He held a white wooden pointer with a red painted tip parallel to the dirt floor of the briefing room.

He turned and tapped a spot on the map tacked to the wall. "This is our ambush site along this canal that draws water off the Vam Co Dong River for irrigation. We've seen lots of trails meetin' up at this point here and Intel reports tell us that it's the first source of decent drinking water the VC come to in-country."

As Caruthers spoke, Scotty looked around the room from his chair near the wall. Six Vietnamese soldiers sat in a semi-circle in front of Caruthers. He had met none of them before. All had come from the Division Reconnaissance Platoon. The fact that they had all volunteered reassured Scotty after all the stories he had heard about South Vietnamese being extremely reluctant warriors.

On the far end of the curved row of folding chairs, Major Pascoe sat squarely, his arms crossed over his chest.

Scotty listened to Caruthers who expertly delivered as good a patrol order as he'd heard since being drafted. Caruthers would pause every few sentences and a soldier in the middle, a sergeant by the rank on his shirt, quietly translated for his fellow Vietnamese who didn't speak English.

Going into combat for the first time and with soldiers who didn't even speak his language added to Scotty's level of anxiety. He felt the sweat trickle from his breastbone to his navel and realized that it was time—his first patrol briefing for his first real ambush.

In a matter of minutes, he'd be outside the Sugar Mill's compound where everyone had to be considered the enemy. He looked at the bright square the setting sun threw on the wall as it poured through the only glassless window in the room. He tried to take a deep breath and let it out without anyone noticing.

Stuffing the small GI notebook into the pocket of his jungle fatigues, Scotty looked across the compound in the direction of that night's ambush. The sweat he built up in the briefing room began running down his chest from his neck and as quickly began to cool from the light breeze slipping gently out of Cambodia to the west. Scotty's mind filled with the sudden reality: he still had plenty to do before the patrol.

He flipped his wrist to check his watch. Two hours and he would be outside the concertina wire. The real thing. It seemed to him it had been a long time coming—the training, studying, practicing and preparing for the first time he would really be in harm's way. The first time he would face someone intent on killing him. He couldn't remember when anything had felt so serious to him. Not since his first parachute jump at Airborne School had he felt such an overpowering sense of responsibility for how things would come out. He could do it right, or he could screw it up. That much he had learned.

He found himself ticking off the last minute details of what he had to do to get ready for the ambush patrol—a process drilled into him in Ranger School. But his first urge was to find some time to finish a short letter to Eileen he had started earlier. And to get one off to Kitty. Even if only a few words for each.

"Hayes!"

Scotty heard his name over the sounds of the road traffic outside the compound and recognized Pascoe's voice. He turned and saluted simultaneously. "Yes, sir?"

"You ready, Sergeant?"

"To go, sir? He nodded toward the front gate of the compound. "Not yet, but I will be."

Pascoe gave him a smile making Scotty feel a bit uneasy with its sincerity. "With Caruthers leaving soon I'm going to be expecting a whole lot out of you, Hayes. We have a big job to do here."

Scotty wasn't sure if Pascoe expected an answer, and if he did, what would be appropriate. He tried something neutral. "I'll do my best, sir."

"Let's walk," Pascoe said, pointing toward the mess hall.

Scotty took up a place to Pascoe's left—as was the custom when walking with a superior. He found himself in step with Pascoe in less than three strides.

Pascoe looked around as if to make sure they weren't being overheard. "You see, Hayes, we set the tone around here. I don't have to tell you how slow these Viets can be at getting their asses in gear. So everything *you* do has to be the way we want them to operate. I expect you to be the first to fight, the first to show them the way we do things. Lead by example. They'll be watching you. You drag butt, so will they. The Army sent us here to put some fire in their asses and some wins in the scoreboard.

"If we're going to create a reputation as a division known for kicking ass it starts with you and me. I want to see you come back here with scalps every time you go outside the wire with the Viets. You got me?"

Scotty nodded and uttered a yes with just enough conviction to keep Pascoe from thinking he wasn't on the team.

Pascoe patted Scotty on the shoulder. "Good, good. I knew I could count on you." He then turned and walked away, toward the operations office, without so much as a goodbye or good luck.

Scotty watched Pascoe's stride. It was as if he knew people were watching him walk across the compound.

"Watch your back."

Scotty turned to find Caruthers standing in the doorway to the mess hall. "What's that, Sarge?"

Before he spoke again, Caruthers stuck his finger in his mouth and pulled out a plug of chewing tobacco. He dropped it onto the ground and pushed it into the dirt with his boot. "Listen, boy. I'm just an old ground pounder, and I don't know much about much." He looked up under the brim of his patrolling cap at Pascoe entered the headquarters. "But I know you better keep your eye on that guy. Don't know why. And I ain't been around him all that much. He's kind of a ghost. He never comes out of his office, never seems to be 'round trainin' much and I don't think he's been on any a' our operations. Wherever he's keepin' himself and whatever he's doing, I wouldn't turn my back on him. If you know what I mean."

"Yeah," Scotty said. He turned from Pascoe to Caruthers. "I hear you, Sarge. He has a real funny way of saying *we* when he means me. *We* got to do this. And *we* got to do that."

"Yeah, he does that a lot with me too. Oh, hey . . . I got something for you." Caruthers reached down into the cargo pocket on the leg of his jungle fatigues and pulled out an envelope striped with an Air Mail red, white and blue border and waved it.

Scotty stepped closer and took the letter, quickly searching for a sign of its writer. Eileen's name in blurred ink filled the lines printed for the return address. He burst into a broad smile. "Thanks, Sarge. I've been waiting for this." He didn't wait for a response but quickly slipped his finger under the flap, opened the envelope and pulled out the small onion skin pages. He spread them with is fingers to see there were three pages—all in beautifully handwritten fountain pen ink.

Caruthers reopened the screen door to the mess hall. "Well, I can see I've 'bout lost your attention, young sergeant."

Scotty looked up quickly from his letter. "Oh, sorry, Sarge." He waved the pages. "My girl. First letter. Since I got here. You know."

"Yeah, I know. I've had me lots of letters like them—Germany, Korea, Panama. You go on and read your letter. But don't be forgettin' we leave here pretty soon."

Inside the NCO hootch, Scotty checked his watch. An hour was all separating him from his first combat patrol. He felt it in his gut but was determined to find some time to read and savor Eileen's words. He flopped down on his bunk letting his legs slant off to the side, avoiding the pile of combat gear he had rigged earlier. Eileen's letter was still in his hand.

He looked at the date on the outside of the envelopes and realized it had taken twelve days for it to get to him. He'd been warned by others the turn-around time for a letter seemed like an eternity, but there was no option—no faster way of communicating. Not even phones.

Scotty touched Eileen's handwriting and read the first line again. She was unsure if the letter would get to him soon and if it would only be read by him. She'd never known anyone else in Vietnam but remembered reading letters were censored in World War II.

He reminded himself to tell her in his letter no one would read her letters but him. He wanted to encourage her to be as candid and as intimate as he could.

She spoke of Kitty's health seeming to improve sometimes for days only to suffer a setback. And she cautioned Scotty shouldn't worry because she would watch out for Kitty as if she were her own mother.

She quickly got around to them and how she missed him even though he had only been gone a few weeks. She had started counting the days and would remind him each letter how many days he had remaining on his tour in Vietnam.

She missed him. He stopped and read the line again. A year until he could see her seemed like such a long time. He thought of the few days they tried to fill with each other before he left, her smile, her laugh and how wonderful she smelled. The ache he felt for her was like nothing he had ever felt for any girlfriend before. She seemed to fill his head, and his body reacted each time he thought of her.

He read the rest of the short letter and was disappointed to hear she had not received any of the letters he had already mailed to her. She promised to try to write him every day. He felt guilty because he had barely been able to find the time to get one out every third or fourth day because of his schedule. He made a promise to try to match her efforts.

He set aside his regrets and feelings of guilt and got onto one end of his wooden footlocker. The other end served as his desk. He wrote as quickly as he could to use the time he had to get the writing he wanted to do done.

"Hey, you goin' to war with us? Or are you going to get all gooey over your letter, young Ranger?"

Scotty jumped at the sound of Caruthers's voice. He looked quickly at the alarm clock near his bunk. "Damn, Sarge. I lost track of time." He leaped to his feet and grabbed his combat gear and his rifle. He folded Eileen's letter to take it with him.

Caruthers pointed at the letter still in his hand. "Better leave it here."

"I can't take it with me?" Scotty asked.

"I 'spose. If you want to turn it into a gob of wet paper and runny ink. This is as dry as you gonna' be for some time. It's your call, boy."

Digging into his shirt pocket, Scotty found his ballpoint pen and put the tip of it down the barrel of his carbine he held between knees. There was no getting away from the roiling dust cloud slipping over the tailgate and powdered everyone inside. Aside from the discomfort, grit down the barrel of his rifle could cause it to jam when he most needed it.

Customary for military transport in Vietnam, the deuce and a half truck they rode in had the canvas cover over the bed of the truck rolled up on the bows to provide shade but still allow the riders in the back to see out. The floor was covered with filled sandbags in the event they drove over a mine—sandbags to absorb the blast and some of the fragmentation.

The six Vietnamese soldiers sat in pairs, chatting—as if there was no war, no Viet Cong, no possibility of a land mine or ambush or someone rushing by on a motorbike to toss a grenade into the back of the moving truck. All of these possibilities crossed Scotty's mind as he kept his eyes on the activities ahead of the truck and alongside the dirt roadway.

Scotty sat next to Caruthers and quietly spoke. "How come the Major ain't coming with us?"

Caruthers laughed. "You shittin' me? The major on a patrol. That's rich!"

"No way, huh?"

"You can put money on never seein' his ass out here humpin' a rucksack or getting uncomfortable with the little people." Caruthers spit a stream of chewing tobacco juice out over the side of the truck bed. "I seen lots like him before. You know, the 'You go on out there and kill a Commie for me' kind.

"In all the time he's been here I ain't never seen him outside the wire 'cept'n when he and Minh are flying over the war at nearly fifteen hundred feet."

Scotty took his eyes off the villagers clogging the edges of the narrow roadway on their way home. He looked at his watch. 1900 hours, seven p.m. civilian time. It was just starting to get dark. He thought of home again. It was seven in the morning the next day in Florida. Eileen would be on her way to Kitty's. Scotty suddenly realized how otherworldly America seemed from the back of the truck on his way to his first combat operation.

After another twenty minutes of driving at a snail's pace, they stopped. Figures inside the bed of the truck were only somewhat blacker than the night when the driver finally stopped alongside the road. "This is our stop, young sergeant," Caruthers's voice announced from the darkness.

Before Scotty could reply he jumped at the sound of a loud metal clanging caused by one of the Vietnamese soldiers, who had unhooked the tailgate and let it slam open against the chassis of the truck.

"Well, if they didn't know we were comin' before, it's fuckin' sure they know now," Caruthers said. He punctuated his irritation by spitting a long stream of tobacco juice out into the ditch alongside the roadway.

"No shit. What now?" Scotty asked.

"We'll get off the road, let the vehicle go back and see if we can get some decent night vision after the truck headlights are gone. Let's go. Out."

After too much milling around and confusion in the dark to suit Scotty's standards the patrol got into its march formation.

Scotty wasn't comfortable with the eight members of the patrol tightly clustered and crouched in a ditch not ten feet from the roadway—now abandoned after dark because of the risk of traveling at night in Viet Cong–controlled areas.

The sound of the truck's engine faded, and Scotty came to the full reality of his situation. It was the day he had known would come from the minute he got orders to Vietnam. From that moment on he could be shot at, wounded, maimed or killed. While the thought was disturbing, he was most concerned with how he would react when the shooting actually started. Would he be able to hold his head up after it was over? Would fear grip him so tightly he would freeze up? Would he embarrass and shame himself? The more he thought about it, the tighter the knot in his gut. He realized his mouth was dry, and he was perspiring even though he wasn't even moving yet.

He tried to remember what he had been taught about this moment. He heard words Sergeant Russell had told them all the day they went through the Infiltration Course, crawling under live machinegun rounds being fired over their heads: "Courage is not the absence of fear. It is doing your job in spite of your fear. Now, suck it up and move!"

Ranger training kicked in for Scotty. He looked at his compass to cross check his rough guess of where he thought they were and what direction he would have to move in to walk the three miles back to the Sugar Mill should the patrol be overrun and the need for escape and evasion arise.

"You ready?" Scotty felt Caruthers's hand touch his arm as he heard his words. "Sure, Sarge. Where do you want me?" Scotty replied.

"I'm fourth in order of march behind the captain, and you are sixth, behind Sergeant Tran."

"The medic?" Scotty whispered.

"Yessir. The very same witch doctor."

It took the patrol almost twenty minutes to get on the move, get stretched out so they wouldn't be clustered up into an easy target and put some distance between them and the few remaining shack houses along the roadway where they had offloaded the truck. Scotty watched as Captain

Nguyen moved from man to man making sure he understood what was expected of him on the move.

Nguyen was a very small man not more than five feet tall. His uniform and equipment dwarfed him. He looked more like a schoolboy than the commander of the Reconnaissance Company.

Scotty had heard plenty about Nguyen. He was quiet, efficient, and unlike many other officers, had earned his job through merit and successes.

The story Scotty got from Caruthers was Nguyen had been an administrator at an orphanage in the coastal city of Phan Thiet. It was funded and run by American Quakers. When Scotty first heard the story, he thought of Sister Bernadine and wondered what had become of her.

It was at the orphanage Nguyen learned some English. Caruthers told him Nguyen was pretty good at it, but unlike Colonel Minh, he rarely used it. Scotty thought it was strange for a man who spoke a language not to use it when the opportunity arose. Especially since Scotty had seen Nguyen reading American military training manuals. Once he even saw him with a copy of *The Last of the Mohicans*.

Nguyen had been drafted into the South Vietnamese Army when the country was split at the 17th Parallel at the end of the French-Indochinese War ten years earlier and rose through the ranks. Many of the Vietnamese troops didn't want to serve with him because he was aggressive and looked for fights. But the same soldiers wanted to be with him if they got into one.

Scotty's eyes had finally adjusted enough to the darkness to be able to make out the huge red cross in the white circle on Sergeant Tran's helmet. Beyond Tran, he was unable to see Caruthers, Captain Nguyen or the two soldiers in front of Nguyen in the line stretching out over a hundred meters in a single file.

In Scotty's mind plenty of things were already wrong with the patrol. But he was neither in a position of authority to say so nor was he unaware picking at their failings would only result in loss of face and no correction. He had learned back at Benning the only recourse he had was to make note of the errors on operations and then incorporate improvements into future training. The only way to sidestep the loss of face was to put distance between the infraction and the correction. He made some mental notes.

His gear was far from broken-in the way he wanted it, and everything was riding wrong, painful, or both. Scotty squirmed to shift his load of combat gear, ammunition and the two quarts of water in his canteens to relieve the discomfort with little success.

Soon the ground beneath his jungle boots began to lose its hardness. The night sounds filled with a harmony of tens of thousands of night insects and nocturnal birds. And that blending was periodically punctuated by the sounds of the labored breathing within the patrol and occasional distant rifle fire and Vietnamese artillery.

After an hour of walking, Tran raised his hand to pass back the signal. They were stopping for a break and a map check. Scotty repeated the hand signal and looked back. He was pleased to see each man in the patrol take a knee or squat in alternating left-right ready positions to provide some security in the event they made enemy contact on the break.

"How you doin'?" Caruthers asked in an almost inaudible tone.

"I want to take my map out and make sure we are headed the right way. But I'm guessing it would be bad form, huh?"

Caruthers gave Scotty a reassuring pat on the shoulder. "Might as well send up a sky writin' plane sayin,' 'We think you got no damn idea what you're doin.'"

"That's what I thought," Scotty whispered.

"We're on course, aw'right. This little guy they got up front with the map is 'bout as good as I've seen over here. Can't get him to leave the whores alone in the village and his peter's sneezin' 'bout half the time with the clap, but the boy can read the shit out of a map.

"What you gotta' do next time is memorize the route before we go, keep a good pace to tell how far we been moving and sneak a peek at your own compass now and then to keep 'em honest. Just don't make a big deal out of it."

An artillery parachute flare burst over the city of Cu Chi miles to their rear to turn the night into day for some other South Vietnamese outpost needing help. A sliver of its light bounced off Caruthers's face. He looked old to Scotty. How many times had he done this in the wars he had been in? How many nights had he too worried if he would ever see daylight again?

Shortly after they started moving again, the ground gave way to abandoned rice paddies and then to marshland. Walking became more and more difficult as the mud came up to Scotty's mid-calf and the water up to his waist. He wondered how far the sucking sounds of pulling their boots out of the dough-like mud could be heard across the flat ground.

He licked his upper lip and felt his skin cool quickly on the right side of his mouth, telling him they were downwind from the ambush site and anyone near there would be unlikely to hear the noise the members of the patrol were making on the move.

The wind got progressively colder, stronger and damper as they moved. Scotty looked up at the black night sky and could see no stars. It meant cloud cover. A chance of rain. Another thing he didn't want that night.

It was nearly one a.m. when Captain Nguyen finally held up the patrol. As planned, he, Caruthers and one of the Vietnamese soldiers went forward to recon the ambush site.

Scotty waited with the others, silently rechecking all of his equipment with his fingers as if on autopilot. He took advantage of the stop to adjust some of his gear rubbing him and causing discomfort over his right hip bone. He pulled his canteen from its carrier, unscrewed the plastic cap, careful not to let its chain clink against the aluminum body of the canteen, and raised it to his lips. The smell of Halazone water purification tablets filled his nostrils while he let the lukewarm water flow over his tongue and fill his throat. He took several large swallows, surprising himself at just how thirsty he was. The thirst and the sense of chill he felt from the mild breeze made him aware how wet his fatigues were from perspiring and wading through the paddy water.

It aggravated him to think even after a few weeks in country he still had not become fully acclimatized to the constant heat and equally oppressive humidity.

He heard some rustling and turned to find Tran had gotten to his feet and was signaling Scotty they were moving out again. If they were on plan, they would slowly move into their ambush position with a minimum amount of noise and motion which might give them away to any Viet Cong who might be in the area.

Slowly, they moved no more than a hundred and fifty meters and came upon the southern bank of an east-west canal. As Scotty got closer to the actual canal, he could see the reflection of the night sky on the surface of the quietly running water. From what he could tell, the canal was absolutely straight for as far as he could see east and west. It appeared to be no wider than a two-lane road and had raised pathway on the far bank.

On Scotty's side of the canal, the bank was hard ground, which simply held the running water in its course. The bank was every bit as effective as concrete having been wet and sunbaked every day for decades.

Captain Nguyen moved back from his position in the file to Scotty and grabbed him by the sleeve to get his attention. He then silently pointed at a spot on the bank where he wanted Scotty to position himself for the ambush. No talking was necessary. Nguyen had made it clear in the briefing he would personally place each man in the patrol to avoid confusion and unnecessary talking at a very critical time.

Scotty gingerly dropped to one knee, then rolled forward on the opposite elbow raising his rifle to a prone firing position, not taking his eyes off the flowing water and the far side of the canal bank.

Nguyen, who had positioned the two other soldiers at the end of the file behind Scotty came back to place himself in the center—now to Scotty's right.

If everyone was in his position, Scotty knew but couldn't see, they faced the water—two Vietnamese soldiers were to Scotty's left, Nguyen to his right, Caruthers to Nguyen's right and two soldiers on the far end of the ambush.

Tran, the medic, had been placed to the rear of the line of ambushers facing in the opposite direction to provide early warning and security in the event someone wanted to sneak up on the ambush's blind side.

Scotty lowered his face as close as he could get it to the ground to see the outline of the man to his left and right silhouetted against the only slightly lighter glow of the night sky. Both Nguyen and the soldier on his left were also in place, ready, aiming their weapons on the water in front of them.

An hour went by, then another. Scotty recognized no matter how wet, sore and fatigued he was, his mind was still moving at a high rate of speed. Training prompted him to think about a thousand things which would never occur to a civilian laying in wait for someone in the Asian night. He tested his memory by recalling the radio call signs and assigned frequencies in the event Caruthers were to be killed or wounded and he would have to take over as senior advisor.

He pulled out his compass and watched the radium dial spin, slow and settle on true north reassuring himself he knew the exact direction of the rally point Nguyen had designated two hundred meters back. It would be the spot where they would all reassemble if they were attacked and had to run to safety.

His elbows began to hurt after still another hour of propping himself up into a ready firing position. While the days seemed to sap his strength with the heat and humidity, the ground at the ambush site continued to draw heat out of Scotty's body. And the dampness of his sweat and swamp water soaked uniform combined with the steady breeze causing him to shiver. He fought back against his growing awareness of just how many places on him were stiff or uncomfortable. And he was more conscious than ever of the tightening in his chest and shortness in his breathing. Though he was motionless, his body was pumping adrenaline, and his instinct was telling him to brace for trouble.

Scotty knew with each passing hour their chances increased for being able to pull off a successful ambush, his first real ambush. He kept forcing himself to rethink his actions, remember the details of the ambush plan and challenge himself about his readiness. Then something struck Scotty on the shoulder. A small rock or pebble. He turned to find Captain Nguyen alternately waving toward him and pointing at something upstream.

Scotty squinted then shielded his eyes from the only slightly brighter skyline to better see the layers of black in front of him. His heart began to pound as he saw something floating in the water—coming toward the ambush position. Whatever it was, it was too far away for Scotty to make out, but it was larger than a man. And it didn't seem to have any sharp or severe dimensions to it, like a boat or a raft.

Be ready, be ready kept flying through Scotty's mind. He first reached out to confirm the position of the three hand grenades he had laid out in front of him on the ground—each with the safety pins straightened out for easy pulling should he need to throw them. Satisfied, Scotty raised the sights of his small carbine rifle to his eye line to place aim on the floating object and flipped the rifle off of safe.

As the floating object continued to get closer to the ambush site Scotty was finally able to see more definition. It appeared to be a large bush or shrub floating along the canal, slowly closing on them. But as he watched and waited it also became apparent to him it was not just an uprooted bush. It was not spinning or randomly floating at the same slow speed the water was moving down the canal. Instead, it maintained its orientation in midstream and seemed unaffected by the turbulence of the water or speed of the flow. It was clear to Scotty someone was controlling the direction of the floating vegetation and keeping it in the center of the flow.

Thinking ahead, Scotty checked his watch and then took a quick look at the horizon before returning to the rear site of his rifle. It was almost dawn and the horizon was beginning to show some signs of pink with the promise of sunrise still over an hour off.

Scotty looked over toward the two South Vietnamese soldiers on his left and was pleased to find them at the ready also looking at the floating bush. But he was equally unhappy he could see them clearly. If he could see them, then anyone who might be floating in and under the bush in the water could see the ambushers too. They were only hidden by the night and once that was gone so was any concealment the darkness afforded them.

The floating bush crossed a point just in front of the upstream end of the ambush patrol and out of the corner of his eye Scotty could see Captain Nguyen holding his palm in the air signaling the patrol to hold their fire.

The bush got even closer, passing in front of the ambushers. Suddenly the night filled with the sounds of Captain Nguyen's rifle spitting automatic fire into the bush and the water around it.

As fast as Nguyen's rifle began to hurl red tracers into the water the others opened fire; someone to Scotty's right pitched a grenade into the water. His ears were assaulted by the ferocity of the sounds of all the weapons firing and spent cartridges ejected from each rifle making chime-like sounds as they hit the others already on the ground next to each shooter.

Scotty found himself already following Nguyen's lead. He became aware of the repeated kick of his rifle butt in the hollow of his shoulder as bullets left his weapon, passed through the bush, and slapped into the into the muddy far bank below the water line with a deep smack-thunk sound.

From somewhere inside the floating brush a burst of flashes angrily leaped out—several rifle rounds and two brilliant green tracers. Scotty watched as the tracers first appeared to be headed directly at him but zipped over his head with the deafening crack of a bull whip.

Suddenly, the surface of the canal erupted into a plume of muddy water as the first grenade exploded under and slightly upstream from the floating bush taking small branches and tufts of vegetation with it and ending the short bursts of returned fire.

Scotty reached forward, dropped the empty thirty round magazine from his rifle, picked up a full one from the stack of three just below it and prepared himself to continue firing when the water falling back to the canal and surrounding banks stopped splashing around him.

He tried to force himself to exhale to regain some pattern of normal breathing recognizing he'd been holding his breath during the short, brutal fusillade of small arms fire. He then coached himself to fight the tendency to get tunnel vision and only see what was within arm's length. He had to relax, keep an eye out for what else was going on around them and make sure to look upstream. Whoever was in the floating brush could be the advanced party for a larger group.

Scotty looked back over the barrel of his rifle to find something of substance to aim at while he surveyed the area and he caught the two soldiers to his left leaping to their feet, throwing off their gear and dropping their weapons to the ground. First one, then the second, jumped from the bank into the water the same time, He heard Caruthers screaming, "Cease fire! Cease fire! Hold your fire!"

As the two half swam and half waded into the center of the canal, first one and then another object surfaced apart from the floating brush. Scotty raised himself up on the heels of his hands and saw two slick black shirts on the backs of two bodies floating face down in the water.

The ambushers in the water talked excitedly while one of them fired a pistol into both bodies as some form of insurance. They then grabbed the floating bodies and tugged them to the near bank almost twenty meters downstream from Scotty's position. There they searched the bodies, pulled some equipment off of them and then climbed back up the slimy bank gleefully proclaiming in Vietnamese they had one enemy AK-47 rifle and web gear containing some grenades.

During the entire plunge and search Scotty tried to watch the two Vietnamese soldiers while listening to Captain Nguyen who spoke excitedly and non-stop in somewhat broken English and Vietnamese. He wanted them all to stay alert, to keep an eye upstream in case there were more and to reload their rifles in case they needed to defend themselves from some yet unseen attackers.

Breathing excitedly, Scotty finally took his eyes off the two wet ambushers and watched the bodies of the two Viet Cong bob in the canal as the slowly turned in the current and floated away downstream. They were the first two dead men he had ever seen. What surprised him most was how easily death had come to what was a quiet dawn.

It was at that point he realized how light it was—he could see a few hundred meters without difficulty. This meant he could be seen too. He slowly scanned the flat, swampy horizon for any sign of a threat to the patrol.

It was only a few minutes past dawn and already he felt the promise of another hot, wet and sticky day.

"We go."

Scotty turned toward the voice and saw Sergeant Tran, the medic back in his place in line waving in the palm-down style unfamiliar to most Americans.

Scotty smiled. "You speak English? Yes?"

The pocket-sized Asian soldier smiled revealing a pair of silver capped front teeth and shook his head. "No speak. We go." And then he looked over his shoulder in the direction of the others who were already on their feet and readying to move out—away from the ambush site.

As quickly as the full sun broke the horizon, the temperature spiked. Scotty wiped the sweat from his face and eyes and looked around at the countryside as it came to life. Dirt roadways silent during the night, save the occasional stray dog and ever present hum of insects, filled with farmers and merchants. They appeared on the roadways from their small farms and thatched houses tucked into the thousands of tufts and clumps of trees offering shade and protecting them. Scotty was sure they had limited hopes: Just to get through yet another day without the war ravaging their lives.

Scotty again scanned the flat terrain to his left and right looking as far out as he could for any signs of enemy activity which might threaten the small patrol walking single file over the marsh turned hardened mud ground toward their pickup point. The night without sleep had taken its toll on all of them as they moved without the spark they had when they left the Sugar Mill the day before.

To Scotty fatigue quickly translated to a lack of security for the patrol. They walked with their eyes focused on the next step rather than the most threatening treeline or possible firing position for a hidden enemy rifleman. Their weapons were no longer at the ready. One of the Vietnamese soldiers up ahead of Scotty even carried his rifle over his shoulder. Scotty would talk to Caruthers about how to correct this on future patrols without giving offense.

Before Scotty heard the chopper, he noticed both Captain Nguyen and Sergeant Caruthers each began talking over their respective radios. Caruthers looked up as he pressed the handset of his radio to his face, searching the sky for the voice on the other end of the conversation.

Minh's chopper appeared as a small but thumping dot on the horizon and grew ever larger as it approached the patrol. Scotty knew they were speaking on separate frequencies: Nguyen speaking to Minh and Caruthers to Pascoe in the chopper which quickly fell into a large loop as it began circling the patrol over a quarter of a mile above them.

Almost as quickly as the chopper arrived it flew off in the direction of the Sugar Mill. Within an hour the patrol reached the small hamlet in a more secure part of the province where they would wait for the truck to pick them up and take them home too.

It seemed strange to Scotty—Captain Nguyen allowing the patrol to wait for their ride in a roadside restaurant. His American training would keep the patrol in some secluded spot in a defensive posture as long as possible to reduce the risk. Each day taught him how different they were, most of them never having known peace.

They each found a chair and either ordered something to eat or broke open their rations—no one in the patrol had eaten for over fourteen hours.

Caruthers sat down next to Scotty, rested his carbine against the wobbly chair and dumped his radio and rucksack onto the top of the table. "Damn, I'm getting too old for this boonie humpin' shit."

Scotty pointed a finger toward the radio. "What was all that about?"

"Who? Oh, the major. He and Minh came out to tell us what a good job we did racking up those two gooks. Pascoe busted my ass with a bunch of questions about 'What were they carrying? Did they have any documents? How were they dressed?' You'd think we fired up Ho Chi Minh's chief of staff. Fuck, they were just a couple a' bad guys slippin' into the country. This guy Pascoe's got to lighten' up, or he's going to burst into flame 'fore his tour of duty is up here." He turned to the restaurant owner and pointed at the row of beer bottles on the wall over the counter. "Gimme' one of them, papasan," using the Korean War term older soldiers tended to pick up in one war and bring with them to the next.

Drinking was something else never done in Scotty's training experience. "Little early for beer, isn't it, Sarge?"

Caruthers playfully patted Scotty on the shoulder. "Son, if'n you don't take y'er pleasures where you can here there'll never be a right time. Hell, you're on duty all day, every day. Nobody's shootin' at me right now, and I'm not likely to get shitfaced on a single beer. I'm tired, hot, sore and I want a fucking Ba Mui Ba." He then laughed, "Shit, what are they gonna' do to me? Send me to Vietnam?"

"That mean beer?" Scotty asked. "That ba mooee . . ."

"Naw, it's Viet fer '33'—the name of the beer." Caruthers spun the bottle the owner had placed on the table revealing the large numerals on the label.

Scotty smiled. "Guess I learned some more Vietnamese today."

Minutes after arriving and still damp, dirty and tired, Scotty and the other patrol members sat in the briefing room at the Sugar Mill debriefing the ambush patrol in detail.

Major Pascoe tapped his pencil on the list of notes he had jotted down in his notebook. He continued to anxiously tap the pencil's eraser against the page as Sergeant Caruthers described each step of the ambush patrol from his own notes.

Pascoe kept interrupting Caruthers.

Scotty watched as Caruthers only gave Pascoe as much as it took to shut him up and not let Pascoe start lecturing Caruthers on what they should have done better. Caruthers was good at holding off the Pascoe.

And Pascoe was very unhappy the patrol didn't kill more VC and capture more weapons, equipment, and documents.

"Major, if we'd let those two guys go on by thinkin' they were just the point element of a larger unit, and we'd a been wrong we'd have no body count at all. I think Captain Nguyen did it right, if you don't mind me sayin' so."

Even if Pascoe didn't agree Scotty realized he wouldn't say so in front of Captain Nguyen because to do so would embarrass Nguyen in front of his soldiers.

It took two hours to cover the ambush, most of it focused on the execution of the violent exchange lasting less than a minute. Out of questions, Pascoe deferred to Nguyen who released everyone to go clean up and get something to eat.

Pascoe stopped Caruthers and Scotty as the debriefing broke up. "You two hang back. I want to talk to you."

Caruthers caught Scotty's eye and shot him a momentary expression of impatience with Pascoe.

"We can do better than this, gentlemen. A body count of two? That's not going to get anyone's attention in Saigon at MACV Headquarters," Pascoe said, his hands on his hips, shaking his head.

"Major, I wasn't trying to impress anyone in Saigon. I was just out there hopin' we could put more fire on them gooks than they could lay on us. I was just hoping to keep from getting my ass shot up because I was thinking I was some kinda' cowboy," Caruthers said.

Pascoe's face reddened. "I don't think I like your attitude, Sergeant."

Old soldier that Caruthers was, Scotty could see he chose not to respond, leaving the next move in Pascoe's hands.

Quickly, Pascoe turned to Scotty. "I expect to see far more out of you. Don't you disappoint me too, Sergeant." He didn't wait for a reply. He just put on his cap, kicked the door open with is boot and walked out into the mid-day sun.

Scotty stood quietly looking at Caruthers.

Caruthers ritually pulled some chewing tobacco from the pouch he plucked from his pocket and tucked it into his mouth. "If that man thinks I'm goin' to stick my fucking neck out for him with as little time as I got left in-country he's dumber than I thought he was.

"Anyway, I wasn't runnin' the damn patrol—Nguyen was. And there's no way in hell I was going to light a fire under a Viet captain. He's about as good as we got in the whole fuckin' division. All I'd a done was piss him off if I'd a pushed him."

Scotty shrugged, not sure if he could offer anything to Caruthers's mood or justification. "Sarge, you'll be out of here soon. Don't let him get to you."

Caruthers moved the plug of tobacco from one side of his jaw to the other with a flick of his tongue, opened the screen door and fired a stream of tobacco juice out into the compound. "Son, he's gonna' be your problem soon. Jus' remember he can kill you, but he can't eat you."

Bugs circled the small desk lamp as Scotty tried to write a letter to Eileen. The desk wobbled, the bugs landed on his writing paper, but his mind was still out on the ambush. Scotty's mind drifted back to the darkness and the gunfire and the sight of two humans floating in the canal.

The fact he had been on his first combat patrol, might have fired a round and killed someone and had seen his first real Viet Cong soldiers was something he had been training for, worrying about and anticipating for so long. Now it was behind him. In soldier terms, he had lost his cherry. He was now a real combat infantryman. He felt a sense of accomplishment tempered with the understanding he would do it many more times before his tour was over. And he might not survive all his future enemy contacts.

Though his head was filled with the ambush, he found himself unsure about what to tell Eileen. He picked his pen and snapped the plunger over and over exposing then concealing its ballpoint. Should he share the details of the two deaths with her? Would he be lying to her if he simply said nothing or glossed it over?

He decided telling her too much would only worry her and put her in an awkward position with Kitty, should Kitty ask Eileen what he had told her about the combat operations. More than most mothers, Kitty was keenly aware of the consequences of a meeting engagement with the enemy gone wrong. So he started writing, mostly asking questions: How was she? How was Kitty? How was her mom? The job, the weather, the old Studebaker. He continued to fill the small notepaper page with blue lines, here and there marked by globs of greasy ink. The pen too was a casualty of the oppressive heat.

At the end, he turned to more personal comments: How he missed her; how much he wanted to spend time with her when he got home and how he hoped she felt the same way.

Before long, it was after midnight, and he wrote the words *Love, Scotty*, put the pen down and rubbed his burning eyes.

Scotty finally folded the letter and slipped it into the envelope. He carefully addressed it and wrote the word *free* in the upper right-hand corner where a stamp would go—one of the few privileges given to soldiers serving in Vietnam, free postage for letters home.

Rain began to pelt the tin roof over his head.

He promised himself he would tell Eileen the whole truth someday when it would no longer frighten her to know what he was facing each time he left the compound.

CHAPTER 17

Spring didn't arrive in Scotty's part of Vietnam without bringing the Monsoon winds, which, in turn, brought the rains. Rain would continue through October or November with a hundred days marking the monsoon's greatest intensity. Paddies had already begun to fill to overflowing; ditches along the roadside swelled with fast running brown water and the compound at the Sugar Mill became a mud bog.

The soldiers knew which months would bring unending torrential rains and had put down makeshift wooden pallets made from ammunition boxes to provide pathways crossing the compound and even some of them were already submerged.

With the approach of the Monsoon Scotty had put more than a dozen combat patrols under his belt learning to apply all of the techniques of soldiering he had learned in training. And with each patrol, his confidence was elevated.

He had been surprised and pleased to see how all the combat techniques pounded into him by Ace Russell and the long list of NCOs Russell had passed him on to had worked when he needed them. He'd seen several more firefights, more deaths and some devastating wounds sustained by both sides. But the things he found most surprising were the dogged determination of the poorly equipped Viet Cong and how well suited he was for the job.

He had come to like the Vietnamese soldiers, even if he often became impatient with their universal lack of sense of urgency. Actual combat—the shooting part, was as terrifying as the first time, but he seemed to be able to call on something inside to control his fears and the constant anxiety he lived with every day he walked the fields and paddies. Wanting to be as prepared as he could be, Scotty picked Caruthers's brain knowing he would only have access to him for a few more weeks.

And he soon enjoyed a comfortable relationship with the Vietnamese soldiers who had been watching him closely before they slowly placed their confidence in him.

The time passed quickly while Scotty was busy but ever so slowly when he thought about how long it would be before he could see Eileen again—which was often.

"Hayes!"

Scotty heard Pascoe's voice and excused himself from the small group of Vietnamese soldiers he sat with in the mess hall. He walked to the doorway where Pascoe stood, obviously unhappy about something. "Yes, sir?"

"Outside."

On the steps of the mess hall, Pascoe looked around, making sure his remarks were not overheard. "What did you learn in NCO school?"

Scotty was unsure what the question meant and tried not to show his irritation with Pascoe who had a tendency to ask nearly incomprehensible questions which always seemed to put him at an advantage. "I'm not sure what you mean, sir."

Pascoe pointed in the direction of the unseen table inside, where he had been sitting with the Vietnamese soldiers. "Does the phrase 'Over-familiarity breeds contempt' ring a bell from your leadership training? Or did you just sleep through that lecture?"

"I'm not sure what you mean, sir."

"I'm getting a little tired of finding you so damn chummy with the Viets. You can't be their friend and also lead by example. Seems like every time I turn around you're in some gaggle with a bunch of them."

"But sir, I'm trying to establish what do you call it, ah, rapport with them. Isn't that part of my job?"

"Sergeant, you can establish rapport without becoming their friend. Getting friendly with them will only undermine your authority. You should know that."

"Sir, I don't have any authority over them. They don't work for me. I'm just an infantry advisor. I have to persuade them. I just can't order them to do anything."

"Don't be a smart-ass, Hayes. I want to see some distance between you and the Vietnamese and that's the end of it. If I find you sitting around shooting the shit with them again, I'll be forced to find some other job for you. And trust me when I tell you it won't be the limit of my actions. You're one of the reasons why I was never keen on this accelerated promotion program for soldiers not ready for the responsibilities being an NCO demands. And if you force me, I'll see to it you don't stay a sergeant for long."

Scotty felt anger rising inside his chest and was sure his face was flushed, giving him away. Still, he knew it was useless to argue with Pascoe. There seemed to be nothing they agreed upon except the undeniable fact: Pascoe was a major and Scotty was a sergeant. And the difference gave Pascoe all the firepower he needed to punish Scotty.

Scotty stood silent.

"Now, get out of here and find Caruthers for me."

Scotty saluted, and Pascoe turned his back and walked away. He knew one thing, he was right and Pascoe was wrong about relations with the Vietnamese soldiers. He wouldn't change how he interacted with them. He would just do it where Pascoe wouldn't catch him. And it would most likely be out of the compound on patrols and combat operations, where he was not likely to find Pascoe.

Pascoe and Lieutenant Colonel Wills stood stiffly under the overhang protecting the doorway to the General's Mess as they watched the glossy olive drab helicopter with the red and while two-star general's placard touch down on the helipad inside the compound.

General Pham Ly, commander of the division and American Brigadier General Pace Devlen, the Senior Advisor to the Vietnamese Corps stepped from the chopper and sprinted to the overhang trying to dodge puddles and return the salutes of the two American officers waiting for them.

His uniform wet from the spray thrown by the chopper blades, Pascoe stood aside and held the door open while the three senior officers entered the mess. He looked back at the chopper and saw Colonel Minh in the command pilot's seat, uncharacteristically making some notations in the chopper's maintenance log book while the turbine engine groaned to a stop.

Inside, the mess was a small island of European splendor. Pascoe had only been in the General's Mess once before. No one on the staff and none of the advisors were allowed to use the mess unless General Pham was dining there. And even though he commanded the division, Pham spent most of his time in Saigon.

Pascoe stood quietly by the door and looked around the room. Three large tables were arranged into a U were covered with clean, stiff tablecloths. Each place was set with bone china, sterling silverware, and three crystal goblets. Napkins stood tented next to the plates and each place setting had a delicate cup and saucer.

The room had plywood fabricated stands which held vases of fresh flowers and the wooden floor had been painted with a thick coat of glossy black enamel.

General Pham took his place of honor at the center of the base table; Devlen took the place to his left.

Vietnamese soldiers dressed in mess steward attire appeared from behind a screen concealing a doorway to the kitchen and fluttered about the Vietnamese general like gnats. One unfolded Pham's napkin and draped it across his lap, while another poured steaming Vietnamese tea into the delicate cup, while still a third plucked sugar cubes from an equally ornate sugar bowl and dropped them into the general's tea.

The general looked up from his tea and waved for the standing Wills and Pascoe to take places on the leg of the U. They sat and the room grew quiet while everyone waited for the commander to finish his endless stirring to take a sip of his tea. He did and simply nodded approval to no one in particular.

General Devlen took the cue and stood. "General Pham," he turned to Wills and Pascoe, "Gentlemen, I have some exceptionally good news for all of you." He nodded to his aide, a thin and pasty looking lieutenant who had somehow slipped from the chopper to the General's Mess without Pascoe noticing.

The lieutenant pulled a manila folder from his briefcase and walked over to Pascoe's place, careful not to draw attention to himself. He placed the folder next to Pascoe's elbow and returned to his post near the door.

The General continued. "I'm thrilled to announce General Pham has been nominated by the Chief of Staff of his army to assume command of Vietnamese III Corps.

Pascoe had barely exchanged pleasantries with the Vietnamese General in the weeks he had been there, and now the man was leaving. His immediate thought was who would replace him? Pham had been aloof enough not to make Pascoe's life miserable. Could he be that lucky again with Pham's replacement?

The door opened, and Colonel Minh entered dripping water all over the floor. He wore a raincoat draped over his shoulders and carried his cap in his hand.

General Devlen waved his hand toward Minh. "What perfect timing. I was just about to announce the second part of my good news. Gentlemen, Colonel Minh has been promoted to general and will be assuming command of the 6th Division from General Pham."

He extended his arm to Minh, "Please, General. Join us for tea in your new General's Mess."

As Minh worked his way around the end of the table to join his boss and General Devlen, Devlen applauded the general. The others followed suit in a gesture of congratulations.

The news hit Pascoe like a rifle shot. He had just found what seemed to him a comfortable working relationship with Minh and now he would be just as likely to get a replacement Operations Officer for Minh who would be difficult to work with and might be a real obstacle to his goal of repairing his faltering career.

General Devlen continued. "My final announcement gives me particular pleasure because it involves someone in my advisory team." He looked at Pascoe and pointed at the folder on the table in front of him. "Open it, Major."

Pascoe opened the folder to find a formal order. His eyes quickly darted down the page, and he found his name, *Pascoe, Eldon H.* The only name on the orders.

General Devlen continued. "I'm pleased to announce Major Pascoe will be moving from his current job as advisor to Colonel Minh in Operations to Division Senior Advisor to again advise *General* Minh."

Pascoe read the words next to his name: *be promoted to the rank of temporary Lieutenant Colonel.*

Devlen continued, "And he will be pinning on the new silver oak leaves of a lieutenant colonel."

Pascoe was confused. There was no lieutenant colonel's promotion board meeting at the Pentagon. He was sure of the schedule. He would have known if he were being considered for promotion.

While he pretended to be focused on Devlen, his eyes slipped back up the page as the General's words became just noise in his head. The orders!

They were *not* Department of the Army orders. They were MACV orders. His eyes searched the page again looking for more clarity. *Temporary!* He was only being promoted to *temporary* Lieutenant Colonel.

It was an *acting* lieutenant colonel's job. He was being *frocked,* an old Army custom invoked by field commanders to give authority to someone greater than his current rank but without permanence and without the pay normally expected of the rank. It was related only to the job and only while in the job.

"Come on up here, Eldon." Devlen reached around and took two oak leaves from his aide who had quietly moved into position to offer them. "I want to ask General Minh to do the honors and pin on your new insignia." He handed the silver insignia to Minh.

Pascoe tried not to show his shock and outrage. He wasn't being promoted for merit. He was being temporarily promoted to give him a rank more appropriate for a general's advisor—so Minh could have a lieutenant colonel. It was to save face. It was political. Pascoe was furious.

As he stepped up to the head table, the three generals stood. While Minh pinned the insignia on Pascoe's collar, Devlen spoke to all but looked Pascoe in the eyes make his point. "I'm sure Colonel Pascoe realizes the importance and the intent of the message we are sending him from MACV Headquarters when we put our faith in his abilities by assigning him to General Minh as his Senior Advisor replacing the departing Colonel Wills."

Pascoe painted a convincing enough smile on his face while he accepted handshakes all around and Devlen went on to say his official goodbye's to Colonel Wills who would be leaving within the week.

When he finished speaking, Devlen and the others sat down while Wills made some remarks about hating to leave and how pleasant he had found the working relationship with General Pham and how welcomed he had felt for the year he had been there.

Pascoe felt Devlen looking at him while Wills spoke. He could see Devlen searching for some sign of recognition in Pascoe's eyes indicating he clearly understood just exactly what had taken place. Only Pascoe and Devlen knew the promotion was not real.

When Wills finished General Devlen invited everyone in the room to come forward to congratulate Generals Pham and Minh and Pascoe on their promotions.

In the glad-handing, Pascoe found himself face-to-face with General Devlen. A man he knew not at all.

Devlen spoke loud enough for everyone within earshot to hear him congratulate Pascoe. But then he leaned in a little closer and lowered his voice. "Major, I think you understand the reason for this temporary promotion. I don't want you to think it is the by-product of your performance to date. Because, I have to say, you haven't really set the world on fire from what I've been able to see in Saigon. I have every confidence things will change. Right?"

Pascoe was almost speechless. He had never seen the man in the 6th Division's headquarters or out in the division's area of operations. Now, he gives him a temporary promotion with one hand and tells him he's doing a shitty job—all while smiling for everyone in the room.

He knew Devlen was talking about at recent attack on a South Vietnamese barracks in Saigon. One of the Viet Cong captured in the attack had admitted his unit had infiltrated through the Sugar Mill area several weeks back. Caruthers had been right. "Ah . . . You can count on me, General," was all Pascoe could think to say. There was no use arguing with the man.

Still, to everyone in the Division, Pascoe was a lieutenant colonel. And the issue was never discussed after that day.

Pascoe sat at the field desk in is room in the Team House, his head in his hands. He looked at the orders again. He wanted to be sure what he was reading actually meant what he thought it did.

On the bottom of the orders, he found a paragraph headed Special Instructions, which read: This promotion remains in effect within the Republic of Vietnam and while the named officer is assigned to the Military Assistance Command. At the time of his reassignment, this order is rescinded, and the officer will revert to the permanent rank of major on the effective date of reassignment instructions.

Pascoe pushed the orders aside and pulled a glass he had taken from the mess hall from under a handkerchief covering it, keeping the dust off of it. He poured himself a half tumbler full of Johnny Walker Black scotch from the bottle he had been nursing for days and drank it quickly. He then poured another.

His mind was crowded with disturbing thoughts. Time was slipping through his fingers. The months were ticking by. And he had done nothing remarkable since arriving in Vietnam. And if he didn't do something quickly he could easily find himself either on the way home or reassigned somewhere where he would have even less of an opportunity to make a name for himself. He took the glass of scotch with him, stood and walked to the tactical map of his province he had tacked on the wall in his room.

He sat down on his footlocker and looked at the map. He thought about the patrols and enemy contacts the division had made since he had been there. They all confirmed Minh's arrival orientation—the enemy continued to infiltrate into Vietnam from a point inside Cambodia almost thirty miles north-northwest of the Sugar Mill.

He had read report after report of enemy forces who continued to move down the Ho Chi Minh trail network into Cambodia in spite of the repeated air strikes designed to interdict the traffic along the trail.

He knew if they could only go into the enemy assembly areas on the other side of the border they would be likely to inflict larger numbers of casualties, find large weapons and equipment caches and, for him, make a mark sure to be noticed. But they weren't allowed across the border unless they were returning fire on enemy positions firing on South Vietnamese patrols or aircraft. And, even then, they were not allowed to expand any contact deeper into Cambodia.

He drank more scotch and examined the map trying to develop some plan, something to produce more impressive results than he had enjoyed to date. Results which would be seen by higher headquarters as positive in his unit. Results he could claim credit for.

Somehow, he had to take advantage of his new job advising a division commander instead of its operations officer to compensate for the time he had spent in country without adding anything remarkable to his record. Having General Minh's ear surely had to hold some promise.

Dinner finished at the end of a long training day, Scotty went back to his room after a beer with Caruthers who elected to stay in the small club they had set up in a small storage room in the Sugar Mill.

Scotty carefully hopped through the compound trying to dodge the deep puddles of water from still another day of nearly constant rain. Inside his room he shucked his shirt and cap, throwing them on his bunk. He sat down on the chair by his desk and turned on this cheap Vietnamese desk lamp before untying his boots.

The light poured onto a small pile of mail someone had left in is room for him. He fanned the envelopes to see two were from Eileen, one was from Kitty, and one envelope was covered with lined out and forwarding addresses. He looked at the return address. All it said was Fitch, A Company, 4th Training Regiment, Fort Benning. The postmark was unreadable because it had been stamped and re-stamped with each time it had been forwarded. Scotty could see it had been sent to him at Airborne School, forwarded to NCO training, Ranger School and then on to his APO address in Vietnam.

He slipped his finger under the flap and opened the letter, not because it was more important than Kitty's or Eileen's, but because he was puzzled what Fitch would be writing to him for. He had not heard from Fitch since they graduated from Basic Training.

The date inside the letter was seven months old. Fitch started his letter with the usual pleasantries hoping it found Scotty well and somewhere he enjoyed. But he quickly got to the heart of his letter. He was stationed at Fort Benning at the time of the writing and had received some bad news he thought the others in their platoon would like to know. He was trying to write to all of them and asked Scotty to let him know if Scotty had any addresses on old platoon chums.

The news was bad. Fitch found out Sergeant Russell had been captured by the North Vietnamese while on patrol inside Laos with Special Forces. There was no other information, but Fitch promised he'd update Scotty if he heard anything. He asked Scotty to return the favor.

It explained why he hadn't received any replies to the few letters he had sent Russell. Scotty just assumed that Russell was on some classified mission and couldn't write—and would when he got the chance.

Scotty put the letter down and began to think the worst. Russell could be dead or suffering unspeakable torture he had heard was commonplace in the prison camps. He looked at the other three letters and decided he didn't want to read them just yet. A spot in the center of his chest felt leaden as sadness and anger seemed to well up inside him. In his life, no man had meant as much to him as Asa Russell. No man had shown as much interest in him or had as much faith in him. Thinking he might be dead or in pain greatly darkened Scotty's mood. He put on his shirt, grabbed his cap and headed back to the club to have another beer with Caruthers.

***

The monsoon season continued to strengthen and influence everything. Pascoe moved into his new job with ease, taking full advantage of the added prestige and influence it brought with it. Now everything done within the advisory team would be of his design. He had not yet found an American major to replace him. But he was satisfied to see Minh's Operations job had been filled by a Vietnamese lieutenant colonel who had been plucked from some obscure and bureaucratic Saigon staff job by Minh. Word was he was related to the Army Chief of Staff, and Minh's arm had been twisted. But he seemed reluctant to do anything Minh didn't wholeheartedly support and seemed to curry favor with Minh whenever he could. For Pascoe, that meant there would be little opposition to his advice to Minh from the Operations section.

For the time being, Pascoe had to wear two hats and keep his hand in his old job. This had its advantages—giving him more influence over the division's operations.

For Scotty, it was training and more training. He and Caruthers took turns preparing and presenting classes on map reading, tactics, first aid and fire direction. The days when they could take the Vietnamese soldiers out into the training fields surrounding the Sugar Mill were few due to the hostile weather. On the bad days, they were all crammed into the small makeshift classrooms. They all suffered from the smothering humidity and tried to hear the instruction over the rain pelting and pounding the tin roofs at the Sugar Mill.

Pascoe got impatient with the weather and gathered the team. "I want to take advantage of the weather and turn it our way for a change," Pascoe said.

Scotty sat next to Caruthers in the sweltering briefing room taking notes on the notebook balanced on his knee.

"Everyone here knows while we can often track infiltrators into South Vietnam in the muddy marshland between here and the Cambodian border. And they can know when we are in the area using the same techniques.

"From intelligence reports I'm reading out of Saigon, I'm convinced more infiltration is going on when we are not out searching the Area of Operations. They may be poorly equipped. But the VC aren't stupid.

"I've been able to convince General Minh we need to run a reconnaissance in force closer to the international border to find out exactly where they are crossing." He turned and tapped his knuckle on the acetate cover

over the black line indicating the border on the tactical map beneath it. "Knowing this will narrow down the area we have to monitor to interdict this movement.

"Right now we're catching the ones we catch when they are many miles into Vietnam and have split up into one, two and three-man teams. If we could get them at the point they cross the border, we're bound to increase our body count. And we can also prove to higher headquarters they're actually staging at specific coordinates inside Cambodia—something Cambodia continues to deny."

All the Americans and the Vietnamese in the room who understood English laughed at the denial. Once they quieted down, Pascoe continued. "The concept is simple. Captain Nguyen will take twenty-two soldiers from his reconnaissance company, Hayes, and Caruthers, and move under cover of darkness to this point."

Pascoe tapped a small point marked on the overlay with grease pencil near an abandoned hamlet named *Doi Bao Voi* less than five hundred meters from the dark black border.

"Here we'll conceal the members of the patrol in the abandoned hootches of the hamlet, and monitor the movement. I hope we can document enemy movement by taking photos of the enemy activity. If we can be persuasive enough, we hope to later mount an effective regimental sized operation with the okay of Saigon.

"I don't need to tell any of you we have to have something big to go after to justify such a large operation so close to the border."

A hand went up next to Scotty. Captain Nguyen, normally quiet in briefings then stood up. "Helicopt?" Nguyen asked in the clipped English sounding more like French most Vietnamese used to refer to choppers.

Pascoe shook his head. "No." He turned back to the map and with a pointer from the map tray traced blue veins on the map indicating the streams which fed all the flooded marshy flatland. "We will go in using small boats. This will make our presence in the area less likely to be discovered by the enemy."

Scotty couldn't help but notice Pascoe included himself in the operation by again using the word *we*. He turned his head slightly and caught Caruthers's eye. They exchanged a knowing glance—both recognizing Pascoe's choice of words and the ease with which he decided to place them in harm's way.

"We will depart this location for the objective area in seven days. In the meantime, we'll be getting some small boats prepared, and I want you all to train your troops in using them."

He stopped and deferred to Nguyen. "Of course, if this meets with your approval, Dai Uy," he said, using the Vietnamese term for captain.

The night before the patrol Scotty wanted to make sure he finished a letter to Eileen so there would be one on the way to her while he was out on patrol. Between swatting moths away from the paper and stopping to think just what it was he wanted to tell her, Scotty felt at a loss for words.

Writing had not been one of Scotty's skills in high school. Since joining the Army, he had only added writing military messages and operations orders to his writing experience. Writing to Eileen was the first time he had ever felt self-conscious about writing at all. Her letters to him were so personal, and he felt so close to her when he read them. She was able to write like it was just the two of them and she made him long for her when she talked about them being together again and how she missed him and missed his touch.

That alone gave him an ache stirring up images of her face and eyes and how much he wanted to have sex with her. Something that just didn't happen in the short time they had before he left. He knew one thing about her, he wanted to spend the rest of his life with her, but saying so was hard for him to do in a letter.

Scotty crumpled up another attempt and threw the balled-up notepaper into the cardboard box next to his desk serving as a trash can. He took a sip of the not-quite-cold beer he had brought to his room from the team club and decided just to say it outright, to tell her he wanted to be with her and tell her he felt awkward with his writing and hoped she would understand he just wasn't much good at it. But she shouldn't think he wasn't filled with thoughts of her almost every hour of the day.

He spent the next two hours writing what would only be a three-page letter. In it, he said more to her about his feelings for her than he had in all of his earlier letters combined.

The boats were each not more than six feet long and four feet wide at their mid-line. They had taken a beating during the few days the patrol members practiced carrying them, loading them, paddling them quietly in unison and righting them when they overturned in a stream near the Sugar Mill.

At first, Scotty was skeptical about boats made from tightly woven bamboo could even float, but they did. Now they were stacked upside down on top of each other in the back of a truck following the members of the patrol all crushed into the lead deuce and a half.

Only a dozen days separated Caruthers from a plane trip home. Though he was senior to Scotty, they decided it was time for Scotty to take over Caruthers's job. This put Scotty in the first boat with the patrol leader, Captain Nguyen, and Caruthers in the second boat with the extra supplies.

They got off to a rocky start putting the boats into a stream feeding the Song Vam Co Dong river year-round. The boats held the twenty-five-man patrol with some added equipment and rations in the center of each boat.

An hour into the slow paddling upstream the boats ran into unexpected trouble. Scotty felt his boat come to an abrupt stop about the same time he felt some pressure against his knees through the thin bamboo bottom.

Three of the soldier-paddlers immediately started chattering about the problem as they leaped over the side to free the boat from whatever halted its progress.

Instead of pulling the boat forward over the obstacle, the soldiers pushed it backward—into Caruthers's boat. It immediately started to float again. Still, they had not cleared the underwater obstacle.

Two of the soldiers from the lead boat searched blindly under the waterline, only their heads above water. Scotty could see one suddenly smile as he began to chatter cheerfully in Vietnamese. He pulled and tugged and finally brought a large knot of tangled reeds, roots and all, from the bottom of the narrow river bed. He and the other two soldiers heaved the bundle up onto the bank, The finder was proud to stand in what had been the high spot to show all he had cleared the channel.

Scotty was glad to see the obstacle gone. But he was concerned about the sound of their voices carrying in the flat of the surrounding area and the fact they had now left evidence on the bank someone had passed that way.

During the night the problem of blocked channels from the increased flow of rain and runoff into the streams and rivers happened three more times. Scotty was pleased to see the change in the behavior and improved noise discipline as they got ever closer to their objective. He just wished they had been quieter earlier.

As planned, the move to the abandoned hamlet near the Cambodian border would take two days. With the passing hours, the pressure on the patrol to find someplace to lay up during the day grew. The lack of adequate vegetation gave them very few options.

Just before dawn on the morning of the second day, Scotty passed the word back to the other boats after Captain Nguyen picked a suitable tree stand which would hide the entire patrol.

It was square and small, no more than fifteen meters on a side, but it was large enough to hide everyone if they stayed down and didn't draw any attention to the cluster of trees.

To hide from sight and reduce the chances their movement into the area would be discovered they emptied their boats of men and equipment before it got light. They then swamped their boats and sunk them in the stream next to the trees which would conceal them.

Scotty stepped out of his boat onto the spongy ground hoping to find some more firmness in the trees. Dragging his combat gear, rifle and his radio with him, he moved slowly, waiting for the sucking muck to release his boots with each step. He found a tree with some exposed roots to sit on he guessed would hold him and some of his gear out of the rotting marsh.

It took almost half an hour for the patrol members to get into the trees, set up a defensive perimeter and settle to avoid being seen once the sun came up.

Scotty knew the daylight hours were going to offer the only opportunity for him to get some sleep. Still, he pulled out his map and spent a few more minutes memorizing the relative positions of key landmarks along their patrol route. He wanted not to have to pull out his map to orient himself should they make unexpected enemy contact along the way.

By nine in the morning Scotty still had not gotten any sleep. The swamps were crawling with small, determined flies. And no matter what he did he couldn't avoid the weather extremes, which alternated between blistering hot when it wasn't raining and bone-chilling downpour when it was. He sat up and looked around the perimeter. Twenty-four other people all trying not to move, not to make noise and not to be seen. From the small clump of trees only marginally concealing them, Scotty could look out in almost any direction across miles of flat marshland untilled, uninhabited and uninterrupted save a few more clumps of trees like theirs.

Scotty tried to fill the time until he could sleep with checking, re-checking and cleaning up his gear—all mud covered or waterlogged from the first night's boat trip.

Three hours later he was out of small tasks to do unlikely to draw attention or make noise. People think it is easy to sit still for hours. But the tempta-tion was great to move about, get comfortable, stretch, scratch, cough even get up to take a piss. Any unnecessary motion was asking for trouble. No one could be sure there wasn't a single enemy soldier somewhere out in the reeds with the sole purpose of keeping an eye out for the approach of patrols like Scotty's.

He looked at his watch, its face so caked with decayed organic matter from the ground he had to scrape it clean with his thumbnail and polish the smeared mud with his fatigue shirt. The watch hands had hardly moved.

He tried to pull his canteen from its carrier without making any large moves or noise. As he put the spout to his lips and inhaled the strong chemical odor of the water purification tablets dissolved in the cloudy wa-ter, he wasn't sure if he was really thirsty or bored and eager to get moving.

Returning his canteen to its carrier, Scotty leaned back on his ruck-sack. Comfortable he had done all he needed to do to be prepared to move out after dark, he let his mind drift to Eileen and home. Simply bringing it to mind tugged at the center of his chest. Belton, Florida seemed so far away and from another time. He closed his eyes and tried to picture Eileen. The first image to come to him was her in school. Her hair was longer then, and she wore skirts with petticoats—attractive skirts, not the matronly ones she had to wear to work at Ronnie's. He let his mind linger on her walking down the hallway of Palms High, her calves tapering into the bobbie socks she wore with her loafers. The image seemed to be even farther back in his past than it actually was. He mentally counted the months then multiplied out the days until he would be going home. No matter how many days he had left, they all combined into months—plural. It seemed like an eternity. It was becom-ing clear to him he had something he'd never thought much about—a future. A future with Eileen.

He let himself dwell on her face as he drifted off to a light sleep.

＊＊＊

"Hayes!"

Caruthers's raspy whisper woke Scotty from a much deeper sleep than he had even thought possible in the muck and rain. "Yeah? What? What's wrong?"

Caruthers's put his hand on Scotty's arm. "Nothing. So far, we're okay. But we're moving out in a hour."

"Got it." Scotty sat up, his shirt sticking to his back, saturated with a paste of water, mud and decayed black slime. He reached around and tried to pull the shirt from his skin. "Great. 'I wanna be an Airborne-Ranger . . .,'" he whispered to himself—the words of the Jody cadence he had sung so many times double-timing in formation back at Fort Benning.

He rubbed his eyes and looked out to the limits of his vision, darkness setting in. He tried to look back to the southeast, toward the small towns and hamlets on the larger river. He could no longer see the day's end traffic of carts, oxen and farmers all headed home. It was as dark where he had come from as where they were going. At that point it hit him: They were really deep in enemy territory. And they were only one day into the patrol.

One more check of his gear and Scotty started on himself. He reapplied camouflage stick to his face, neck, hands and exposed forearms. The rain and sweat had removed most of what he had applied before dawn to get him through the day. As he stroked his skin with the huge lipstick-like tubes of makeup, he began to inventory the toll the patrol was already taking on him. His hands and arms were covered with small cuts from the sawgrasses. Everywhere he had lumps and bumps from mosquito bites. He found several spots where an attacker was effective, some still stubbornly attached to his skin.

He pulled his plastic bottle of bug repellent from his shirt pocket and squirted it onto his hands, drenching them and then rubbing the excess on his neck and face. The solvent in the repellent made the camouflage stick's waxy pigment dissolve a little and go on more smoothly without crumbling.

He checked his work with the metal signal mirror he kept on a small chord around his neck. In the dark his image was far from clear, but what he could see showed him where he had missed exposed white skin sure to give him away and compromise the patrol or even cost him his life. If he could see anything in the mirror so could the Viet Cong.

While some of the soldiers slipped out of the tree stand and back into the stream bed to refloat the boats, Scotty turned to Captain Nguyen to make eye contact and let him know he was available, should he need him.

Nguyen simply acknowledged Scotty's readiness with a slow nod.

Scotty couldn't quite figure Nguyen out, yet. He seemed to understand more English than he spoke or let on and was a man of few words in either language. He treated Scotty as an equal despite the great difference in their ranks. And he never seemed to pester Scotty with endless requests for personal favors. But he was not afraid to approach Scotty when he wanted to know something with his three-word question: "Show me, please."

He could have ended up with a much worse counterpart than Nguyen. For this, Scotty said a small thank you.

Proximity was everything. The closer the wobbly boats got to the objective area the more vigilant they all became. Scotty couldn't make out many faces in the full-on darkness, but he could see the postures of the soldiers. Those who were paddling were careful not to clunk the wooden paddles together or hit the side of the boat. Those not paddling, entrusted with the security of the boats, held their weapons high and ready—their heads on near swivels watching for the slightest irregularity in the surrounding terrain. And the soldiers in each boat tasked to empty the bilge by scooping out water using number ten vegetable cans from the mess hall did so quietly. They took care to first scoop without scraping the bamboo bottoms awash with seepage. Then they quietly dipped the cans into the water over the side, turning them upside down to empty without splashing. Training was paying off.

Scotty turned to look over his shoulder. Navigation in a small boat at night was one of the most difficult skills any infantryman had to master. At least walking the soldier could check his direction with his compass and his distance by counting his pace. The first thing every Ranger learns is his own pace—how many steps it takes for him to move one hundred meters in the bush. Scotty knew his cold—one hundred and twenty-one paces would put him at the hundred-meter mark on flat land, more going up or down hill. But his pace was no good to him in a boat moving at a speed he could not calculate. And without landmarks along the banks to help him, the best he could do was stay oriented on where they had come from. The small towns behind them threw a faint glow of light up onto the cloud cover letting Scotty know they were still heading west—toward Cambodia. But he was uncomfortable now knowing exactly where he was on the ground.

They continued paddling, first turning off on one tributary to the stream, then, another hour later to an even smaller stream—all flowing out of the west.

His neck ached, and the small of his back began to burn from kneeling in the boat for so long. Scotty scrubbed the face of his watch against his leg again to clear the new layer of dirt and mud from it and held it up to see the marginally readable radium dial. Zero one hundred hours military time—one a.m. and they were still paddling.

Scotty craned his neck and straightened up to see over the heads of the others in his boat. The blackness: Cambodia was out in front of them— somewhere. No towns, no inhabited villages and visible signs of life. But every man on the patrol knew they were heading toward a sanctuary filled with hundreds, if not thousands of enemy soldiers, way stations, ammunition caches, hidden training areas, mess and sleeping facilities. All concealed and now covered again by a second cloak—darkness. Scotty's guess was they were pretty close to their objective—the abandoned hamlet.

Captain Nguyen held up the small armada. He turned to Scotty, said, "Boats here," and pointed at an overhang on the inside of a turn in the stream. According to their patrol plan, they would submerge the boats and walk the rest of the way to the hamlet using the streambed to conceal their tracks.

Offloading all the gear, weapons, rations and ammunition from the boats to the patrol members' backs took nearly a half an hour to do quietly. Scotty was impressed with the further increase in noise discipline within the patrol. He knew what they knew—anything, any slip, clank, bang or splash, could unleash enemy fire and get them killed.

While four of the soldiers finished tying the boats to underwater roots, Nguyen took Scotty and three others forward to find the hamlet. Caruthers stayed behind with the remainder of the patrol waiting to be brought forward after the advanced party found the hamlet.

Unlike a linear ambush, Nguyen put the two dozen soldiers into a tight perimeter inside the small hamlet consisting of four abandoned single-room thatched huts and one larger hut which appeared to have once been someone's home on a few hectares of soggy farmland. The onetime owners had planted trees all around the small cluster of structures and erected a broken down fenced pen to hold livestock. His efforts provided some concealment for the patrol members. The owners had been gone for years, but the trees grew anyhow.

Scotty walked around the entire perimeter at a crouch to lower his profile against the blue-black sky and checked each soldier's field of fire more to see where everyone was than to oversee Nguyen's placement.

By the time Scotty got back to the command post where Nguyen, his radio operator, Caruthers and the medic had set up it was nearly dawn and time for everyone to freeze in place and see what the day would bring. Scotty hoped the south side of the perimeter would offer a good view of any infiltration trails coming out of Cambodia.

Knowing their survival would depend entirely on staying hidden, each man in the patrol began pulling grasses and reeds from the ground to camouflage themselves, replacing the wilted vegetation they had picked up the day before.

Back in the command post, Scotty unpacked his ammunition and began to inspect it. The last thing any soldier wanted was to suffer a stoppage in the middle of a firefight because he had neglected to keep his ammo clean. As he inspected each magazine, he realized he was beginning to feel an even greater sense of danger. Just a couple of football fields from the Cambodian border put him closer to the largest enemy threat he had faced since arriving in Vietnam. He knew full well the hamlet they had chosen was easily within the range of enemy mortars on the other side of the imaginary dividing line. And his division's artillery was not able to reach out to help the patrol. This gave the enemy an advantage and sanctuary.

He pulled out his map and dropped in onto the flat side of his radio in front of his knees. With a single spin, he oriented the map to true north and matched up the few landmarks on the map with the reality of his surroundings.

Finally, he checked the receiver of his rifle for a round well seated into the chamber and set it aside before he touched up his camouflage makeup again.

The day droned on with the hum of insects and small birds in the flooded fields surrounding them. Scotty shielded himself from the intense periods of sun between the rain squalls by tucking himself and his equipment into a fragile and still partially thatched lean-to which must have once served to keep dried fish and grain up above the waterline. As he gazed out onto the flats between the hamlet and the border he spotted something unusually black. The motion fired up his senses making him reflexively raise his rifle to the ready. It was a shiny black. The glimpse alerted him to the chance of a Viet Cong soldier in wet black pajamas they called *ao ba*.

Scotty pulled his binoculars from his rucksack and trained them on the small dark spot almost two hundred meters outside their perimeter. With his naked eye, he could see some movement, not unlike someone crawling close to the ground. But with his binoculars, he could see it clearly. It was not just black. It was steel blue, black and the darkest of nighttime violets. It was a crow—a large common crow. Scotty relaxed and felt a little silly.

The crow was busy attacking something out of Scotty's field of view, something obscured by the marshy grasses and reeds. Whatever it was, the crow ripped small pieces of whatever he was standing on and ate them with gusto and urgency.

"Corbeau?"

Scotty pulled his glasses away from his face and looked to find Captain Nguyen. Vietnamese was still an alien language to Scotty. But when the officers slipped easily from Vietnamese to French and then to broken English it was even more difficult. He followed Nguyen's eye line out to the bird ripping at its prey. "Oh, *crow*, right?"

Nguyen nodded and smiled, something rare for him. "Oui." He tried to copy Scotty, "Crauw."

"Good enough." Scotty nodded and smiled back.

Nguyen pointed back at a place he had made for himself under the overhang of a thatched wall which once stood upright on one of the decayed structures.

Scotty nodded and whispered, "Okay, Dai Uy. I got it," in answer to the unspoken request for Scotty to keep an eye on things while Nguyen got some sleep.

Scotty spent the better part of an hour scanning the terrain in all directions—with emphasis to the west but often returned to the crow. He was entertained by the crow's tendency to project courage. The bird failed to show any sign of fear about predators that might be around him. Still, he ate while constantly looking about for threats to his survival—as Scotty had been doing. But the crow seemed much cooler about it. No, the crow had a haughtiness about him and an arrogance announcing he ruled his territory and it was his lunch time.

The weather seemed not to be a problem for the crow either. As Scotty watched the clouds boiled up and poured for several minutes and then stopped again. Rain or not, the crow ate and held his head up with attitude.

Once he had finished, the crow took flight and was quickly joined by a second crow Scotty had not seen before. This bothered Scotty—somewhere near the first crow and near the patrol some other motion had taken place he had not noticed. He tried to reassure himself the second crow must have been in a somewhat deeper depression or hidden behind a larger tuft of marsh grasses, but the fact remained with him—something had happened within a few hundred meters of his location, and he missed it.

He watched the pair of crows soaring, flying together but not in unison like ducks or geese. They found thermals, climbed onto them eliminating the need to flap their wings as they rose to higher altitudes searching the ground below for more food. As they circled, they adjusted their direction by making ever so slight changes to the large splayed feathers at the ends of their wings and a twist of their tails.

As the breezes continued out of the east the crows' orbits moved farther and farther away until they were specks in the sky and their irritating caws were smothered up again by the return of still another rain squall over Scotty.

As night fell, Scotty, Caruthers, and Nguyen moved from their centrally located command post in the center of the cluster of crumbling hootches to positions on the south and west of the perimeter. This to add firepower and extra eyes to the job of watching the border for activity. Their assumption was any Viet Cong who had crossed the border the night before was well east of them, had been laying up during the day and would continue to infiltrate deeper into Vietnam once darkness fell again. Those they could do little about.

But new infiltrators would cross as soon as it got dark enough for them to feel they could move without being seen. Scotty knew it would be another long night of watching and waiting. At least it was a reconnaissance patrol, and they were not expected to bring back any scalps or put a major battle victory on the books before they were finished. If they could just confirm the often-denied claim the Viet Cong were staging out of an assembly area only a long stone's throw from their positions, they would accomplish their mission.

Even before it got completely dark, the mosquitoes begin to feast on Scotty and the others. Scotty pulled the olive drab cravat from his neck and his bottle of bug juice out of his pocket. The cravat was actually intended to be a sling in a first aid packet in its first life. But soldiers in Vietnam had learned it made an effective and lightweight sweat rag and kept bugs and twigs from slipping into the necks of their fatigue shirts while out in the field.

Scotty crumpled up his cravat, squirted it liberally with insect repellent and then retied it loosely around his neck. The smell of the repellent filled the air around his face and gave him some temporary relief from the insistent attackers.

Dusk had turned into an inky darkness and the night took on a different symphony of harmonizing insects, night birds and the sounds of distant thunder. The thunder was somewhere so far off it was only a rumble now and then. Scotty periodically looked back in the direction of the Sugar Mill some thirty miles to their rear for any sign of light or evidence of approaching rain.

If he could see the glow from the lights of the populated strip along the highway bouncing off the clouds, he knew there was a high enough cloud cover to allow helicopters to fly to them if they got into serious trouble.

Sometimes the glow gave him reassurance. Other times during the night he could see no sign of light meaning the ceiling had dropped enough to isolate them and keep help from coming should they need it.

With nothing he could do about the division's ability to respond to contact, Scotty decided to dismiss it and focus on the task at hand. To do anything else would just make him more anxious with no way to change things.

He strained to see anything moving out in the flatland to his front. Simply distinguishing the sky from the ground was nearly impossible because it was so dark. He raised his binoculars to his face knowing they sometimes helped make the darkness only slightly easier to see through because of the optics' ability to intensify ambient light and detect movement. He scanned the terrain to the front and then swung around to the right—the west.

As he did, a streak of light slashed across his binoculars' field of view in the opposite direction. Not sure what he had seen, Scotty slowly retraced the arc until the slash appeared again. He steadied his elbows, took a breath and slowly let half of it out to eliminate as much binocular movement as he could then scanned back to the west, again.

Bingo! He found it. It *was* a light. A single, weak and distant light. Scotty quickly pulled his rifle from its place next to his elbow and laid it on the ground pointing exactly in the direction of the light. He needed some reference point to help him find the same spot to watch should the light go out.

Back inside the narrow field of view set by the limits of his binoculars, Scotty found the light again. It appeared to be a single gas lamp or candle, but he was sure if it was beyond the border. Still, he couldn't be sure at all how far away it was. With nothing to compare it to and no knowledge of the size of the flame, his guess could be from three to five hundred meters. Not useful for much except the inherent fact there was life where there was a light. And the life was most likely Viet Cong. He felt his pulse begin to quicken.

By the time Scotty got to Nguyen's position it had started raining hard again. All he could do was tell the captain what he saw and wait for him to call it in to Division Operations. Neither of them could see the light through the downpour even if it was still burning out in the downpour.

Around midnight the rain let up again. Scotty pulled his binoculars from inside his shirt where he had been trying to keep it dry to prevent condensation from forming inside the lens barrels. He reached out and found the short section of bamboo pole he brought back to his position from Nguyen's. He had replaced his rifle with the bamboo and trained his binoculars in the direction the stick was pointing hoping to find the light again.

No luck. It was dark in the lenses of his binoculars even though the air between him and the original source of the light was clear and free of fog. He searched for twenty minutes and then rested his eyes before trying again.

Scotty wondered how many VC had been able to slip by the patrol under cover of darkness helped by the curtain the rain had been placing between them. He began to wonder if they would be able to see anything at all. The patrol was scheduled to stay in the abandoned hamlet for two nights and three days. Any longer would just increase the chances they would be compromised and become a target for the Viet Cong. He knew the chances of success rested on the weather. If the rain continued, they would have no more success in the remaining night of the patrol than they had the on the first night. Visibility was everything.

Suddenly, Scotty heard movement to his front. Sloshing, someone or something was moving through the tangle of weeds and low brush. He looked to his left and could see the Vietnamese soldier next to him had also heard the noise.

They waited. And the noise continued—who or whatever was making it moved slowly and deliberately. Scotty turned to move to Nguyen's position to tell him of the noise and found him already crawling his way on his hands and knees.

Scotty and Nguyen continued to watch, seeing nothing, they continued to listen as the noise got farther and farther away—headed in the direction of Saigon.

Nguyen cupped the handset to his radio to his mouth to reduce the chance of being heard as he called for artillery support. While they couldn't fire an explosive round far enough to kill or injure whoever was moving through the marshland, they could light up the night.

In a matter of minutes, the night air was cut by the ripping arc of an artillery flare shell, which burst high over the marshland and several miles east of the patrol's position.

The flare wobbled under a small parachute which extended its time of descent and allowed Scotty and Nguyen to see more clearly the terrain in front of them. They searched it first for anyone else moving toward them and then turned to look in the direction they guessed the trespasser had gone.

Scotty trained his binoculars on the marshland now rendered spooky by the artificial light hanging above it but saw nothing.

Nguyen tapped Scotty on the arm and directed his attention to a point back toward the border.

There, illuminated by the flare, were the faces of three Viet Cong soldiers spaced nearly fifty meters apart, down on their bellies in the swampy water for security but unable to resist looking around themselves for any sign of South Vietnamese soldiers.

They were more evidence of infiltration. Scotty looked down at the stick he had placed on the ground to orient himself on where he had last seen the lamp. The stick pointed almost directly at the distant infiltrators.

CHAPTER 18

Scotty could tell it was not going to be good news when he saw Caruthers crawling toward him. "What's up, Sarge?"

Caruthers stopped crawling and got up on one elbow to pull his map out of his pocket. "Got some new marchin' orders from the Sugar Mill."

Scotty picked up the handset to his radio, pressed it to his ear and pressed the press-to-talk switch a couple of times. "Didn't hear it on mine."

Caruthers squirted a wire-like stream of chewing tobacco into a nearby clump of grass and shook his head. "I wouldn't count on hearing much with that antenna." He was referring to the difference in antenna lengths between his radio and Scotty's. The second radio with Scotty could be counted on to talk to Caruthers's radio but not the Sugar Mill's.

"So what's up?" Scotty asked.

"Well, *Colonel* Pascoe got me out of a good dream to tell me to pass on a change of mission to you and Nguyen, like I'm some kinda' fuckin' messenger boy."

It was obvious to Scotty Caruthers still wasn't convinced Pascoe deserved a promotion by the sarcasm he attached to Pascoe's title. "What's he want?"

"He ain't happy. Ain't happy about the VC what slipped by us. Ain't happy we haven't been able to find Ho Chi Minh's whole fuckin' headquarters out here and he ain't happy he couldn't get you on the radio."

"Shit!" Scotty replied. "Give me better equipment, and I could talk to Saigon!"

"Gets worse," Caruthers added.

"How so?"

"Seems he convinced General Minh to tell Dai Uy Nguyen to send out a small detail to see what's what over there." He pointed toward the border. Toward where they had seen the three infiltrators and where he had seen the light.

He thought of the crows. "What? There's no way to keep from being spotted moving out there if you're over a foot tall. Hell, the only tree stands are hundreds of meters apart where there aren't even any between us and that location."

Caruthers tapped a spot on his map where the two countries met. "Yeah, it may be, but he wants a small recon party to sneak on out after dark and move closer to the bad guys."

"That's damn near suicide!" Scotty said, trying to keep his voice hushed.

"I'll go out with 'em. We'll be okay," Caruthers said, tucking his map back into his pocket and spitting more tobacco into the marsh.

"No. I'm Nguyen's counterpart now. You're too short. If you got shot up out there—"

Caruthers interrupted Scotty. "One condition. If you go with Nguyen's party I want ta' reorganize the stay behinds back here as a reaction force, jus' in case y'all make contact."

"I can't imagine Nguyen would have a problem with that."

"Good," was all Caruthers said before scooping up his rifle, spitting again, spinning on his stomach and crawling back toward the command post.

Later, back at the command post in the center of the perimeter, Scotty, Caruthers and Captain Nguyen stretched out on their bellies, heads only inches apart under a poncho. With the poncho keeping the light from the red filtered flashlight being visible in the night, they all looked at the map on the group between them. Nguyen took a grease pencil and drew a black loop from the hamlet to a point right at the Cambodian border and back to the hamlet.

Not coming back by the same way they went out needed no discussion between them. They all knew it was the fastest way to get ambushed.

"Good, Dai Uy," Scotty said, even though he wished there was some kind of terrain features to conceal their movement—hills, ditches, treelines—anything but two foot high reeds sticking out of stagnant marsh water.

Nguyen circled a small blue dashed symbol on the map. It signified an intermittent stream. They could only tell if it was a good enough stream or not by going to take a look at it. "Maybe rain," he added.

Scotty raised his hand and twisted his fingers together. "I'll keep my fingers crossed," he said, also hoping for some advantage the rain would give them to keep from being spotted.

Nguyen looked at his hand and then back to Scotty, puzzled.

"Oh, it means you hope for good luck."

Nguyen nodded. "Yes. Custom?"

"Yes," Scotty said, feeling a little foolish.

***

The next day was spent like the earlier ones—re-rigging gear, getting some rest and checking ammo, weapons, and radios.

It was almost nine p.m. of the second night in the abandoned hamlet when they finally left the perimeter. Scotty, Nguyen, Sergeant Tran—the medic and a soldier named Khoi. They carried only weapons and ammo, no headgear or rucksacks as the crawled forward into the stream bed nearest the perimeter. The rain had swelled it enough to be a source of concealment and a way to move more quietly than slogging through the mud.

Scotty followed Nguyen into the stream bed not much wider than his shoulders. The two-foot deep water hardly moved as it followed the stream's channel meandering in easy turns with no abrupt changes in direction. He held his rifle up out of the water with one hand while half crawling, half floating along the stream bed.

The four moved for not more than thirty minutes before Nguyen held them up to listen. It was so dark they all knew unless they stumbled upon an enemy ambush set for them they would be more likely to hear a threat moving in the dark marsh than see it.

While they were listening, Scotty checked his compass to make sure he knew where the perimeter was in case they had to escape contact and run back to where the others still remained in the hamlet. He raised his head and looked back in the direction of the hamlet but could not make it out in the darkness. His guess was they had moved about four hundred meters to the west which put them within a few hundred meters from actually being inside Cambodia. Knowing exactly where the border was was not possible. It wasn't like it was marked. On one side it was swampy, marshy Vietnam, and on the other side, it was the same swampy, marshy terrain.

Once Nguyen was satisfied it was safe to move on, he led the four onward by simply moving out, letting the other three follow. Their movement was slow, and the water was beginning to chill the small patrol.

Captain Nguyen stopped them after another thirty minutes of very deliberate movement. He moved back to Scotty and pointed off to the west and then touched his ear. He had heard something.

Scotty strained to hear something, anything. It began to rain lightly. The sounds of the patter on their wet uniforms created even more ambient noise to complicate hearing something far off. Hearing nothing, he simply shook his head to let Nguyen know.

The captain pulled out his own compass, took a reading to help orient himself and then got up to his knees on the stream's bottom and looked around in all directions. He looked back to Scotty. "We stay here."

Scotty pulled the radio handset from inside his shirt where it had been traveling wrapped tightly in a plastic bag which once held the radio's battery. He put the handset to his ear and without speaking pressed the transmit key four times to send the prearranged signal back to Caruthers and the rest of the patrol in the hamlet they were stopped at their observation point, and all was still okay.

After a few seconds, he got a single voice response transmission from Caruthers, "Roger. Understand you have reached the objective and your SITREP is negative. If that is correct reply with two squelch breaks."

Scotty squeezed the press-to-talk button on the handset twice causing the constant hissing of the rushing noise in the earpiece of the handset to be interrupted by silence twice at each end.

Caruthers took the initiative to end the transmission. "Roger that. Out."

The four climbed up the slick bank of the stream bed to get out of the running water for what was left the night even if only to trade it for muddy, marshy grasses next to the bank. They positioned themselves in a starlike pattern covering all four cardinal directions of the compass, their feet nearly touching in the middle. Scotty found himself facing the border.

They would spend the night not moving, not making any noise if they could avoid it while they watched and listened. It was silent beyond the night creatures and the rain which sometimes slacked but never really stopped.

Nguyen tapped Scotty and then Khoi to get their attention. He put his hands prayer-like up against the side of his face and closed his eyes to tell them he wanted them to get some sleep.

Scotty's nervous system was on full alert for any sound, smell, or noise promising danger. He found it hard to sleep with most of his body in water two inches deep on top of a bed of rushes and mud the consistency of cake frosting. He found himself fighting his body's competing demands for rest and alertness. He felt himself drift in and out of full consciousness. Wanting not to miss a radio call, he cradled the radio handset in the crook of his neck.

Every hour he heard Caruthers report the situation was negative back to the Division Operations Center at the Sugar Mill. They had arranged for Caruthers to make the reports and if he heard nothing from Scotty and Nguyen he'd simply pass on they were seeing and hearing nothing by submitting a negative SITREP.

Just before dawn, Scotty began to think about what they needed to do to get back to the hamlet before the skies became too light to conceal their movement.

He heard the handset crackle and looked at his watch. It was not on the hour—the specified reporting time for Caruthers to call Division. The transmission was weak and broken, but he recognized the voice. It was Pascoe back at the Sugar Mill. He told Caruthers to pass on to Nguyen and Scotty General Minh wanted them to stay out on their reconnaissance one more night.

Though the transmission was weak and intermittent on Pascoe's end, Scotty heard Caruthers argue with Pascoe. He told him they'd been out in the water long enough and would be in a terribly exposed position during the day if they waited it out to stay another night. His words did nothing to persuade Pascoe. Finished arguing with Pascoe, Caruthers finally conceded. He then called Scotty only to find out through a fluke in the atmospheric conditions most of the transmission from the Sugar Mill had bounced out enough to allow Scotty to monitor the conversation with Pascoe.

The change in plans meant Scotty, Nguyen, Tran and Khoi would have to spend the day on their back or bellies to keep from being seen by anyone. There was nothing tall enough near them to conceal them should they sit up or stand.

Scotty resigned himself to the mission change and welcomed the warming sunrise. Still, he was conscious of the fact daylight would bring a greater risk of being detected only a stone's throw from the Viet Cong staging area on the others side of the invisible border.

By noon Scotty's skin was white with wrinkles from the water and he, along with the other three, were trying to shield their faces from the sun baking them between the rain squalls passing in a hurry to get somewhere else. He felt the pain of wet fatigues sticking to his ankles inside his boots—the folds making creases in his skin. His waist burned from the rubbing of his belted trousers and pistol belt cutting into his now more fragile skin with every small move.

His body was a bundle of distracting sensations, aches, and pains. While his face and neck were burning in the sun, his butt was cold and sore from sitting in the wet marsh. The water constantly running from the ground beneath him to the nearby stream pulled heat from the core of his body.

His stomach grumbled. The thought of eating was at once appealing and unappetizing. All the members of the Advisory Team had accepted Pascoe's policy of eating what their Vietnamese counterparts ate. This meant not carrying American C-Rations. Instead, Scotty had a single meal in his shirt pocket, a meal of cold rice and fish. He knew he had to eat and remembered he hadn't eaten for almost twenty-four hours.

Scotty looked over at Nguyen and Khoi who were finishing their meals and decided he could start. At least two of them needed to be ready to return fire at any time. They couldn't all be eating in case they were suddenly attacked.

He opened the wrapper containing his meal. The rice was gooey and clumped inside the banana palm wrapper. Some of it was even soggy from water that seeped in through the plastic bag he had tried to protect it with.

He ate with is fingers, at first avoiding the four anchovy-size fish laid in parallel fashion across the rectangular loaf of cold rice. They looked up at him, head, scales, eyes and all. He girded himself for the worst and popped the first one into his mouth knowing it would be the only source of protein he would have all day. The small patrol would not eat again until they returned to the hamlet with Caruthers and the others.

The rain came and went again in the same pattern it had been demonstrating for almost a week. The sky was dark with clouds and the sun finally cooled behind the passing clouds as it dove for the horizon off in the direction of Cambodia. The four prepared for another uncomfortable night in the marsh.

As the sun was setting Nguyen elbowed Scotty. They both heard it. A metallic clunk, then another.

How far off was hard to tell with the rain falling slowly and steadily. The sounds gripped Scotty's chest like a huge claw sending even more demanding messages through his system. They all signaled him to ratchet up his vigilance one more notch. The sounds meant people, and that meant enemy troops close, maybe within rifle range.

Then the sounds stopped as quickly as they started. Scotty turned to look at Nguyen to see if he might be hearing anything Scotty was missing. He found an equally puzzled look on Nguyen's face.

Without warning the night went from silent to a series of loud metallic thunks. Four, then five, then six thunks. These were followed immediately by the equally unmistakable sounds of outgoing mortar rounds. Each sliced through the coming night air over the four men huddled near the stream bed.

Scotty spun around to look in the direction of the hamlet and held his breath for what he knew was inevitable: The first four, then the fifth and then the sixth mortar round hit the hamlet with ear-popping crack-thump explosions visible as dark smoke and large sprays of water.

As quickly as the mortars stopped detonating at the hamlet, intense automatic small arms fire broke out. Scotty got up on his knees and could see the exchange of green Viet Cong AK-47 tracers and Vietnamese red tracers. The streaks of color skimmed along hugging the ground and either burned out, went into the mud or ricocheted into the sky in wild and unpredictable angles and arcs.

It was clear to Scotty Caruthers's perimeter had been spotted. They'd been targeted, and now they'd been attacked by an enemy force Scotty estimated to be greater than fifteen riflemen and three machine guns. Scotty's heart pounded as his first impulse was to get up and run in their direction. Before he did, he heard his radio come to life. He stuck a finger in his free ear to drown out the shooting sounds and pressed the headset to the other. It was Caruthers's voice speaking to the Tactical Operations Center back at the Sugar Mill.

He was remarkably calm but concise and clear. "Contact! Contact! Incoming mortars and ground attack. Estimate platoon, maybe company size assault. I've got wounded. Lots of wounded. Need help. Now! Over."

There was no answer on the other end.

Caruthers's voice came back on the radio. Not as calm. "Is anybody fucking awake back there, goddamnit? We are under attack, and I have wounded. I need gunships, and I need MEDEVAC now!"

A timid voice with a heavy Vietnamese accent replied, "Roger. Stand-by."

Scotty leaned over and whispered into Nguyen's ear to tell him what he had heard on the radio and then asked what his orders were.

Nguyen shook his head. "We stay. Cannot help."

The words cut through Scotty's belly. He knew the captain was right. The only way they could get there in time to help with four more rifles was if they ran. And if they ran they would surely be spotted and cut down before they got close. So far it didn't appear the Viet Cong knew there was a smaller patrol detached from the patrol base they were attacking.

"Gunships?" Pascoe asked.

"They come from Tay Ninh," General Minh answered as he lifted his chopper off the helipad at the Sugar Mill.

Pascoe looked out over the wall surrounding the compound at the final traces of sunset throwing a very pale pink glow over the landscape. He tried to calm his anxieties as Minh turned the chopper west toward the encircled troops in the hamlet.

Pascoe's mouth felt dry, and his gut began to cramp up. He had been in Vietnam for months, except incoming fire at the compound, he had never been near an actual firefight nor had he been in a chopper taking enemy fire. He knew that was about to change. His eyes drifted to the altimeter as if encouraging Minh to hurry up and get the chopper to a safer altitude outside the effective range of most small arms fire.

He looked over his left and right shoulders outside the chopper. "General, where are the extraction ships?"

"We meet them there," Minh replied nodding his head in the direction of the beleaguered hamlet.

The two were interrupted by Caruthers's voice in their helmet headsets. His voice was raspy, and the strain was obvious. In the background, they could both hear the continuing gunfire as Caruthers's spoke trying to be distinct: ". . . six KIA, five seriously wounded and need immediate evacuation. Can you give me an ETA on the MEDEVAC?"

Pascoe knew Caruthers had probably taken control of the defense of the hamlet since the senior Vietnamese soldier was a sergeant who only spoke Vietnamese and in Caruthers's opinion was ill-equipped to take charge. He had complained about the soldier often in training.

"Where the hell are the MEDEVAC choppers?" Caruthers asked.

Pascoe pressed the transmit button on the floor of the chopper with the toe of his boot. "They're coming. Stand-by . . ." He looked over at Minh who pointed to the north with his gloved index finger.

Just then the headset came alive again with another voice. "This is Dustoff 25, over." The MEDEVAC choppers were trying to contact Caruthers.

Caruthers answered using his radio callsign. "Dustoff, this is Sample Pirate 9, over." He seemed to be yelling over the voices of at least two Vietnamese soldiers speaking excitedly in the background.

"Pirate, this is Dustoff," the MEDEVAC pilot somewhere in the night replied. "We are inbound to your location with an ETA of fifteen minutes. Can you bring me up to speed?"

Looking through his windscreen, Pascoe spotted the rotating beacons of the two MEDEVAC choppers approaching from the northeast.

He kept his eyes on them as they crossed the sky in front of Minh's chopper and approached the firefight on the ground. Pascoe was watching the beginning of a ballet that would be played out thousands of times before the Vietnam War would end. Soldiers on the ground were trying to guide air ambulances to their location to pick up gravely wounded comrades while also trying to suppress incoming enemy fire long enough for the choppers to land safely and evacuate the wounded.

As Minh's chopper got close to the firefight site, Caruthers gave the information to the MEDEVAC pilot as two heavily laden gunships called hogs for their ungainly appearance flew by racing to the aid of the soldiers on the ground.

Pascoe finally saw the smoke. For all the noise and excited voices over the radio the small spot on the flat marshland appeared to be no more than something fairly small burning from fifteen hundred feet up and a mile away.

The gunships began coordinating with Caruthers and the MEDEVAC to determine the source and direction of the enemy fire and the greatest threat to the first MEDEVAC chopper. As they spoke, the first MEDEVAC chopper was already lining up half a mile out for an approach most likely to achieve success and draw the least amount of enemy fire.

Minh spoke to Pascoe over his chopper's intercom: "Why do we hear Caruthers? Was your new sergeant—ah, Hayes Captain Nguyen's advisor on this patrol?"

Pascoe stumbled over his answer quickly coming up with some excuse to explain why Hayes wasn't responding from the middle of the frantic firefight below them. "Ah . . . He might be helping with the wounded. I think he has more medical training than Caruthers."

Minh reached down on the console between them and checked the radio frequency dialed in. "I will try to get Nguyen on the other radio and find out."

The firefight went on for more than forty minutes while Scotty and the small detached party could only wait and watch the night light up with angry tracers and grenade explosions.

Scotty felt helpless, too far away to do any good but close enough to hear the fight and see the shooting. He kept the radio handset pressed to his ear and monitored the few hurried exchanges between Caruthers and the division radio operators. From what he heard Caruthers was told to wait for gunships to help him overcome the enemy fire and MEDEVAC choppers to pick up his wounded. That didn't satisfy Caruthers who kept calling for help every couple of minutes.

Scotty watched from the bog barely concealing the four members of his small detached party. With darkness painting away the daylight the night and the oncoming rain squall were all that hid them from the nearby enemy.

He realized they could not go to the aid of the embattled occupants of the hamlet. And their own survival depended entirely on being able to stay low in the water hoping that none of the enemy in the area discovered them. And hoping their own choppers didn't mistake them for VC.

The choppers quickly clustered and assumed their roles without added radio chatter. Minh's chopper took up a counterclockwise circular track in the sky as if on unseen rails. From it, they would oversee the operation.

The gunships zeroed in on the enemy firing positions with pass after firing pass, raining down machinegun bullets and rockets with each run.

The first MEDEVAC ship started bleeding off altitude as it slowed its approach to spot in the hamlet sure to draw the attention of everyone for two miles around and the fire from any Viet Cong within range.

Scotty raised his binoculars to his face and peered over the vegetation on the bank of the stream concealing him. He found himself holding his breath as the chopper emblazoned with a huge red cross on its nose turned on its landing light, flared a few feet short of the touchdown point, slowed even more and settled into the marsh grasses.

In the last few feet of its descent enemy fire shifted from the belea-guered patrol in the hamlet to the chopper in an attempt to bring it down.

The chopper disappeared behind some of the small trees in the hamlet, and Scotty held his breath as if doing so would increase the chances of getting the wounded out before the chopper got blown out of the sky.

As he watched, he heard General Minh's voice in the headset he held to his ear. He didn't understand what he was saying in Vietnamese, so he stretched his arm out and passed the handset to Captain Nguyen also watching for some sign the chopper was loaded with wounded and com-ing out of the hamlet safely.

Nguyen listened for a moment and then started talking hurriedly, clearly irritated. At the same time the chopper's blades reappeared over the trees hiding them, and its bulky fuselage soon followed.

Scotty started talking to himself, urging the pilots on. Coaching them out of earshot: "Come on. Come on. You can do it."

Enemy fire and occasional tracers reached up from the marshes to knock the bird from the sky. A section of the plexiglass chin bubble in front of the pilot's pedals in the right seat shattered and rained chunks of plastic as the chopper climbed and came in the direction of Scotty's four-man patrol huddled in the stream bed.

As the chopper screamed over Scotty's head, a second MEDEVAC chopper entered the hamlet landing on the spot vacated by the first. From what Scotty could see it too was taking on wounded and a half mile be-hind it a third chopper was lining up to land as soon as the bird on the ground cleared the trees.

From his position on the ground, there was no way for Scotty to know Sergeant Caruthers was one of the seriously wounded being loaded onto the MEDEVAC chopper, enemy bullets having found his leg in the open-ing seconds of the firefight.

Inside Minh's orbiting chopper Pascoe watched the three choppers conducting the medical evacuation—one in the air, one on the ground and one lift ship getting ready to land to pick up more. He couldn't help but overhear the heated conversation between Minh and Captain Nguyen on the ground.

Minh ended his transmission to Nguyen and turned to Pascoe to do something Vietnamese rarely did by custom—he looked Pascoe directly in the eyes. "Did you tell Nguyen to take small party closer to border?"

Pascoe stuttered. "Ah, no." Panic gripped him. He decided to just play dumb. "I mean . . . I thought you had instructed them to go. I ah . . . just assumed when I talked to Caruthers about it you had given instructions. But *I* didn't direct them to do anything." He wasn't sure if Minh could tell he was lying or not.

Minh didn't reply. Instead, he started speaking rapidly into his mouthpiece to the other pilots and to Nguyen on the ground.

Finished, he came back on the intercom and told Pascoe: "The gunships have been successful. Enemy fire has stopped." He pointed down at another chopper passing beneath them landing where the third chopper had just lifted off and continued, "He will pick up other soldiers in the hamlet."

Pascoe knew that the other four soldiers on the ground a thousand meters away were still there, still at risk and now more vulnerable than ever. "What about Nguyen's party?"

Minh watched the fourth chopper take on the remaining troops and then replied. "I sent my gunships back to rearm and refuel. When they return, we will pull out Nguyen and the others."

As fast as the chaos had occurred, it calmed. Scotty looked around at Nguyen. His face was red, and he was as aggravated as Scotty had ever seen him. He asked already knowing the captain had lost many of his soldiers, was not with them during the fight and was stranded on the ground with three others. "What is it, Dai Uy?"

"When gunships come again, we go."

"They're going to extract us?" Scotty asked for clarification.

Nguyen nodded yes and turned to tell Tran and Khoi to get ready.

Scotty looked up at the solo copper circling the area somewhere around two thousand feet above them—Minh's chopper. He felt like he should be doing something. But the others were gone, many dead and wounded and the four of them just had to wait and hope they weren't discovered before the next pickup chopper got to them or took effective enemy fire lifting off with them inside.

He checked his weapon again to make sure it was ready in case he needed to use it and looked back to the other three. They too were watching Minh's chopper slowly circle a safe distance from the ground.

Scotty checked his watch, trying to gauge how much longer they would have to wait for the gunships to rearm, refuel and then return to pluck them from their exposed position in the marsh. Then he heard it, a sucking noise. Someone was trying to pull a foot out of the muck. Someone not more than fifty meters from them. Scotty tried to look over the grasses without giving his position away.

Out of the corner of his eye, he caught Nguyen moving up next to him, his rifle at the ready. He too had heard the movement between them and the now evacuated hamlet.

They waited. Scotty didn't have to ask Nguyen why he didn't call the General's chopper to tell him they had heard movement. The risk was he'd be heard, and the movement just might be the Viet Cong soldiers from the hamlet trying to get back to their base area across the border without getting caught by the choppers.

They held their breath and Scotty wondered if Minh and Pascoe could see anything from their orbit. Before he could speculate on how hard it might be to see men in black pajamas moving cautiously through the muddy marshes from above the first burst of enemy fire crossed near his right ear and hit its mark. Sergeant Tran gave out a clipped cry as he fell forward, his face dropping into the muddy stream forehead first.

Scotty turned to make eye contact with Nguyen as he slammed the radio handset to his face and called out for the only help they could count on.

Inside the chopper, Pascoe heard the voice "We are taking incoming small arms fire and have no, I say again *no* cover. One KIA!"

While Pascoe replied over the radio, he could hear Minh screaming at someone in Vietnamese over his. He assumed it was about the return of the gunships, which could make the difference between the survival of the three remaining soldiers on the ground and them being overrun by the enemy forces escaping from the hamlet contact back to the border. "Roger your situation. Stand-by."

Minh craned his neck to look out the side window in the door of the circling chopper for signs of the three huddled in the streambed. "We cannot wait."

"What do you want to do?" Pascoe asked.

"Tell your sergeant to throw smoke."

Pascoe realized that asking Hayes to throw a smoke grenade meant Minh wanted to be able to pick them out on the ground because he intended to fly in to pick up the survivors himself—even though they were still under attack and even though the gunships and the lift ships had not returned. He turned to Minh and stalled. "Are you sure you want to do this, General? You need not take this risk. Maybe we should wait for the gunships."

Minh gave Pascoe a clear expression of disapproval. "Colonel, I have soldiers down there. *You* have a soldier down there. We will go down. Get me smoke."

Pascoe made one more look over his shoulder toward the Sugar Mill searching the sky for the other choppers while he called Scotty using his radio callsign. "Sample Pirate 9 Alpha I need you to throw smoke and prepare for immediate extraction. Over."

There was no answer. He repeated the call.

On the ground, Scotty helped Nguyen pull the medical gear and ammo off of Tran's body. The radio handset bounced on Scotty's chest, the coiled cord wrapped around his neck to keep it out of the water.

Two more sharp bursts of automatic fire crossed over the three remaining in the streambed. It became obvious that there was more than one Viet Cong and they had the three in a crossfire.

Khoi jumped to his knees and angrily returned the fire of one of the Viet Cong but couldn't spin fast enough to fire on the other before he cut Khoi by down placing two AK-47 rounds in his midsection.

Scotty saw Khoi fall and picked up the handset only to hear Pascoe's voice telling him to throw a smoke grenade. He dismissed the instructions feeling he should tell Pascoe their situation had worsened, and they needed someone to get the VC off their backs before attempting to get them out.

Pascoe told Scotty to stand-by again and tried to change Minh's mind one more time. "General, Hayes says they're taking fire, and he needs suppressive fires first."

Minh did not respond. He looked out and down. He heeled the chopper over into a steep descending left turn.

Pascoe watched the altimeter unwind as the ground started to rush up toward the chopper. Just below twelve-hundred feet he heard a sharp metallic clap and hoped it wasn't what he thought it was. "General, I think we are taking fire."

Minh scanned the instruments searching for any sign of flight systems failures and kept the chopper on a steep and steady glide path toward Scotty and Nguyen. "I can see them."

Scotty gathered up as much as he could—half of the extra gear from the two dead soldiers. He turned to Khoi and began to lift his lifeless body as he kept an eye on the chopper closing on their position.

Nguyen grabbed Scotty's arm, looked at Khoi and shook his head.

Scotty was unsure. Over the firing and the growing sounds of the thumping chopper blades he asked, "Leave them?"

"Yes." Nguyen helped Scotty slide Khoi back down into the stream bed.

Pascoe felt the chopper slowing, its nose coming up, as it approached the two stranded soldiers waiting on the ground three hundred feet below and a few hundred meters in front of him. Suddenly the sky outside the came alive with bright bursts of red and green tracer fire much of it heavier than AK-47 rifle fire. He knew what it was but didn't want to believe it. They couldn't be taking such potentially lethal fire. They just couldn't.

He looked out the side window of the chopper. About five hundred meters to the west he saw it. There, inside Cambodia, a 12.7mm anti-aircraft machine gun manned by two helmeted gunners was spitting hundreds of bullets a minute at the descending chopper. Each round was the size of his thumb and longer than his fingers. Each capable of tearing huge chunks of the chopper away as it ripped through the aircraft's thin outer skin. Pascoe found himself completely frozen in fear as rounds zipped by the front of the chopper, and they kept flying nearer to the path of the enemy fire. He couldn't believe they were still in the air. He looked over at Minh, hoping he would break off the approach and get out of the enemy's gun sights.

Minh's gaze was fixed on a landing point he had selected on the ground. His fingers opened and closed repeatedly on the hand-grip of the cyclic control as the chopper neared the landing zone.

Nguyen and Scotty forced themselves to dial out the enemy fire coming from several directions and gauged the distance to the same spot the chopper was headed for. They jumped to their feet and began to run to meet their rescuers hoping to arrive at the chopper's touchdown point the moment it landed.

The enemy fire got worse. Scotty and Nguyen tried to spray fire back at the shooters more concerned with how much fire they could put out than how accurate it was.

Once the chopper came into better range, the enemy riflemen shifted their fires to the larger target.

Nguyen stopped long enough to drop to one knee, fired and cut down one of the Viet Cong soldiers foolishly standing in the marsh firing at the oncoming chopper.

The two kept running toward the chopper gasping for the air the needed to fuel their straining muscles.

As the ground got closer and in spite of the growing sense of panic he was feeling, some of Pascoe's training kicked in. He lightly and automatically put his hands on his matching set of controls and his feet on the pedals in the event he had to take over the flying. He held his breath and watched as Minh flared the chopper to bleed off forward speed and land it in the muck.

Scotty and Nguyen were still twenty long strides from the chopper, each step made more complicated by the extra weapons and equipment they carried while running in water a foot and a half deep. They splashed muddy water into their own faces as they ran, making visibility that much more difficult for them.

Pascoe watched the two struggling soldiers slog through the muddy marshes and heard himself urging the two on in his head. Come on. Run! Faster! Hurry! We can't wait . . .!

The long waiting moment inside the cockpit was jarred by the explosive sounds of two enemy rounds coming through the windscreen on Minh's side of the chopper. One round struck him just below the collarbone, and the other went into his helmet above his left eye.

Minh's blood and brain tissue flew across the cockpit hitting Pascoe face and shoulder. He was stunned. He watched Minh's head slump forward and felt the cyclic come free in his hand as Minh's fingers went limp, released their grip and fell from his matching flight control.

The unrelenting enemy firing continued throwing up spouts of water as rounds hit the wet ground around the chopper. Pascoe wasn't sure where the fire was coming from, but he was sure if he stayed there one more second he would meet the same fate as Minh.

He looked out at Nguyen and Hayes fighting to stay on their feet as they slogged through the marsh burdened by their awkward loads.

The longer Pascoe sat there waiting for the two soldiers the more intense the enemy fire became. He looked out the door, and his eyes met Hayes' running as fast as he could toward the chopper. They were wide and wild.

Pascoe just couldn't do it. He couldn't wait that few more seconds for them to take the last strides needed to get them to his waiting chopper. There was just too much enemy fire. They'd all perish.

While his mind spun clear of rational thinking, focusing instead on the extreme danger he found himself in, his hands and feet committed him to action. He sucked the collective control up under his left arm putting maximum power into the turning chopper blades and pushed forward on the cyclic stick between his knees quickly bringing the chopper's tail up off the ground.

The powerful aircraft continued to respond to his touch as the toes of the skids immediately broke ground and cleared the landing zone. Pascoe leaned his controls over and added body English putting the aircraft into an ascending left turn. As he climbed out of the landing zone he watched the ground fall away below—Hayes' and Nguyen's darkened images getting smaller as he did.

Pascoe pushed the chopper beyond its safe flight limits to tap out its power and speed his departure. He quickly put as much distance and altitude as he could between him and the lethal spot on the ground where they took the fire that killed Minh.

Finally, leveling up and rolling off some of the top end power, he reigned the nose around and headed in an easterly direction, careful not to get any closer to the heavy machineguns still capable of reaching up to snatch his chopper out of the sky.

Scotty wiped his face to clear the muddy spray from his eyes. He was sure he was mistaken. How could the chopper leave without them? They were just a few strides from the cargo door when the added power to the blades created a wash of swampy water and a blast of rotor wash blowing the two of them backward and blinding them.

He wasn't completely sure what was happening. The chopper had landed to pick them up and almost before it stopped rocking it lifted off again and headed away.

Exposed in the open landing zone, Nguyen and Scotty ran for the nearest clump of thick brush and dove into it. Inside the thicket they turned back to back, each taking responsibility for half the terrain outside the brush.

As the chopper put more and more altitude and distance between it and the enemy gunners Pascoe looked over at his slain counterpart. General Minh's head bobbed, his body restrained by the waist and shoulder harness holding him upright in the seat.

Pressing the transmit button on the floor, he called back to Operations again to ask what the hell happened to the other choppers. He was told they were grounded by a low ceiling and heavy rains. But he got a promise from the Vietnamese duty officer the choppers would be dispatched back to his location as soon as the weather conditions permitted.

There was no telling how long that would take. Pascoe's mind raced. He had a dead co-pilot. His chopper had taken hits but was still flying. He scanned the flight instruments and saw he was low on fuel. All this and he had two soldiers on the ground in the middle of a hornet's nest sure to turn on him again should he make another attempt to pull them out.

He set the chopper up a high orbit east of where he'd last seen Hayes and Nguyen and tried to clear his head and decide what to do.

On the ground, Scotty cupped the radio handset to his mouth in order not to be heard in the now silent marsh and called Pascoe's chopper.

He got no answer even after several more tries.

In the chopper circling only a few miles away, Pascoe heard Scotty's hushed voice over the radio and didn't answer. He told himself he would answer as soon as he had something to tell Hayes, but he didn't have anything yet. After the third try, the sound of Scotty's voice grew weaker —his battery was dying. Pascoe still did not answer. He had nothing to tell Scotty and was becoming more convinced he couldn't possibly survive another touchdown near the border to pluck the two off the ground.

He looked back in the direction of the landing zone and saw no tracers. But he knew enemy gunners were still there, and they expected another rescue attempt. He convinced himself that it was over. He couldn't get in, and they couldn't get out. He looked over at his compass and laid the chopper over into a turn taking him northeast—away from Scotty and Nguyen and even away from the Sugar Mill.

Thinking his radio was not working, Scotty shrugged off its harness and started looking for some reason why he could not raise a chopper.

Nguyen tapped Scotty on the back and pointed off at the chopper—

Minh's chopper. Both were puzzled by its flight path—it was flying farther away from them. They watched as the navigation lights and rotating beacon got smaller and dimmer.

Scotty gave up on the radio. He had no other battery, and the radio was filled with water from their run to the aborted chopper rescue. He tossed it aside and took a breath. They were in trouble. Low on ammo, far from home and in a place sure to be known by all enemy forces in the area. He looked at his watch. It was almost eight p.m. He whispered to Nguyen, "We must move."

Nguyen didn't take his eyes off the terrain outside the thicket watching for anyone looking for them. He nodded and spoke softly, "Yes."

In only minutes on its new heading, the chopper was close enough to Nui Ba Den for Pascoe to see the mountaintop clearly—even in the dark. The charcoal layer of clouds only a few hundred feet above the chopper promised more weather dangerous for any aviator to try to fly through, especially one who had done as little bad weather flying as he had since graduating from flight school many years earlier.

He knew a few facts: The weather was too bad back at the Sugar Mill for him to fly there and land. He certainly was not going to put down out in some bad guy's rice paddy to wait for it to clear up and he had less than twenty minutes fuel left on board. Nui Ba Den was the only place he could put down with some margin of safety and wait for the weather to clear around the Sugar Mill.

The landing pad on top of the mountain Minh had taken him to his first week on the job came into clearer view. He set up to make a pinnacle landing and felt his gut and his grip tighten. There would be no second chance. If he didn't put the chopper down safely on the right spot, he would probably roll the chopper down the far side of the mountain and surely die.

CHAPTER 19

The turbine whine quieted as the blades of the chopper spooled down to a stop. Pascoe finished a hurried and half-hearted checklist of shut down procedures then turned off the main battery power.

He sat back in the seat and tried to take his first real breath in nearly a half hour since Minh had tried to take them into the hot landing zone to pick up Scotty's small patrol.

The only noise he heard was the light rain ticking on the tinted plexiglass windows over the pilot's seats and a light wind blowing. He looked up at the cloud cover for some sign it might clear up between the mountaintop and the Sugar Mill but couldn't see much since the bulk of the aircraft blocked his view having landed the chopper into the wind.

Pascoe checked his pistol to make sure it was loaded, picked up his carbine from its place, slung over the back of his seat and stepped out of the chopper.

True to his training, he walked around the front of the chopper as was every pilot's habit to stay clear of the tail rotor, turning or not. As he passed the shattered windscreen in front of Minh's body still strapped into the seat, he avoided the sight of his dead counterpart. He couldn't look at the man. He was even angry with him. Had he not insisted on trying to pull those soldiers off the ground he might still be alive and Pascoe would not be in the mess he found himself in.

Pascoe found a large rock near the chopper and leaned up against it. At first, he looked around the hilltop for any sign there might be someone there bent on doing him harm. He shielded his eyes from the rain and looked out over the paddy land surrounding the mountain. He started with the Sugar Mill for some hope the clouds would clear soon. Since it was dark, he could not see much and had to hope there would at least be enough visibility and a high enough ceiling for him to follow the highway flying low level all the way back to the Sugar Mill.

He decided to walk around the chopper to see how much damage had been done. Clouds or no clouds, if the aircraft was too damaged to take off from the mountaintop it wouldn't make any difference if the skies completely cleared out and the moon lit up Vietnam.

He let his fingers follow his eyes as he touched, looked and inspected the critical areas of the chopper involved in flight control, avionics, engine, and hydraulics. In addition to the holes blasted in the windscreen killing Minh and the two holes in the tail boom he found another in the horizontal stabilizer. It was a small caliber hole not near anything vital. And it had done no damage short of puncturing the thin chopper's skin.

He continued to search the other side of the chopper and the less damage he found, the more concerned he became. Other than the death of Minh, there was no evidence they had actually been involved in intense enemy fire, or they had been the target of very much shooting. In short, there was little to support a decision to abort the extraction and return to the Sugar Mill. How could he explain returning? How could he explain not holding on the ground long enough to pick up the stranded soldiers? He tried to control his sense of panic. There had to be a way.

It came to him. He knew how dangerous it was. Pascoe pulled the pistol from his holster and stood back from the chopper. He picked out a spot on the fuselage unlikely to be critical to flight and fired a shot into it. That would do it. He would make the chopper look like it had been through far more intense combat. They needed to see how truly volatile the landing had been. He found another spot on the nose and fired again, and another aiming point on one of the skids and fired a hole in it.

He emptied his pistol into the non-critical parts of the chopper and followed that up with half his carbine magazine. He wanted to save some ammunition should he need it later.

The strip of trees was no more than twenty feet wide but was almost thirty meters long. Scotty crawled from side to side to get a feel for how large their small sanctuary was. He discovered the stand of brush had once been planted to provide a weather break for the adjacent but long since abandoned rice paddies. In the years since the farmers had left the land, the original trees had been joined by a tough and wiry cluster of thorny weed-like bushes, which concealed him and Nguyen from view.

Scotty could see east and west from the narrow axis of the tree stand, but he and Nguyen were virtually blind to anything north and south because what concealed them also obscured their view.

Scotty returned to Nguyen, reported what he had found and asked him if he had a plan.

Nguyen reached for the radio and Scotty shook his head to let him know it was useless. "Okay. We wait."

The word *okay* sounded awkward coming out of Captain Nguyen's mouth, but he was right. Nguyen's informal tone was for a definite purpose—to inspire confidence.

Still, they had no other choice. They were concealed and unless the Viet Cong had seen them slip into the tree stand they would be good there until choppers from division returned to pull them out again. Surely they would do that. And they wouldn't want to confuse the returning pilots by moving to another more distant location and not being able to tell them with no working radio.

Unaware of Minh's death, Scotty trusted there was a reason Minh and Pascoe aborted the pickup before he and Nguyen could reach the chopper. And he was sure they would return.

Their only problem, other than being discovered, was not being able to speak to the choppers and guide them to their location. Scotty knew they would have to figure out a way to signal the pilots when they returned. He reached into his pocket and pulled out two packs of GI matches. If he could dry them out, he could use them to start a fire. They would be useful at night or if it was overcast. He still had his signal mirror around his neck to get a chopper's attention in daylight.

Nguyen recognized what Scotty was doing, and the two began breaking small branches off the trees and the thicket to be ready to start when the next rescue attempt started.

Certain he couldn't wait longer for the weather to clear and still be able to explain where he had been and why he had not been reachable on the chopper's radio, Pascoe climbed back into the aircraft and restarted it.

He watched the instruments carefully to make sure he hadn't done any serious damage to the flight systems while firing rounds into the aircraft.

As quickly as he fired up the chopper, his helmet headset came alive with radio calls from Operations for him to reply. He decided to ignore the calls until he got the chopper safely into the air.

His anxieties over making a pinnacle landing were matched by his uncertainty about taking off from the mountaintop at night in the rain. He put the chopper in motion and found it responsive and his skills adequate to get it off the peak of Nui Ba Den and into straight and level flight en route to the Sugar Mill.

Once in the air, he found the ceiling too low to offer him much visibility in the direction of the Sugar Mill. He maneuvered the chopper over the main north-south highway running from Tay Ninh to the Sugar Mill and followed its path at a dangerously low altitude.

No longer able to ignore the radio calls he pressed the transmit button and reestablished communication with the radio operator at the Sugar Mill. He quickly explained away the half hour of silence by claiming the weather had been severe enough between them that while he had heard most of their calls, he was unable to overcome the radio interference created inside the nearby thunderstorms to understand or reply.

The radio operator asked him where he wanted the gunships and pickup choppers to rendezvous to rescue the remaining troops on the ground.

Pascoe hesitated then replied, "Turn them around if they have already lifted off. There are no survivors. I say again, there is no one to pick up." He paused, then added, "I also have one crewmember casualty—KIA."

There was silence on the other end of the radio. Pascoe could only guess the radio operator knew what the obscure reference meant—the only other crewmember in Pascoe's chopper was Minh. And he was dead.

The radio operator came alive again in Pascoe's headset and responded with a simple reply in broken English, "Roger." Pascoe rescanned his instruments, checked his fuel level and followed the roadway below now more aware of the dead man next to him still strapped into his seat than the line he had crossed with his explanation. He blocked the ultimate violation of the oath he had taken seventeen years earlier as a cadet at West Point from his mind: Cadets would not lie, cheat or steal; nor tolerate those among them who did.

In the treeline, Scotty and Captain Nguyen began to inventory their resources. They had less than fifty rounds of ammunition, two rifles, four grenades, two maps, two compasses, Tran's medical kit and no radio.

The marshes seemed to have gone quiet save the noises of the night which somehow returned after each violent clash of soldiers and machines. They didn't need to talk about the danger they were facing. They had to stay hidden until choppers returned to find them. Then, the hardest part would be making it from the treeline to the pickup choppers without getting cut down by enemy fire while out in the open. Then they would hope the chopper could climb out of the pickup zone without being blown out of the sky.

***

Pascoe went over the explanation he would have to give on arrival at the Sugar Mill as he continued to follow the road below. He would have to have his side of the story down pat. He was sure he'd be asked to repeat it many times before the night's events would be behind him.

He convinced himself there was no chance the two soldiers on the ground could have survived after he flew away. There had been too much fire, too many Viet Cong in the area and they had been completely compromised by stepping out into the open to reach the chopper. And even if they had survived by some stroke of luck they were not only in a place where they couldn't be rescued, they were more than likely in the hands of the Viet Cong. Prisoners—that early in the war meant impossible to rescue.

The lights were all on around the helipad at the Sugar Mill as Pascoe slowed the chopper's forward speed to set up for his landing. As he crossed the walls, he could see a reception party waiting for him on the steps of the headquarters building. Generals Pham and Devlen had obviously been notified of his arrival because of the report of Minh's death. Next to them stood two small Vietnamese medics dutifully wearing their Red Cross marked helmets holding a folding stretcher almost twice their height.

Nearby, a crowd of Vietnamese soldiers stood in a cluster, morbidly curious to see what the chopper held.

Pascoe put the chopper onto the large H on the ground inside the compound and ran through his shutdown procedures still focused on what his demeanor should be once he stepped from the chopper. He surely needed to be disturbed by the losses, by Minh's death and he should make a point out of stressing how hard they tried to find and rescue the remaining soldiers out on the ground.

General Devlen stood a few strides from the chopper surveying the damage to the aircraft as Pascoe unbuckled and stepped down onto the toe of the skid to get out of the chopper. He saluted Devlen and said nothing more than a salutatory, "General."

The general returned his salute and shook his head looking back at the shot-up chopper. "Goddamn, son. How did you get this thing to make it all the way back here without falling out of the sky?"

Not missing the opportunity to downplay it, Pascoe looked over his shoulder at the chopper and shrugged. "They are tougher birds than we think sometimes, General."

The two medics scurried around the front of the chopper, pulled Minh's body from his seat and placed it on the stretcher. Before they moved it, one of the soldiers took a cloth from his pocket. To Pascoe, it looked to be a handkerchief or napkin. He draped the cloth reverently over the dead general's face, as was the custom designed to keep family and friends from being shocked by the vision of the deceased.

Pascoe and Devlen stood silently as they carried the body to the dispensary on the other side of the compound. A scream broke the silence. Pascoe looked at the woman standing by the Vietnamese general's quarters, once the home of the Sugar Mill's owner. She was Minh's wife. Pascoe had only met her once at a reception for the local mayor.

She broke into a run across the compound, her shoes throwing up muddy water with each stride staining the back of her white satin pants under her dark blue ao dai.

She reached the body of her fallen husband and threw herself across his chest while the two medics tried to carry their burden. It was an awkward sight as the two soldiers were unsure if their duty was to get the dead warrior's body out of the drizzle to a more respectful place or if they should stop long enough for his widow to wail and pour out her grief for the world to hear.

"Colonel?"

Pascoe turned to find General Devlen gesturing toward the headquarters building and the Vietnamese Corps Commander standing under the overhanging porch.

"Shall we join General Pham inside? I'm sure he would like to hear how this happened," Devlen said.

Inside the conference room, the three officers sat at a large table topped with a map of the division's area of operations. The two generals sat on one side while Pascoe sat on the other facing them. He knew whatever he said was critical to how he would be treated from then on.

General Devlen made it all that much easier for Pascoe to embellish and depart from the actual facts with his opening words. The general waved at a young soldier in the room but spoke to Pascoe. "Are you okay with us doing this now? Would you like something to drink?"

Pascoe nodded yes to both questions. "Yes, sir."

The soldier brought a bottle of Coca-Cola with a tumbler and placed it near Pascoe's elbow.

"Colonel, we understand you and General Minh made valiant attempts to extract all the members of the patrol on the border. And I want you to know General Pham, and I will be sure to take steps to see that you and General Minh are appropriately recognized for your heroism in the face of such overwhelming enemy fire.

"Now, if you feel up to it, we'd like you to walk us through the events of the last twenty-four hours. We are sure there are plenty of lessons to be learned from this action. And maybe we can extract some wisdom from the losses we regret we have sustained."

Pascoe took a sip of the drink and paused to show he was concentrating on the details as well as focusing on accuracy. He began by summarizing the initial mission of Nguyen's patrol to recon the area near the border, sure they knew that much. Then he reached a point where he told his first lie: ". . . then General Minh decided it would be useful to detach a smaller patrol to get even closer to the border since the hamlet was a bit too far away and not actually on the path of the infiltrators."

Then he added his second lie. "I was a bit surprised to find the destination he picked for the smaller patrol was just inside the Cambodian border. I asked him about it, and he told me the precise location of the border was not that firm and showed up in slightly different orientation on different maps."

General Devlen nodded his head not so much as in approval as if to tell Pascoe to go on, he was listening.

Pascoe explained the routine details of the patrol being split into a larger and smaller elements and added that after the first night without any success on the part of Nguyen and Hayes, General Minh decided to let them watch the border one more night—Pascoe's third lie. He compounded it by adding Minh had asked him to pass his instructions through Caruthers to both parts of the split patrol. He knew his name would be somewhere on the radio log kept at the headquarters. Every transmission sent or received was carefully recorded with time and date. Not so conversations between him and his counterpart.

What went unnoticed was the fact that Pascoe didn't ask about the other soldiers who were extracted with Caruthers.

The mud beneath Scotty was warm and clammy from his body. The night had cooled off a bit, but the parts of his clothing not immersed in the water and muck were still as wet as when he had drifted off around one in the morning.

He raised his head off his upper arm and immediately felt the stress he must have been holding in his neck through the night. It was stiff and hurt. He twisted it slowly to free it up. As he did, he felt sweat roll from his hairline above his ear back behind it and down his neck, disappearing somewhere under his collar. The day was already heating up.

Shielding his eyes with his hand, he raised up on his elbow and scanned the flat terrain around him. In some places, he could see steam wafting from the mire. A mud crane attacked a stalk of some kind reaching beyond the other grasses for some sun. Scotty continued his sweep until his neck could no longer follow his eyes. He rolled over onto his stomach hearing the sucking sounds of mud reluctantly releasing his hip and the squishing sounds of his abdomen and hips settling back onto the mud-speckled with grasses and living and dead bugs of several varieties.

The continuation of his scan of the terrain revealed nothing. He rolled back onto his elbows and tried to clear his head to focus on his plan for the day. His mouth was dry, and his stomach growled, begging to be filled. He needed something, anything, to maintain his flagging strength if he hoped to make any progress before nightfall.

Scotty pulled his trousers up over his knees to make a quick survey of his growing number of scrapes and bites—most of which were already infected. An ulcer on his knee had started as a scratch a few hours out of the Sugar Mill was growing worse. It was becoming a crater with a waxy looking ochre center rimmed in angry red inflammation. He prodded the flesh around it with his finger and could feel the large pillow of fluid collected under the center of the ulcer threatening to burst through the fifty-cent piece sized crust.

He tried to calculate how long they had been out. It seemed to him to be longer, but it was just short of a week since they had left the Sugar Mill. Both Scotty and Nguyen were beginning to suffer from lack of sleep, lack of food and sheer exposure to the elements. He felt extremely fatigued and couldn't explain the pains in his joints. Scotty sat upright in the treeline, shook off the malaise and continued his inventory of bumps and bruises. The skin above his boot tops was raw from exposure to the water and dotted with the perfectly round bloody circles where leeches had attached themselves, gorged on his blood and then dropped off. Two were still searching for a place to feast. He pulled them from his leg before they got started and flicked them off into the grasses.

He looked at Nguyen who was using a small piece of rag to clean the dirt from his rifle as he kept watch on the narrow ribbon of marsh separating them from Cambodia.

Scotty looked at the same horizon searching for any sign of renewed threat. The long abandoned paddy fields were silent. Only morning birds and distant roosters broke the silence as Scotty kept alert for the welcomed sounds of approaching choppers he hoped would come. He realized how much he wanted a moment away from the threat he knew waited nearby and let his mind wander to Eileen and Kitty and home. Would they ever see each other again? Was Kitty okay?

Eileen's face formed quickly in his mind's eye. He wanted so badly to be with her, out of the stinking thicket, away from the war and home in Belton.

He looked back in the direction of the unseen Sugar Mill for signs of helicopters. The sky was mostly clear. Gone even were the rain clouds. He hoped they might get a respite from the rain allowing the sun to dry them out and give them some relief before the next predictable rains.

With the arrival of the choppers, he could count on getting back to the Sugar Mill, to a shower, food, and sleep. He let his mind drift back to Eileen while his eyes scanned the ground between them and the Viet Cong.

Pascoe left his room in the team house and walked out into the compound. His first instinct was to look at the sky to see if it would be still another day of more rain than not. But he was pleased to find the sky intermittently broken with clouds and patches of the brilliant blue Vietnam could be proud of.

He heard voices and found several young Vietnamese soldiers looking at the damaged hulk of General Minh's chopper. They appeared to be amazed at the number of bullet hits in the chopper and fascinated with the shattered windscreen and blood-covered seat where their commanding general had met his fate.

As they saw Pascoe, one of them called the group of six to attention, and they all saluted the American colonel as he continued on his way to the headquarters building.

Pascoe returned the salute and said good morning to the group but couldn't bring himself to look at either the bullet-riddled chopper or the ripped and bloodied seat of its now missing command pilot.

He promised himself to check on how soon the chopper would be sent to maintenance for repairs. At least there it would be out of his sight and wouldn't remind him of the day before.

Inside the headquarters, a Vietnamese soldier hurried after Pascoe who had just entered the building and was threading his way through the corridors to his office.

"Trung Ta?" he called out for Pascoe using the Vietnamese for lieutenant colonel.

Pascoe turned to find the soldier behind him stopped and standing stiffly, one hand extended to give him an envelope. Pascoe thanked the soldier and dismissed him. He looked at the careful handwriting on the envelope and wondered what it could be. Everything else in the headquarters was in multiple copies typed with old typewriters all with crooked keys and fading ribbons. The envelope was heavy stock, and the handwriting was done in what looked to him like brush and ink in the Asian style.

Once inside his office, he dropped his cap on his desk, sat and opened the envelope. In it, he found a hand-lettered invitation from General Pham's office to a parade in Saigon where Brigadier General Duong would be installed as the new commanding general of the division.

Pascoe had wondered who would replace Minh. General Duong had been the Assistant Division Commander under Minh but had spent all of his time in Saigon handling administrative and logistical matters for the division.

Pascoe also worried about the impact on the morale and effectiveness of the division going through three division commanders in a matter of weeks. He had the same feeling of anxiety he had felt when he had heard General Pham was moving until he found out Minh would replace him. Now Duong was almost a complete unknown, and Pascoe would have to make sure he quickly established a good working relationship with him to please General Devlen.

He tried to remember if Minh had said anything about Duong which might be useful in cementing good relations. He had time before the parade to do some boning up on the new general.

Scotty looked at his watch again, then at the sky. It was clear and had been for most of the day. But it was getting late. He looked at Nguyen checking the border through binoculars. Nguyen must have been thinking the same thing because Scotty saw him check his own watch.

He tried to run through all the reasons why someone hadn't come to pull them out yet. He had ruled out weather and could only think they might be preparing a ground element to secure the area while they extracted him and Nguyen. With no radio and limited understanding of the politics in a Vietnamese infantry division he had to trust they would come and whatever the delay was it would make sense to him once they got back to the Sugar Mill.

Nguyen poked Scotty and handed him a dirty clump of cold rice—obviously the end of his rations.

Scotty took the rice and ate it in one bite. Even though it was mixed with dirt, slimy and most of its grains had been crushed into a paste, he enjoyed it. They were completely out of food—a problem in not too many more hours if they weren't picked up. They needed the nourishment for the hours of vigilance, lack of sleep and what seemed like gallons of adrenaline they were pumping.

Scotty wiped his hands across his face and felt the stubble. He realized how dirty and nasty he was after so many days in the rotten wetlands without a shower. At his throat, his fingers found the lymph nodes under his jaw line were enlarged and tender. This added to his concern. He didn't need to get sick. He was sure they'd be back at the Sugar Mill soon, and he would be able to get it looked at then.

Pascoe looked out the window at the gathering clouds, absentmindedly clicking his ballpoint pen over and over again. He heard General Devlen's parting words the night he briefed them on the action at the border. He tried to impress on Pascoe the importance of preparing a detailed report of the combat action which would be viewed by far more people in the chain of command than a normal after action report. The increased interest would be because of the proximity to the Cambodian border and because American and South Vietnamese soldiers might not be dead. They could have been captured. The report would go to the Embassy in Saigon.

He also recalled Devlen patting him on the shoulder and saying no matter how good a job he did, the Ambassador would have heartburn. It was as if they were combat soldiers standing together against the civilian oversight of their duties.

Still, Pascoe recognized Devlen had drastically understated the problem. It would be more than heartburn. It could be the source of an international diplomatic flap. His only defense was Minh called all the shots and when Minh was killed it was Pascoe's decision to return to the Sugar Mill. He was certain he had convinced Devlen the two on the ground were most likely prisoners of war if not dead. There had just been too much firing and too many Viet Cong soldiers in the area for them to have survived once they had left their concealment to run to the aborted chopper pickup. And once he lost contact with them a second try would have surely ended in failure and more likely the total loss of his chopper. His assessment was a downed chopper inside Cambodia was going to make a firefight gone bad into a serious international incident with the chopper as proof.

Either way, he couldn't pull them out if he could no longer find them. But he certainly would have continued to try in spite of the withering enemy fire he faced and the border issue.

All he had to do was keep his story straight on paper. He leaned back over the lined pad on his desk and began writing.

It was almost dark, and Scotty couldn't believe they had not heard any aircraft all day. He kept searching his mind for a reason no one had come to get them. He finally gave up, spun on his stomach and moved up alongside Nguyen who had been watching in the opposite direction. He whispered to Nguyen, "No choppers."

Nguyen nodded. "We have trouble."

"What?" Scotty asked, thinking it had to do with their water or ammo. Instead, he saw Nguyen's reach out and point toward the most distant clump of trees.

Scotty looked hard for something. But before he saw anything he heard voices. High pitched and somewhat excited, someone was yelling directions in Vietnamese. It took Scotty no time to figure out what it meant. Any enemy force concealed by darkness and comfortable about making noise was convinced they had a superior force to whatever they might encounter and not worried about giving away their position. He had to assume they knew only two of them were still hiding somewhere in the area.

Nguyen pointed off in a slightly different direction at a small light. A flashlight. It was in the abandoned hamlet once occupied by Caruthers and the rest of the patrol before they were attacked then evacuated. The Viet Cong were searching the hamlet.

Scotty heard the first shot. AK-47 fire. Then another. They were shooting first before looking in any place in the hamlet where someone could be hiding. There was some nervous laughter and the sound of hollow metal objects clanking together. They must have found some empty canteens or ammo cans left behind.

Nguyen and Scotty remained motionless. Their tree stand offered them concealment but no protection if the enemy soldiers started firing on them.

The light turned on and off and moved out of the hamlet—closer to the two in hiding. The shooting continued sporadically and got louder—closer.

Scotty took both his hands and shielded his eyes from the slightly brighter night sky to see something to their front. He first saw the white reflection of water splashed up by a soldier walking nearly two hundred meters away.

He strained to focus and was then able to see there were nine of them, all about ten meters apart walking toward Scotty and Nguyen. Scotty touched Nguyen and pointed in the direction of the oncoming squad to make sure he too had seen them.

Nguyen nodded.

"Do they know we are here?" Scotty whispered.

"Maybe yes. Maybe no. We wait."

The soldiers keep moving toward the two in the thicket. But as they had done in the hamlet, they began shooting again. They didn't pass up the chance to shoot into anything else that just might conceal someone. They would approach a bush or a large clump of sawgrasses and fire a few rounds into it. Getting no return fire they moved on to the next. They did this to eliminate one potential hiding place after another.

Scotty and Nguyen didn't need to be told what was happening. An old technique used to flush out hidden enemy, reconnaissance by fire—shooting to get a response from a possible enemy in hiding. If they received returned fire, they would all concentrate their rifle fire on the spot to kill whoever might be in hiding.

Scotty and Nguyen couldn't move. The enemy squad was headed in their direction and closing. Within the next few minutes, their hiding spot would be the target of one of the approaching soldiers. There was vegetation to conceal them but no cover to protect them. The ground inside the thicket offered no fault or fold to shield them from incoming small arms fire. And there was no way they could overpower the approaching Viet Cong soldiers with two rifles and limited ammunition. All they could do was stay low, remain perfectly still and hope for the best. Scotty knew hope was surely not an approved infantry technique, but they had no options. They had to hope the approaching Viet Cong would change directions, overlook their thicket or just get lazy and miss them.

It took the approaching squad ten minutes to get to a point where Scotty and Nguyen's hiding place might be their next target. Scotty knew if he had a move he'd feel a whole lot better. Even if the odds were awful, they'd still be odds. His felt his gut tighten even more. Scotty raised his rifle and took aim on one of the soldiers.

Nguyen reached over and put his hand across the receiver of Scotty's carbine to make sure they were in agreement. They wouldn't fire unless they absolutely had to. Firing before their lives were really at risk would surely give them away.

The soldiers kept coming, kept shooting and kept talking nervously as they approached.

Scotty felt sweat dripping from his face to his chin and ultimately dropping off onto the back of his hand firmly gripping the small of his rifle stock.

The enemy soldiers got close enough for Scotty to see the expressions on their faces. Their voices were clear. They displayed no fear of discovery by a larger unit. They were not worried about being ambushed or facing sniper fire. They showed their lack of concern for security in their recklessness—walking in the open and making so much noise.

Scotty hoped for the only chance he thought they had. Soldiers are soldiers. They tend to take the path of least resistance and do the minimum to get the job done. If they were well commanded, they would carefully search the area rather than taking the lazy way out—reconning by fire. Maybe their laziness would save Scotty and Nguyen. It was a crap shoot.

Scotty held his breath as they got even closer. The nearest enemy soldier was not more than a hundred feet away. He swung his rifle to his left and casually fired a shot from the hip at a clump of bushes twenty meters or more from Scotty's thicket. Getting no reaction out of the target he scanned the area in front of him for something else to shoot at.

Scotty was sure they would be next. It only made sense the soldier would fire at the next thing in front of him, and that meant the thicket hiding Scotty and Nguyen.

The soldier swung his rifle to the front, and Scotty found himself looking directly into the barrel of an AK-47 not more than sixty feet in front of him. His heart pounded and his chest tightened. He felt his finger take up the slack on his trigger while his brain kept saying: Hold it. Steady. Hold it.

The soldier tried to fire, but his magazine was empty. He dropped the empty one from his rifle's receiver, replaced it with a full magazine and took aim again.

Scotty found himself looking directly at the business end of the VC's rifle again. He was sure he couldn't be lucky again. Then, one of the soldiers on the other end of the line hollered something. Scotty didn't understand it, but there was excitement in the enemy soldier's voice.

The other soldiers looked at the excited soldier. The soldier in front of Nguyen and Scotty was also distracted from his next target and looked away—to his right—away from Scotty and Nguyen.

Nguyen leaned over and whispered into Scotty's ear. "Boat."

Scotty got it. They had found a boat. One of the boats the patrol had hidden the night they set up in the hamlet. The soldier who alerted the others about the boat must have told them to come to his location—nearly two hundred meters from Scotty's position.

Scotty watched as the soldier whose rifle had been pointed at their thicket changed directions to follow orders. Scotty wanted to scream, "Yes! Yes. Go. Go look at that boat. Go. Enjoy yourself." He held his breath then noticed the soldier hesitate. Something wasn't right for the soldier. Something told him not to turn his back on the thicket in front of him. As if it were almost an afterthought, the soldier, now even closer, swung his rifle back toward the thicket again.

Scotty heard the click the rifle as the soldier switched from single shot to automatic mode. Then without any real point of aim, the soldier fired off a burst of six rounds into the thicket.

The bullets cut through the brush above and on both sides of where Scotty was pressed to the muddy ground. Each one snapped by with a frightening crack seeming even closer than it actually was. Scotty held on and hoped to be spared. Small pieces of twigs and leaves fell inside the thicket—each severed from its branch, ripped from its own source of sustenance. It was over as fast as it started. Scotty searched his senses for any alarms telling him he had been hit and felt nothing. He raised his head and looked at the Viet Cong soldier.

The soldier hesitated, waiting for something to happen. When he saw nothing, he threw his rifle up onto his hip and turned to join the others. His bare feet sunk into the mud and came loose with a sucking sound with each step he took toward the others and away from Scotty and Nguyen.

Scotty held his breath and silently commanded the soldier in his head: Keep going. Don't stop. Go over with the others. Go. Hurry. He found himself mentally trying to help the soldier place each foot forward and pull the trailing one out of the capturing mud to hasten the soldier's departure. He watched anxiously as the soldier's image got smaller and harder to distinguish in the night.

It took the squad of Viet Cong soldiers only moments to clear the area in front of the thicket. It seemed much, much longer for Scotty. Once they were gone, he assumed they were searching the area where they had found the boat for anything else they might find.

He relaxed his grip on his rifle and turned to Nguyen to share an almost joyful expression of relief. But what he found was not Nguyen equally frozen over his rifle. Instead, he found Nguyen sitting up, bending over holding his hands low across his midsection.

Scotty could make out Nguyen doubled up but not moving. He heard Nguyen's breathing. It was extremely labored. He had been hit by the enemy fire and was trying not to make noise or alert the departed enemy squad.

Scotty searched the muddy ground for the medic's aid kit and found himself silently praying the wound was superficial and not life threatening for Nguyen.

CHAPTER 20

Eileen sat quietly in the examining room while Doctor Gordon looked skyward, listening to Kitty's lungs through the stethoscope.

He moved its bell from place to place on her small back. "You getting enough rest?"

"That's about all I do," Kitty replied.

Eileen made eye contact with the doctor and gave him an almost imperceptible head shake contradicting Kitty's words.

"Why don't I believe you, Kitty Hayes?"

"Because you're just a man and beautiful women intimidate you," Kitty said, trying to lighten the moment.

"Well, you're going to be in charge of this disease, Kitty. What you do to keep it under control is going to have far more influence on your condition than the pills or me. So I don't want to hear it if things get worse and you aren't taking care of Kitty."

Kitty rolled her eyes. "Okay, okay . . . You are worse than having a nagging husband, Doc."

"I'm not sure a man in your life wouldn't be a good thing right now. At least he could force you to take better care of yourself and make you get more rest."

"He'd play hell trying," Kitty said.

"Well, I'm going to deputize Eileen here to keep a closer eye on you because I'm afraid you're showing some signs of complications."

"What? Is something else wrong?" Eileen asked.

Doctor Gordon took off his glasses and surrounded Kitty's hands in his. He looked at her but spoke to both of them. "One of the problems with this disease is it won't stay put. It isn't just a disease confined to the lungs. It has affected your heart. One of the chambers of your heart is enlarged, and this is *not* good."

"Hell, Doc . . . I'm tougher than that," Kitty said, not convincing Eileen. "I can handle it."

The doctor released her hands and pulled his pen from the pocket of his lab coat. He scribbled a prescription on a pad he plucked from the other pocket and ripped it off. "Well, as tough as you think you are, this might help a bit." He handed the piece of paper to Eileen and said, "You see to it she takes these every day." He continued to speak as if Kitty were not in the room. "If she doesn't, remind her that I'll put her in the hospital and I'm sure she won't be happy about that."

Pascoe finished his first scotch while drying off after his shower. He threw his wet towel over a hook on the wall and put on a clean, dry pair of GI boxer shorts.

He needed the liquor to temper his mood. He filled his tumbler with two more fingers of scotch and sat down at his makeshift desk. It was the first moment he had really had to collect his thoughts. His mind had been racing since Minh had taken their chopper into the enemy fire. He was now more sure than ever he would have died too had he not acted quickly and pulled the chopper out of the landing zone. There was strong justification for his actions he simply couldn't reveal. But he knew.

Pascoe was sorry Minh was dead, but he thought the decision Minh had made was reckless, and he was even a bit angry Minh had risked both their lives to save two soldiers on the ground. They probably would not have been able to make it to the chopper anyway with all the enemy fire directed at them and the chopper. Minh should have waited for the gunships to return. Even if it meant leaving the two out there in hiding for another night or until the weather cleared.

He was equally sure his decision not to try a second time was right. Even so, his decision was borne out when he later couldn't see them or hear them on the radio. All he could have done by going in again was lose a chopper and get himself killed for two soldiers most likely already dead or captured and on their way to the Viet Cong sanctuaries inside Cambodia.

Tossing back the scotch and pouring himself a third, he reminded himself he had to quit worrying about what was done. It was behind him. He had to move on.

He was tiring of the endless editing of his report of the night's actions. He needed something to distract his attention. On the corner of his desk were the last three letters he had received from Karen. That's what he would do. He would write to her. She knew nothing about what he had been through, and he now had some combat action to tell her. Some combat action painting him in a favorable light.

The story he told General Devlen was carefully crafted to place any responsibility for the decisions made the night of Minh's death on Minh while still leaving some room for interpretation leading to an assumption Pascoe had been somewhat heroic and dedicated to the rescue of those still on the ground.

His paper version was clear, fact-filled but it told little. It was in many more words but was far less forthcoming than the version he had told Devlen. Pascoe knew the paper version would be around for a long, long time.

He stood and stepped to the locker. From it he pulled a cigar off the shelf holding the last of the stock of cigars he had inherited from Colonel Wills before he left for home. He sat back down at the desk and thought over what he might include in his letter from the two versions of the night's events he had already given. True to his habit, he jotted down the topics in a laundry list manner on a separate piece of paper. He lit the cigar and found a place to begin the letter—telling her about the events surrounding Minh's death.

As he began his letter, to Karen he chose to tell her only part of the incident. He focused on how heated the combat had been, how dangerous the situation he and Minh found themselves in. And he wrote with less specificity about the patrol on the ground. And he didn't mention the loss of Nguyen and Hayes at all.

He shifted from the topic of the combat action to changes at the division as they affected him. He shared with her his concern about a new division commander and a new counterpart for him. Finally, he asked about financial matters, if the car was running well, if the quarterly insurance payments were taken care of, if she had been able to find a source for his favorite cigars, and how soon he could expect some more since he was running low.

He finished the letter without asking her about how she was doing, how she was handling the separation or about her health or well-being.

True to his training as an academic and before folding and stuffing the letter into an envelope he proofread it. As he read his account of the aerial combat over the stranded patrol and the intense rescue effort, he was impressed with how well he came off. Feeling the scotch, he took a puff off of his cigar and blew it skyward as he unconsciously nodded his head in approval and then folded the letter.

There was no way they could use a light to explore the extent of Captain Nguyen's wound. Careful not to give away their position making noise, Scotty tried to encourage Nguyen in as low a whisper as he could muster. "Hold on. Just hold on," Scotty said. He pulled a combat dressing out of the aid kit. "You hit anywhere else, Dai Uy?"

Nguyen didn't speak. His face contorted in pain, he shook his head.

Scotty continued applying the best first aid he could under the circumstances. He was sure they were a long way from being in the clear as far as alerting the out-of-sight but still nearby enemy soldiers searching the battle area. Training took over. Words filled his head: *Stop the bleeding, clear the airway, protect the wound, treat or prevent shock.*

The wound was actually at the very top of Nguyen's thigh almost where it connected to the hip below the socket. Scotty wiped as much of the mud and water as he could from his hand on his shirt and felt for blood. In the dark it was hard to tell what was blood and what was muddy marsh water. He realized he'd have to wait until daylight to make a better assessment of Nguyen's wound.

Still, he couldn't wait for any longer to find out if the bullet which pierced the front of his upper thigh had come out somewhere else making an even larger exit hole. He started behind Nguyen's knee and felt his way up the backside across his buttock and around his kidney.

He methodically returned to the outside of the knee and worked his way up past Nguyen's hip bone to his rib cage. Again, no exit wound. Finally, he searched the area of Nguyen's inner thigh and was fairly confident there was no exit wound anywhere. Scotty knew this was a mixed blessing. On one hand, there was no other wound bleeding externally. On the other, the bullet could have gone anywhere in Nguyen's body tearing more tissue and blood vessels in its path causing more internal bleeding.

Worried about bleeding he couldn't see, Scotty placed the combat dressing over the wound and the clothing covering it and pressed down just to stop the bleeding. As he did, Nguyen winched sharply at the added pain.

"Roll over," Scotty whispered. He wanted Nguyen to put the weight of his pelvis onto the combat dressing and provide his own pressure to stem the flow of blood.

Nguyen groaned and emitted a wheezing sound between his teeth as he tried to follow Scotty's instructions.

Scotty grabbed the back of Nguyen's belt and helped him roll over. He searched for what to do next.

Breathing. Scotty could hear Nguyen's breathing labored by pain but otherwise unobstructed. He realized that step needed no attention.

Shock. Shock was as much a killer as a shot in the head could be. He had to get Nguyen's head down below his heart, and he needed to cover him to conserve his body heat. He felt for Nguyen's wrist to check his pulse. It was too dark to get an accurate count without his watch. Nguyen's pulse felt fairly strong to Scotty if not a little elevated. There was no way he could tell if Nguyen's skin was damp and clammy in their muddy hiding place. They'd been that way since they got out of the boats on the first night of the patrol. Scotty knew if he could keep Nguyen alive until daylight he'd have a better chance of seeing just how badly he was wounded and figure out what he could do to keep him alive until they got back to the Sugar Mill.

He had to believe a rescue was planned, something was in motion, and someone was going to come looking for them before much longer. Scotty took off his harness holding his gear and ammo pouches. He then removed is shirt and placed it over Nguyen's back to help him hold in his body heat in the dampness of the bog. All the while he heard himself repeating, "You're going to be okay. We're going to get you home. Just hold on, Dai Uy," under his breath.

Pascoe felt awkward sitting in the back of General Duong's helicopter. He would have preferred to be in one of the pilot's seats. He looked around inside and saw the chopper was in far better condition than General Minh's chopper had been. Pascoe assumed the maintenance was the responsibility of the two Vietnamese pilots flying the chopper.

Duong sat on the canvas bench seat reading some documents, which had preoccupied him since they lifted off of the helipad at the Sugar Mill. It was the first time he and General Duong had actually met, and the man was pleasant enough but had to talk to Pascoe through his interpreter, a young sergeant who sat in the single jump seat behind the pilots. This made everything more complicated.

Pascoe hadn't yet been able to get a good fix on Duong. He was an unlikely looking general officer, portly and balding with unusually thick glasses. His arrival at the Sugar Mill was a surprise. Pascoe had been instructed to wait for a chopper to take him to Saigon for the ceremony to install Duong as the new division commander replacing the dead Minh. Pascoe never expected to find the general on the same flight. He wanted to know where he was coming from, but questions seemed awkward for Pascoe through the interpreter who said nothing unless spoken to first.

Could it be the general was making a gesture of welcoming his new senior advisor by meeting Pascoe at the Division Headquarters? He was becoming aware of the often deliberate gestures of the Vietnamese to honor customs and protocols not common in the American Army. Some were borrowed from the French and others were of their own invention.

Pascoe took the opportunity to look at the countryside between the Sugar Mill and Saigon as they flew. It was quite different than the drier terrain he had first seen the day he first flew to the division headquarters with Minh. On this trip, the streams were out of their banks, and all of the rice paddies were flooded with brown water, some of it from the local rains, the rest of it from deep inside Asian mountain chains at the origins of the Mekong River.

He was happy to see the clouds had thinned for the morning allowing them to fly without weather problems and keeping him from getting his starched khaki uniform drenched. It was the first time he had worn anything but fatigues since his arrival in Vietnam. The occasion was formal for the Vietnamese, and it was only appropriate he wear the equivalent uniform for the ceremony planned that morning.

The chopper slowed and then circled a manicured parade ground with a helipad at one end and a formal wooden reviewing stand and set of bleachers at the other. The bleachers were filled with a mixture of military and civilian Vietnamese faces shading their eyes and craning their necks to see the approaching chopper.

All were there for the ceremony. Out in front of the reviewing stand stood twelve hundred Vietnamese soldiers in strictly regimented ranks awaiting the arrival of the chopper and their new commanding general.

The two battalions flanked a six-man color guard holding the flags of the division, the corps, Vietnam and the United States. On one end of the troop formation was a six cannon salute battery and the other a forty-man marching band.

The pilot maneuvered the chopper to a point immediately in front of the reviewing stand and put the aircraft down gently, an expert at his job.

Pascoe took the general's lead and followed him and the interpreter from the chopper to the two-foot high reviewing stand.

On the stand were several dignitaries, all of them general officers. He recognized Pham and Devlen and just assumed the others were from the headquarters of the Vietnamese Corps located in Saigon.

Salutes were rendered and answered all the way around and an efficient looking Vietnamese major pointed at the two chairs on the reviewing stand where he wanted General Duong and Pascoe to sit. Pascoe was
surprised to find himself in the front row with Pham, Devlen, and Duong.
With no one to ask, he simply took his seat and said nothing, smiling at
the others as they did the same.

As they took their places the Vietnamese band played more western
music he from John Philips Sousa. They were awful. Their execution was
awkward and amateurish sounding more like a junior high school band.
Pascoe had been spoiled by the accomplished bands he had become accustomed to while at West Point.

From either side of the bleachers, behind the reviewing stand, two
large trumpet-like green loudspeakers crackled with the words of a well-
rehearsed voice who spoke first in Vietnamese and then in English. "Ladies and gentlemen, will you please rise for our national anthem."

Everyone got to their feet, and the Commander of Troops located in
front of the ranks of soldiers called them to attention. With the first note of
the Vietnamese anthem, everyone in uniform saluted and held the salute
until it was over. But instead of dropping the salutes at the end, the band
went right into a very bad rendition of the United States national anthem,
and it too received the honors rendered the earlier anthem.

The music stopped, the voice over the speaker asked all to sit. General
Pham stood and stepped to the microphone centered at the front of the
reviewing stand. Though the visitor-spectators were all to his rear, he directed his remarks to the troops assembled in front of the stand.

As he began, speaking in Vietnamese, the interpreter quietly knelt
down next to Pascoe and handed him a piece of paper. It was a typed
translation of General Pham's speech. It became obvious to Pascoe there
were too few Americans at the ceremony for the entire speech to be interrupted by a translator repeating the general's words in English.

Pascoe read the speech as the general spoke. It was filled with hopeful
remarks about the ultimate victory of the Republicans, the term the South
Vietnamese used to refer to themselves, over the communist insurgents
who surely would fail in their attempts to enslave the free people of the
South. He went on to praise the support and advice they were getting from
Washington and made a point of how sure he was the friendship between
Saigon and America would last for a thousand years.

Toward the end of his remarks, he reminded everyone assembled they were there to honor General Duong who had been selected by the Premier over many other well qualified general officers to become the new commanding general of the well respected and often feared 6th Infantry Division. He made sure to include mention of their nickname, *the Tigers of the Delta*.

The general finished his speech. And on some unseen cue, the band struck up again and played more martial music. While they played, Generals Pham and Duong descended the steps on the front of the reviewing stand and marched to a point in front of the color guard.

There they halted and waited for the bandmaster to stop the music. Once done, General Pham took the flag of the Division from the hands of the color bearer, turned and handed the flag's six-foot staff to General Duong.

Pascoe has seen many such ceremonies in his army put on to pass command of a unit, activate new units or install new commanders. They were pretty universal in armies the world over. While everyone was focused on the generals, he took the opportunity to look around the ceremony. There were so many dignitaries he couldn't recognize and the bleachers held a dozen unfamiliar American officers and NCOs all wearing Military Assistance Command patches hanging from the pockets of their khaki shirts. The large number of unknowns reminded him he was out on the country's border pretty much alone while the faces at the ceremony were enjoying Saigon, relative safety and spending their days making decisions which had great impact on what Pascoe did in his job.

He fought the urge to be irritated seeing so many senior NCOs fatcatting it in Saigon when he couldn't get an NCO to replace Caruthers and now needed a replacement for Hayes. He wasn't sure if he should take Devlen's new found familiarity and pleasure with his performance as an opportunity to complain about staffing.

Pascoe was snapped out of his thoughts by the band striking up again after General Duong handed the flag back to the color bearer who had been holding it in the first place. As they played, the two generals returned to the reviewing stand. Pascoe was pleased to see them return thinking they were surely near the end of the ceremony and it might break up before the very humid heat got worse as the sun climbed much higher in the sky.

But the generals did not mount the reviewing stand. They stopped short of it by two paces and stood shoulder to shoulder facing the stand and the bleachers behind it. Then, General Devlen stood and walked to a position to General Duong's left.

Pascoe wasn't sure what was next. He had never liked the uncertainty situations like this brought to him. He watched the three stand there for an awkward moment before the sound of a new voice blared out of the tinny speakers. "Ladies and gentlemen, General Pham, General Devlen and General Duong would like to take this opportunity to share with you an occasion of importance."

He recognized the voice as that of General Devlen's aide, also unseen at the site of the hidden microphone somewhere under or behind the bleachers. But what occasion could it be? Pascoe looked around to see if anything else was happening near the parade field which might give him some clue. He found nothing.

The lieutenant's voice continued. "At this time we'd like to ask Lieutenant Colonel Eldon Pascoe, Senior Advisor to the 6th Infantry Division to step down from the reviewing stand and take his place in front of the general officers."

Pascoe wasn't sure what was happening but stood, descended the steps and walked to a spot in front of the three generals. He stopped at a point centered on and five feet in front of the trio. He stood there, searching the eyes of all three generals and found all three were smiling.

The voice was replaced with that of General Duong's interpreter. "Ladies and gentlemen, distinguished guests—General Duong and General Pham are pleased to take the occasion to award Lieutenant Colonel Pascoe the Vietnamese Cross of Gallantry with Palm for his courage and bravery in the face of the enemy in the vicinity of the hamlet of Doi Bao Voi in Hau Nghĩa Province . . ."

Pascoe couldn't believe what he was hearing. He watched a Vietnamese sergeant and an American soldier with a camera come into view and walk around the four standing at attention. The sergeant carried a velvet-covered board used to carry medals for presentation. The soldiers stopped at General Pham's side, and the General reached over and pulled the large orange medal and its ribbon from the board.

As the General approached Pascoe, the voice continued to read the details of the citation in Vietnamese. Pascoe could only pick out enough words to know it was the citation but not much more.

Pham stopped in front of Pascoe and waited until the citation reading was complete. He then pinned the medal to the pocket flap of Pascoe's shirt just beneath his silver aviator's badge.

Pascoe's felt himself standing taller and straighter as he realized they had turned the corner. He had drawn favorable attention to himself and had been awarded his very first combat medal for bravery. He wanted to yell out something as childish as a loud yahoo! But decorum was everything, and he struck a proud but humble pose while the general finished pinning on the medal. That done, the general reached for Pascoe's hand to shake it.

Pascoe quickly wiped the moisture he felt in his palm on the side of his trousers then took the general's hand. As they shook hands, Pascoe spotted the Vietnamese soldier with the velvet-covered board move to General Devlen's side.

The voice over the public address system changed again to the American lieutenant who spoke enthusiastically. "And General Devlen is proud to be able to also award to Colonel Pascoe the American Army's Silver Star Medal."

Another medal? Pascoe couldn't believe it. A Silver Star? He was floored by the announcement. It was what he came to Vietnam for, recognition, contradictory evidence of his worth to overcome the single bad efficiency report he had received. He watched Devlen repeat the process Pham had just finished. Devlen plucked the medal from the board and pinned it to Pascoe's shirt pocket next to the Vietnamese Gallantry Cross. He then stepped back and stood silently while the voice over the speakers finished reading the citation in English. ". . . for gallantry in action involving close combat with an armed hostile force in the Republic of Vietnam. Lieutenant Colonel Pascoe distinguished himself by heroism while participating in aerial flight as the pilot of a helicopter under intense and sustained enemy fire . . ."

Pascoe was stunned by the moment—being recognized by both the US Army and the Republic of Vietnam for heroism in combat.

He listened as the voice finished the citation. ". . . making repeated attempts to extract encircled friendly elements under heavy and sustained enemy fire. His courage and selfless devotion to duty reflects great credit upon himself, Military Assistance Command and the United States Army." He knew those words were forever permanent and would soon be part of his record at the Pentagon. The citations would surely be there before the next lieutenant colonel's promotion board would meet. And the citations would certainly be accompanied by an impressive efficiency report from General Devlen. After all, how could the general award him a Silver Star and not also write him an outstanding efficiency report?

Though they had gotten off on the wrong foot, Pascoe was determined to impress the general with his performance of duty in the time he had left in the advisory team. Doing so would be sure to influence the general to write an impressive efficiency report on him to go along with his two medals for heroism in combat. It would be insurance.

The presentations complete, Pascoe saluted the three generals, and the music started up again with a bang.

The generals and Pascoe returned to the reviewing stand where all four stood shoulder to shoulder facing the troops. The Vietnamese Officer standing in front of the formation, the Commander of Troops, yelled out the series of commands to get the troops to shoulder their rifles, then turn, then step off in a column to perform the age-old custom of *passing in review*.

With the first step, the band in front of the column started playing another selection more appropriate for soldiers to march to at exactly one hundred and twenty steps per minute.

Pascoe wanted to look down at the two new medals pinned on to his shirt but resisted the urge. He stood stiffly and proudly next to the three generals while they all watched the Commander of Troops maneuver the long column of companies into two left turns lining them up with a path taking them all past the front of the reviewing stand to render honors to the VIPs.

Daylight finally filtered into the trees concealing Scotty and Nguyen. Before Scotty did anything else, he moved to all four margins of the thicket binoculars to look for any signs of enemy forces still in the area.

That done without seeing any indication the Viet Cong were near, Scotty returned to Nguyen. As he crawled back to the captain's position, he wasn't looking forward to what he would find in the daylight. Scotty knew he was in a really bad situation. Something told him not to expect choppers to come looking for them after days of waiting. If they hadn't already tried to pick them up, there was little chance they were coming at all. He had to assume they thought he and Nguyen were dead or captured. What else would explain the lack of effort to rescue them?

He reached Nguyen's side. "How you doing, Dai Uy?"

Nguyen's color was pale. His breathing was shallow, and he was perspiring heavily. Not something Scotty was used to seeing from a local. They always seemed to be immune to the extremes in the weather Scotty found difficult to become acclimatized to.

"Not good," Nguyen said.

"I'm going to have to roll you back over to check you out." He grabbed the captain's belt and shoulder and waited.

Nguyen nodded, made a face in preparation for the added pain and let Scotty roll him onto his back.

The pain was severe, but Scotty wasn't surprised the tough little warrior was able to keep from crying out. As Scotty untied the tails of the combat dressing holding the blood soaked pad to Nguyen's hip he heard Sergeant Asa Russell's words: One day you're a private in an eleven-man rifle squad. The next you're one of the few left alive, and you're in charge— responsible for the lives of others. All that time you are up to your ass in bad guys trying to shoot holes in your ass.

How sure Russell had been the same thing would happen to Scotty and how unlikely the scenario felt to him that night in the Company Orderly Room at Fort Benning.

Nguyen was now Scotty's responsibility. He might not be able to keep him alive, but without Scotty's help, he surely would die. As he pulled the dressing back from the wound, the bleeding continued. Turning its edge back even more, Scotty could see the top of the wound in Nguyen's leg. What he had guessed might be a round bullet hole in his leg was instead a more ragged hole, longer than wide and deep—to the bone.

Scotty looked more closely and saw not only torn tissue but a deep groove cut into the thigh bone. He guessed Nguyen had not been shot directly. Rather, the round hit the ground before it ricocheted across Nguyen's upper leg. The impact with the ground itself had distorted or flattened the slug and cut through the tissue like a machete rather than puncturing it. The round had gone in the tissue and out—good news. It meant there was not a bullet still in Nguyen.

Scotty felt only slightly better about dealing with the wound he found in the daylight. Now he had a long list of lesser problems: How was he going to keep the wound from getting infected? How was he going to keep Nguyen's strength up without food and adequate nourishment? And the worst of all, how was he going to get him to safety and competent medical attention? There was no way Nguyen could walk. Scotty wasn't even sure he could stand up.

He sat back and wondered what Asa Russell would tell him. He shrugged. He knew what he'd tell him. He'd tell him to figure it out, not sit on his ass and worry about it. It was clearly a case where doing nothing would surely cost Nguyen his life and might get Scotty killed too. Doing something surely couldn't be much worse.

"How much pain are you in Dai Uy?"

"Is painful. Yes."

Scotty rummaged around in the aid kit looking for something to help the wounded captain more comfortable. He found three small glass ampules of morphine wrapped in a paper envelope also containing a glass syringe and needle. He also found a tin of Darvon with codeine. He held both up so Nguyen could see them and he pointed at the Darvon.

"Okay," Scotty said. "Darvon it is. But you know we have the morphine if it gets that bad."

"Yes," Nguyen said. He tried to raise himself up on his elbows.

Scotty pulled his canteen, handed him the pills and waited for him to wash them down. Then both waited a few minutes for the Darvon to kick in before Scotty tried to rebandage Nguyen.

Scotty looked at the sun filtering through the trees lighting up the area of the wound itself. He was sure the sunlight wouldn't hurt the wound and might even help to keep bacteria from growing in the wound. In the brighter light, he could see the bone was severely compromised. The ratty edges of the wound were beginning to dry out, the larger ligaments were lacerated but bleeding seemed to be under control. In short, the leg was going to be useless to Nguyen until got treatment to repair the damage. Treatment far beyond Scotty's first aid skills.

Scotty pulled his map from the cargo pocket on his leg and flopped it open, spinning it to orient it to true north. He knew he just had to assume there was no other rescue effort planned. With no way to communicate with anyone since their radio had died, Scotty knew they didn't even have two choices. To stay meant Nguyen's death. And his own elevated temperature, swollen lymph nodes, aching joints now made him worry how much worse he was going to get. Staying put was not going to work. No, he was sure. His only choice was to get the two of them back to some American or South Vietnamese outpost. He didn't care if it was a military post or government office. He just had to get them back to civilization.

Nguyen must have realized what Scotty was thinking and shook his head. "You go. Come back."

"No, sir. I can't do that. I leave you here without food, water or medical attention you won't last half the time it would take me to get to help and get back." Scotty nodded toward Cambodia, still only a stone's throw away. "Even if you did survive, the VC are going to be coming through this area. It won't be that long before an infiltrator finds this thicket just like we did."

He didn't wait for Nguyen reply. Instead, he decided he'd waited long enough for the pills to kick in and opened another battle dressing to place over Nguyen's open wound.

He looked at his watch and started planning their day. "Dai Uy, I want you to get some sleep. I'm going to find the shortest path to the next thicket in the direction of the Sugar Mill and we'll slip out of here tonight."

He stopped speaking long enough to hold up the map and pointed to a curved line of abandoned farms, tree stands, canals, and streams. "This is a long and wide swing out of our way, but we might be able to move from point to point, working back to the highway where we can find help."

"How?"

"I guess I'm going to have to carry you."

"You cannot do," Nguyen said.

"We don't have any choice, sir."

Having removed all of his gear except his ammo, canteens, and binoculars, Scotty took black mud marinating in the stagnant water and smeared it on his face, neck and hands to replace the camouflage sticks he had run out of. It smelled disgusting, but Scotty had no option. He couldn't be seen. It was clearly one of those moments Russell had pounded into him in training: If you can be seen, you can be hit. If you can be hit, you can be killed.

He made one more check of the sleeping Nguyen's temperature making sure he wasn't exposed to too much drying sunlight, picked up his rifle and started out. He knew he had to plan carefully if he hoped to have any success in getting them back to safety without being seen moving across the marshland. It would almost be a cross between hopscotch and chess. They would need to move from one place of concealment to the next and not leave a trail. A tall order, but what else could he do?

It took him several minutes just to move to a spot in the thicket where he could see across the marshland to the east and north. He hoped the map was accurate and there would be another clump of trees close enough for them to move to and rest before moving on again.

Just inches from the edge of the thicket Scotty stopped and listened for any movement. Nothing. Other than the sounds of birds and insects humming and chirping in the reeds it was quiet. This was good news. He had learned early in training wildlife can be a great source of information. When it is completely quiet, there's a good chance the insects and birds are aware of some danger or tension in the area. Hearing noise gave him confidence.

He put his binoculars to his eyes and began a quick and methodical sweep from left to right looking at everything in his view. He needed to make sure no one was watching him before he picked the exact path they would take to get to the next cluster of trees. He was happy to find the terrain actually matched the nine-year-old map.

His eye caught something unnaturally dark nearly a hundred meters out in the open terrain. He raised his binoculars to focus on whatever it was. It might have been something left behind by the Viet Cong who shot Nguyen, maybe something useful. Cranking the binos into sharp focus, he saw it was a crow. A dead crow. It was large and blue-black glossy. Could it be the same crow they had seen so many days earlier? Did the crow fall victim to the random shooting? And was there a mate somewhere waiting for him to return?

Scotty wondered if he and Nguyen would end up dead in some paddy. Or if anyone would ever know. He quickly bristled at feeling sorry for himself, took a deep breath and shook it off. Self-pity was something neither one of them could afford. Of that he was sure.

The companies passed in front of the reviewing stand one at a time in step to the music. As they did, the young Vietnamese captains in command of each company saluted the dignitaries on the reviewing stand.

Pascoe returned the salutes in unison with the generals and felt his chest swelling when the color guard passed with the US and Vietnamese national flags.

The last company passed, and the voice of the interpreter came back over the loudspeakers again. "Ladies and gentlemen, this concludes the ceremony. The Corps Commander, General Pham, would like to thank you for coming today. A reception is planned in the area immediately behind the bleachers. You are all invited to attend." With that, the sound system clicked off, taking with it the hum that had been under every announcement.

Pascoe was unsure of the next move since he had started the day thinking he was only going to a change of command ceremony for General Duong. It never occurred to him the day could have turned out to be so important to him. Without thinking about it, his fingers touched the two ornate pendants hanging from the colorful ribbons of his two new medals.

"Congratulations."

Pascoe realized General Devlen was standing by him reaching out to shake his hand. "Oh, sir. Yessir. Ah, thank you." He took the general's hand for the second time that day and tried to give him a firm and manly shake. "I was completely surprised by all this."

"Well, you earned them. And we rushed the Silver Star through so too much time wouldn't elapse between the action and the award. You see, we don't get too many chances to recognize the service and heroism of our advisors because they don't command the troops they advise and aren't in a position to make heroic and difficult decisions as you did."

Pascoe tried to be humble in his reply. "Well, sir . . . I didn't really do all that much. It was General Minh who made all the hard choices out there. Heck, I was more of a passenger in that chopper."

The general reached over and patted Pascoe on the arm. "Well, you can brush it off if you want, but we feel you deserve the medals. Now, let's go over to the reception and get some refreshments."

As they walked to the reception area set up behind the bleachers, General Devlen turned to Pascoe. "Oh, Colonel, Headquarters has classified your Sergeant Hayes as MIA."

"I'm sure that'll be very upsetting for his family," Pascoe said. "I hope we can resolve his status one way or the other soon so his family can get some peace of mind."

"I agree. This was supposed to be an advisory effort, and now we have more than a dozen Americans we think are in the hands of the VC. I'm hoping Washington can bring enough pressure on Hanoi to force them to release our people."

The general stopped at a table topped with champagne glasses, tended by a young Vietnamese girl wearing a beautiful rose colored ao dai. He took a half filled glass from the girl and waited for Pascoe to do the same. Raising the glass, he made a toast. "Here's to better days ahead and more Vietnamese generals like Minh."

Pascoe raised his glasses to meet the toast. "I'll drink to that. I'll miss him." He sipped the champagne and tried not to make a face at the truly horrible quality of the Vietnamese wine, which was lukewarm.

"Where do you see your division going from here?" the general asked.

"I guess a lot depends on what General Duong wants to do," Pascoe replied. "And I don't know much about him yet."

General Devlen looked around, making sure they were not overheard. "Well, I do. I think he will need a stronger hand than Minh. He's not spent much time with troops. He has a long and respected resume as a staff officer, but the command of troops combat is going to be something new to him." He looked Pascoe directly in the eyes. "I expect a lot from you in this. I want to see you lead this man to success and make it look like it was his idea. That will take some finesse, but I'm sure you can do it. Right?"

"Oh, yessir. You can count on me sir," Pascoe said.

"I'd like to hear how you are planning on doing this soon."

Pascoe put the glass back on the table and took the chance at spring-boarding off the general's instructions to bring up something important to him. He didn't know when the opportunity would come up again. He carefully picked his words. "General, do you think fleshing out my advisory team will present a problem for your headquarters?"

"Why? What's the problem?"

"Well, I'm terribly short of manpower in my team and replacements seem to be slow in coming."

"Short in manpower?" the general was surprised. "I wasn't aware you were having difficulties."

"I never got a fully qualified replacement for Caruthers, and now he's gone. His replacement is gone—"

"That's the youngster who's MIA?"

"Yessir, Hayes. And there's still the matter of my replacement. Once you moved me up to be the division's senior advisor that put a hole where my job was in Operations." He then took care to make it sound like something other than a complaint. "Of course, I realize how thin you must be. My guess is you are stretched all over with the demands on MACV expanding and the slowness of the replacement pipeline from the States."

Devlen's eyebrows knitted in a slight scowl. Then he raised his index finger, his glass still in hand to catch the eye of a large colonel swabbing his forehead with a damp handkerchief a few paces away in the crowd. "Mike? A minute?"

Colonel Mike Wright acknowledged the general, put his own drink down and came over to the General and Pascoe. "Yessir."

Pascoe recognized the colonel as the same man who had assigned him to Minh when he first arrived in Vietnam.

General Devlen pointed his glass at Pascoe. "Mike, I think you know Pascoe here. He tells me there's some kind of hold up on replacements for his advisory team out with the 6th Division. Can you tell me what the hell the hold up is in getting him the people he needs?"

The portly Colonel stuttered searching for a reply. "Yessir. I remember Pascoe." He glanced at him. "How you doin?" Then back to the General. "Sir, I'd be happy to assign some more bodies to the 6th if I had them. We aren't getting 'em in as fast as we're losing them to injury, wounds and illnesses."

The General was silent for a moment. He then put his glass on the table and dropped his more pleasant tone. "Well, Colonel, that's not going to cut it. I want to see you in my office in three days with a plan to solve this problem. I want all the facts and figures, and I want something I can take up the chain of command—to Washington if I have to. Do you understand me? I want ammunition."

The Colonel's face reddened, and he began nodding before the General even finished speaking. "Yessir. I will do that. I'll make it a priority."

Pascoe felt better about bringing the subject up and not repeating his efforts to get more manpower through normal channels which started with Colonel Wright.

Well-wishers stopped by to shake Pascoe's hand and congratulate him on his awards while also taking the opportunity to rub elbows with their commanding general.

Pascoe was somewhat overwhelmed by the attention. In his years in the Army, no one had ever made such a fuss over him. And now he was getting handshakes, well wishes and pats on the back from senior officers and peers recognizing him for his bravery in combat.

A young American soldier carrying at large press camera and wearing an armband identifying him as part of the PIO office stopped in front of General Devlen and Pascoe and asked if he could get a picture. The general looked to Pascoe. "I think this would be a good idea. You will want to remember this day. And we need to recognize good work in pictures." He took Pascoe's hand, accustomed to staging handshake pictures over his years as a general officer."

Pascoe smiled into the camera while the soldier licked the base of a flash bulb and stuck it into the socket on the large reflectored flash attachment on the side of the cumbersome camera. The thought of putting a picture of him up in his office some day back in the States appealed to Pascoe. He broadened his grin and turned his torso slightly in to make sure the medals showed in the photo.

Once the photos were taken General Devlen spotted General Pham arriving at the refreshment table and excused himself with Pascoe to go talk to the Vietnamese corps commander.

Pascoe again caught sight of the photographer taking more pictures of the festivities—young Vietnamese girls dressed in their finest. As he approached, it looked to Pascoe like the soldier was doing more hitting on the girls than picture taking. But he knew one thing true about most Vietnamese—they loved having their pictures taken. They saved their money to add to their collections of photos of themselves. A soldier with a camera had a built-in opening line.

"Soldier?"

The photographer turned to find Pascoe at his shoulder. "Yessir?"

"What's chances of getting a copy or two of your photos of today's ceremony for my files?"

The soldiers started nodding even before he started speaking. "Sure, Colonel. No problem." He added a well-worn phrase which had somehow become commonplace among the English speaking Vietnamese, "Can do, easy."

"Great. That'll be great," Pascoe said.

"And don't worry, Colonel. I'll make you look good."

Pascoe didn't know how to respond to the soldier obviously used to officers asking him for photos. He just smiled and let it go. "I'll look forward to seeing them soon. You can just send them to me at 6th Division Headquarters."

"Yessir. I'll have a bunch going out to General Duong. I'll slip yours in the Pony Express pouch too," the soldier said, poking fun at the slow-moving message distribution system which moved correspondence and reports from headquarters to headquarters.

"Pascoe!"

Pascoe turned to find Colonel Wright standing unusually close, his red flushed face pushed close to Pascoe's. "Let me tell you something, asshole. The next fucking time you hang my ass out to dry with General Devlen you're going to think a goddamn building fell on you. You got a problem with personnel—you call me. You don't go whining to the general you piss ant son of a bitch!"

Pascoe tried to reply while pulling back from the aggressive attack of the large colonel. He tried lying. "It wasn't like you think. He asked me if I was doing okay in the manpower department and I just couldn't lie to him."

"You could have fucking told him we were working on filling the vacancies—which we were."

"I didn't mean to—"

"You got my root in a ringer, and I'm not going to forget it, *Major*," the Colonel said, emphasizing Pascoe's real rank and reminding him of the difference in their relative authority.

CHAPTER 21

Scotty crawled back to Nguyen's position satisfied they could make it once night fell. It would only be a few hundred meters, but it would be a start, and it would be a test run on moving Nguyen incrementally. If they were able to make it that short distance without too much difficulty, they might be able to increase the distance the next night. And the ones to follow. He looked up at the sky peeking through the trees as if doing so might bring on a flight of several choppers. But he'd resigned himself to the fact it wasn't going to happen. If they were coming, they would have already been there.

Reaching Nguyen, Scotty checked him for fever and then held his canteen to his lips. He knew even if they made the trip to safety and neither the Viet Cong nor Nguyen's wound got them, dehydration could.

Scotty mentally put filling canteens on his list of things to do before they left the thicket that night. He had been working on the list since making the decision to move both of them in hops toward safety.

"How are you feeling?" he asked Nguyen.

"Not matter. We must go. We stay, we die."

"Well, I'm not going to let that happen, Dai Uy," Scotty said as he peeled back the corner of the combat dressing to take a peek at the wound.

"Not easy," Nguyen said.

"Well, you can buy me a Ba Mui Ba beer when we get back," Scotty said then he laughed slightly.

"Bier LaRue," Nguyen corrected, raising himself up on one elbow to see what Scotty could see under the bandage.

"What's that?"

"Good beer. I buy you."

Scotty released the dressing back and sat back and looked around. "I've got a lot to do here before we leave. If anyone comes this way they'll know we have been here."

Nguyen tried to sit up. "I will help."

"No. No, Dai Uy. If we need anything, we need you to be as rested as you can be. You stay," Scotty said.

He took a few minutes to sort out what they would keep and what they would leave behind. There was no way he could haul all they had managed to bring to the muddy den. He pulled an aluminum canteen cup out of the bottom of its canvas carrier and looked for a place to start.

A few feet from where they sat there was a spot void of growth, mostly because it was a pool of stagnant black water. Scotty crawled to the spot, scooped most of the water out of the shallow and began digging the mud out underneath it. He needed a hole large enough to bury things they would leave. What they couldn't take they'd bury and then he'd try to conceal the burial spot.

Scotty dug for nearly thirty minutes producing a hole only a foot and a half in diameter and about as deep. The earth was mud, some light gravel, and plenty of knotted weeds and roots, most the size of threads. By themselves, they were easy to break. But in the bundles, he found they were hard to cut up with the lip of a canteen cup.

Perspiration ran down his face but didn't cool him. His own temperature was on the rise, and he kept ignoring it simply because there was nothing he could do about it other than drink as much fluid as he could force down.

The only good news about needing water was he could find it in every direction. It was foul and more black than clear. But it was water, and between him and Nguyen, they still had dozens of tiny water purification tablets to dissolve in the marsh water to reduce some of the bacteria, which might otherwise buckle them over with acute diarrhea or vomiting. Giardia was the most likely to get them. The paddies were filled with the waterborne microscopic invaders capable of bringing down a grown man with ease.

Scotty looked around at Nguyen's rifle, scraps of field dressings, extra socks, an extra but long dead radio battery and a second pistol once belonging to the medic, Tram. All would be dead weight for him on the move.

He hated burying one of the rifles and the extra pistol. He would take his rifle and Nguyen's pistol with them. If they had to defend themselves at close range or if they needed to use them to keep themselves from being taken prisoner more weapons wouldn't be much more help.

He thought of Russell and wondered what it was like for him. Had he fought off enemy forces until he was simply overpowered? He stifled a laugh. Of course, Russell would fight as long as he had strength in his body. Scotty knew he would have to do the same. He was the only person able to save their lives and if he failed it would not just be him who suffered. He stuffed the stay-behind gear into the hole then spent another half hour covering everything with mud.

That done, he gathered deadfall and scattered it over the freshly turned mud to conceal the hiding place.

"Want some more ice tea, hon?"

Kitty shook her head as she swallowed the last of the glass. "Nope. Anymore and I'll be up all night. Thanks."

"You sound better today."

"Listen, if I have to fake it, I will. I'm not letting that damn doctor put my butt in the hospital," Kitty said.

"Well, if you keep taking your medicine and getting enough rest you might be able to keep out of there."

Kitty waved a dismissive hand at Eileen. "Now you're starting to sound like him too."

"Well, whatever it takes to keep you healthy I'll do. You need to do the same, and you know that, Miss Kitty."

"Yeah. I hear ya'—but I'd still kill for just one cigarette."

"Kitteeee . . ." Eileen replied. She took the tall tea glass from Kitty, spun and placed it in the sink. She reached up and parted the runner of the Creeping Charlie hanging in the small kitchen window behind the faucet to be able to see out the window. She was surprised and alarmed at what she saw.

"What? What is it, sweetie?" Kitty asked.

Eileen knew it would not be good news, no matter what it was. She saw an Army captain get out of the olive drab sedan. "Nothin.'" She pulled the apron from her waist, folded it and placed it over the lip of the sink. "Somebody just pulled up out front. Stay put. I'll get it."

She walked the few steps to the front door almost praying the officer had the wrong address or was looking for someone else's house. Not waiting for him to ring the doorbell, she opened the door and shielded her eyes with her hand from the blinding Florida sun. "Hello. Can I help you?"

The captain looked at an envelope in his hand. "I'm looking for Mrs. Jacob Hayes. Might she be your mother?"

"No, I'm Eileen Carter, a friend. Is it about Scotty? Her son?"

"The captain took off his cap and put the envelope inside. "Yes, but I need to speak to her."

"Can you wait here a minute. I want to . . . I mean, she's not been well—"

"Sure. I understand."

Eileen left him standing on the front steps while she went to prepare Kitty.

"Who was it? Kitty asked, not looking up from the TV Guide crossword puzzle she worked on with a ballpoint pen.

Eileen walked around in front of Kitty, kneeled down, took the pen out of her fingers and held Kitty's hands between her own. "Kitty, now I don't want you to get upset, but there's someone here from the Army about Scotty."

Kitty's hand broke loose from Eileen's as she covered her mouth and her eyes began to flood with tears. "Oh, my God. Not my baby. Not my baby too."

"Just sit here, and I'll bring him in."

***

The captain pulled the envelope from his cap and checked the details on the military telegram inside. "Yes, ma'am, it was three days ago they declared him missing in action. But he is not missing and *presumed dead*. I want you to understand that. There's still a chance they may find him. This is only a preliminary designation and not a final disposition for your son."

Kitty blew her nose in the tissue Eileen had placed on the kitchen table. She took the official looking document from the captain and spread it out the table, fighting to read it through her tears. "He's alive. I know my boy is alive."

Eileen stood next to Kitty and hugged her to let her know she was right. Eileen prayed she was right. She released Kitty and pointed to the cup in front of the captain, "Can I get you some more?"

"I need to be alone," Kitty stood unsteadily and walked out of the room.

"You need some help, hon?" Eileen asked.

But Kitty didn't reply. She clutched the telegram to her chest and walked toward her bedroom.

Eileen waited until Kitty was out of earshot and turned back to the captain, coffee pot in hand. "What happens now?"

He held his palm over his cup to decline her offer. "There'll be a Survivor's Assistance Officer assigned to come explain things."

"What kind of things?"

"Mrs. Hayes will begin getting Sergeant Hayes' paychecks and the SAO will be her contact for anything regarding her status as his dependent and any further information about Sergeant Hayes' status."

"No. I meant, is someone looking for him? What does the Army do about Scotty?"

"Ma'am, I don't have any information about that. I would assume there's something going on within his unit, but they don't tell me that."

"Who can?" Eileen asked, her tone becoming more demanding.

"Why don't you let me find out for you and I'll get back to you. I can call the Pentagon and get some more details if you'd like," the captain said.

Eileen couldn't fight the tears welling up in her eyes. He reached over and put her hand on the captain's. "I'd appreciate that. She's not well, and any hope we can give her will do her a world of good."

***

Nguyen and Scotty took turns taking short naps during the afternoon as they waited for darkness to fall. Both were suffering from lack of nutrition and were extremely weak because of it.

Scotty woke Nguyen after dark. "We need to move early. Anyone coming from Cambodia is just leaving there now, and we need to be moved and stopped before they come anywhere near us."

"Yes." Nguyen sat up with difficulty.

Scotty knew they would be unable to completely cover their tracks. His only hope was to make it appear they were not who they actually were. That meant trying to look as much like infiltrating Viet Cong soldiers as possible. He took a small twig and scraped the mud off the laces of his jungle boots and unlaced them. He would walk barefoot and hope anyone coming across his tracks wouldn't be able to tell his foot size from the average Vietnamese's.

His feet were white and wrinkled from a week spent in the water and the mud of the marshes. The breaks in his skin from leeches were beginning to get more infected.

Tying his laces together, he slung his boots around his neck and then the sling to his rifle. The next part was the real test. Could he lift and carry Nguyen?

Nguyen awkwardly pulled himself upright, standing on his good leg, which allowed Scotty to put his shoulder into Nguyen's midsection. Without words, they both coordinated their movements—Scotty bent his knees and thrust upward while Nguyen leaned well over Scotty's back.

They made it. Nguyen was draped over Scotty's shoulder, steadying himself with a hand on his pistol belt.

Scotty reached out with his free hand, took hold of a sapling and began the slow process of getting out of the thicket. He said a silent prayer.

It took the two twenty minutes to move to the margin of the thicket. Scotty stopped only long enough to ask Nguyen if it was just too painful for him to go on.

Nguyen's words came with little force. "Go. We go."

The first step out into the open area between the thicket and then next clump of trees was shakier than Scotty had expected. The ground was soft mud under the two inches of standing water. And he had no trees or bushes to hold onto with his free hand to steady him. The added weight threw him off, and he quickly realized unless he compensated he would wobble and fall to his left or right. He tried widening his stance and taking shorter steps.

At first, it felt completely awkward he was sure he would fall. After ten more steps he was gaining confidence and a rhythm the new stride, even if it was slower than he had hoped he could move across the open area.

After the first hundred meters, his left arm and shoulder began to suffer under the weight of his Vietnamese passenger. He had cut off some of the circulation in his left shoulder somewhere, and his entire arm was going numb. He needed to shift the load. He stopped, took as steady a stance as he could, turned his head and whispered to Nguyen. "Dai Uy. I'm sorry, but I gotta' move you."

Not waiting for a reply, he flexed his knees, thrust upward momentarily lightening Nguyen's load on his shoulder while simultaneously moving him to a spot only millimeters off the point which had been taking the bulk of the weight.

Nguyen tried to suppress the gasp, the pain, and the shifting caused, but wasn't completely successful.

It worked. Scotty felt blood returning to his arm and the feeling to his fingers. He opened and closed his hand. "Hold on, Dai Uy. We're moving."

It was late enough for his presence in the Intelligence Section of the Division's headquarters to not be under much scrutiny. Most of the staff had gone to bed, and only a single radio operator manned a bank of radios and telephones in the far end of the large room.

As Pascoe had done every day since Minh's death, he carefully read every intelligence report forwarded to his division from MACV Headquarters. They were English translations of information collected by all of the Vietnamese units in the corps area. He had read so many he was able to recognize what six digit grid coordinated where anywhere near the area were Scotty and Nguyen were last seen. He read the documents looking for any sign they had either been actually captured or, more likely, their bodies had turned up somewhere. The last thing he wanted was to be surprised about any possible news of Nguyen and Hayes that could blow back on him.

He found more reports of continued infiltration of Viet Cong across the no-man's-land on the near side of the border but nothing about the two missing soldiers. He rubbed his eyes and finished the last of the phone-book-sized stack of carbon copies of the documents which had originated in Saigon and called it a night.

Returning the reports to the in-box he had found them in, he looked around for something to clean the carbon ink from his fingers. The roll of toilet paper used to clean the grease pencil markings from the tactical map on the wall was the only thing available for the task, but it had the habit of moving to a new location each night. And even it would only take part of the stain from his hands. He would have to scrub the rest off in the shower, as he did every night.

He stepped to the tactical map mounted on the wall and studied the red boxes indicating enemy units, still looking for the seeds of a plan he could devise and suggest offer to the new division commander with some degree of promise of success. He knew it wouldn't be long before Devlen would ask him how it was going. He needed to come up with a plan, get Duong enthusiastic about it and then let Devlen know he was following through on Devlen's instructions.

He put his cap down on a field table, pulled his pen out of his pocket and found a lined pad to take notes. He spent the next two hours working on two assumptions: One, that the infiltrators had to be as human as anyone else and likely to show a pattern of movement related to using the easiest way to get from Cambodia to their underground units around Saigon. And the hundreds of tiny hamlets and farms had to be filled with South Vietnamese who would be able to help point out infiltrator traffic when they found trails in their rice fields. Pascoe was sure some money would encourage them to be more forthcoming with information. If he could get the money, he could get the information. And with the information, they could set up more effective ambushes in the most likely infiltration routes.

This would mean the ambushes would need to be set closer to the inhabited parts of the province. He liked that too. The more distance he put between himself and the heavy firepower the communist forces had just inside the border, the better.

He sat back and looked at his notes. They showed promise. Satisfied, he needed a drink.

Reaching out for a tree branch as they got to their first new hiding spot, Scotty stopped and to listen for movement anywhere near them over the sound of his rapid and labored breathing. The movement from the thicket to the first new one took almost two and a half hours even though it was only eight hundred meters.

Scotty could tell Nguyen was in pain during the entire move, but he said nothing and just held on. They would rest up and do the same thing again the next night.

Inside the new clump of trees, Scotty found a place to put Nguyen down. But when he helped Nguyen slip off his shoulder he found Nguyen was unable to stand under his own power. Scotty helped him to a more comfortable position on the ground. "How you doing, Dai Uy?"

Nguyen waved his hand to let Scotty know he would be okay, but Scotty knew better. "We need some food, Dai Uy. Soon as it gets light, I'll look for something we can eat."

Sergeant First Class Peter Jackson and Major Keith Laury sat silently waiting for Pascoe to speak.

Pascoe leafed through the files each brought and collected his thoughts before saying anything. He tried to conceal his anger from the two sitting in front of his desk. From their appearance and the contents of their files, it was clear to Pascoe they were not only completely unqualified to serve as advisors, they were not likely to be trainable during the time he had left in Vietnam.

"How much do you weigh, Sergeant? Pascoe asked.

"Well, sir. I'll admit I'm a little overweight—"

"A little overweight?" Pascoe's face reddened. "You're a goddamn whale. You've got to be over three hundred pounds!"

"But, sir, I'm trying to lose weight, and I'm sure I can get it down."

Pascoe looked back at the sergeant's records. "You've only got four months left in-country. How damn much weight do you think you can lose by then? No, don't answer that. Let me tell you how much. If you stopped eating now," Pascoe pointing to the unseen rice paddies outside the building, "you wouldn't lose enough to be able to make it a day out there on patrol with the Vietnamese. I'd be hauling your ass out of the paddies with heat exhaustion or a heart attack.

"Where the hell have you been that you could get this big and no one said anything to you?"

The sergeant looked down and his hands, toying with his cap. "I've been an Assistant Mess Sergeant at MACV since I got here."

"What?" He looked down at the sergeant's records again. "You're not even an Infantryman?" Veins stood out on Pascoe's neck.

"No, sir. I was. I was for ten years, and then I hurt my back in Germany in a Jeep accident, and they reclassified me."

Pascoe leaned forward and spoke slowly. "Well, Sergeant, here's how it's going to work here. I want you to get your ass out of my office right now, and I want you to find a notebook. I want you to write down in that notebook everything you eat every day. And I mean everything. And I want you to spend an hour each morning and each evening out in the compound exercising. I want to see you out there sweating every time I go to breakfast and every time I head to my quarters at night. You got that?"

"Yessir."

"And I want to see the log you keep every other day. On my desk. You got that?"

"Yessir."

"Now, get out of here and find that notebook."

The sergeant got to his feet and saluted.

Pascoe returned the salute and watched the huge perspiring soldier waddle through the door to the hallway. He then picked up the second folder on his desk to take a second look.

The major sitting in front of him waited while Pascoe took an uncomfortably long time with his records.

"What am I supposed to do with you, Laury?"

Surprised at the question, he replied. "Sir? I was sent here to be your Operations Advisor."

"Get up."

"Sir?"

"Get up and look out that window." Pascoe pointed to the glassless window.

The major stood and looked out the window across the compound.

"Look up," Pascoe said.

"Up?"

"Yes, up. Now, what do you see?"

Laury looked at the sky gathering with clouds. "Nothing, sir."

"Do you see any North Vietnamese aircraft? Any Viet Cong choppers?" Pascoe asked.

"No, sir. They don't have any aircraft in South Vietnam," Laury answered.

"That's right. So what am I going to do with an Air Defense Artillery-man in an Infantry Division?" He didn't wait for a reply. "Sit."

Laury took his chair again.

Pascoe slammed the folder closed. "You have no experience with troops, do you? No, don't answer that. I can tell from your file you haven't done shit. You are neither airborne nor Ranger qualified. You've been an ROTC instructor and an Assistant Post Exchange Officer. But the high-light of your career to date is that you've been the Recreation Officer at Fort Bliss, Texas.

"Well, Laury, what are you going to do for me here? Hand out soccer balls?"

Laury searched for a reply. "Sir, I volunteered for this job. I know I don't have any combat or infantry experience, but I can learn."

"This isn't school, Major. It's the real thing. Vietnamese soldiers are poorly trained, poorly equipped, poorly motivated and poorly paid. Do you think they deserve to be poorly advised?"

The major broke eye contact with Pascoe and looked at the floor. "No, sir. I guess not."

Pascoe leaned back in his chair and let out a sigh of resignation. "Well, I've got you. So here's what we're going to do." He nodded across the com-pound. "I want you to go over there and get out every After Action Report on every operation this division has conducted in the last two years and read them cover to cover. I want you to know the manpower, training and equipment status of every company in this division.

"I want you to talk to these troops—use the interpreters if you need to—but find out what they do and don't do, what they are good at and what they can't get their heads out of their asses to do. I want what you find out to guide you in making recommendations to the new Operations Officer for what he should prioritize in setting up his training schedules."

Pascoe then turned around in his chair and pulled a beige paperback book off the shelf. He threw it across the room to Laury who caught it. "I don't care what your religion was when you came here. That's your new bible now—the Division Operations Manual. I want you to memorize it. I want you do know every word in and be able to quote it to me if I ask. You got that?"

"Yes, sir."

"Go," Pascoe said.

The major stood, saluted and left Pascoe's office not waiting for a returned salute.

As Laury got to the door, Pascoe stopped him. "One more thing . . ."

The major stopped and turned back to Pascoe. "Yessir?"

"Everything you read—I want you to have that whale of an assistant of yours read everything too. You got that?"

"Yessir." Laury left the office.

Pascoe turned to look out the window trying to calm his anger. Colonel Wright had done it. He had gotten back at him for embarrassing him in front of General Devlen. He knew he couldn't complain to the general. But he would come up with a plan to make it backfire on Colonel Wright. Maybe if he let the General see the two new replacements at his next visit, their malassignment would be obvious to General Devlen, and he would take action. It also wouldn't hurt if the Vietnamese complained through their channels.

Somehow, he would make Colonel Wright pay for screwing him.

The day's haul was disappointing. After getting some sleep, Scotty spent the better part of the afternoon catching tadpoles and small frogs in the marsh water. He had caught several but knew they would yield less than two ounces of edible meat. Still, it was food.

While he was catching supper Nguyen had been separating the edible parts of a pile of water lilies. He then sorted lily parts and waited for Scotty to skin the small amphibians to salvage enough edible protein.

Nguyen served the tasteless Asian swamp salad on a large flat leaf Scotty couldn't identify and encouraged Scotty to simply combine the small slivers of raw meat with the lilies and eat it all.

Scotty fought the urge to gag putting the first bite in his mouth. He'd eaten worse in Ranger School, but he never thought back then there was a real reason for it in training. He had always thought it was one way to separate the men from the boys. Now he was living the very reason for the extreme cuisine he had eaten in the Florida Ranger Camp tucked into the swamps—survival.

He found he was so hungry for anything the food soon took away some of the cramping and some of the light headedness. He washed it all down with more than half a canteen full of the brackish water heavily overpowered by the chemical taste of the purification tablets. In the back of his mind, he was hoping whatever purification the tablets held for water would extend to the food and protect him from whatever evils the marsh vegetables and uncooked paddy life might possess.

After eating, Scotty cleaned up any signs of having prepared a meal and buried all the scraps as he had done with the excess equipment in the first thicket.

Before dark, he checked Nguyen's wound and rationed out more Darvon to help him with the unending pain. Nguyen thanked him for the care and the dinner, but Scotty told him he needed to rest and not talk. After dark, they would be moving out again. Things seemed to be going as well as could be expected, then Scotty heard it: Rain.

Her watch told her it was almost time to leave for her shift at Ronnie's. Eileen was worried Kitty had been in her room since late afternoon and it was getting dark.

Ever since they got the news about Scotty Kitty's constant smile was gone. Eileen worried about the impact of Kitty's mood on her health.

She tried to slip into Kitty's room without making any noise in case Kitty was sleeping. The room was dark—the lights out and curtains drawn. Eileen tiptoed across the floor, but before reaching Kitty's bedside, she saw her turn over.

"Eileen? That you, hon?"

Eileen sat on the edge of Kitty's bed and stroked her hair. "Yes. Hope I didn't wake you. How you feeling?"

Kitty sat up a bit in her bed and pulled yet another tissue from the box on her nightstand. She blew her nose and wiped tears from her eyes before replying. "I just don't know if anything in this world could break my heart more than this."

"You know, Kitty, if he were here he'd say you can't let this get to you so bad it makes you sicker. You know that, don't you?"

"Of course he would. He's grown up so much since high school, and he's the best son . . . But he's missing." She broke out in quiet heaving sobs and tears streamed down her face again.

"You're going to think I'm completely crazy, but I think he's alive too. I feel way down in my gut he's not dead and he's gonna' be okay. Is that crazy, because I believe it as if I know it's true?"

Kitty took Eileen's hands in her own. "It's because you love him and your heart won't let you think anything else.

"I want him to be okay, and I want him to come back to me, to us. I want you two to have the time together you deserve."

"Then you need to keep your spirits up and stay healthy so we can welcome him home."

"Do you pray, honey?" Kitty asked.

"I didn't. I do now."

CHAPTER 22

It took Scotty and Nguyen three more days to move only four miles. They held up in what remained of a small rice farm which looked to Scotty to have been abandoned back when the French were still fighting in Vietnam. The structures which had once been the farmer's home and his livestock pen had collapsed and were overgrown with weeds and brush winding up through the thatch and bamboo once offering shelter for his family and his animals.

Scotty had moved them into what remained of a lean-to once the shelter for the farm's stores of rice, water, and edible roots. After searching the few earthen crocks, Scotty was only able to find a few handfuls of rice which had somehow survived the years. He knew they couldn't start a fire to cook the rice, but at Nguyen's suggestion, they soaked the rice in water for several hours to soften it—making it palatable if not pleasant tasting.

Over the week and a half they had been moving, both Scotty and Nguyen's health were showing the toll. Nguyen's wound had crusted over and was slowly oozing awful smelling pus from a raging infection. But he refused to complain and refused to quit. Each time Scotty asked him if he needed to stop longer he would insist Scotty not be concerned but to focus on their survival. Scotty had never seen real courage before—not like Nguyen's.

Scotty's condition worsened. He couldn't remember all of the earmarks of malaria but assumed it was what he was suffering from. He ached everywhere and alternated between periods of fever and chills he could shrug off.

After a night of more chills than fever, Scotty yearned for the sun to come out to help warm him up. But with the dawn, the skies filled with rain clouds. He would spend another miserable day waiting for darkness to fall.

Scotty got no rest during the day. Whatever he had was getting worse. His eyes hurt, and he couldn't fall asleep because he was experiencing pain in his lower back.

Certain he would not be able to sleep, he crawled to the margins of the brush hiding him and Nguyen for the day and scooped water from the flooded paddy field and poured it over his face and neck to try to bring down the fever.

He looked up at the sky hoping for rain which would bring cooler temperatures and make him feel better.

Pascoe looked through the doorway of the mess hall and saw the low ceiling hanging over the compound. He tried to remember the dry season which had been in its waning days when he arrived at the Sugar Mill. Knowing there was absolutely nothing he could do about the coming rain, he pushed the screen door open and stepped out into the compound.

As he walked to his office to start his day he saw Sergeant Jackson sitting on a porch across the compound with a Vietnamese sergeant. As they spoke, Jackson took notes. Pascoe also noticed Jackson mopping the perspiration from his face even though it was still the cool part of the day. He made a note to check on Jackson's weight program.

The pile of paperwork on Pascoe's desk never seemed to end. As quickly as he would read and respond to the endless demands from MACV headquarters for input regarding operations, training, equipment, enemy sightings and funds expenditures he would find more of the same replacing them.

He looked up from his desk and caught sight of Sergeant Jackson across the hall in the Vietnamese operations section talking to a file clerk. "Jackson!"

The sergeant turned toward Pascoe's voice.

"Come in here."

The sergeant found a spot in front of Pascoe's desk. "Yessir?"

"Sit down."

The sergeant took the single chair in front of the desk and sat waiting for Pascoe to speak.

"Tell me about your weight."

"Well, sir, you know we don't have any scales around here. Weight doesn't seem to be somethin' these people concern themselves with," he said, referring to the Vietnamese soldiers.

"Are you on your diet and doing your PT?"

The sergeant leaned back and hooked his thumb into the waistband of his trousers pulling them away from his ample belly. "All I can tell you, Colonel, is I've been able to tighten my belt, and my pants are a little roomier in the ass end."

"Well, I want you to keep at it. We need to get you down to a weight where you can get out in the bush with the troops.

"Now, what was all that with you and that Vietnamese soldier on the steps of the supply room?"

The sergeant became uncomfortable with the question, and his tone changed noticeably. "Oh, I was just talking to him about, ah . . . training."

"What training?"

"I wanted to know what he thought they needed," the sergeant replied, not convincing Pascoe.

"You read those After Action Reports?"

"Yessir . . ."

"How far back?"

"Six months."

Pascoe sat back in his chair. "So, tell me. What have you learned?"

"I think they need lots more training in patrolling and marksmanship. They don't seem to find many bad guys out there and when they do they can't seem to hit them when they shoot. "

"I agree. Have you discussed this with Major Laury?"

"Not yet, sir," he said, starting to get up.

"Tell him I agree when you see him this morning."

"I won't be seein' him today, sir." He started moving toward the door.

"Why?"

"He's up in Tay Ninh talking to the chopper pilots about possibilities for more training with aircraft."

"Good. Good. Well, tell him when he returns." Pascoe stood and picked up his cap off his desk. "I'm going over to see General Duong. If anyone needs me, I'll be there." He tapped the pile of papers in his outbox. "I need you to get these to Saigon."

Jackson stood and said, "Yessir," eager to leave.

Scotty crawled to Nguyen to alert him they needed to move again. It was getting dark and had been raining for most of the day. If it continued, it would help conceal their movement and some of the sounds they made moving.

"You have fever," Nguyen said.

"I'll tell you, Dai Uy, I think it's malaria. It probably won't kill me, but I feel like shit."

"No."

"No? No what?" Scotty asked.

"Not malaria. Is Dengue."

"Dengue fever?" Scotty asked, surprised at the captain's diagnosis.

"Yes. You have pain in head?"

"Yeah, and my back and my joints."

Nguyen nodded his head. "Dengue."

"Shit! This is going to get worse. Isn't it?"

"Yes, my friend. It can be very bad."

Scotty racked his brain trying to remember his medical training and vaguely recalled Dengue could be fatal in its worst form—hemorrhagic fever. "Well, there's not a damn thing I can do." He got up to pick up Nguyen. "So I got to live with it. Let's go while I can still lift you."

They moved for most of the night without a break. Scotty wanted to put as much distance between them and the Cambodian border while he could still carry Captain Nguyen.

Toward dawn Scotty slowed partially catch his breath and reposition the captain slung over his shoulder and to look at something confusing ahead of him.

"What is wrong?" Nguyen asked.

"I don't know," Scotty whispered. "I think we've got a road or something up ahead." He turned around in a complete circle just to see if anyone else might be moving hidden by the rain and darkness.

Turning back to their direction of travel, he took several more labored steps and recognized an irrigation canal. The near bank was void of vegetation, obviously used by small wildlife in the area.

On the far bank, a stand of Nipa palm trees sprouted out of a head-high cluster of bushes and weeds.

Scotty put Nguyen down and then slid over the side of the canal into the water just a foot below the top of the bank. The canal, only waist deep, held running water which though cloudy was clear of debris compared to what they had been drinking for days.

He immediately welcomed the cooling effect of the water on his body. His fever had sapped his strength and made him nauseous for most of the night. He moved to the far bank and pulled himself out of the canal to check out the vegetation on the other side for a place they could lay up during the day coming on in a matter of minutes.

There he found the high ground was neither marshy nor muddy. The falling rain was running off the grasses there, and to him, it looked like a four-star hotel room.

Scotty crossed the canal again, picked up Nguyen and carried him in his arms to the new hiding place.

Once there, he flopped onto the ground to try to marshal needed to get through their next day.

After resting long enough to get his wind back, Scotty got to his feet and told Nguyen he wanted to look around.

On the far side of the new treeline hiding them was a bomb crater. He crawled out of the trees far enough to look into the crater and out over the terrain beyond.

The inside of the crater was half filled with quiet standing water broken only by the light rain still falling. It was sixteen feet across, and Scotty guessed it to be not more than nine feet deep. The pockmark in the paddy was perfectly round and the sides were steeply sloped. Satisfied no one was hiding in the crater, Scotty took a long, slow look at the terrain around their hiding place. To the north, he saw something irregular in the distant paddy. He dug his elbows into the muddy ground to steady his binoculars and looked again. There, silhouetted against the black skyline was the outline of two Viet Cong infiltrators walking slowly, half bent at the waist.

He guessed they were far enough away not to be a threat to Scotty or Nguyen if they maintained the same heading. They did remind Scotty of how perilous their own trip was and how much chance was involved in them being safe or being discovered.

He watched for a while hoping to see where they would hold up for the upcoming day but lost them when their route took them behind some small trees. Then he heard a splash. Then another. There were fish in the man-made hole. Fish!

When Scotty returned to his position inside the treeline, he found Nguyen dozing. "You okay, Dai Uy?"

"Maybe you go. Leave me. Come back."

Scotty sat near Nguyen. "What? I can't leave you. What if the VC stumble on you?"

"What if VC find now?"

Scotty knew Nguyen had a good point. Two of them were not more likely to be able to survive enemy contact anymore than one would. He knew what Nguyen was getting at. It wouldn't be long before he wouldn't be able to carry Nguyen another step. Scotty's strength was waning, and he was beginning to suffer from bouts of violently cramping diarrhea. He needed to make it as far as he could with Nguyen and then consider hiding him somewhere and getting help to recover him. But he wanted to try one thing first.

"Listen. How about this?" He pointed over his shoulder. "There's a bomb crater just outside the trees with fish in it. Let's lay up here for an extra day or two and see if we can do a little drying out, catch some fish to eat and get some rest. Then we move on. We're bound to be more rested. How does that sound, Dai Uy?"

Nguyen was quiet for a long time. "Good," was his only reply.

Scotty spent the early hours of the morning trying to catch the small fish in the crater using his hands. After an hour of unsuccessful attempts, he decided to try something else. He took his trousers off, tied the ankles of each leg in a knot and used them to scoop up large quantities of water. As the water leaked through the fabric, it left behind the small fish he had scooped up. Within two hours he had collected more than a dozen sardine-sized fish and took them back to his hiding place.

The two ate the raw fish and spent the remainder of the day resting. It was the first time in days they had been able to get enough protein to compensate for the demands they were placing on themselves. That coupled with not moving for two more days helped them delay the unavoidable toll the journey was taking on the two of them.

Scotty moved Nguyen to a spot where the light slipped through the trees and uncovered his wound to allow the sun to beat down on the torn and inflamed flesh. He hoped sunlight and fresh air might help dry out the tissues which had been wet since he sustained the wound.

While letting Nguyen take in some sun, he took the other already used combat dressing to the canal and washed the dried blood, mud, and dirt from the large gauze pad. Clean or not, the pad was anything but sterile. At least washing it and letting it dry out would provide better protection for Nguyen's wound once he replaced it.

With the afternoon came the seasonal rains. And with the rain came the cold. It was relative, but a thirty-degree drop in temperature as the light rain turned to steady rain and then to a downpour was enough to set both of them shivering. Scotty and Nguyen huddled together, back to back, to share their body heat, a trick Scotty had learned in Ranger School, keeping his kidneys as warm as possible circulated warmer blood and helped fight off the cold.

By dark, they were both shivering uncontrollably. Scotty wasn't sure how much of his was cold and how much was Dengue fever. He hoped their plans to get some rest by staying put for an extra day or two were not wrecked by the cold rain which would keep them from sleeping.

Eileen sipped her coffee sitting at the kitchen table at Kitty's. As she did, she looked at a small snapshot of Scotty she kept in a plastic covered pocket in her wallet.

"I miss him too, honey."

Kitty had slipped into the room quietly and stood over Eileen's shoulder.

Eileen looked up at Kitty, tried to speak and suddenly realized tears were streaming from her eyes.

Kitty pulled Eileen to her waist and hugged her. She stroked Eileen's hair and tried to calm her. "He's gonna' be okay. Sure as I'm standing here, he's going to come back to us. I lost a husband to a war. I ain't goin' t' lose a son to one."

Eileen leaned back and looked up into Kitty's eyes. "Oh, Kitty. This hurts so bad. I don't know what I'll do if I don't ever see him again."

"Shhh," Kitty said as she wiped the tears from Eileen's face with the cuff of her bathrobe.

"I can't take this waiting, and I'm ashamed I'm not stronger," Eileen said, sniffling then hugging Kitty tighter.

"Do what I'm doing."

"What's that?"

"Just start planning for what you want to do when you see him again. You got t'get your head right about this. You got to just think of nothing else but seeing him again soon. You got to believe as hard as you can he'll be coming home to you and me," Kitty said kissing Eileen on top of her head.

"How can you be so sure?"

"You and I both knew that boy when he was livin' here. And we saw how different he was after the Army got hold of him. He's strong. He's stubborn, and he's got a good heart. I have confidence in him. That's how I'm sure.

"Now, what is it you want to do when he comes home?" Kitty asked.

"I want to spend the rest of my life with him."

Kitty smiled, "Then you better get your dowry together, girl. 'Cause I know he's coming home."

Eileen laughed then found some worn and crumpled Kleenex in the pocket of her waitress apron to blow her nose. "Look at me. I'm a mess." She pulled a compact from her purse and looked at herself in the small round mirror. Her mascara had run down her face. "I look like a raccoon."

They both laughed, and Kitty rubbed Eileen's shoulders reassuringly. "Don't you need to be gettin' to work?"

Eileen checked her watch. "Oh, God yes. But do you have everything you need? You hungry? Need me to get anything at the store for you?"

"Go. Go do what you gotta' do. I'll be okay."

Eileen stood to go, and there was an awkward moment of silence. She looked at Kitty one last time, her unspoken questions were clear: Would he really return? Would he really be okay?

"I'm right about this. Now you go to work and make some plans. Plans for you two when he comes home. Now, go on, git."

Kitty closed the door behind Eileen and walked back into the kitchen. She pulled a mug from the cupboard over the sink and poured herself a cup of coffee. She took a sip and began to quietly cry for her boy.

With sunrise came relief from the bone-chilling cold during the night's rains. Scotty looked through the trees hoping to find more blue sky than clouds but had to settle for a little of each. At least it had stopped raining.

The day and the one following was a repeat of those before. They tried to rest and conserve some strength. Scotty dried out some of the small fish, wrapped them in his cravat and stuffed them in his pocket to take with them.

By dark, they had decided to try something new. The canal next to where they were hiding was going in the general direction of the Sugar Mill. Scotty wanted to see if he could make better time if they got into the canal and he pulled Nguyen along using Nguyen's buoyancy to relieve Scotty of the burden of carrying him.

They emptied their canteens to turn them into floats. Scotty screwed the tops back on and tied them about five inches apart with is boot laces. He then placed Nguyen on his back in the canal and slipped the two canteens under the small of the captain's back. They offered enough floatation to raise his hips off the bottom of the canal.

Scotty took hold of Nguyen's collar and began to draw him gently through the water, careful not to allow the water to swamp his face as they moved.

In an hour they had covered more ground than any earlier night. Scotty was encouraged by the progress but worried about the cold water on Nguyen. He stopped several times and asked if Nguyen wanted to get out of the water and warm up.

Nguyen wouldn't complain though his lips were blue.

They kept moving until just after midnight and found the canal suddenly taking a turn to the north, no longer in their intended direction. Scotty left Nguyen on the bank of the canal and waded ahead for another hundred meters hoping the canal might switch back. It didn't. He gave up for the night and looked for a place to conceal them. Within twenty minutes he found a depression in the paddies with plenty of vegetation growing in it. It was wet, but offered the concealment they would need the following day.

Scotty and Nguyen got little sleep that night—each taking turns staying awake to watch for anyone stumbling on their site. Scotty's attempts at sleep were fitful. His fever came and went only to be replaced by uncontrollable shivering and chills. He knew he was losing strength rapidly. His challenge beyond avoiding capture was to hold on long enough to get the two of them back into South Vietnamese hands. The rest would just be luck. He had more confidence in his ability a few days earlier. That night he was no longer sure he could do it. They had been in the marshes for over two full weeks. He looked over at the sleeping Asian officer knowing his failure would surely mean Nguyen's death. He told himself he had to put failure out of his head. He had to drive on. This was what Asa Russell would expect of him.

About an hour before dawn Nguyen woke Scotty who thought it was his turn to take the watch. It wasn't.

Nguyen pointed out at three figures moving carefully through the reeds. Their direction of march put them on a collision course with Scotty and Nguyen.

They stayed still, watching the soldiers close on their position, moving to within fifty meters.

Scotty looked over at Nguyen who shook his head, indicating Scotty shouldn't shoot. He held his fire and let them continue to approach.

Suddenly, one of the soldiers said something and pointed in the direction of Scotty and Nguyen. Scotty was sure he would have no choice. He would have to fire on the three before he lost a clear line of sight to each. But another pointed off to the south, disagreeing with the first Viet Cong soldier. What ensued was an argument between the two over their direction of travel. It finally became apparent to Scotty the second soldier won the argument. The three suddenly changed direction and walked south—away from Scotty and Nguyen.

As the three put more distance between themselves and Scotty and Nguyen, Scotty was overcome with nausea again. He tried to suppress the urge to vomit but was unsuccessful. The onset was sudden, his stomach was virtually empty of everything but some water, and the attack passed quickly. Still, he was afraid the three Viet Cong soldiers might have heard him. He snapped his head back up and looked in the direction of the soldiers moving away from them and saw the one closest to their hiding place halt temporarily as if he heard something. He listened then seemed to shrug it off and continue to move away.

The waves of nausea came and went for the next two hours, and Scotty had nothing left to vomit. He splashed water in his face hoping to make himself feel a little better and looked over to Nguyen. He was looking at his wound. "What's wrong, Dai Uy?"

"Am okay. You rest."

Scotty moved to Nguyen and lifted the corner of his dressing covered with mud. What he found was disgusting. The wound was infested with maggots feeding on the deadened flesh surrounding the center of the injury. "Oh, man. This is not good."

"We home soon. I be okay," Nguyen said.

Scotty felt Nguyen's face with the back of his hand and could tell the captain was spiking a temperature greater than he had experienced since being wounded. Their trek, the elements, and their diet were all conspiring against both soldiers. It was decision time for Scotty. He was certain he had to outrun his own disabling disease and the accelerated spread of Nguyen's infection.

During their journey, Scotty lost much of the confidence in his estimates of the distance they had traveled and how much ground they still had to cover. He pulled his map from his pocket and tried to orient it but knew it would be difficult since there were so few good landmarks to use to plot his position precisely.

He rolled over to the margins of the thick weedy hedge concealing them and parted the leaves enough to look out in the direction of the Sugar Mill.

What he saw surprised him. Traffic. People. Walking. He could see tiny motor scooters and miniature ox carts moving barely three miles ahead of him along a dirt roadway hugging the bank of a river running generally north and south. It had to be the Vam Co Dong River—the one the Sugar Mill was built on. He couldn't see anything looking like the Sugar Mill, but he could see small, single-story buildings of stucco and thatch—hamlets—South Vietnamese hamlets.

If they could get there. If they could only get to that river without being caught, shot or tripping a booby trap, they would survive. They could get help. He and Nguyen could get much-needed medical attention. If only he could get them across the final three miles of dangerous open ground.

He looked for available way stations where they could hide out, as they had done since leaving the border. There were none in a direct line from where he hid to the closest point on the path following the river. There were some to the north and some to the south. To take advantage of them would mean covering almost half again as much distance to get to them just to hide in them.

Scotty looked back at his map and had a better idea of where they were, now that he could see a turn in the river ahead of him. Excited, he turned to Nguyen. "Dai Uy. Look. Here." He pointed in the direction of the river.

Nguyen could hardly raise his head. The strength he needed to move to Scotty seemed outside his reach.

It was certain now, Scotty really needed to move faster. He needed to get this man to help before the infection killed him. He crawled over to Nguyen. "Can I drag you over here to look? Can you just tell me what I'm seeing is what I'm seeing?"

The captain nodded weakly.

"Don't move. Let me." Scotty hooked his hands under Nguyen's arms and slid him to a point where he too could see through the vegetation at the people walking, unafraid, unarmed but with a purpose to places important to them.

Nguyen's eyes kept closing as if he didn't have the strength to stay awake. He fought the urge to let his body take him into restful sleep and looked in the direction Scotty was pointing. He seemed to smile, ever so slightly, and said something Scotty couldn't quite hear.

"What? What did you say?" Scotty asked, putting his ear only inches from Nguyen's lips.

"An Ninh . . ."

"An Ninh? Did you say An Ninh?" Scotty asked.

Nguyen nodded affirmatively and closed his eyes.

An Ninh, Scotty ran his finger up the river depicted on his map and found it—An Ninh. It was a small village not more than a mile north of the Sugar Mill. He remembered driving through there. He remembered there was a major roadway through it. He'd been there. He'd just never seen its skyline from that angle.

Excited, Scotty turned to Nguyen to share the good news he'd confirmed on his map only to find him asleep. He reached over and felt his skin again. It was burning.

Scotty pulled his cravat from around his neck, soaked in the swamp water, wrung it out and placed it on Nguyen's throat—next to his jugular hoping to help cool him down.

He looked at his watch. It was getting late. He had to make a decision quickly. He knew if he carried Nguyen the rest of the way, as weak as he was himself, it would take them three more days—at least. Where would they hold up during the daylight? He had no good options.

But he might be able to make it by himself in half that time, get some help and come back. He knew the decision was his to make. Nguyen wouldn't be able to discuss it with him. And even if he could, what would be the point? He had learned a lot about the little captain in their time together. He was incredibly brave, stoic and unselfish. He would surely argue for being left behind.

Scotty would do it. But what needed to be done first? He couldn't just walk off and leave Nguyen. He needed to put a plan together to leave Nguyen with whatever Nguyen might need. Once that was done, he needed to move fast.

Before he made any final decision and made arrangements to leave, he needed some rest. He knew it was dangerous to try to get some sleep while Nguyen was sleeping, but he couldn't wait for the captain to wake up and spell him. Even if he did wake up, how long could he stay awake? Scotty had to take the chance. He propped himself up against a small stand of pygmy bamboo and rested his rifle across his knees. He desperately needed to rest, but he also needed to be very vigilant and use his hearing to warn them of the approach of anyone while he tried to rest.

He closed his eyes and listened. The air was still, birds were chirping at a distance and insects chimed in. Then he heard it. Choppers. He heard helicopters. Not close and not coming their way, but close enough to hear. He was that close to safety but still in grave danger.

Pascoe was pleased he had been able to convince General Duong to go along with his new plan to pay for information from previously uncooperative villagers and then exploit the information to concentrate their ambushes on the most likely enemy infiltration routes. The plan still needed to be blessed by MACV. It would be US money they would spend. That meant convincing General Devlen of the promise the plan offered. He knew he'd have to put on a good sales pitch. He was pleased with the content of his briefing, but he was far from patient with his new senior sergeant. "Goddamn it, Jackson. Stay with me!"

Sergeant Jackson stood between a large paper easel with a list of points written on the attached pad in large block letters and the tactical map covered by acetate and marked with areas of interest Pascoe was referring to.

Pascoe stood nearby at a plywood podium off to the side of the visuals

Jackson was pointing out with a long white pointer and picked up his place in the prepared text he was reading.

Both men faced an empty briefing room with the chairs arranged neatly in rows, and GI butt cans made from empty coffee cans painted red, filled with a few inches of water and placed on wooden stands every three chairs.

Pascoe read a sentence from his text and then looked over at Jackson to see if he was pointing to the place on the map or the point on the bulleted list Pascoe was referring to. "We are going to rehearse this until it is letter perfect. I don't care if we have to do it twenty times. When I say something requiring you to point it out, I want you to do so without hesitation and without error. You got me, Sergeant?"

"Yessir," the sergeant replied, large ovals of perspiration staining the armpits of his uniform becoming evident each time he extended his arm to point.

"And I want you in a fresh uniform when we brief General Devlen. You hear me?"

"Yessir."

Pascoe gathered up his text, flipped it over to the first page and began again, speaking to the empty chairs.

"*General Devlen, General Duong, distinguished visitors, welcome to the 6th Infantry Division headquarters. This morning's briefing is to familiarize you with the division's plan to increase its effectiveness to interdict enemy movement through the area of operations and gain your support and the resources necessary to gain the desired results . . .*"

They went through the entire twenty-minute briefing four more times, and Pascoe told Jackson to plan on doing it again the next day—until it was perfect.

CHAPTER 23

It took much of the afternoon for Scotty to gather enough dry leaves and grasses to make a nest for Captain Nguyen. Scotty picked the highest spot inside the stubby trees to reduce the chance the water would rise and swamp Nguyen and to increase the chance any new rains would quickly run off and away from him keeping him as dry as possible.

After helping the weakened and feverish Nguyen onto the bed he had made, Scotty began covering him with more leaves until he had made a blanket. It would help reflect his body heat and keep Nguyen warm during the cold nights and rains he would surely face while Scotty was gone.

He left his canteens filled and within reach. He could drink out of the paddies and streams along the way.

In a canteen cup, Scotty left rice they had come across, softened in water and made into a pasty mush. In a second cup, he placed fingerlings and two freshwater prawns for Nguyen.

Scotty checked his carbine to make sure it was loaded and operating smoothly. He emptied his pockets of the three remaining twenty-round magazines and put them in Nguyen's shirt pocket where he could get at them easily. He finally rested the rifle across the captain's thighs.

Nothing needed to be said between them. The fact Scotty was leaving his rifle with Nguyen reinforced their understanding about their relative vulnerabilities. If Nguyen were to be found, he would have to defend himself as long as his could hold out. If Scotty were to be discovered in his last efforts to cross the paddies to get help, he would be unlikely to win a shootout with more than one Viet Cong. And he was unlikely to run into only one enemy soldier. For him, a rifle would just slow him down and might cause him to be mistaken for a Viet Cong soldier. Any South Vietnamese soldier wouldn't think a lone figure walking through that area with a rifle would be an American. He would protect himself with Nguyen's pistol but keep it concealed in his shirt.

Sitting back on his heels, Scotty looked at Nguyen. "What am I forgetting, Dai Uy?"

"I be good here. You go."

"You gonna' be okay?"

"Yes. You go."

Scotty stood and looked directly into Nguyen's eyes, even though it was not done in the captain's culture. "I promise you I will come back to get you. I promise."

Nguyen smiled, his voice weak, "Yes. I know."

***

His feet hurt from days of exposure, constant immersion in water and cutting fibers of roots and small rocks each time his bare feet sliced into the mud. The speed Scotty had hoped to pick up by not carrying Nguyen was offset by his continuing deterioration. The spiking fevers and joint pains had been accompanied by ever increasing back pains, nausea, and pounding headaches. He even experienced pain when he moved his eyes. Pain which compounded the severity of his headaches.

He had been moving for an hour when he felt another wave of nausea and the urge to vomit. He knew this was the worst. It was almost impossible to vomit quietly.

Luckily, it had started to rain again. The rain helped cover the retching sounds. On his hands and knees, he tried to vomit into his own footprints to cover up some of the evidence he had passed that way and make it a bit easier by only having to shove mud into the hole rather than dig one.

Closer to midnight Scotty simply had to sit down. His legs couldn't hold him up. He'd been staggering for almost two hours when he did stop.

As he sat in the middle of an old rice paddy, too tired to move to a nearby dike which might offer some added concealment, the water covered his legs up to a point just below his navel. Though feverish, he began to shiver, rain pounding on his head and neck and plopping loudly in the paddy water. He thought of Nguyen and wondered if he was doing okay or if the rain was as bone-chilling for him. He hoped the blanket of leaves he had prepared for him helped him hold the little body heat he had left.

Ahead, Scotty could see the tiny lights from lamps and lanterns in the houses along the far bank of the river. In the rain and the dark, it was hard for him to tell how far away they were. He couldn't tell if he would have to walk yet another night to reach the river's edge.

He had never felt so exhausted. Nor had he ever felt such little confidence in what he had to do. He shivered violently and considered his options. If he got back up and continued, he could count on the effort to move to warm him up. But what if that same effort proved to be too much and he found himself collapsing before reaching help? He promised Nguyen. He thought of Eileen and Kitty.

It took considerable effort to get from sitting to standing and then walking again. But he did it. As he walked, each step more painful and more demanding than the last, he heard Ace Russell's voice in his head. "What's wrong with you, boy? You some kind of sissy or something? Get your ass moving soldier, or I'll put a boot in it for you." He hoped Russell's night was going better than his.

A few steps and he began hearing his own words though they were barely audible. "You can do this, Hayes. You can do this. Just pick up your foot and put it down. You can do it . . ."

He had no idea what time it was and didn't want to look at his watch. It was still dark. He had to keep moving as long as it was dark. As long as he could walk.

Suddenly, Scotty felt himself falling forward. Damn! He had tripped over something and was falling. The ground was going to hurt. He was sure of that. With the aches in his muscles and joints, the impact would hurt. Jump School flashed through his head. Falling was falling. Hitting the ground was all the same, with or without a parachute. He tried to twist his torso to expose the same body parts he would use making a parachute landing fall—calves, thighs, buttocks, pushup muscles. But he never got that far, and the ground never happened.

He landed in a small stream with an awkward splash. It was moving water. Water jetted up his nose and made him gag. He snapped his head up to get some air and clear his mouth and throat and found himself floating. Floating! Floating in the general direction of the river. It was a tributary feeding the river he wanted to reach. He had tripped over a dike holding the water on its course.

Scotty searched below the water's surface with his hands and found the stream was two feet deep and about as wide as he could reach with both arms extended. The sides of the stream were exposed roots he could use to navigate his drifting and help keep him from dragging bottom.

The help in moving was what he needed to overcome his flagging endurance, but the water chilled him to the core. The rain fed the stream which moved even faster the closer he got to the river—and the water got much colder too.

He decided to stay in the water as long as he could stand it then get out and warm up by walking along the bank. Once the walking became too taxing, he would get back in the streambed. At least, that was the plan.

Scotty was very disappointed in his ability to stand the cold. He'd been in the water for half an hour before he couldn't stop his teeth from chattering. He grabbed some roots below the water line to stop, pulled his legs up under him to a kneeling position with difficulty. He crawled to the stream bank and fell over its edge, rolling into the adjacent paddy, completely exhausted. He laid there in the mud half-submerged the rain pounding him in the face and rolling off into his ears.

He knew he had to go on. He wanted so badly to sleep, to find some warmth and just sleep. He knew sleep would kill him. He would drown in the paddy water or be discovered once at sun up. He started yelling at himself in his head. Get up, Ranger. What's wrong with you? You some kind of pansy, Ranger? Roll your ass over and get up. Now, Ranger! People are counting on you, Hayes.

On his stomach, pain stabbed his lower back as he fought to keep his face out of the water. He had to get up. Getting on all fours was extremely painful, but he did it. Once there, he rested for the next move. He sucked up as much air as he could hoping to flood his muscles with the oxygen he needed. He had to get up. He had to move.

He found the strength somewhere and got to his feet again. Unsteady, dizzy and still shivering, he took a step. Then the next. And the next.

It was still dark when Pascoe left the mess hall with a cup of coffee in hand. He had learned many years earlier the lesson of any classroom or briefing. If you don't rehearse and check on all your training aids, you are sure to find something missing, wrong, or out of place when it is time for the briefing. With Generals Pham and Devlen coming that day to hear the plan he and General Duong had put together, he would not be embarrassed by being unprepared. There was still time for one more rehearsal.

The only bright spot in Pascoe's day was finding Sergeant Jackson and Major Laury waiting for him in the briefing room. "Jackson," he said, a clear tone of displeasure in his voice.

The portly sergeant leaped to his feet from a folding chair in the front row. "Yessir?"

"What the hell is wrong with you?"

"Sir?"

"The sun isn't even up yet, and you are sweating like a pig. Look at your uniform," Pascoe said, moving close enough to Jackson to make him lean back.

"Sir, it's hot here."

"By now you should be acclimatized and not look like a bag of wet rags. Remember, I want you in a fresh uniform before we start the briefing. You got that?"

The sergeant nodded his head and avoided eye contact with Pascoe. "Yes, sir. I'll do that."

"Now," he turned to Laury, "let's get started. Major, I want you to sit in General Devlen's chair and raise your hand every time I say something and Jackson here doesn't point to exactly the right point on the charts or map. Have you got that?"

Laury guarded his expression, moved to the general's chair and replied, "Yessir. I've got it."

Pascoe took the podium, pointed at the spot where he expected Jackson to be and began reading his briefing text while the sergeant took his position.

He could hear the thunder in the black boiling clouds which had passed over him earlier and were now many miles inside Cambodia. Throwing his arms out to his side to steady himself and keep from falling, Scotty looked up for a sign of dawn. On the horizon, he could see a thin line of pink separating the dark night sky from the broken horizon now dotted for him with hamlets and villages.

The river he fought to reach was still a mile off, and he needed to move faster to get there before being discovered walking through the dangerous no-man's-land. He knew it meant getting back into the freezing stream swelled that much more by the rains over the past three hours.

The water was colder than before. New rain, new runoff and the increased speed of the current chilled him within seconds of returning to the stream. He would have to move faster to beat the sunrise and generate some heat deep in his torso. He reached down and grabbed handfuls of roots on the bottom of the stream and increased his speed by pulling himself along, aided by the current.

As he crawled along the streambed, letting his body half-drag and half-float behind him, he held his head above the water trying to push the pain of his crushing headache out of his mind by focusing on the most pleasant thing he could think of—Eileen's face. He saw her in his mind, and he heard her words. He recalled sentences from her letters and tried to imagine her long, slender fingers writing the words she sent to him.

He crawled faster and tried to imagine her scent and the soft silky texture of her hair. All the while he was unaware of the fact he was talking as he moved, encouraging himself to move faster and not stop and to pull harder with his arms. It didn't even sound like his voice. It was low and guttural and raspy. He had to get to that river. He couldn't lay up in the paddies another night. He couldn't last another night.

That much he knew.

The sky was clear enough, even though there were large gray-black threatening clouds still clearing on their way to Cambodia. Pascoe could hear the deep rhythmic thumping of the approaching chopper resonating in the heavy, moist air. The speck on the horizon kept getting bigger as he waited for the generals to arrive for his briefing.

As he waited, he repeated the words he had rehearsed in his room. Words of welcome for the two arriving general officers. He was a little uncomfortable with the fact General Duong had still not arrived to welcome Pham and Devlen. He turned and hollered into the briefing room through the open glassless window. "Jackson. Get on the horn and call over to the command post. And see what the hold up is with General Duong. Let his people know the chopper is inbound."

Before Jackson could cross the room to make the call, Pascoe saw General Duong step out into the compound from the headquarters office complex. He was wearing his best combat fatigue uniform, complete with a general's belt and a holstered .45 caliber pistol with tortoise shell hand grips.

Pascoe was not happy Duong had not heard the briefing yet. He wanted there not to be any surprises for Duong which might embarrass him in front of Devlen. But Duong had seemed to be uninterested in the details.

The chopper circled the compound and set up for a landing. Pascoe could see it was Devlen's chopper flown by American pilots and not General Pham's. He envied Devlen, having a new D Model Huey. Pascoe realized he had not seen Minh's chopper since the day he returned it to the compound. The repairs needed were extensive enough to require it be sent to Long Binh. Even as old as it was, it had been the best chopper in the division.

Scotty shivered as he pulled himself along the stream bottom in somewhat of a trance. He blocked out the pain and ignored the nausea, exhaustion, and danger he still faced. No longer able to hold his head up because of the pain in his neck, he kept his chin just below the water line and his eyes focused on its surface.

Suddenly his hands found something under the water which snapped him out of the fog pain and sleeplessness had brought on. It was wooden— man-made. He looked around at a platform on the bank connected to a slot under the water line. It was a crude device to divert water into a catch basin next to the stream where fish could be trapped.

He raised his head and saw he was not more than a hundred feet from the junction of the river and the stream. Not wanting to be swept into the faster-flowing river, Scotty crawled out onto his belly in the adjacent paddy. He looked around. There were people on the bank of the river starting out their day. They carried loads of produce destined for market. To the south, a boy with a long thin switch herded a water buffalo into a paddy and nearly fifteen giggling young women carrying small bundles appeared to be heading off to school.

No one on the river bank had seen him yet. He was the same color as the muddy paddy hiding him from notice. He knew he had to get on the roadway quickly before he became so exhausted he would be unable to stand or walk.

Scotty looked around in every direction. He was sure his situation was less threatened by the Viet Cong. Unless a hidden sniper were willing to risk exposing himself to get a shot off at Scotty he was unlikely to face enemy fire the last few strides to the roadway. But his mind began to spin as he realized he could still blow it all if he were to be mistaken as an enemy soldier coming out of the no-man's-land. He looked up and down the bank and quickly found what he assumed would be his only immediate threat. Downstream a small single-lane bridge crossed the river, and a sandbagged guard post held two armed South Vietnamese soldiers. They were from a local unit posted to permanent sites often threatened by the Viet Cong.

Scotty knew they were poorly trained and poorly equipped, making them more likely to spook and shoot at anything they felt might threaten them. He would have to get onto the roadway and mingle with the civilians to avoid being singled out as a target by the two soldiers leaning against their guard post smoking and laughing.

Getting to his feet was harder than he had anticipated. His head spun as he stood and he needed a few seconds to regain his balance.

**

The pilots put the general's chopper on the helipad with little flair or difficulty. The rains had kept the dust down, and the pathway from the chopper to the briefing room had been covered with a raised wooden walkway to keep the visitors out of the mud.

A gaggle of Vietnamese soldiers and staff officers escorted the two generals from the chopper to the briefing room and saw to it each was offered coffee, tea or a soft drink.

Pascoe felt a touch of stage fright as he looked out across the briefing room now filled with the visiting dignitaries and members of the division staff.

He looked at Jackson, standing stiffly, if not awkwardly, in a fresh set of fatigues between the easel and the tactical map in the front of the room.

The room quieted down as Pascoe took the podium to begin his briefing.

Scotty stepped onto the well-worn trail next to the river and began walking for the first time in seventeen days on hard packed earth. In front and behind him the nearest Vietnamese civilians were not closer than fifty meters. None of them showed any recognition he was there. Scotty knew they saw him, but could understand them not getting involved with a strange looking staggering American, bearded, barefoot and covered with mud. He walked toward the bridge keeping his eyes focused on the two Vietnamese soldiers guarding it. He wanted to be able to raise his hands to show he was not a threat to them, if needed. If that didn't work, he walked close enough to the roadway's edge to be able to jump back into the rice paddies to take some cover should the soldiers fire on him.

Each step was more painful than the last. Skin was sloughing off his feet after days of softening and deadening in the mud and water. His nausea wouldn't go away, and he wobbled as he walked. He tried to straighten up and not look like a drunk fighting to keep from falling off the trail as he approached the soldiers at the bridge.

One of them spotted Scotty, stared as if unsure what he was looking at and then poked his partner.

Scotty heard words in his brain as he silently prayed for help. God, don't let this end here. Please don't let me spook them. Then he thought it would be up to him. He held his hands where they could see they were empty as he walked the last ten paces to their bunker and forced a smile so they'd be more likely not to see him as a threat.

The two soldiers stood there frozen with curiosity at Scotty's approach and unsure what to do. They said nothing as he walked past them to cross the bridge.

Scotty considered stopping but realized he didn't know enough Vietnamese to explain his problem. And he could see they had neither a radio nor a phone in their small, open-topped sandbagged enclosure. So he nodded politely and walked onto the bridge.

He heard them talk to each other as he passed and turned to make sure they weren't expecting him to halt. The last thing he wanted was to be shot in the back.

As he turned around, he saw what they were talking about. He was leaving bloody footprints with each step.

He entered the heavier flow of traffic on the asphalt roadway on the other side of the bridge and keep urging himself to keep moving. He only had a thousand more meters to go to get to the Sugar Mill, and he could feel his knees getting more wobbly. He turned around and hoped he would find some soldiers or a military vehicle headed to the compound but found only merchants and farmers quickly moving past him all in a hurry to be somewhere else.

Scotty couldn't stop. He continued walking unsteadily down the roadway conscious of the stares he was getting from Vietnamese along the road. Then he heard something behind him. Shuffling footsteps. He turned to find an old man wearing black pajamas, a conical hat and badly repaired flip flops on his feet. The man led an ox pulling a cart which was a flat wooden platform on top of salvaged car tires and an axle. The small cart had six bamboo cages all holding chickens and roosters.

The old man smiled, revealing almost no teeth and pointed to the cart, inviting Scotty to get on.

Scotty mimed a question for the man to make sure he understood the man's intent.

The old man responded by stepping back to the cart and patting it to show Scotty where to sit.

Scotty smiled and bowed thankfully at the old man and used what flagging strength he had to climb onto the worn wooden bed of the cart.

***

Through the briefing room window, the guard gate raised. Its motion caught Pascoe's eye from his place at the podium. He also heard the commotion coming from the guard gate as a handful of Vietnamese soldiers all began talking excitedly.

The activity at the gate also distracted everyone in the briefing room. All three generals turned to look at what was going on.

Pascoe, unsure about what to do, stopped speaking, hoping the soldiers would quiet down. But they didn't. Instead, he saw them part as if to allow a large vehicle to enter the compound. But in the center of the wide path they cleared through the front gate walked Scotty Hayes, half staggering.

The sight of the American sergeant shot a bolt of lightning through Pascoe's chest. What would he do? How could he explain this? What was Hayes going to say?

The word of Scotty's return quickly spread through the briefing room and the generals got their feet and went out into the compound.

Scotty noticed the officers at the doorway to the briefing room but ignored them. Instead, he staggered directly to the parked helicopter and the two American pilots sitting inside the cargo compartment. One was reading a magazine, and the other was writing a letter home. "I need your chopper, sir," Scotty said to the First Lieutenant closest to the open cargo door.

The lieutenant looked at the American sergeant, surprised painted all over his face. "What?"

Scotty raised his arm as if it were filled with wet cement and pointed off to the west. "I have a Viet captain I couldn't bring out with me. In need to go get him. He's out in the paddies."

The Warrant Officer threw on his flight helmet as the two pilots looked at each other and needed no more convincing. The lieutenant got out, helped Scotty into the chopper and got into his own seat in the cockpit. While his co-pilot ran up the turbines on the chopper, the lieutenant looked over his shoulder at Scotty. "How far out?

Scotty climbed into the chopper and then onto the canvas bench seat with great difficulty and nodded west. "A couple of miles. I can show you. We need to hurry. He's badly wounded, and I'm afraid he's in pretty rough shape."

The warrant officer looked back at Scotty. "If he's any worse off than you are, Sarge, we'll put a rush on it. Hold on back there."

Pascoe didn't know what to do. He rushed to the side of the idling chopper and looked in at Scotty. "So, you escaped? This is great news."

"*Escaped?*" Scotty asked. "Escaped, hell!" He pointed off toward the unseen border. "I walked here from where you left me, you asshole!"

Pascoe's color drained from his face. "I can see you are not yourself. We can talk about that later. Right now you need help."

Scotty ignored Pascoe's comments and buckled himself in the chopper.

Pascoe looked at the chopper and back to Scotty. "Where are you going with this chopper? Are they evacuating you to medical help?"

"No, Major. I'm going to do for Captain Nguyen what you wouldn't do for us, you son of a bitch! I'm going to go pull him out."

Three Vietnamese soldiers somehow understood enough of what was going on in the compound to run get their weapons and climb onboard the chopper with Scotty.

Scotty looked around at the faces and realized they were soldiers he had been on patrols with. Soldiers he had been chastised by Pascoe about being too familiar with. Now, when he needed them, they didn't even wait to be asked. He smiled and gave each of them a thumbs-up.

The chopper lifted off leaving Pascoe standing in the middle of the compound unsure how much of the conversation the general officers standing outside the briefing room had heard. However much it was, he knew it would take some quick thinking to talk himself out of the situation he had put himself in. He felt blood rushing to his face as he made eye contact with General Devlen—whose look told him Devlen had heard enough.

Scotty tried to keep from vomiting on the short flight out to Nguyen's position. He crawled up between the two pilot's seats and pointed them toward the area where Nguyen was hidden.

He became disoriented for a moment and had to move about the chopper to look out, first finding the small bridge and then getting the pilots to fly dangerously low so he could find his own trail in the mud which would take him back to the stream which had helped him get to safety.

His training kicked in at his moment of greatest need. Scotty found the location. Barely able to speak, he pointed at what seemed so much smaller from the air. "There! That's it. Land there!"

The pilot looked at Scotty and yelled over the noise of the rotor blades, "We're going to make one quick circle before we put it down. We'd just like to know there's nothing down there to surprise us."

Scotty nodded and sat back on the floor of the cargo deck hoping they would find nothing. The chopper descended, and the dwarf trees hiding Nguyen were soon visible out the left door. Scotty tried to be another set of eyes to make sure there was no one laying in wait to ambush a chopper coming to rescue Nguyen. As he looked out at the trees and the chopper got closer, he noticed several crows flying out of the treetops. He hoped they were not signaling what he most feared—Nguyen dead. He told himself they were not vultures; they were just crows. He hoped he hadn't taken too long to get help. He hoped he had left enough water and food with Nguyen to sustain him. And he found himself again asking God for help.

The chopper pilots put the aircraft down in the flooded rice paddy next to the trees hiding Nguyen, the chopper's blades not more than forty feet from the violently whipping branches.

Scotty slid across the floor of the cargo compartment then stepped out onto the muddy ground with little concern for the pain he felt in his feet. Instinctively, he looked around for anything or anyone who might threaten the rescue party. Seeing nothing obvious he pointed at three likely spots where the Vietnamese soldiers needed to position themselves to provide some modicum of protection for the helicopter crew now so vulnerable sitting on the ground at flight idle.

As the soldiers took up their positions, Scotty moved to the trees. With each step, he was announcing his desires. "Let him be okay. Let him be okay. Let's get him home."

His eyes took a few seconds to adjust to the darkness inside the thicket. At first, he couldn't see Nguyen where he had left him. But he forgot he had covered him with leaves and deadfall to keep him warm and hidden. His eyes finally detected the unnatural shape of the butt of Nguyen's rifle. He fell to his knees and crawled to his side, still half speaking, half hoping. "Dai Uy? You awake? We're going home. We're getting out of here."

Nguyen's body was still, his eyes closed.

Scotty reached out and touched him. He was wet and clammy. But his skin was hot. Scotty was thrilled to find the man still had a fever. "Dai Uy . . . Come on. Wake up," he yelled over the sounds of the nearby idling chopper.

The captain moved his hand, tried to open his eyes and moved his lips as if to speak. But no words came. At least, none Scotty could hear.

"Get ready. 'Cause we're leaving now!" Scotty grabbed the captain's arm and with great difficulty, pulled it over his neck to get him up to a point where Scotty could boost him up on his shoulder into a fireman's carry.

He picked up the rifle with his free hand and bounced once to adjust the captain on his shoulder then turned to leave the thicket.

The first steps screamed alarms to Scotty: That he probably wasn't strong enough to make it to the chopper. And he had to move now and move quickly if he hoped to get the man to help.

He stepped forward more worried about his balance than his safety as the thorns, snags and branches reached out to tear and rip at his face and neck. He kept moving until the trees gave way to the daylight, now revealing still another downpour. He looked at the chopper which hadn't seemed that far away when it landed.

The pilot was waving for Scotty to hurry. Scotty could tell he had already started to increase the RPM of the turbine engine to take off as soon as possible. The new rain streamed off the tips of the spinning rotor blades throwing a widening circle of water.

Each step was less steady than the last, and the chopper seemed not to get closer fast enough. Scotty kept talking to himself: "Move. Faster! Get to that chopper." He felt a knee buckle and then the other. It was as if his legs had turned to jelly. Not five paces from the chopper he went down in the mud.

He found himself on his knees, still upright, still holding Nguyen on his shoulder but on his knees when he should still be moving forward closing on the waiting aircraft. As much for himself as for Nguyen he yelled, "Don't worry. We're gonna' make it, Dai Uy. Don't worry."

Scotty struggled to maintain his balance while he pulled one leg up to place his barefoot on the muddy paddy beneath the water and discovered how much less stable he became in that posture. At the moment he thought he had lost control of himself and his load he felt a hand under his armpit. It was one of the Vietnamese soldiers. Then a second grabbed him by the other arm.

Between the two of them, they got Scotty and Nguyen up to take the last few strides to the chopper. Scotty rolled Nguyen's limp body onto the cargo deck of the aircraft then tried to raise his own leg to get in. He couldn't. He just didn't have the strength. He tried again and could only get the knee half as high as the first attempt.

The two soldiers and the American door gunner reached out and grabbed Scotty by his shirt and pulled him up and over the mud-slimed edge of the chopper and onto his stomach inside the aircraft.

Scotty wasn't even sure he even had the strength to roll over and sit up when the chopper suddenly lurched forward, tail up, tilting the cargo deck violently. The pilot, now clear of the ground, yanked the chopper violently to the east changing the pitch of the slick floor, threatening to spit Scotty out the door to the paddies now a hundred feet below. He felt himself sliding, out of control, toward the console between the pilots—the floor now as wet, muddy and slippery as the paddies they were leaving.

He crashed into the console. But there he was able to get a grasp on one of the legs of the pilot's seat to keep himself from sliding toward the gaping open cargo door during the ride.

Scotty got a better grip, turned over, pulled himself up to a sitting position and found all three Vietnamese soldiers attending to Captain Nguyen. One was trying to cover him with his own dry shirt. One was attending to his wound and one was holding the captain's head while pouring water into his mouth from his own canteen.

Rain blew in the cargo doors and sprayed Scotty as he looked around. The two pilots were completely focused on getting the chopper to the Sugar Mill. At the other end of the chopper's cargo bay, the two door gunners sat in their side-mounted jump seats. They trained their two machineguns on every danger spot they passed over ready to eliminate any threat to the chopper. Scotty closed his eyes, dismissed his shivering and heard himself say, "Thank you."

CHAPTER 24

Kitty . . .?" Eileen wasn't sure if she was awake but was sure if she wasn't she'd want to be awakened. She called her name again in the dark, quiet room. "Kitty, darlin', are you awake?"

Kitty answered in a small and sleepy voice, "What is it, hon?"

"Gonna' turn the light on. Mind your eyes," Eileen said before she flipped the switch on the wall.

Kitty rubbed her eyes and looked at Eileen. "What? What are you smiling at? Oh, no. Is it Scotty? Is there some word about Scotty?" She sat up, unaware she had clasped her hands in front of her chest in a prayer-like pose.

Eileen nodded enthusiastically as she ran to Kitty's bedside, sat on the edge of the bed and took Kitty's hands in hers. "He's okay. They've found him."

"He's okay? Tell me he's okay. Please, please tell me he's okay," Kitty pleaded, tears flooding her eyes and as quickly streaming down her cheeks.

"I told you. He's okay. *He's okay*. Our Scotty's okay."

Kitty wiped her eyes with the sleeve of the sleep shirt she wore. "Oh, my God! How wonderful! He's okay!" She slipped her hands from Eileen's, placed them on the back of Eileen's neck and pulled her face to her chest. She held her closely and rocked her back and forth repeating, "My baby's okay. He's okay."

Eileen started to cry with the same happiness and sheer surprise at the good news. "He's coming home. I don't know all the particulars. I only know he's already on his way to the States."

Kitty pushed Eileen out to arm's length, sniffled and asked, "How do you know? Could this be a mistake? Who told you this?"

"Whoa. Kitty, whoa!" Eileen said. "Captain Jeffries called. He told me Scotty was at a hospital in Saigon yesterday and would be leaving soon. He said he'd come tell you in person later and give you all the details, but he wanted you to get the good news as quickly as he could."

Eileen whipped back the cover and swung her legs over the side of the bed.

"Where are you going?" Eileen asked.

"Scotty's coming home. We've got things to do." She unconsciously reached up and touched her unkempt hair. "You 'nd me got to get gorgeous for that boy."

"Before you get too excited and throw a rib out of place, know he's not going to be here right away."

"Why not?" Kitty asked, worry returning to her expression.

"Captain Jeffries said he's going to spend some time in a hospital in Japan to get him some rest and some medical treatment before the long trip to the States to—"

"'Medical treatment?' What's wrong with him? I thought he was okay? Oh, please tell me he's not wounded," Kitty said.

"He's exhausted, and he's sick. But don't worry. They say he hasn't been shot or anything. It's just going to take another couple of weeks for him to get here."

Kitty stood up. "Well, we still got lots to do. Don't we?"

Eileen stood, hugged Kitty and kissed her on the forehead. "Yes, we do. We sure do."

The colonel looked freshly dispatched from some protected headquarters—new fatigues, no tan and leather boots, not canvas topped jungle boots. His shirt didn't even have a nametag on it. His collar insignia gave him away as a member of the Judge Advocate General's Corp—an Army lawyer.

He took out a small card with a list of the legal rights he was obligated to read to Pascoe and began to read verbatim: "No person subject to the Uniform Code of Military Justice may compel any person to incriminate himself or to answer any questions the answer to which may tend to incriminate him . . ."

Pascoe couldn't believe it. *He* was being investigated? This would have consequences far more damaging than the single bad efficiency report he got at West Point. He heard but didn't hear the colonel continue to read him his Article 31 rights. "No person subject to the Code may interrogate, or request any statement from an accused or a person suspected of an offense without first informing him of the nature of the accusation and advising him that he does not have to make any statement regarding the offense of which he is accused or suspected and that any statement made by him may be used as evidence against him in a trial by court-martial . . ."

Pascoe had to think of something—some way of sidestepping the finger being pointed at him. Something he could lay off on Minh or, or some explanation for whatever it was he was really being suspected of. His mind frantically searched for a solution without success.

The colonel continued. "No person subject to the Code may compel any person to make a statement or produce evidence before any military tribunal if the statement or evidence is not material to the issue and may tend to degrade him. No statement obtained from any person in violation of this article, or through the use of coercion, unlawful influence, or unlawful inducement may be received in evidence against him in a trial by court-martial.

"Do you understand these rights as I have read them to you, Major?"

He heard the sarcastic emphasis in the colonel's voice when he said the word *major*. Pascoe felt panic setting in. He stammered, "Yes, ah no. This has to be some kind of mistake. I'm not guilty of anything. I haven't done anything wrong. I, ah . . . I—"

"Major. I'm going to ask you again. Do you understand these rights as I have read them to you?"

Pascoe became combative. "Of course I do!"

The colonel corrected him. "'Of course I do, *sir*.'"

His thoughts tumbled out of control. There had to be someone who could come to his aid, someone who could get this off his back, someone who could make it all go away. But no name came to mind.

And the colonel pulled a lined pad out of his briefcase. It had questions written on it. He pushed the pad aside and prefaced his questions with a statement carefully chosen to follow the process. "Major. You are suspected of violating Articles 99 and 107 of the Uniform Code of Military Justice. The purpose of this investigation is to determine if there is enough evidence for me as investigation officer to recommend a trial by courts-martial to the convening authority, who in this case is the Commander of the Military Assistance Command."

"What? You can't be serious. Someone's accusing me of cowardice?"

"Technically, *misbehavior before the enemy* and filing false official statements."

"We have statements from Sergeant Hayes and Captain Nguyen. We also have sworn statements from the command pilots of the helicopter elements supporting the operation incident to the loss of General Minh and several Vietnamese soldiers. And all these statements appear to contradict your account of what happened that night."

The colonel then pulled a small stack of documents from his briefcase. "I'd like to start by asking you if you recall preparing and signing these statements concerning specifics of the enemy contact in which General Minh was killed and two soldiers went missing that night." He shoved copies of the report Pascoe he had written across the table to Pascoe.

The first thing Scotty noticed in addition to the stethoscope clasped around the doctor's throat he was a bright silver Parachutist's Badge over his breast pocket and a Ranger tab on the shoulder of his starched khaki shirt. He'd been ushered into the room only two hours earlier after transport from an Air Force plane had brought him to Fort Benning.

Scotty sat up quietly waiting for the balding Army doctor to finish reading the half inch thick file of medical forms and test slips clamped into an aluminum folder which had been hanging at the foot of his bed.

Without even making eye contact with Scotty the doctor put the earpieces of his stethoscope into place and motioned for Scotty lean forward. He listened to his lungs then poked at his tender kidneys. Pushing Scotty back, he pulled up the bottom of his GI pajama top and probed his liver with his fingers. "Tender?"

"Yessir," Scotty replied.

The doctor made a few notations in the medical file and tucked it under his arm. Finally, he looked at Scotty. "I'm Doctor Owens. I'm going to be looking after you while you're here at Fort Benning."

"Just how much *looking after* am I going to need, sir?" Scotty asked, still unsure exactly how sick he was. He had been poked, probed, shuttled, transferred and moved from bed to bed and hospital to hospital for almost three weeks.

"Well, let me see . . ." The doctor flipped the metal lid of the file open again and rifled through the pages. "Somehow you've managed to get yourself pretty well dehydrated while you were in Vietnam. And you've picked up a good case of Dengue fever; you're suffering from lots of odds and ends symptoms of exposure and prolonged immersion. And . . . And you got yourself a pretty stubborn case of intestinal parasites. On top of all that, we haven't yet ruled out worms, but we're working on all of it."

He flipped the file closed, dropped it on the bed and looked at the flow rate on an upturned bottle of saline solution on its way to Scotty's bloodstream by way of a plastic tube and needle in the back of his hand.

"What? I mean will I . . ."

"The answer is yes," Doctor Owens said. "*Yes*, you'll be okay. *Yes*, we can fix all this. And *no* you aren't going to like some of the medications. And you are going to be a bit impatient, but you didn't get all this overnight."

Scotty looked out the window of the eighth-floor ward at Martin Army Hospital. "How long will I be here, sir?"

The doctor looked at the chart one more time. "I'd say we need to keep you here for at least another two weeks . . ." He looked sternly at

Scotty. "If you follow my instructions to the letter, Sergeant. If you don't, you'll be here that much longer.

"Then we're going to send you home for a month on convalescent leave and treat you as an outpatient. How does that sound?"

Scotty grinned widely. "That sounds great, sir."

The doctor waved his finger at Scotty. "That doesn't mean you are well. I'm sending you home with a rucksack full of medications you'll have to take religiously and some restrictions on your diet. Your stomach's not ready for Buffalo wings or tequila or Tabasco sauce. As a matter of fact, no booze for you for at least six months. We need to take all the load we can off your liver."

"That'll be fine with me, sir. You can count on me."

"Then I'm going to want to see you after your leave, and I'll decide if you are ready to return to duty. How does that sound?"

"Airborne, sir!"

The doctor reached out and shook Scotty's hand. "Welcome home, Ranger."

Scotty woke in late afternoon from a disturbing dream which had slipped in when he dozed off. In it, he saw himself unable to carry Captain Nguyen to the chopper and the chopper lifted off without them. He shook off the dream knowing it was just a dream and Nguyen too was getting good care in Vietnam.

He looked around the six-bed ward. The only other bed in the room with a patient in it was at the far end of the room. The patient was a large man with his back to Scotty, sleeping soundly and snoring lightly.

Scotty became aware of sounds coming through the window next to his hospital bed. Outside and several floors down a company of basic trainees was double-timing along the range road headed back to the cantonment area from a day's training. As they ran, they yelled Jody cadence under the direction of an unseen drill sergeant.

Scotty thought he would never love hearing that sound again. His mind wandered to his days on the same range road, to Russell and Fitch and how awkward and unsuited to that life he felt back then. He wondered if Russell had been as lucky as he had been. If he might be in some military hospital somewhere also itching to get released.

He recalled how humid he had thought Benning was. Now the breeze coming through the open window was pleasant by comparison to the crushing humidity of Vietnam. He moved his hands across the clean rough GI sheets and thought about going home to Belton.

Footsteps outside his room caught his attention. They were coming down the long hallway from the elevator. They clicked crisply on the tile floor. A women's footsteps, he thought. But not the nurse's. They all wore white rubber soled shoes which were nearly silent and part of their white Army uniforms and nurses' caps.

The footsteps stopped at what Scotty guessed was the nurse's station. He heard but could not make out what was said. Then the footsteps continued and got closer. Until they stopped in the doorway to his ward.

Scotty looked up, and there was Eileen. Not the Eileen he had left so many months before. An even prettier Eileen stood there. She had her hair up, makeup on and wore pumps. He had never seen her in high heels and had never seen a skirt like the one she wore. Words like miniskirt and hullabaloo had all been minted while he was in Vietnam. The short skirt showed off her long beautiful legs.

"Scotty?" she said tentatively.

"Oh, my God, you are beautiful," he said.

He watched her movements as she rushed to his bedside and then abruptly stopped once there. She looked at the IV bottle and the tubes. She seemed unsure if she should touch or embrace him. He reached up, grabbed her arm firmly and pulled her to him. She sat on the side of the bed, and they held each other tightly, quietly as she tucked her face into the crook of his neck and let her long pent up tears of relief and joy flow.

Scotty pulled his face away and kissed her hair, then touched it with his fingertips. "There was a time I thought I'd never be able to do this again."

She sniffled, rummaged around in her purse, found a tissue and blew her nose. "I knew. I was sure you were coming home. You might think I'm crazy, but I was sure."

He looked at her for a long time, silent, taking her in and not missing a single strand of hair, nuance of her makeup or the wonderful way she smelled.

"Scotty?"

"Yeah."

"Are you okay? Tell me you are going to be okay."

"As they say in Vietnam, 'Can do, easy.' Yes, *I am* okay. They're going to let me out of here in a couple of weeks, and I can come home on leave. And be with you."

Excited, Eileen bounced up and down on the bed and then caught herself. "Oh, I'm sorry. Did that hurt?"

Scotty laughed. "Are you kidding me?"

She laughed and wiped another tear from the corner of her eye.

"How's Kitty?" he asked.

"Your mom's a tougher old bird than I thought she was. When it was bad, she hung in there. Once she heard you were coming home, she was like a teenager. She's been cleaning the house and baking for weeks."

They both laughed.

"That's good. You've been so good for her—"

Eileen took Scotty's hands in hers. "We can talk about Kitty and all that later. When do I get to spend some time with you all by myself?" No sooner had she asked, she blushed at the forwardness of her question.

Scotty leaned back and smiled as if he knew a secret. "Well, we can find some time while I'm home on convalescent leave, but I've got a much better idea."

She brightened up even more. "What? What idea?"

"I've been told I have to go to Honolulu to testify in a trial in about three months. Why don't you come with me? You've never been there, have you?"

"No. I mean yes. I mean no, I haven't been there, and yes, I want to go with you."

He was silent for a while then took her hands in his. "While we're there, why don't we get married?"

"What? Oh, yes. Yes, yes, yes!" She threw her arms around Scotty's neck then took his face in her hands and kissed him.

CHAPTER 25

NOVEMBER 1965

His emotions shuttled between anger at Pascoe and his pain over the loss of so many good soldiers because of Pascoe's cowardice under fire. Scotty sat in the gallery of the courtroom at the Schofield Barracks headquarters building in Oahu with Eileen by his side. Everyone involved had been called back into the room after the court martial board had met in closed session for two days after a week of testimony.

Finished with their deliberations, the officers shuffled back into the courtroom. The grinding sounds of their combat boots and the scuffing of their chairs on the raised platform, built just for the trial, broke the silence. Two colonels, three lieutenant colonels and one major flanked Brigadier General Ben Stratton. They silently took their seats.

Stratton slipped on his reading glasses. He opened a piece of paper folded once at the midline and read to all assembled in the room, "As President of this court-martial it is my duty to inform you the members of the court, two-thirds of which were present at the time a secret written ballot was cast, have reached their verdict."

Scotty looked over at Pascoe, standing behind the Trial Counsel's table with his military attorney. His color was ashen, and his eyes were fixed on a point on the wall above and behind the members of the court.

The general looked up at Pascoe and then continued reading: "As to the charge of violation of Article 107 of the Uniform Code of Military Justice, Making False Official Statements, the court finds you guilty.

"As to the charge of violation of Article 99, Misbehavior Before the Enemy, the court finds you guilty.

"For these violations, you are sentenced to: Suspension of all pay and allowances, confinement at the United States Disciplinary Barracks at Fort Leavenworth, Kansas for a period of no less than fifteen years, reduction to the rank of Private E-1 and a dishonorable discharge."

The general looked up from his notes and scanned the completely silent courtroom then turned back to Pascoe whose expression gave away the shock of his sentencing. The general took off his reading glasses and plopped them on the table. "Major Pascoe, I've been a soldier for thirty-one years. This is certainly not the first time I've been president of a court-martial board. But I have to say I have not seen such an egregious violation of the trust soldiers must have in their officers as you have committed. Every man who carries a rifle faces an enemy or risks his life to execute the orders of officers appointed over him deserves the full measure of unwavering protection and unqualified loyalty his officers can give. Every soldier needs to know he will never be left behind on the battlefield as long as there is even the slightest chance he might be rescued, or his remains might be recovered. You, Major, have broken that trust, and for that crime, you deserve the disdain and the scorn of your peers and all those soldiers who have ever served with you.

"I, for one, will lose no sleep over your confinement and dishonorable discharge. You do not deserve to be a field grade commissioned officer. You do not deserve the privilege of command of combat soldiers. And you certainly do not deserve the respect your rank should entitle you to.

"Soldiers will forgive just about any failing in an officer but cowardice. You have shamed yourself, the officer corps and your alma mater—the United States Military Academy."

The general picked up his glasses and closed the bound maroon Uniform Code of Military Justice Manual before him. "This concludes all matters before this court and we are adjourned."

The members of the court stood and followed the general out of the room while everyone else waited for them to leave. Scotty felt Eileen give his arm a supportive squeeze as they both watched the two military police take Pascoe into custody, place him in handcuffs and lead him down the center aisle of the courtroom to the doorway leading to the street.

As Pascoe passed the row where Scotty and Eileen stood he stared at the floor in front of him and avoided making eye contact with Scotty.

SPRING 1968

Still dark, Scotty tiptoed into his infant daughter's bedroom and looked at her sleeping soundly in her crib. Though she was only eight months old, Scotty still stood in amazement every morning finding himself so blessed to be where he was and to have her and Eileen in his life.

Though it had been thirty-six months since he and Captain Nguyen had made it through the marshland along the Cambodian border, and he had already served one more year in Vietnam with an American Airborne Brigade, the time they were lost was still on his mind. How close they came to death, how great the possibility seemed that he would never stand over the crib of a baby daughter safe in Army quarters at Fort Benning, Georgia never left him.

He walked into the kitchen for a last sip of coffee before heading out to work. There he found Eileen, her hair pulled back into a ponytail wearing his pajama top which hit her about mid-thigh. "Morning, sunshine."

She stretched her arms over her head and then reached out for him. "C'mere. Let me give you a hug before you leave."

"Okay, as long as it's only a hug. You know what happens when it is too much of a hug."

They both laughed.

He embraced her and she put her head on his chest. "How's our baby girl doing? She awake yet?"

"No. And I wanted to hold her before I left for work."

"Hold me, and I'll pass it on later."

"Deal." He kissed the top of Eileen's head and smelled the sweetness of her hair.

Eileen leaned back held him at arm's length and looked up at him. "You better get going. You're gonna' be late?"

"Got a whole new gaggle of trainees arriving today. Don't wait up for me. You know how first days are."

She gave Scotty a kiss and released him. "Got to go check that baby girl."

Scotty put on his Drill Sergeant's hat and gave Eileen an affectionate pat on the behind as she walked away. "You two have a great day."

Dawn was breaking. Sergeant First Class Scotty Hayes stood on the Orderly Room porch of Company E, 1st Battalion of the 3rd Training Regiment at Fort Benning. He sipped lukewarm mess hall coffee from the mug he had brought with him from breakfast.

He watched as two hundred and thirty brand new Army recruits were hustled off the olive drab buses parked in the company street and herded into their first sloppy military formations by junior NCOs with the group.

Once they were somewhat organized and quieted down, Scotty put his cup down on the railing and automatically checked his to see his pockets were buttoned and his campaign hat was set squarely on his head, low over his eyes.

That done, he walked down the three steps to the cinder topped roadway to a point in front of the assembled recruits.

As the company's senior Drill Sergeant he took his position in front of them, the remaining noises, shuffling and mumbling within the ranks ended—each man looking at the sergeant obviously in charge of their futures.

Scotty raised his voice to reach every man in the formation and heard Sergeant Russell's words slipping from his lips. "Welcome to E Company and your first day of Basic Training. My name is Hayes. We're going to spend the next two months together. And you're not going to like me. But I won't lose any sleep over that . . ."

EPILOGUE

Scotty and Eileen Hayes—had three children, two boys and a girl named Kitty. Sergeant Major Scott Hayes retired from the Army in 1993, after he returned from the first Gulf War. He and Eileen settled down in their hometown of Belton, Florida.

Kitty Hayes—died quietly in her sleep in 1975 after having become a grandmother three times over.

Eldon Pascoe—was released from the United States Disciplinary Barracks at Fort Leavenworth, Kansas in 1981 and took a job teaching history in a private boy's school in Oklahoma. He was fired two years later without explanation.

Sergeant Asa Russell—was the second American to escape from an enemy POW camp in Laos. He stayed in the Army and retired as the Command Sergeant Major of the 82nd Airborne Division in Fort Bragg, North Carolina.

Sergeant Caruthers—lost his right leg from wounds he suffered in the attack on the hamlet of Doi Bao Voi and went home to start a successful fishing camp in Lake of the Ozarks, Missouri.

Captain Nguyen—was promoted to major and became the Operations Officer of the 6th Infantry Division. In 1974, with the fall of Saigon to Communists forces, he became a boat person and ended up owning a liquor store in Costa Mesa, California's small Vietnamese community.

Karen Pascoe—divorced Eldon Pascoe three months after his court-martial conviction and later remarried an old high school sweetheart. She became a successful real estate agent in Peekskill, New York.

Malcolm Striever—was drafted in 1968 and sent to Vietnam as a helicopter door gunner in the 1st Cavalry Division. While serving there, he was killed in a helicopter crash.

ABOUT THE AUTHOR

Dennis Foley retired from the army as a lieutenant colonel after several tours in Southeast Asia. He served as a Long Range Patrol platoon leader, an Airborne Infantry company commander, a Ranger company commander, and a Special Forces "A" Detachment commander. He holds two Silver Stars, four Bronze Stars, and two Purple Hearts. In addition to his novels, he has written and produced for television and film. He lives in Whitefish, Montana.

DENNIS FOLEY

FROM OPEN ROAD MEDIA

OPEN ROAD

INTEGRATED MEDIA

Find a full list of our authors and
titles at www.openroadmedia.com

FOLLOW US
@OpenRoadMedia